Thirty and a Half Excuses

Also by Denise Grover Swank

Rose Gardner Mysteries

The Chosen Series

On the Otherside Series

Curse Keepers Series

Off the Subject Series

The Wedding Pact Series

Thirty and a Half Excuses

A Rose Gardner Mystery

Denise Grover Swank

CROOKED
LANE

NEW YORK

Copyright © 2013 by Denise Grover Swank

Published in the United States by Crooked Lane Books, an imprint of The Quick Brown Fox & Company LLC.

Crooked Lane Books and its logo are trademarks of The Quick Brown Fox & Company LLC.

The Library of Congress Cataloging-in-Publication Data is available upon request.

978-1-62953-221-9
978-1-62953-377-3

Cover design by Louis Malcangi
Book design by Jennifer Canzone

Printed in the United States.

www.crookedlanebooks.com

Crooked Lane Books
2 Park Avenue, 10th Floor
New York, NY 10016

First Edition: October 2015

10 9 8 7 6 5 4 3 2 1

Chapter One

I had never been more scared in my life.

Sure, I'd been frightened out of my wits before, like when I was sure Daniel Crocker was going to shoot me or when Jimmy DeWade planned to take me to the woods outside of town and kill me. But after those momentary flashes of terror, my life returned to normal. Well, as normal as my life got.

This fear had seeped into every cell of my body, and it clung to me day and night, gnawing me from the inside out.

This time I wasn't afraid of dying.

I was afraid of failing.

"Tomorrow's gonna be a big day. I think we're ready."

I jumped at the sound of Violet's voice and spun around. She was leaning on a broom, surveying the abandoned floral shop we'd rented for our business.

I nodded, trying to swallow. "Yeah."

Three months, several hundred thousand dollars, a small business loan larger than both of our houses put together, and lots and lots of hard work had resulted in this moment: the eve of the grand opening of the Gardner Sisters Nursery.

"We're still waiting on that shipment for flowering kale, but I think we're all set with the traditional flowers people expect." Violet set the broom in the corner and straightened a pot of *Kalanchoe* that was already perfectly arranged. Her eyes found mine and she smiled. "This is happening."

I took a deep breath, feeling like I was about to hyperventilate. "Yeah."

When Violet had first mentioned the idea of opening the nursery several months ago, her husband Mike had just announced he was leaving her. I had other plans at the time—I was supposed to move to Little Rock with my boyfriend Joe—so when she asked me to be her partner, it took me a while to warm to the idea. But once I did, I realized I wanted it as much as Violet did.

Now I was scared to death. There was more than me and my dog Muffy to worry about if the nursery failed. Violet was hinging her two children's futures on this venture.

She grabbed my hands and squeezed. "We're gonna be great."

Violet had spent most of her life taking care of me and reassuring me. I'd made tremendous progress over the last four months, but right now I needed my big sister's support. I nodded. "Yeah, you're right."

She squeezed again. "Trust me. We've done our homework. We know what we're doin'."

Violet had done most of the homework. She'd researched her plan for the nursery for over a year before ever mentioning it to me. She was the brains and the backbone behind this venture, and I was the capital, investing the money my birth mother had left me in her will.

Violet had always poured her all into being a wife and mother. But now that her marriage was failing, she needed to devote her attention to something else. It turned out that she had a head for business, which gave her the confidence to thrive. I'd never seen her happier or more fulfilled. But sometimes I wondered if there was something else making her happy that I didn't see.

"You almost done there?"

I patted dirt around the plants I'd just finished potting. The container was overflowing with fountain grass, pansies, marguerite daisies, and coral bells. "Yeah, I just need to clean up."

Violet rested her hand on my arm. "Rose, relax. We're going to be fine."

I searched her eyes and some of the confidence I saw there soothed my nerves. Deep down I believed we would be successful, but I was finding it hard to overcome more than two decades of being told how worthless I was and how I'd never amount to anything. Every time I tried something new my mother's voice would fill my head, stealing all my confidence and joy. But I'd wasted the first twenty-four years of my life giving her power over me. I wasn't going to give it to her anymore, even from the grave. I lifted my chin. "I know." And I meant it.

Violet dropped her hand and walked to the counter as my peripheral vision began to fade to black. A tingling filled my head, a sure sign a vision was coming on, and I tried to relax—fighting them did no good. I'd had visions since I was a child, and there was no stopping them when they came. Whenever I had a vision, I saw it from the perspective of the person closest to me, a talent that had gotten me into more trouble than most people face in a lifetime.

Everything faded away, and I was standing in the nursery parking lot, surrounded by a crowd. A man with highlighted, poufy hair and a too-perfect tan shook my hand, his bright-white teeth nearly blinding me. He turned to the crowd and smiled, saying, "As a new member of this community wanting to support local businesses, I'd like to order enough flowers to cover the entire grounds of the New Living Hope Revival Church!" The crowd broke into loud applause.

As the vision faded away, I blinked. "We're gonna get a huge order."

Violet was bent behind the counter. She stood, her eyebrows lifting. "What?"

I offered a soft smile. "I just had a vision that Henryetta's newest minister is going to order enough flowers to cover the grounds of his church." One of the inconvenient side effects of my visions was that I always blurted out what I saw. Usually I wished I could keep it to myself, but this one I would have wanted to share anyway. Visions containing good news were rare.

"Jonah Pruitt? The televangelist? Do you know what this means, Rose? *The publicity we could get*?" Violet squealed and danced in place. "I told you!"

I inhaled deeply. "My visions don't always come true, Violet."

"This one will. I feel it in my bones." She put her hands on her hips and cocked her head with a huge grin. "We're gonna be great!"

I lifted the pot off the table and set it on the floor. "Funny, that's what Joe said."

"I've always liked him."

I snorted as I swept the loose dirt on my worktable into a plastic bin. "Yeah, that's why you set me up on a blind date a couple of months ago while he was in Little Rock."

Violet frowned. "We didn't know anything concrete about Joe then, and he refused to tell us."

"Well, you didn't like him anymore when you pinned him down, and he finally told us about his family."

She put her hands on her hips. "And you know darned good and well why. You still haven't met them, have you? I'm telling you that little Rose Gardner from Henryetta, Arkansas, will not meet the approval of his rich, socialite, political family in El Dorado. Mark my words."

"And yet you still have the audacity to say you always liked him?"

She laughed. "Okay. I guess he grew on me."

"Me too." I started to fold up the soiled newspaper on the table, when a headline caught my attention. *Elderly Woman Found Dead*. Leaning over the table, I scanned the article in the week-old paper. "Did you know our old Sunday school teacher, Miss Laura, died last week?"

Violet's eyes widened. "What? No! How?"

I read more before glancing up. "It says they found her dead in her house. Her air conditioner was off. They think she died from heat exhaustion."

"That's so sad. I loved her."

Amazingly enough, I did too. She was one of the few people at the Henryetta Southern Baptist Church who had been genuinely kind to me. "Why do you suppose her air conditioner was off?"

Violet shrugged. "Who knows? You know how miserly old people get. Look at Momma."

I resisted a shudder. I always did everything in my power *not* to think about Momma. "It just seems weird, don't you think? It's been hotter than blazes outside. They're calling it a record heat wave for September."

4

"She probably figured it was autumn, so it was time to turn off the air, temperature be damned."

"But her windows were closed . . ."

Violet pointed her finger at me with a stern look. "Your problem is now that you've had two run-ins with criminals, you think *every* death is suspicious."

My mouth dropped. "That's not true!"

"Why, just a couple of weeks ago, you thought that Old Man Hurley's death needed to be investigated."

I scowled. "You have to admit it looked strange. A grown man found dead sitting in his lawn chair in the backyard, not wearing pants."

"Lots of old men don't wear pants. Remember Mindy Draper's grandpa?"

I pursed my lips. "He was senile."

Violet bent down and grabbed both of our purses and walked around the counter. "You've got plenty of trouble in your own backyard is all I'm sayin'." She handed mine over. "You don't need to go borrowing more."

"What's that supposed to mean?"

She opened the door and paused. "Nothing. Forget I said anything."

I followed Violet outside and waited while she locked up. "What aren't you telling me?"

Her mouth twisted to one side as she considered what to say. Finally she lowered her voice. "There's rumors going around town is all. But don't you worry about it. That's what I love about you, Rose. You don't care what people say."

That wasn't true. I cared plenty. I'd been the topic of Henryetta gossip for as long as I could remember. But there wasn't a thing I could do about it.

She kissed me on the cheek. "It's nothing anyway. I'm the one people should be talking about." She gave me a wicked smile. "Me and my scandalous almost-divorce."

"I thought you and Mike were just separated."

Violet ignored my statement, walking away from me. "I've got to get home to my babies, and you need to go home and get some rest. We've got a big day tomorrow!" Then she hopped into her car and pulled out of the parking lot.

I watched her drive away before getting into my old Nova and driving toward home.

When I turned down my street, my heart leapt with joy. Joe's car was in the driveway. He sat on the front porch with a beer in his hand and a big grin on his face, filling the chair with his tall frame. He'd gotten his dark brown hair cut since I'd seen him on Sunday, his natural copper highlights not so prominent now.

I parked behind him, barely swinging the car door closed before I ran up to the porch and threw my arms around his neck. "Joe! What are you doin' here?"

Joe lived in Little Rock, over a two-hour drive away. We spent every weekend together and only occasional weeknights. It was an unusual occurrence for him to show up on a Tuesday night without warning.

His arm wrapped around my waist and held me close as he lowered his mouth to mine. He kissed me thoroughly before lifting his head to stare into my face. "Tomorrow's a big day for you, Rose. Where else would I be?"

"You came for our grand opening?"

"Of course. I love you, darlin'. I wouldn't miss it."

I kissed him with all I was worth, certain my elderly neighbor Mildred was at her window with binoculars. She'd probably call the Henryetta Police Department about me fornicating in broad daylight. "You know Mildred's watching, don't you?"

Joe grinned against my lips. "I'm counting on it."

I leaned back and swatted his arm. "You're terrible."

A devilish gleam filled his brown eyes, making the scattered dark flecks stand out more than usual. "You know we're her main source of entertainment. We've got to give her something to talk about while I'm gone."

My smile fell, my joy short lived. "So it's official. You're going undercover?"

Joe nodded. "I'm sorry."

I pushed him down onto one of the chairs and sat on his lap. "Don't be sorry, Joe. You're just doing your job." He'd warned me he had a big undercover job coming up soon. We wouldn't be able to see each other until he was done. I smoothed an imaginary wrinkle out of his T-shirt, then looked into his eyes. "I knew you were a state police detective when I met you."

He grimaced. "Well, not exactly when you met me."

"True." Joe had been undercover then too. He'd moved in next door to me while he was investigating a state-wide car parts ring. Through a host of unusual circumstances, he'd thought I might be involved. But then we became involved in a completely different way, and he ended up saving my life. I saved his too. We'd been together ever since. A little over four months. "But when I found out the truth, I had to accept your job for what it was. It's what brought us together. I can't begrudge you for that."

Smiling softly, he lowered his face, whispering against my lips. "You're amazing."

I didn't feel so amazing. Leaning my forehead against his, I searched his eyes. "So how long will you be gone?"

He pulled back, shaking his head and releasing a long sigh. "I don't know. Maybe one week, maybe three."

He hadn't even left yet, and I already ached with loneliness. The longest we'd been apart was five days, and that had been almost impossible to bear. "Will we be able to talk on the phone?"

"I don't know. Maybe a few times. If I can risk it."

"So it's dangerous then, what you're doing?"

He cupped my cheek. "Every day I'm a state police detective is dangerous."

Anger singed my chest. "Don't do that. Don't pretend like this isn't a big deal. It is. The last time you went undercover like this you fell in love with me, and you almost got killed. What if . . ." My voice broke, and I couldn't finish.

Joe's eyes narrowed in disbelief. "What if what? What if I fall in love with someone else?" He shook his head. "Rose, there's only you, darlin'. Only you."

I wish I had more confidence, but I wasn't sure I'd ever be totally confident where Joe was concerned. He'd always feel out of my league. But this time I was more worried about the dying part. "It's still dangerous, no matter how you spin it."

7

"I'll be careful. I love you, and I don't want to risk losing that."

I wanted to say if he really felt that way, he'd never go undercover again. But I didn't want our last night together to be sad or full of anger, and I knew it wasn't fair. "You can't tell me what you're doing?"

He shook his head.

"Can you at least tell me where you'll be?"

He hesitated. "El Dorado."

I gasped. "Where your parents live." I let the news sink in. "Will they know you're there?"

"No. I have no intention of seeing them anyway." A few months earlier Joe had confessed that his family came from oil money. He was mostly estranged from them, though he hadn't yet told me why.

"You'll have to see them sometime."

"The longer I can put it off, the better. My mother keeps calling and insisting that they meet you."

The prospect of meeting his parents made me almost as nervous as Joe going undercover. "Do *you* want me to meet them?"

"I'd rather put it off as long as possible."

I knew Joe didn't get along with his parents and avoided seeing them, but a small part of me worried that he didn't want me to meet them because he was ashamed of me.

"You said you'd have to do your father a favor." I swallowed my guilt. "Because of me." When I was on a jury for a murder trial in July, I found out through one of my visions that the defendant was innocent. I started investigating the case on my own to prove what I knew to be true, and after the judge found out, he threw me into the county jail. It took Joe; the Fenton County assistant district attorney, Mason Deveraux III; and apparently Joe's dad, who wielded political influence, to get me out. Later Joe told me that he was waiting for his father to collect on the favor.

"Trust me, the favor will be much bigger than bringing you to dinner." He took a deep breath. "But I'd do it again in a heartbeat."

And he would. Joe loved me so much, he'd do anything for me. Which is exactly why I needed to be supportive now. "That's one of the many reasons why I love you." I placed a gentle kiss on his lips. "You're going to do great. You're going to get the bad guys, and you're going to shut them down. Or whatever it is you're doing."

He laughed. "You're more confident than my boss."

My smile fell along with my stomach. "Then why are you doing it?"

His face hardened in determination. "Because it needs to be done."

I knew that look. Joe wasn't usually a stubborn man, but when he'd made up his mind about something, he was going to do it. There was no convincing him otherwise.

A loud engine revved as a big muscle car sped down the street past my house.

Joe watched the car pull into the driveway of the house on the corner across the street. "That boy drives too fast."

I watched Thomas get out of his car and slam the door shut. "The only good thing about having a teen with a loud car who drives too fast in the neighborhood is that he gives Mildred someone else to complain about besides us."

Joe's eyes lit up in a playful challenge. "Is that right? Then I'm not doing my job well enough." He pulled me back to his chest and lowered his mouth to mine.

I laughed and pushed him away. "Oh, no you don't. I'm hungry. Do you want me to cook dinner?"

He grinned. "I've already got it started."

One of the perks of having Joe as a boyfriend is that he not only cooked, but he cooked really well. "What are we having tonight?"

"I fired up the grill. We're gonna have steaks."

"Be careful. Mike will think you're invading his territory." The words were out before I thought about what I was saying.

Joe sobered. "What's the latest on Violet and Mike's separation?"

"Vi thinks he's about to file for divorce."

Joe winced. "And how's she doing with that news?"

I shook my head, twisting my mouth to one side. "Better than I expected. She's devoting all her attention to the nursery and the kids."

"I guess it's good that she's got something to focus on."

"Yeah." The breakup of her marriage still shook me up. I had thought Violet and Mike had the most stable, happy marriage of anyone I knew. But it turned out their relationship wasn't all peaches and cream. There were problems she and Mike had been sweeping under the rug for years. It made me even more determined to make sure Joe and I were honest with one another.

I looked around. "Where's Muffy?"

"She's playing with the boys."

My little dog was an ugly mutt nobody wanted until I saved her from a farmer about to take her to the pound. She looked like a cross between a rat and some sort of terrier with her pointy ears and snout. Her short gray and black fur had become softer and less wiry since her adoption. She had been timid and scared at first, a lot like I was at the time. Both of us had come a long way in the last four months.

She loved playing with the little boys who'd moved into the house next door. The house where Joe had lived for a little over a month while he was undercover. Remembering that piece of information set my stomach rolling. "How long can you stay?"

"I'll be around for the grand opening ceremony, but I have to leave by noon."

I grabbed his face between my hands, holding back tears. "I'm gonna miss you."

He sighed. "Me too."

We were subdued for the rest of the night. Joe reassured me multiple times that the nursery would be a success. But I knew he couldn't guarantee that. No one could. Besides, since my visions made me the town pariah, I couldn't help thinking that my involvement could potentially hurt our business. My vision about the televangelist gave me hope, but when I told Joe about it, a frown wrinkled his forehead. "Be careful in any dealings with Jonah Pruitt, Rose." The way he said it caught my attention.

"You know something about him?"

He's eyes leveled with mine. "You know I can't discuss state police matters." His voice lowered, making sure his full meaning came through.

Jonah Pruitt was being watched by the Arkansas State Police. That was interesting news. We'd just have to make sure he paid up front.

Chapter Two

The next morning, I was so anxious I could hardly eat breakfast. The nursery opening had me on edge, but Joe's assignment worried me more. If the nursery failed, it was only money. But there was only one Joe.

"I'm gonna be fine, Rose." Joe could read my mind like a book, or more accurately, he could read my face. "This isn't the first time I've gone undercover. Or even the tenth. I know what I'm doing or I wouldn't be doing it."

I nodded. He was right. But I was still scared to death.

I let Muffy out one last time before we left, my gaze drifting to the end of the street. School had already started for the day, but Thomas's car was still parked in the driveway. His mother was going to be fit to be tied. He already had a raging case of senioritis, and it was only September. It would be a miracle if he graduated in May.

After I put Muffy in the bathroom, Joe and I drove to the nursery separately. Violet was already there when we arrived at around 8:30. As I started uncovering the flowers on the sidewalk, Aunt Bessie pulled into the parking lot. She wouldn't have missed this for the world, so Violet and I had recruited her to work the register after the ribbon cutting ceremony.

When she got out of her car, she was grinning ear to ear. "Look at you, Rose! A business owner!"

"I know, hard to believe isn't it?"

She pressed her lips into a smug smile. "Not so hard for me. You're smart, and you love flowers. And if you use your gift to your advantage, you'll increase your sales even more."

I stared at her in confusion. "What are you talking about?"

She leaned in close, lowering her voice. "You can read them, child. Find out what their yards look like and make suggestions."

My eyes widened. "That doesn't seem right, Aunt Bessie."

Tsking, she walked into the shop. "There's no sin using the gifts God gave you."

I had always trusted Aunt Bessie, but she was suggesting that I purposely try to have visions. I usually did everything in my power to *not* have them.

I wiped my forehead with the back of my hand. It was going to be another hot day. Opening in the fall had seemed like a good way to ease into the business. But it sure didn't feel like fall with this heat wave. The forecast was for a high in the low nineties. I worried it would keep people from buying their autumn foliage.

Our fall hours were nine to six, and the official ribbon cutting ceremony had been set for eleven, so we had a couple of hours to prepare, which was a good thing since Violet was all a tizzy. The mayor and several members of the city council were coming, but the more important guests were the Henryetta Garden Club. Little did I know that Violet had been wooing them for over a year.

Even though our official opening was later in the morning, several customers showed up when we opened the doors at nine. Violet had done a great job with marketing and promotion, and the whole town was talking about our store. Our location helped too. We'd taken over an abandoned floral shop on the edge of the town square that came with a parking lot and a dilapidated greenhouse. Joe had spent the past several weekends working on the greenhouse, and it looked amazing. I understood why he wanted to be there for the grand opening. He was almost as much a part of the nursery as I was.

Mike's parents arrived at around 10:45 with Violet's kids, five-year-old Ashley and nineteen-month-old Mikey. They saw Violet and squealed, running across the parking lot to her. She squatted and scooped them in her arms, kissing each one of them on the cheek.

I stood next to a chrysanthemum display, my heart bursting with envy.

"How many kids do you think you want?" Joe had snuck up behind me, his gaze on my niece and nephew.

My mouth parted in surprise. We'd never discussed children before other than the generic *we both want a family someday*. We'd barely begun skirting around the idea of something permanent. I hesitated, worried I'd scare him off if I told him three or four. "How many do *you* want?"

He draped his arm around my shoulders and looked down into my face with a grin. "A houseful."

"Me too."

He planted a kiss on my nose. "Just one more reason we're perfect for each other."

"Ewww . . ." Ashley groaned. "Aunt Rose is kissing her boyfriend."

Joe held me close and winked at her. "So what's new about that?"

Ashley giggled. Joe dropped his hold on me and chased her around the building, trying to tickle her.

Days like today filled me equally with contentment and the want for more.

A crowd began to gather, and I stood by the corner of the building. While most of the citizens of my town preferred for me to keep to myself, there were a few exceptions, like my best friend Neely Kate. As soon as she jumped out of her car, her face lit up.

"Look at you! You're a small business owner now!"

Neely Kate had gotten married a couple of months earlier, a big event that had matched her larger-than-life personality. The wedding was beautiful, just like I'd seen in a vision. She'd planned on quitting her job after her honeymoon, but then her boss, Jimmy DeWade, was arrested for murder and two counts of attempted murder—on me—and Neely Kate had to take over his position. She hated every minute of working in the courthouse, but thankfully, she didn't blame me for it. She had reason to: I was the one who discovered that her boss was a murderer.

I put my hands on my hips, allowing a little excitement to override my anxiety. "I think we're ready."

She spotted Joe over by the greenhouse, and her mouth turned up into a wicked grin. "I see your man is here."

"He's just as much a part of this as I am. Heaven knows he's put in enough time and manual labor."

She nudged my shoulder and winked. "I bet he got paid back with a different kind of manual labor."

"Neely Kate!" I laughed, then shook my head with a pretend scowl. The garden society ladies were beginning to arrive, and I had enough strikes against me.

"I won't be able to stay long, but I had to come wish you good luck."

"Well, be sure to get a piece of cake before you go. I ordered a sheet cake from the Piggly Wiggly bakery, and they put our logo on top."

Neely Kate smirked. "You didn't use Ima Jean's bakery?"

"She was gonna charge twice as much." I had to pinch pennies where I could.

She shook her head, puckering her mouth in mock sympathy. "You'll pay for that and more, in ways other than money."

I had a feeling she was right.

Several minutes later, the mayor arrived and Violet showed her first signs of nervousness, running her fingers through her hair and tugging at her skirt. She hurried over to Neely Kate and me, glancing over her shoulder. "Do I look okay?"

"You look beautiful, Violet." Neely Kate beamed. "He's bound to notice."

I turned my confusion to Neely Kate. "Who are you talking about?"

Violet shook her head. "Never mind. Have you seen Miss Mildred?" She bit her lower lip and surveyed the crowd.

"No, but I wasn't lookin' for her either." The less I saw of that woman, the better.

"She promised me she'd be here. As president of the garden club, if she doesn't come . . ."

"She loves you, Violet. If she said she was coming, she'll be here. Maybe she had trouble getting her car started. You know how old that thing is."

"You and I both know that old Cadillac is like a cockroach. Even a nuclear bomb couldn't kill it." Violet took a deep breath

15

and smoothed a hand over her stomach. "I'm so nervous I feel like I'm gonna throw up."

I grabbed Violet's hands. "You are *amazing*, Violet Mae Gardner Beauregard. You created this from nothing! Two months ago it was an abandoned building, and look at it now! It's bursting with flowers and happiness. *You* did that."

"No, Rose. You're just as much a part of this as I am. You and Joe."

"But *you* had the dream, Violet. You did the homework. This would never have happened if it weren't for *you*." I looked at the assembled crowd. There were over fifty people present, and I suspected they weren't just here for the sheet cake. "The towns-people of Henryetta love you, Violet. That's why they're all here, ready to cheer you on and buy flowers from us. They're here to support *you*." Part of me was a tiny bit jealous of that fact, but I'd lived with it for long enough to accept it. This was Violet's moment, and I wouldn't begrudge her that. "Now get up there and cut that giant ribbon."

Her eyes flew open. "We're doin' it together."

Violet's world was hanging on this business. Mine was hanging on the man walking toward me. "I'll come up there with you, but I'm gonna stand to the side and let you do all the talking."

She nodded and turned to face the crowd, smiling as she walked to the front of the store. Someone from city hall had draped a red ribbon across the sidewalk in front of the entrance and tied it to the racks holding flats of flowers.

When Joe reached me, he was beaming with pride. "It's your big moment, darlin'. Now get over there with Violet."

Neely Kate's eyebrows rose. "He's right. You earned it."

"After all the work you've done, you're coming too." I slipped my hand into Joe's and pulled him with me.

Brody MacIntosh, the recently elected mayor, stood at Violet's left, holding a ginormous pair of scissors. Brody was a good-looking man, and newly single since his wife had taken off with the manager of the Walmart in Lafayette County. Every unattached woman in Fenton County was after him, and a good portion of the married ones too. Since he owned the local lumber yard, he had looks *and* money, and his newly gained political position also gave him power. Although, for the life of me, I couldn't see how being able to vote on the trash pickup day made him more attractive.

I kept to the side and let my sister have her moment of glory. I hated to be the center of attention, but it would be odd if I wasn't at the front with Violet since it was the Gardner *Sisters* Nursery. I scanned the crowd, thankful almost everyone was focused on my older, more beautiful sister. My gaze stopped when I locked eyes with Mason Deveraux, the assistant district attorney, and he offered me a hesitant smile.

I had been introduced to Mason when I was picked for—and then kicked off of—the jury for Bruce Wayne Decker's murder trial a couple of months ago. Mason and I had a rocky start after I literally bumped into him in the courthouse, but we ironed out our differences and became friends. That's why I found it odd, and more than a little hurtful, that he'd practically ignored me the few times we'd run into each other since then. Whenever I mentioned Mason's behavior to Joe, he'd just scowl and change the subject, not that I was surprised. The two of them had known each other in Little Rock, but they refused to elaborate on the circumstances. In any case, it was clear that their acquaintance had been less than amicable. As far as I knew, the only time the two of them had gotten along was when they worked together to get me out of jail.

Jonah Pruitt was also in the crowd, standing toward the front with his too bright smile and some of his church people flanking him. A cameraman stood next to them, his camera pointed at the ground.

I scanned the crowd for Miss Mildred, surprised to see her hobbling over to the crowd from the sidewalk. Her face was red, and she looked flustered. Maybe the heat was getting to her, because despite what I had told Violet, Miss Mildred was never late for anything.

Brody got everyone's attention and gave a little speech about Henryetta being built on entrepreneurial spirit and how supporting the Gardner Sisters Nursery was supporting the determination and drive of single mothers, starting right here in our own hometown. He gave Violet an appreciative grin and although her back was turned to me, I could feel her practically swoon.

Violet was not immune to the Brody MacIntosh charm.

He handed her the scissors, and the two of them cut the ribbon together.

Joe tensed, and I grabbed his hand. I knew he was feeling indignant on my behalf, but it didn't bother me. Much.

The crowd broke into applause when the ribbon fell, and Jonah Pruitt immediately walked sideways toward Violet, making sure not to turn his back to the crowd. The cameraman had his camera pointed at the reverend as he stepped in front of Brody and snatched up Violet's hand in a handshake. Turning to the camera, Jonah flashed his toothy smile. "I'm Reverend Jonah Pruitt, the pastor of the New Living Hope Revival Church. As a new member of this community who wants to support local businesses, I'd like to be your first customer and order enough flowers to cover the grounds of the New Living Hope Revival Church!" The crowd broke into loud applause.

Violet's smile spread across her face. She cast a glance over her shoulder at me, but Joe's hand tightened in mine. He leaned into my ear. "I mean it, Rose. Be careful with that man."

"I have every intention of being careful." I was gonna insist on at least half down. Maybe two-thirds. I had seen his church before, and I knew there were a number of landscape beds around the building. The income we could make from this job would be more than we'd budgeted for the entire month.

"And can you plant them as well?" Reverend Jonah asked.

Violet's eyes widened as she looked over at me.

I nodded. "We sure can." We'd figure something out.

"Rose," Joe grunted my ear.

Brody pushed his way around Jonah's side, trying to regain the limelight and take control of the event. "Well, look at that, folks. Our new-to-town televangelist has stepped up to show his support! Thank you, Reverend Pruitt."

Jonah flashed his mega-watt smile. "Just doin' my part."

Miss Mildred pushed her way to the front, thrusting an elbow into Jonah's side to get him out of the way. Everyone wanted their moment in the spotlight. "As president of the Henryetta

Garden Club, we welcome Violet and the Gardner Nursery as an asset to the town."

The crowd clapped politely.

Joe tensed beside me and muttered under his breath. "That's Gardner *Sisters* Nursery."

I squeezed his hand. "Joe, it's okay." Miss Mildred had not only made an appearance, but she'd given our business the Garden Club's stamp of approval. Violet had to be ecstatic.

"The hell it is."

He started forward, but I tugged him back and ran my hand up and down his upper arm. "Joe, it's really okay. I'm used to it."

"Well, you might accept that attitude from the people in this town, but I sure don't see Violet correcting her."

My stomach cramped. Joe was right.

"Miss Mildred," I said. "I'm so glad you could make it. Looks like you arrived right in time."

Her head jerked and her hands shook. "I have no idea what you're talking about. I was here early."

"But . . ."

Violet tilted her head with a syrupy smile pointed at me. "What does it matter when she showed up, Rose. The important thing is that Miss Mildred is here now." Violet looped her arm through Mildred's. "Let me show you around, Miss Mildred. We have a collection of orchids in the greenhouse that I'm sure will interest you."

They hobbled off toward the greenhouse and Joe fumed. "I have no idea why you want to live in this godforsaken town."

Some days I wasn't so sure either.

The crowd dispersed and began to wander around, checking out the plants we had lining the sidewalk and throughout the greenhouse. We encouraged everyone to go inside our gift shop to get a piece of the sheet cake Violet's mother-in-law was handing out. I figured if we could get the people inside to eat cake, they might find something they wanted to buy. Aunt Bessie was bustling with activity behind the cash register, serving a steady stream of people at the checkout line. I was pleased as punch that my plan had worked.

Violet and I greeted our new customers and helped them find what they needed. After mingling with some of the crowd and filming something with his cameraman, Reverend Jonah cornered Violet at the end of the row filled with flats of pansies. I made a beeline for them.

"—have it in by next week?"

"Um . . ." Violet's eyes looked wild, searching me out.

I reached a hand toward Jonah. "Hi, I'm Rose Gardner, Violet's sister."

He offered his hand. His grip was loose and slightly sweaty. "Reverend Jonah Pruitt. I'm pleased to make your acquaintance. If I'd known Henryetta was full of so many beautiful women, I would have moved my church here several years ago."

Violet giggled, but I was more interested in business. "About your flower beds—"

"Ah," he winked. "I can see you're the businesswoman of the team."

That wasn't necessarily true, but in this case, the way Violet was all atwitter, it certainly was.

Violet and Mike had been high-school sweethearts, and it looked like Violet was making up for all those years she'd been with one man.

I needed to get this back on course. "Well, you *were* our first official customer. We want to make sure you're taken care of." I wasn't about to tell him we'd had seven sales before the ceremony.

"That attention to customer service will ensure your success." He preened then cleared his throat, turning more serious. "Yes, we need to discuss how soon you can get the flowers planted. We're having a revival on the church grounds next week—tent and all—and I'd like to have the lot covered in flowers. It's fittin', don't you think? All those flowers representing the New Living Hope Revival Church?"

Violet nodded, but I kept my gaze on him. Let him worry about the symbolism. I wanted to talk money. "What kind of flowers were you thinking, Reverend?"

His hand rested on my arm. "Jonah, my dear."

My dear, my eye. He was trying to make himself sound older, but I knew Jonah Pruitt was in his mid-thirties, which meant he was probably no more than ten years older than me. Reverend Jonah Pruitt could obviously sweet talk himself into and out of anything. I hoped I would have been resistant to his charm even without Joe's warning. "What kind of flowers were you thinking, Jonah?"

He laughed. "I don't know the first thing about flowers. I thought I'd leave that to you lovely ladies."

Violet gave him her sweetest smile. "If you're wanting them planted by Monday, we'll have to go with something traditional. I'm not sure I have enough stock to plant your entire grounds, but I can get the more traditional plants in time."

I knew for a fact we didn't have enough. We were going to have to put in a rush order of chrysanthemums by the end of the day, the only plant we could get in a large enough quantity on time.

"We're going to need half down on the flowers," I said, trying to sound business-like.

His eyes narrowed. "And you can guarantee they'll be planted by Monday afternoon?"

"Yes."

Violet's eyebrows rose, but she stayed silent.

Jonah laughed. "Well, alrighty then. You've got yourself a deal." He extended his hand toward me. I gave it a good shake, probably squeezing tighter than necessary, then pulled away.

"We'll be out this afternoon to figure out how many plants we need, and we'll have an estimate by the end of the day. Where can I find you to get the deposit?"

He grinned, shaking his head. "You really are a stickler for business, aren't you, Rose?" He winked at Violet, then turned back to me. "I'll be in my office the rest of the day. You can find me there until five-thirty, when I have to leave to get ready for the evening service."

"I'll be there to get a check."

"And I *very* much look forward to seeing you again." He moved onto a group of elderly women in the garden club who giggled when the semi-famous televangelist started talking to them.

Violet's eyes sparkled with excitement. "Do you know what this means, Rose?"

"It means a heck of a lot of work."

"But to have *our* flowers at his church? They'll be on his TV show!"

I suspected none of his TV viewers would ever know they were our flowers, but I didn't see the point of taking her glory from her. "I'll go measure the beds, and then we can figure out what to plant and how many flats we need before I give him our estimate. And get his check."

She scowled. "Why'd you do that? Insist on getting money down? You know we can buy those flowers on thirty-day credit."

Violet wanted this order, and so did I, Jonah Pruitt's questionable character aside. But I saw no reason to tell her about that part. "Just think what we can do with the early cash flow. Besides, we have to hire someone to help plant all those flowers. You and I can't do it ourselves."

Worry wrinkled her forehead. "What are we going to do about that?"

I patted her arm, watching Jonah work the crowd. "I have a couple of guys in mind."

Violet heaved a sigh of relief moments before a woman pulled her aside with a question.

I wasn't so sure she'd approve of the two guys I had in mind, but with such short notice, beggars couldn't be choosers. Besides, their characters might benefit from a little time spent working on church grounds.

"He sure does know how to work the older women of Henryetta."

Mason Deveraux stood next to me, eyes fixed on Jonah.

"Does he? It looks like they love him."

"Oh, they sure do." There was a suspicious note in his voice.

I looked up at him with a grin. "Are you worried you have even more competition for most eligible bachelor of Henryetta?"

His eyes widened in confusion, but I wasn't sure why. He was a fine looking man from a respected Arkansas family. With his dark blonde hair, hazel eyes, and fit physique, the women in town were trying their darnedest to get his attention. Rumor had it he hadn't dated at all since his arrival, which only added to his allure.

I shook my head. "Surely, you know you're on the list of the most eligible bachelors in town. You and Brody MacIntosh."

Mason's face reddened. "That explains all the baked goods that keep appearing in my office."

"And that explains the five pounds it looks like you've gained."

His eyes widened again, this time in alarm.

I leaned my arm against his. "I'm joking. You look great, Mason."

His shoulders sagged with relief.

I shot him a glare. "Why have you been avoiding me the last couple of months?"

It was my day to shock him. "Um . . ." A frown creased his forehead. "I'm the wrong person to be talking to about that."

"Then who is?"

"I think you know." Mr. No Nonsense was back, the man I'd met at the beginning of Bruce Wayne Decker's trial, not the man I'd gotten to know. Without a backward glance, Mason walked toward the cars parked in the street.

Who was he talking about?

And then it hit me.

Joe.

Chapter Three

When I found Joe, he was carrying a flat of asters to the street and loading it into the car of one of the garden club cronies. The sight of him being so helpful made my irritation fade slightly. How many boyfriends would be so helpful? As the woman's car drove away, Joe made his way toward me, and my irritation won out.

"What did you say to Mason about me?"

"What?" He narrowed his eyes in confusion.

I grabbed his arm and pulled him to the back corner of the building. "Did you tell Mason not to talk to me?"

Joe recovered his senses and had the nerve to look angry. "What did he say?"

I put my hands on my hips. "He didn't say anything, but I think you just answered my question."

"Rose." He inhaled, a hard look filling his eyes. "There's a lot you don't know about Mason and me."

"Then tell me."

He glanced at his watch and groaned. "I don't have time. I have to go in a few minutes."

Crossing my arms over my chest, I shot him a glare. "How convenient."

Joe gripped my arms and tugged me to his chest. "Rose, I love you, and I'd never do anything to hurt you. Yes, I did ask Mason to stay away from you, but I have my reasons."

I leaned my head back and cocked my eyebrows. "And those are?"

He whipped me around the back corner, out of sight of the customers, and pushed me against the wall. His lips covered mine, and he kissed me so thoroughly I forgot what we were talking about. But then again, that had probably been his plan. He knew I couldn't stay mad at him for long when he kissed me like that.

Lifting his head, he sighed, worry in his eyes. "Mason and I have a history that I don't have time to get into right now. When I get back, I promise to tell you everything."

His news wasn't a total shock. After Joe's overreaction to finding me with Mason on my porch the night I was first attacked by Jimmy DeWade, I had since suspected they had a past together. "Why haven't you already told me about it?"

He grimaced. "It's not something I'm proud of."

My stomach dropped. What could Joe have done to make him so ashamed? "I don't get why you don't want Mason to talk to me."

"I don't want you to get hurt."

"How could talking to Mason hurt me?"

"I was scared he would tell you about what happened in Little Rock. I want to be the one to tell you, but I wasn't ready yet. It was wrong, and I'm sorry." He ran a hand through his hair, leaving a ruffled mess and looking miserable. "Darlin', I have to leave in less than five minutes, and I don't know when I'll see or talk to you again. I'd rather spend that time kissing than dredging up my miserable past. I'll explain it all later, okay?"

No, it wasn't okay. He should have already told me, but he was right. I didn't want to spend these last few minutes talking about something upsetting. It bothered me enough that he was leaving.

He brushed the hair out of my face, gazing into my eyes. "I love you, Rose, more than I think you even realize. You see me as Joe McAllister, the man you met four months ago, but there's more to Joe Simmons than you know, parts I'd like to leave behind. You make me want to be Joe McAllister."

"You *are* Joe McAllister to me."

He hesitated. "I'm thinking about quitting."

My chest froze. "Quitting what?" I whispered.

"The state police."

I blinked, sure I'd heard him wrong. "What?"

His hand cradled my cheek. "I miss you. I want us to be more permanent than just weekends and some weeknights."

I closed my eyes as guilt rushed in. Two months ago, I'd agreed to move to Little Rock with Joe, but then I'd realized I wasn't ready. And now that I'd opened the nursery with Violet, I was stuck in Henryetta. With Little Rock two hours away, our situation was far from ideal. "I'm sorry."

He kissed me again, a sweet kiss full of love and tenderness. "No, don't be sorry. You love what you're doing now, and I think you'll be great at it. Plus, I've had fun helping you get ready to open the store. I wouldn't dream of taking this from you."

"But if you quit, what will you do?"

"I put my application in with the Fenton County Sheriff's department a few weeks ago, and I had an interview yesterday afternoon. That's part of the reason I'm here."

My stomach tumbled with excitement. "Why didn't you tell me?"

"Because you know my attempt to transfer here with the state police didn't work out. I didn't want to get your hopes up, only to disappoint us both. They have an opening for a deputy, though, and I'm sure they're going to offer me the job." He smiled. "This is the last time I'm going undercover. I never want to purposely be gone from you this long again."

I wrapped my arms around his neck. "Oh, Joe. I don't know what I'm going to do without you."

His mouth found mine and I clung to him, unshed tears burning my eyes. I told myself the most he'd be gone was a few weeks, and I'd more than likely get to talk to him several times, but the dangerous part of his absence terrified me. What if he didn't come back?

"Be careful." The lump in my throat made my voice tight.

"Always, darlin'. I've got too much to lose." He wiped the tear escaping down my cheek, his eyes becoming more stern. "And I'm serious about being careful with Jonah Pruitt."

Joe's tone gave me second thoughts about doing business with the man. "Is he really that dangerous?"

"No, nothing like that. I don't think he'd physically hurt someone—not that I know of anyway—but watch him with your financial dealings." He lowered his voice. "I've already told you more than I should have."

"I told him we need half down, which more than covers the cost of the flowers."

He gave me a tight smile. "That's my girl."

I rested my cheek against his chest, the dull thud of his heartbeat in my ear. I soaked in his presence, trying not to think about the dangers he was going to face over the next few weeks. Instead, I had to trust that he'd do everything in his power to come back to me.

I walked Joe to his car and gave him one last kiss goodbye.

"I love you, Rose. Don't ever doubt that."

I forced myself to be strong and not break down. "I love you too, Joe. If anything happens to you, I'll make you regret it."

He chuckled and ducked into the car. "I'll keep that in mind. Stay out of trouble while I'm gone."

"It's not like I go lookin' for it."

He shook his head with a grimace. "That's the part that worries me the most."

I watched him drive away, my heart leaving with him. At least getting the store up and running would fill up my time and keep me from missing him too much.

We had a steady stream of customers for the next several hours. We'd hoped to sell plants for fall beds, and we were doing better than we'd expected. But then again, the only other places to get bedding plants in Henryetta were Walmart and the hardware store.

Around two o'clock, things died down so I could get away to measure the New Living Hope Revival Church beds. Neither Violet nor I had thought to bring a measuring tape to the nursery. I had one in my kitchen junk drawer, so I decided to swing by and pick it up on the way there.

As soon as I pulled onto my street, I knew something was wrong. A small crowd had gathered on the sidewalk in front of Miss Opal's house, Miss Mildred's next-door neighbor. A police car and an ambulance were parked at the end of the street, their flashing lights swirling. Over the last few months, anytime there was a vehicle with flashing lights in our neighborhood, it always stopped in front of my house. The ladies of the Busybody Club—a.k.a. the neighborhood watch—had to be confused.

After I parked in my driveway, I walked across the street to find out what was going on. I lived in an older neighborhood, and the bungalow homes on my street were mostly occupied by elderly women. The only residents under retirement age were me, the neighbors in Joe's old house, and the house on the corner, the one belonging to Thomas's family.

The elderly women huddled in a tight pack, all of them staring at Miss Dorothy's front door. The front of her house was filled with several emergency personnel. She lived between Opal and Thomas's family. Mildred stood in the middle of the pack, not surprisingly in the position of ringleader. She lifted a shaky hand to her mouth. "I knew something was wrong when I didn't see Dorothy at Violet's nursery this morning. She'd been planning on going to that grand opening since she found out what Violet was up to. She always loved that girl."

My next door neighbor Heidi Joy waddled up to me, her right hand on her back, supporting the weight of her pregnant belly. Her nine-month-old baby was perched on her left hip. "What's all the commotion about?"

"It's Dorothy," Opal answered from the ranks. "Mildred found her."

Heidi Joy's eyes widened. "What do you mean *found her*?"

"She was lying on her living room floor." Mildred's voice shook. "Dead as a doornail."

Gasping, Heidi Joy covered her mouth and wobbled.

I grabbed her elbow to help steady her. "Do you want to sit down?"

She shook her head, but her face had paled. I lifted the baby from her arms and set him on my own hip. He grabbed a handful of my hair and promptly stuffed it in his mouth.

"What happened to her?" I asked.

Mildred's face was almost as pale as Heidi Joy's. "I don't know. I just found her lying there."

A dark sedan pulled up to the curb behind the police car. The driver's door opened, and Mason got out, surveying the crowd. His eyes landed on me for several seconds, but he was wearing his no-nonsense face.

Mason was here as the Fenton County assistant DA.

"Who's that?" one of my neighbors asked.

"Mason Deveraux III, the assistant district attorney," Mildred answered before I could. "He's from a good Little Rock family."

I nearly groaned. I didn't know much about Mason's upbringing, other than he came from money. But in this part of southern Arkansas, it wasn't necessarily whether you had money or not. It was where you were born, as well as where your parents and grandparents were born. The further back in the Arkansas state birth records your family went, the more social status you achieved. My family went back pretty far if I didn't take my birth mother's Louisiana heritage into account. But then again, only a handful of people knew about my birth mother. I'd only found out about her back in June, and I hadn't told anyone other than Violet and Joe. My aunt and uncle had known all along.

Mason disappeared into the house as we kept our vigil. I considered leaving since I had plenty of work to do, but I was curious about what was going on. Besides, Heidi Joy still looked peaked, and I wasn't sure she should be holding a twenty-pound baby. As I shifted him to the other hip, I wasn't sure *I* should be holding a twenty-pound baby. I had no idea how Heidi Joy did it, pregnant to boot. Then I remembered that this was her sixth pregnancy. She'd had plenty of practice.

Several minutes later the paramedics came out the door, bumping a gurney down the steps with a sheet-covered body strapped on top. Several women gasped. Perhaps they hadn't trusted Mildred's medical assessment.

I couldn't help remembering when I was on the other side of the line—the watchee instead of the watcher. My mother's death had drawn a larger crowd, but then again, there'd been no doubt she'd been murdered. And it was a Saturday night.

Mason came outside a few minutes later, walking down the steps and toward his car. He caught my eye and shifted his eyes to the side.

I handed the baby back to Heidi Joy and left my post to meet him at the driver-side door of his car.

He stopped in front of me, a soft smile raising his mouth. "Rose, you looked domestic with a baby on your hip."

"Is that a good thing or a bad one?"

"Neither, just an observation."

"What happened to Miss Dorothy?"

He looked back at the house before turning toward me. "I suspect natural causes."

"You mean like Miss Laura?"

He frowned. "That's why I'm here. But the damn paramedics had already moved her to the gurney by the time I showed up."

"And that's bad?"

"If she truly died of natural causes, no. But with all the bungling that's gone on with the police department since I've come to town, I've requested that they notify me whenever there's a death. That way I can investigate the potential crime scene too."

"Oh." I couldn't help wondering if Mason would have presumed that I was guilty of my mother's murder like the entire Henryetta police department had done. I'd like to think he would have been fair. "Do you really think Miss Dorothy and Miss Laura died of natural causes? Doesn't it seem suspicious?"

"You know this is official business, and I'm really not supposed to be telling you. But after everything you've been through over the last few months, I suspect you need some peace of mind." Glancing back at the house, he lowered his voice. "I think they both died of natural causes because I've got nothing to make me suspect that they didn't. No break-ins. No sign of stolen belongings. There's nothing for you to worry about."

"What did they find in Miss Laura's autopsy?"

"They didn't do one. The county is strapped for cash, and it costs several thousands of dollars to ship the bodies to Little Rock and back and pay the pathologists. We don't do autopsies if it looks like natural causes."

"Oh." I'd never considered that.

He leaned his hip against the side of his car. "Congrats again on the opening of your nursery."

My eyebrows shot up. "So does this mean you're officially through with ignoring me?"

He studied the ground, a sheepish grin spreading across his face, then looked me in the eyes. "That was quite unlike me. I don't usually let other people dictate my behavior."

"So why start with Joe?"

Mason paused. "We have history." I expected him to continue, but he stared at the baby instead.

"So he said."

His eyes widened as his gaze shifted to me. "He told you what happened?"

"No" was out of my mouth before I could stop it. I'd probably just blown any opportunity to get information out of Mason, but I wasn't willing to give up yet. "Why don't you tell me your side of the story?"

He reached for the handle. "Good try."

I grabbed his hand and pulled it away from the door, surprised he didn't resist. "Mason, if this involves me, I have a right to know."

"With all due respect, Rose, it really doesn't involve you. If Joe said the only reason he warned me to stay away from you was because of the history he and I have, he's lying."

My mouth dropped. "Warned you? As in physically threatened you?"

Mason's mouth pursed.

"Why would he do that?"

His voice lowered. "Isn't it obvious?"

"No. It's not."

He closed his eyes and inhaled before returning his gaze to me. "I'd rather keep that chapter of my life closed for good." His face hardened. "But if I was in a serious relationship, I would share it with the woman in my life. She would have a right to know." He started to say something, then swallowed and pinched his lips.

"What? What aren't you telling me?"

"The question isn't what I'm not telling you, it's what's Joe not telling you?"

Anger rose in my chest. "That's not fair."

"Isn't it?"

"We've only . . . we're . . ."

Mason leaned closer, lowering his voice again. "It's obvious how you two feel about each other. Do you know I field at least two calls a week from your neighbor Mildred about your public displays of affection in your front yard?" His shoulders tensed. "But what do you know about Joe's family? What do you know about his life in Little Rock before you two were together? The man I see with you isn't the man I knew in Little Rock, but the reality is that he's still the same guy."

Before I could get my wits about me to ask about the Joe he knew, Mason had climbed into his car and driven away.

Chapter Four

My conversation with Mason shook me up more than I cared to admit. I checked on Heidi Joy to make sure she wasn't going to pass out, then went home to let Muffy out. When I came back outside with my dog, Heidi Joy's four-year-old son Keith stood in her front yard, staring at the police car.

"Was that a dead body?" he asked.

I looked down the street at Heidi Joy. I knew her husband was at work. "Where are your brothers?"

His face scrunched with irritation. "Was it a dead body or not?"

"That was Miss Dorothy. And yes, she died. Now where are your brothers?"

"Andy Jr.'s at school, and Benny and Tommy are sleeping."

"Why aren't you napping?" Heidi Joy had to be really shaken up to have left them alone. That was so unlike her. She wouldn't even let them leave their yard.

His eyes narrowed. "I ain't no baby." He craned his neck to get a better view. "How come she's dead?"

"She was old, and old people die." I suddenly wondered if I should have said anything. When I was four, I had no concept of death. This was a subject better left for Heidi Joy and Andy.

"Did she have a heart attack?"

"I don't know."

"Do people yell when they die?"

I shrugged. "I suppose some people do." I'd never thought about whether my mother yelled when Daniel Crocker hit her in the head with her rolling pin. If she did, no one heard her. That thought sent a shiver down my spine. "Why would you ask that?"

"I heard yelling."

I swung my gaze down to him. "What?"

He looked at me like I was stupid. "There was yelling coming from her house this morning."

"How do you know it was coming from her house?"

His face lowered, and he refused to look me in the eye. "I was across the street."

I turned my attention to the crowd and realized Thomas's car was gone. Maybe he'd made it to school after all. "Across the street from her house?"

"That's what I said, ain't it?" Keith meant to sound defensive, but he sounded nervous instead.

"Were you supposed to be down that far?" I knew for a fact he wasn't. I'd heard Heidi Joy yell at the boys several times a day not to leave their yard. But now I'd scared him, and he'd never tell me anything. "I won't tell your mom."

He looked up through squinted eyes. "Why not?"

"I thought you and I were friends. I let you play with Muffy don't I?"

"Yeah, but you always let Andy Jr. be in charge."

"Well, how about when Andy Jr. is at school, *you* can be in charge?"

His eyes widened. "You mean it?"

"Yeah. See, we're friends."

Keith grinned with a smug look.

"So tell me about the yelling."

He squatted and petted Muffy. "I heard two people shouting."

"What did they say?"

He shrugged. "I don't know. I couldn't understand them."

"Were they happy yelling or angry yelling?"

"There's happy yelling?"

"Well, yeah. You know when you're really excited about something. Like you and your brothers when you're running around with Muffy."

"Oh." His mouth pursed. "Mad yelling."

"Did you see anyone? Do you know who it was?"

He shook his head, frustration wrinkling his brow. "I don't know."

"You don't know if it was a man or a woman?"

He shook his head again. "No, when I heard yelling, I ran home."

Keith was pretty fearless, so if the yelling scared him that much, it must have been loud. I rubbed his head. "That's okay, Keith. You were a huge help." What was I going to do with this information? The police would never listen to me, and I could only think of one person who might. "Hey, I need to go inside and make a phone call. Would you mind watching Muffy for me for a minute?"

"Would I?" He squatted next to Muffy, rubbing her head a little too hard, but I bit my tongue. She jumped up and licked his face, so she obviously didn't mind.

When I went inside, I left the kitchen door open to keep an eye on them. Heidi Joy was still down the street, and I wasn't about to leave Keith and Muffy totally unsupervised.

Grabbing my phone out of my purse, I called the number I'd stored in my phone for Mason, thankful he'd given it to me after saving me from Skeeter Malcolm at the pool hall. His number went straight to voicemail, and I tried to figure out what message to leave him as I listened to his voicemail recording.

"Hey, Mason. This is Rose." I paused. "I might have some information about Miss Dorothy. You can call me back on this number."

I wasn't sure what Keith had heard or if it even had anything to do with Miss Dorothy's death. When I was investigating Frank Mitchell's murder in my attempt to help prove Bruce Wayne innocent, Joe had taught me that sometimes things aren't what they seem to be. I couldn't presume this meant Miss Dorothy had met with a foul end. For all I knew, Keith had heard her television.

After I sent Keith back in his house, I found my tape measure in my junk drawer. I grabbed a pad of graph paper, and then tucked Muffy into the bathroom. Thankfully, Heidi Joy was on her way back when I was ready to leave. I never would have left Keith and his napping brothers alone.

I met her in the driveway. "Keith came outside and asked about Miss Dorothy."

Her eyes flew open in horror. "Oh my word! I just ran off and left them! You must think I'm the worst mother in the world."

"You?" I scoffed. "You're a *wonderful* mother. You were just startled about Miss Dorothy. Did you find out anything else?"

She shook her head. "No, thank goodness. Everyone's saying it was natural causes. I'm not sure what I'd do if there was an actual murder on our street." Her hand flew up to her open mouth. "Rose, I'm so sorry. Sometimes my mouth starts flappin' before I know what I'm saying. Your mother . . ."

Too many memories of my mother's murder had been dragged out of the vault I'd locked them in. "Don't worry about it. I understand. You have your babies to think about." I gave her a smile, even if I didn't feel like offering one. "I have to get going. You should go lie down. You still look pale."

She nodded and took the baby inside.

I had a lot to mull over on the drive to the New Living Hope Revival Church, but my conversation with Mason took precedence. What had Joe and Mason done that neither wanted to confess? When I let myself dwell on it, a ball of fear took root in my stomach. I wouldn't have taken the situation this seriously if both of them hadn't been so adamant about not telling me. What worried me the most was Joe's comment he'd randomly made over the last couple of months that he wished he were Joe McAllister, the name he'd used while living undercover next door to me.

Could Joe Simmons really be so different?

The site of the New Living Hope Revival Church had only recently been christened with its new name. In its previous incarnation, the church had been the First Presbyterian Church of Henryetta. The Presbyterian Church had lost a lot of members to the Southern Baptist Church, and their income suffered, forcing them to find a smaller building. This one had been empty for two years when Reverend Jonah Pruitt came to town three months ago. Jonah secured the lease, and then promptly began to add followers to his fold, many of whom were lured there by the cameras. He had a small television following, but since coming to Henryetta, he had begun to attract the notice of the national media. The fact that the new Henryetta members came from the town's existing churches didn't sit so well with many of the townsfolk. I was certain that this had played a factor in Jonah's decision to support Violet and me. He probably wanted to look more community friendly. As long as he paid us, I didn't care about his motives.

There were a few cars in the parking lot—a couple of run-down older ones and a white Cadillac with the license plate *Rev JP*. Classy. I parked in the shade of a giant oak tree and began to survey the grounds, pad in hand. While there were landscape beds on all four sides of the large church, many were full of over-grown bushes in need of pruning. I'd add weeding and grooming to the list of things we could offer the reverend.

After I sketched the building on the graph paper, I began marking the beds and how many flowers they needed, then listed all the labor. Half the beds were filled to the brim with bushes and perennials, but they were neglected and overgrown, and it was going to take some work to get them ready.

When I got back to the nursery, Violet and I drew up a plan. The lack of flower beds disappointed her, but we came up with several options to increase our profits, including potted plants to put around the grounds and revival tent to add a bit of color.

"This is great, Rose," Violet said, lifting the hair off the back of her neck. "But look at all the manual labor that needs to get done. How are we gonna do that *and* work here?"

"I told you I had a couple of guys in mind."

She squinted. "Who are they?"

I hesitated. "Let me see if they are available first. If they aren't, I'll check with the temporary employment office." Violet started to protest, but I interrupted her. "Miss Dorothy died."

She placed her hand on her chest. "*What?*"

"An ambulance and police car were in front of her house when I went home to get the tape measure."

"What happened? Was it . . ."

"Murder?" Funny how Violet gave me a hard time about looking for the worst when her mind went there too. "Mason said it was natural causes like Miss Laura, but it sure seems like a strange coincidence."

Violet shuddered. "Mason? Why was Mason there?"

"He said he's been going to all the scenes where they find a dead body."

"Don't talk about Miss Dorothy that way." Tears filled her eyes. "Poor Miss Dorothy. I wondered why she didn't come to the opening."

"Mildred said she was planning on going. That's why she checked on Miss Dorothy when she got home. And then she found her lying on her living room floor."

"We'll have to make a casserole," Violet mumbled.

My squinted my confusion. "Who are we gonna make a casserole for? She didn't have any kids, and last I heard, her niece moved away."

"Her sister lives at Happy Meadows in assisted living."

"Oh." I wasn't surprised Violet knew this. She'd been close to Miss Dorothy when she was a kid.

Glancing at the clock, I realized it was close to five. If I was going to get a check from Reverend Jonah, I needed to get to the church within the next half hour.

But first I had to stop at the Piggly Wiggly.

Chapter Five

David Moore still worked as a bag boy at the Piggly Wiggly. I'd first discovered that he worked there after being kicked off the jury of his best friend's murder trial. David had been a witness, and I'd once cornered him in the parking lot, looking for information. Since David and Bruce Wayne Decker didn't have the best work history, I was surprised he was still working there two months later.

He was at the end of register number five, packing a plastic bag with canned green beans. His eyes widened when he saw I was heading straight for him. "I didn't do anything. I swear."

"What are you talking about? I'm here to offer you a job."

Confusion flickered in his eyes as he looked down at the bag he was packing. "I have a job."

"The job I'm offering is a temporary one. Planting flowers." I'd leave the pruning and digging as a surprise. He hesitated, so I pressed on. "What about Bruce Wayne? Does he have a job?"

He twisted his mouth to the side. "Well . . ."

I took that as a no. "It'll only take you a couple of days. And as soon as the job is done, I'll pay you cash."

The cashier, an older woman, gave me a dirty look as David put the bags in the customer's cart. "I dunno," he mumbled. "It sounds hot."

"Bruce Wayne is living with you, right? If he's not working, then how's he going to pay his share of the rent? The first of the month is coming up, and your rent's going to be due. I bet you that you'll earn enough to pay a good part of your rent in the two days I need you. And think of what you could buy with the extra money." I arched my eyebrows, hoping he caught my drift. They were both infamous potheads.

Unconvinced, he scowled. "I'll have to talk to Bruce Wayne."

"So Bruce Wayne *does* have his rent money?" I put my hand on my hip.

David groaned and stepped to the side. "What time do we start?"

I resisted the urge to grin. "Show up at the New Living Hope Revival Church at ten tomorrow morning."

His eyes flew open. "Ten? That early?"

"Half the world's awake by ten, and the other half is sleeping in China."

"Wait. Ain't that the new church with that Reverend Jonah TV dude?"

"Yep, that's him."

A smile spread across his face. "Any chance we'll be on TV?"

"You just never know." I winked. "Bring some water and sunscreen. And be ready to get dirty."

He didn't look too happy about that part, but I left before he could protest.

I pulled into the church parking lot at five-fifteen, surprised to find more cars there than there'd been earlier. When I entered the foyer, strains of guitar and drum music filtered through the doors to the sanctuary. So the New Living Hope Revival Church had a live band. No wonder it was stealing all the Henryetta church-goers. The younger families anyway.

When I walked into the church office, Jonah's secretary eyed me up and down with a look of disapproval. She had salt and pepper hair and had to be in her late fifties, although her ultra-conservative long-sleeve blouse buttoned to the top and her long skirt suggested she'd walked straight out of the early twentieth century. "You're one of the Gardner sisters, aren't you?" Her tone confirmed she didn't like what she saw.

I hesitated, unsure what she knew about me. "I'm Rose."

She curled her lip, momentarily hiding the dark shadow under her nose. "He's waiting for you. Go on in."

Jonah's office door was ajar and after the secretary's less-than-friendly greeting, I tentatively pushed it open. Jonah's mouth was pursed as he studied the computer monitor on his desk, his fingers tapping the keyboard.

"Excuse me, Reverend."

A smile spread across his face. "Rose, so good to see you again." He stood and walked around his desk. "And what did I tell you about calling me Reverend? It's Jonah."

I grimaced. "That feels disrespectful."

He leaned his backside on his desk and crossed his arms across his chest. "And I bet you grew up on fire and brimstone, didn't you? You had the fear of God put into you every Sunday morning whether you needed it or not."

He had no idea.

Lifting his shoulder into a half shrug, he grinned. "That's what makes us different than most of the churches in town. No hell fire and damnation. No condemnation here."

My mouth parted before I quickly hid my shock, but I guess I wasn't fast enough.

He laughed. "I can see that catches you by surprise. Most people have that reaction, and it often takes them a while to get used to us. Especially our older members."

I had to admit his concept sounded wonderful. And also too good to be true.

"I take it you're here for a check?"

"Um, yeah." His unique views of church had momentarily made me forget the purpose of my visit. "I have a few options to show you first."

"Options are always great." He pushed away from his desk and motioned to a small round table in the corner, bordered by two chairs. "Have a seat, and I'll take a look at what you have."

I sat down and Jonah took the chair next to me, keeping a respectful distance. I placed the sketch on the table and slid it toward him, explaining why I'd made certain choices and giving him estimates. The first involved only installing flowers in the beds. The second included flowers in the beds and trimming the bushes and existing landscape. The third included the flowers and landscape trimming, plus pots filled with flowers spread around the grounds.

Jonah didn't even blink at the price. "You have a good eye for design, Rose."

"Well . . . thank you."

He leaned his elbow on the table and turned to look at me. "But then again, that shouldn't be a surprise. You are a beautiful woman, so it stands to reason you'd appreciate God's beauty in nature as well." I couldn't form a coherent answer, but he didn't seem to notice. "I'll take the third option. I like the idea of having lots of flowers around."

While I'd presented the most expensive option, I hadn't expected him to take it. Momma had complained plenty about the Henryetta Southern Baptist Church's budget, so I knew how frugal most churches were. "Okay, then. We're gonna need half down on the supplies."

"I'll tell Rhonda, my secretary, to write you a check."

I gathered my papers. "Okay."

He leaned back in his seat, a grin spreading across his face. "Now that we have business out of the way, tell me a little about yourself, Rose."

I blinked in surprise. "Well, there's not much to tell."

"I find that difficult to believe."

I didn't answer.

"Well, let's start with the most obvious question for a man of the cloth. Do you go to church?"

That was a sticky question. I may have been born and raised in the Henryetta Southern Baptist Church, but I'd never felt any sense of belonging there. The main reason was my visions. They had started when I was six, and despite the fact that my paternal grandmother had experienced visions too and had been declared the Oracle of Lafayette County, Momma had decided I was demon-possessed by the time I was eight. She soon started locking me in the hall closet whenever I had a vision. Several pastors over the years had prayed for the salvation of my soul, but by the time I was a teenager, they'd all given up. "Off and on."

"Have you ever attended a church like mine?"

My eyebrows rose as I shook my head. "Uh, no."

"That's not surprising. But you should try it sometime." He winked. "You might like what you see."

"I don't know about that."

He held up his hands in surrender and laughed. "I know when to back off. Let's move on to another topic." His voice lowered. "I heard about your mother."

My mother's murder wasn't something I wanted to delve into. Not after all the strange feelings Miss Dorothy's death had dredged up. "Well, I need to get goin'." I stood up, nearly dumping the drawing onto the floor. "I need to get this check deposited at the bank."

Jonah grinned as he rose from his seat. "There's no hurry, Rose. The bank closed at five."

"Oh, that's right." He had me flustered. Between the concept of his church, him calling me pretty, and the topic of my mother's death, my stomach was churning.

His voice softened. "Does the thought of coming to my church frighten you, Rose?"

No, but staying with Jonah Pruitt a minute longer sure did. "I've had some . . . difficult situations in church."

"All the more reason to try our church out. The New Living Hope Revival Church is dedicated to providing a home for the castoffs of traditional churches. Giving them hope to live their life. That's what the name of our church is all about."

I backed toward the door. "I will definitely keep that in mind, Jonah. Now if you'll excuse me . . ."

I backtracked to his secretary's office as he followed me with an amused grin. Jonah stood in the doorway, his hand resting on the door frame, looking like he was posing for a photo shoot. "Rhonda, Ms. Gardner needs a check made out to—?" He glanced at me, raising an eyebrow in question.

"Gardner Sisters Nursery."

"Oh, yes." He drawled, his Southern accent sounding heavier than usual. "The lovely Gardner sisters, both as beautiful as the flowers they were named after."

Rhonda opened a desk drawer and pulled out a checkbook, her mouth puckering into a frown. She frowned even more when I told her how much to make it out for.

Jonah brushed past me. "I have to get ready for tonight's service. I hope to see more of you, Rose." His gaze rested on my face as he headed for the door, leaving me behind with his grumpy secretary.

She ripped the check out of the book and shoved it at me. "I don't know what you're up to, but I know your kind."

I took the check and held it close to me in case she changed her mind and tried to snatch it back. "My kind?"

Sneering, Rhonda shook her head. "I've been with Reverend Pruitt for a long time. You're not the first pretty girl to catch his attention. Jonah Pruitt is a man of God, so you can take your whorin' ways with you."

I could have made the argument that I'd only slept with one man, which hardly constituted whoring, but the fact that I was fornicating at all probably wouldn't help my case. Instead, I turned around and left as quickly as I could in case Jonah changed his mind and tracked me down.

I drove back to the nursery, sorting through my confusion. While I had firsthand proof that all the older women of Henryetta loved Jonah Pruitt, I hadn't heard much gossip about the younger ones falling for him. At least not like they fawned over the town's other prime bachelors, like Mason and Brody. I'd seen three sides to Jonah Pruitt today. The showman who'd showed up for the ribbon cutting ceremony. The minister who seemed to sincerely welcome all people to his church, reserving judgment. And the man who seemed interested in me for more than just the transfer of my church membership. But that had to be an overactive imagination at work. Why would Jonah Pruitt be interested in *me*?

Violet was closing up when I went inside. She turned to me with excitement. "Well . . . ?"

"He picked the big one. The potted plants and all."

She squealed and danced in place. "Did he give you a deposit?"

I pulled it out of my purse and handed it to her.

She danced for several more seconds, then stopped, cocking her head. "Why do you look so strange?"

I hesitated, wondering if I should tell her what happened. "I think Jonah Pruitt's interested in me."

44

Her nose scrunched as she watched me, still confused. Then her eyebrows rose. "Oh!" Confusion returned. "Oh." She paused. "What happened?"

"He invited me to church."

Rolling her eyes, Violet shook her head. "Good Lord, if that's *interested in you*, then that means Reverend Martin has hit on every woman in town." She giggled. "Can you imagine?"

I leaned my butt against the counter. "That wasn't all."

"What else?"

"He said you and I were as beautiful as our names."

Violet laughed. "Rose, you're so cute." She patted my arm and walked around the counter. "He wasn't hittin' on you. He was trying to secure our business."

"I don't know . . ."

She put her hand on her hip. "How many men have you dated?"

"That's not fair." She knew I'd only dated Joe. I refused to count the two blind dates she'd set me up on. "How many men have *you* dated?"

An ornery grin lit up her eyes. "Only a few, but I'm changing that tomorrow night."

My breath stuck. "What does that mean?"

"It means I have a date."

"A date? With who?"

"Brody."

I wasn't sure why that surprised me. They'd flirted at the ribbon cutting ceremony. And Violet seemed ready to move on from her relationship with Mike, even if *I* wasn't ready for her to move on. "That's . . . great."

"Don't sound so excited."

"It's just . . . so soon."

She rested her arms on the counter and leaned forward, lowering her voice. "I think he's dating someone."

"Who's dating someone?" Then I realized she meant Mike. "*Oh.*" Try as I might, I just couldn't picture either of them with someone else. It didn't seem right. But if Mike really was dating, didn't Violet deserve to move on too? "What about Ashley and Mikey?"

"It's Mike's night to have them."

This was all too weird for me, but Violet did seem happy. "Good for you, Vi. Brody seems like a great guy. At least, most of the women in town seem to think so."

"He was three years ahead of me in school. I was a freshman when he was a senior. Of course, he didn't know me back then."

I grinned. "Sounds like he wants to know you more now."

Violet giggled and straightened up the counter. "The Gardner Sisters Nursery had a great first day. Tomorrow we need to figure out how to get all those flowers to the church." Her mouth dropped open. "Oh! Did you find someone to plant them and trim the landscape?"

I tried not to cringe. "Two someones."

"Who are they?"

"David Moore and Bruce Wayne Decker."

Her face screwed up. "I don't know them, but why does the second guy sound familiar?"

I moved to the door and said over my shoulder, "Because I was on his jury." Then I hurried out to start covering the plants on the sidewalk.

Violet followed me out the door. "*You hired a murderer?*"

I shot her an indignant look. "He is *not* a murderer. Remember? Jimmy DeWade was the murderer."

"He's still a criminal!"

I shook my head. "For little things. Pot, DUI, shoplifting."

She leaned against the door, crossing her arms over her chest and puckering her mouth. "What if he shoplifts at the church? That's gonna look bad on us."

My head shot up. "What's he gonna steal, Violet? The communion plates? Copies of the Bible?"

She fumed as she tried to find fuel for her argument.

I tucked the tarp in the corner and cinched it with a padlock. "Look at it this way: maybe working for a church will be good for 'em. Build their character and all that." With any luck at all, Jonah Pruitt would invite *them* to his church. But then again, if he gave the guys the hard sell, they might run off before the job was finished.

Violet wasn't entirely convinced, but seeing as we didn't have anyone else, she relented. She planned to ask her father-in-law if she could borrow his truck to haul the bedding plants to the church. Together, Violet and I would load the truck, and then the guys would help me unload. Violet would order more flowers from the supplier, who had pledged to have them delivered to the church by Friday.

After we got everything locked up, Violet and I stood in the parking lot, staring at the sign above the front door.

"I think this is really gonna work," Violet whispered, squeezing my arm.

I turned to her, my eyebrows shooting up. "You had doubts? You've been Miss Positivity since the moment you announced this crazy idea." And then I realized the truth: Violet had faked her confidence the entire time we were getting ready to open the nursery.

She'd faked it in her marriage too.

In some ways, I didn't really know Violet at all.

Her smile returned. "Of course I never doubted, silly. I knew all along it would work."

We got in our cars and I watched her drive away to her home and her kids, wondering what else she had faked. How much of what I saw was the real Violet? The last several years of our lives raced through my head as I considered our past through this new lens.

I was lost in thought, driving home, when Mason called. "Sorry, Rose. I was in court this afternoon. What did you have to tell me?"

"My neighbor heard arguing coming from Miss Dorothy's house this morning."

"Did your neighbor happen to hear what the arguing was about?"

"No, he couldn't make it out."

"Would he be willing to go down to the police station and give a report?"

I paused. "Uh . . . that might be a little difficult since he's only four."

"Only four what?"

"Four years old."

Mason was silent.

"Well?" I finally asked.

Mason paused a few more seconds. "Rose, a four-year-old child is hardly a reliable witness."

"Come on, Mason. You have to admit that two elderly woman dying within two weeks of each other is a little odd."

"Both deaths were from natural causes." He paused. "Or as natural as a heat wave can be."

"But why now? This entire summer has been bakin' hot. Why are people dying now?"

"I don't know." He sounded exasperated. "Maybe they don't expect it to be this hot since it's late September. Both women had their air conditioning off."

"But were their windows shut?"

"Well, yeah . . ."

"If they turned off their air conditioning, why wouldn't they have their windows open? They may have been old, but I know they weren't senile. Are you really not going to follow up on this lead?"

"You canvassing the neighborhood and finding a toddler who *might* have heard something is not a lead."

My irritation took root. "You make it sound like I was interrogating the neighbors. I didn't ask anyone anything. Keith just told me."

"Keith? The four-year-old?"

"Four-year-olds have ears, Mason."

"But they're not very reliable witnesses in court, Rose."

"Court? Who said anything about court?"

"That's what it would come to. He'd be called as a witness. I can tell you right now, I wouldn't call a four-year-old to the stand unless he had something I couldn't live without. And it's sure not overhearing an argument he can't remember. How do you know it wasn't someone's TV? How do you know it was even her house?"

Defensiveness shot through me. "Don't be jumpin' down my throat. I was just calling to tell you what I heard. Excuse me for trying to do my civic duty."

He sighed. "I'm sorry. You're right. I had a rough afternoon in court, and I'm taking it out on you. You did the right thing by calling me."

"Thank you." I tried not to sound miffed.

"I'll have Detective Taylor ask some of the other neighbors if they heard anything, but I don't think anything is going to come from it. There was no forced entry. No sign of violence. She was lying on the floor as though she'd collapsed with a heart attack." His voiced warmed. "Your neighborhood is safe."

After the last several months, I wasn't sure I'd ever consider my neighborhood safe. "Thanks for believing me."

He sighed. "It's not a matter of believing you, Rose. It's a matter of whether the four-year-old actually heard something. But like I said, I'll have Taylor do some checking."

"He won't like it. Especially when he hears it was me who told you."

Mason's words were clipped. "He'll do his job, and he won't know it came from you."

"Thanks."

"Anytime. But just in case . . . be sure to lock your doors, okay?"

"Yeah." He didn't have to tell me to lock my doors. I made sure to do it every night. Not that it had done me much good. I was pretty sure my back window had a flashing neon *Welcome murderers and thieves* sign over it.

Chapter Six

After I made a sandwich, I sat on the front porch watching Muffy do her business in the yard. I snuck a glance down at Miss Dorothy's house, wondering why someone would want to kill her. Or Miss Laura for that matter. Mason said that in both cases there'd been no forced entry and nothing had been stolen. How could someone make the old ladies' deaths look so natural that they didn't arouse the suspicions of the Henryetta Police? Not that much made the police suspicious of anything. Unless the suspect was me.

I had to admit that even though it looked suspicious to me, it just didn't add up to murder.

Muffy kept looking longingly down the street, and a wave of guilt made my stomach knot. I'd neglected my little dog too much over the last few weeks while Violet and I were making the final push to have everything ready for the opening. The boys next door had "dog sat" her over the weekends, but I knew for a fact they hadn't taken her on walks. The only thing I had to do tonight was laundry. Maybe a walk would help me sort out my unsettled feelings.

When I approached Muffy with her leash, she got so excited I had trouble getting the hook attached to her collar. Once she was connected, she took off running, and I nearly tripped trying to keep up. She sniffed and peed over half the surfaces we passed, practically shaking with excitement. My plan had been to take her a square block, but she still had a ton of energy when it was time to turn back. The truth was that I wasn't ready to go back to my empty house yet, so we just kept going. I spent the next forty-five minutes thinking about my encounter with Jonah Pruitt. I hadn't been to church since Momma's funeral, which hadn't even been a service. I'd turned my back on church, but Jonah Pruitt's church sounded like everything I'd ever dreamed of in a church. A place where everyone was wanted and accepted. Shoot, I'd spent my entire life looking for that. Violet, Aunt Bessie, and Uncle Earl were the only ones who'd ever truly accepted me until Joe had come into my life.

Wishing for Momma to accept me had been a wasted effort. Boy would she be surprised to see me now—Rose Gardner, business owner.

The sun began to rapidly sink toward the earth, casting shadows, and I realized I was close to the park where I'd spent time the night of Momma's murder. Instead of going home to her, I'd sat on a bench to write my wish list. If things had gone differently, Momma might not have been killed.

More wasted thoughts.

I turned Muffy around, and we took the same path I had taken that fateful night. Truth be told, I was sorry Momma got murdered, but my life had changed a lot since that night in May, and I wasn't sorry about that. Why hadn't I tried to change things before I thought I was going to be killed?

A half a block away, I hesitated at the street corner, staring at the house where I'd lived since I was a baby. Tonight was so similar to the night Momma had been killed—same time of day, same path, no porch light on—I suddenly felt sick to my stomach.

Muffy stood next to me, looking up in confusion. Why was I standing still when we were so close to home?

I was being paranoid. I made myself put one foot in front of the other and crossed the street, chiding myself for acting so silly. I'd had a busy day, and the elderly women's deaths had me on edge, not to mention all the weirdness about Joe and Mason. All I needed was a good night's sleep.

But Muffy had other ideas. She bolted, jerking the leash from my hand, and tore across the street toward Miss Dorothy's house.

"Muffy!"

She ignored me, running between the deceased woman's house and Thomas's on the corner.

I took off, chasing after her. "Muffy! Come back here right now!" But Muffy had her own plan and stopping wasn't part of it. She sped around the corner and into the backyard. I stood at the edge of the property, letting my eyes adjust. The sun had almost set and the house was completely dark. It didn't help that Miss Dorothy had sheets hanging on a clothesline in the back, obstructing my view of the yard.

"Muffy!"

I heard her low growl over by the house, and my breath came in short bursts. My little dog only growled when there was danger. I considered turning and running for my house, but I couldn't leave her there, and I felt like a coward for even considering it. Muffy would never leave me.

"Muffy!" I whispered, but my voice was drowned out by a sudden chorus of locusts. I pushed between two sheets on the laundry line, finding a row of house dresses. Just when I was about to push through those, Muffy growled louder, and a figure burst through two of the dresses, plowing into me. I screamed and fell backward into the sheet hanging behind me. The man fell with me, landing on my stomach and knocking the air out of me.

Muffy jumped on the man, snarling as her teeth sank into the attacker's upper right arm. He shoved her away, cursing under his breath, and then jumped up and ran off before I could gather my wits enough to react. I worried Muffy would run after him, but she came over to me whimpering instead.

Her cries got me moving. I sat up and ran my hands over her body, fearing that she may have been injured when the attacker threw her. But I couldn't find anything wrong with her, and she stopping whining when I got to my feet.

Muffy had been whimpering because she was worried about me.

My butt was sore from the fall, but I was more frightened than hurt. I was on autopilot as I walked home, flipping on the kitchen light before I stepped inside, already planning to run to Heidi Joy's house if it didn't turn on. But the room flooded with light. No one was waiting in the dark to finish me off. I breathed a sigh of relief.

After locking the door, I grabbed my cell phone out of my purse, calling the first number that came to mind. He answered on the second ring.

"Rose, is everything all right?" Mason's worried voice filled my ear.

"I don't know. Someone just attacked me behind Miss Dorothy's house." My voice was strangely calm.

"Have you called the police?"

"No. I called you."

"Where are you now?"

"In my house."

"Lock the doors and don't open them until I get there, okay?"

"Okay." I nodded, only realizing as I did it that he couldn't see me.

"Are you hurt?" His voice sounded tight.

"Not really. More scared."

"I'll be right there."

I sank into a kitchen chair as my legs turned to limp spaghetti. I felt lightheaded, so I laid my head on the table as Muffy drank massive amounts of water from her bowl. A new fear filled me. "Muffy, you shouldn't have run off like that. You could have been killed."

She looked up at me like I'd just said the most ridiculous thing in the world.

"I mean it, Muffy. I don't know what I'd do without you." My voice broke when I thought about what could have happened to her. Muffy lifted her paws onto my knee, and I rubbed her head. "Good girl. I love you too."

Sirens filled the night air, coming closer and clinching my stomach. I wasn't sure I'd ever get used to the sound of sirens. Especially when I knew they were coming because of me. Instinctively, I had known Mason would call the police, but their presence still made me nervous.

Pounding on the front door made me jump, but Mason's voice followed. "Rose! It's me!"

I stood, waiting a second to be sure my legs would hold my weight, chiding myself for being such a baby. I'd been in worse fixes than this.

When I opened the front door, Mason's worried face filled the opening. Flashing lights filled the street behind him. "Are you okay?"

I nodded. "Yeah. I'm fine."

He looked over my shoulder, hesitating. "Can I come in?"

"Of course," I answered, stepping backward to let him in.

He led me to the sofa. "Sit down and tell me everything that happened."

I sank into the cushions while he sat in the overstuffed chair next to me. "I took Muffy for a walk, and we went farther than I'd planned. So it was gettin' dark when we started for home. When we passed Miss Dorothy's house, Muffy jerked the leash out of my hand and ran behind her house." Muffy jumped onto the sofa and pressed her body against my thigh, resting her chin on my leg. "Miss Dorothy's laundry was still hanging on her clothesline so I couldn't see Muffy, but I heard her growling. I was in the middle of a bunch of sheets and house dresses when someone burst through and knocked me down and fell on top of me. I don't think he meant to attack me. He was just tryin' to get away. But he landed on me, and Muffy thought he was trying to hurt me, so she bit him. He threw Muffy to the side, got up, and took off. Thank goodness, she stayed with me."

Mason listened intently, showing no obvious reaction. "And then you came home and called me?"

I nodded.

"Why didn't you call the police?"

"You very well know why. The same reason I called you this afternoon: They hate me. And not only do they hate me, but they usually try to pin whatever's going wrong in this town on me."

He leaned forward, resting his arms on his legs, his brow wrinkled in confusion. "Rose, you didn't do anything wrong. How could they pin this on you?"

I shrugged. "How could they pin the break-in of my house on me? Surely you can see why I don't trust them."

He sighed, looking guilty. "That was a different situation. You were a suspect in your mother's death. There's no reason to think you were involved in anything this time."

I wasn't so sure.

"Did you get a good look at the guy?"

I shook my head. "No, it was dark, and he caught me by surprise."

"Can you describe him? Was he short or tall? Did you see his hair color or any distinguishing features?"

I sighed. "Not really. He was dressed in a black long-sleeved shirt and jeans, and he was kind of hunched over when he ran toward me, so I couldn't tell how tall he was. But he was bigger than me when he landed on top of me." I closed my eyes trying to remember what I'd seen. "It all happened so fast. Just about the only other thing I remember seeing was a knit hat covering his head."

Mason's hand covered my knee, and I opened my eyes in surprise. "It's okay. But you might remember more as it all settles in. Do you feel up to going over there with me?"

I hesitated. "I guess."

"It's perfectly safe."

I knew that. Only a fool would stick around with all the commotion going on outside, even if it was the Henryetta police. The police were the reason I didn't want to go. I was being ridiculous, and I knew it. But knowing something and feeling something are two entirely different things. Still, I wasn't going to live my life cowering in fear. I'd left those days behind me, and I wasn't about to pick up old habits now.

I stood. "Let's get this over with."

"I'll be with you the entire time."

His statement gave me more comfort than I'd expected it would. But he'd been the one to save me in July when Jimmy DeWade had tried to kill me, and he'd offered me comfort then too. Especially when Joe wasn't giving it to me.

Muffy wasn't happy that I left her behind. Mason walked next to me, keeping a polite distance. I showed him where I was standing when Muffy took off and retraced my steps. The backyard was lit up this time, and Detective Taylor and Officer Ernie were there, snooping around the back of the house.

When they saw me, Detective Taylor approached with a notebook. "What exactly did you see?"

I swallowed my resistance and told him everything I'd told Mason.

"Did you notice what direction he went?" the detective asked.

Shaking my head, I looked behind me, getting a face-full of a sheet. "No, I was more worried about Muffy after he threw her off." I peeked through a gap in the housedresses. A couple had fallen off the line, either in the attacker's flight or after the police's arrival. Ernie was checking out the back door. "Was he trying to get into Miss Dorothy's house?" I asked.

Taylor puffed out his chest. "We're looking into that right now."

Ernie glanced over his shoulder. "It looks like he had just gotten the door pried open before he was interrupted." He narrowed his eyes at me.

Mason stared at the back door before glancing back at me. "I'll walk you home, Rose."

"I'm perfectly capable of walking home. It wasn't like he was after me. I was just in the wrong place at the wrong time."

"That seems to happen to you an awful lot," Mason muttered.

"Tell me about it."

Neighbors had gathered on the sidewalk when I walked to the front of the house. Miss Mildred was front and center again, looking just as worried as she had earlier in the day. It had to be upsetting to an eighty-two-year-old woman to find her neighbor and friend dead, and then discover the police had been called to her house again. Heidi Joy and Miss Opal were there too, and there were some new faces in the crowd—the younger couple who lived down at the other end of the street and worked during the day and Thomas. He leaned against his muscle car with crossed arms, watching the commotion impassively.

"What's going on?" Heidi Joy asked.

I looked back at the house, surprised to notice that Thomas was looking at me with interest.

"Someone tried to break into Miss Dorothy's house tonight. Muffy must have seen or heard something, because she pulled her leash out of my hand and went back there to confront the intruder."

Miss Mildred shot me a look of contempt. "I'll be notifying Animal Control first thing tomorrow morning about your dog running around loose."

I rolled my eyes. "I just gave Detective Taylor and the assistant DA an admission of guilt to that very charge. Don't you think calling the dog catcher is overkill?"

Miss Opal tsked, shaking her head. "Good heavens, Mildred. Don't ya think we've got more important things to worry about?"

Mildred scowled but remained silent.

"What do you think they were after, Rose?" Heidi Joy asked, clutching the edges of her robe to her chest.

"I don't know. But I'm sure the police will get to the bottom of it." I didn't ordinarily have much faith in them, but maybe they'd get things done with Mason riding their behinds.

I didn't feel like standing outside with the crowd, so I went home and checked Muffy out again, just to make sure she wasn't hurt, and then put on my pajamas. I was still wound up from the excitement, so I turned on the television. Hopefully it would help me forget about my strange day. I'd just started to get drowsy when Mason knocked on my door. "Rose, are you still up?"

Cracking the door open, I stayed inside. I'd stirred up Miss Mildred enough tonight without going out in my nightgown.

His face appeared in the opening. "Did you happen to lose a piece of jewelry when the thief knocked you down?"

My eyes widened. "No. I never wear jewelry." The only pieces I owned were the diamond engagement ring my birth mother had left me, a few pieces of costume jewelry, and the crucifix necklace Aunt Bessie had given me when I was baptized in the sixth grade.

"Okay, just checking. We found a piece out in the grass, a necklace with a St. Jude's medal with something engraved on the back, and wondered if it was yours."

"Do you think it belonged to the thief?"

Mason shrugged. "Maybe. Or it could have been in the yard for a while, although it doesn't look weathered. Detective Taylor thinks that it was recently dropped."

I didn't trust Detective Taylor to investigate himself out of a paper bag. "Do you agree with him?"

"Yeah. I do." He shifted his weight, looking over his shoulder at her house before turning back to me. "Are you okay? Do you feel safe? I can have Taylor assign a patrol car to keep an eye on your house and the neighborhood. Do some drive-bys tonight."

I was sure the Henryetta police would love that. "Nah. I've got Muffy as my guard dog. Besides, you're probably right. I'm sure it was just a random intruder."

"If anything else happens or you feel unsafe, promise me you'll call 911 first. They can get to you before I can."

I smirked. "Not tonight."

"You're lucky I was still working."

"You work too much."

He laughed. "Now you sound like my mother."

"I'm not sure if I should feel insulted or flattered."

"Definitely flattered. My mother is an amazing woman."

I grinned. "Then I'll take the compliment." I leaned against the door. "Thanks for coming tonight."

Mason took a step closer. "You know I'm here if you need anything. I don't mind. But the police can do more than I can. I mean it, next time call them before you call me."

"You're presuming there will be a next time."

An amused grin spread across his face. "You're suggesting there won't be?"

I lifted a shoulder into a half-shrug. He had a point; if history kept repeating itself, there would be.

He shook his head with a chuckle. "Goodnight, Rose."

"Goodnight, Mason."

I watched him drive away, and then locked the door and went to get my small jewelry box from my dresser. Sitting on the bed, I lifted the lid to the white box and a tiny ballerina with a net skirt popped up. The box was more fit for a preteen than a twenty-four-year-old woman, but Daddy had given it to me for my thirteenth birthday. I'd never replaced it for two reasons:

One, it was one of the only things he had ever given me outright, without Momma's inclusion. And two, I didn't have much of anything to put in it. My birth mother's ring had come in a ring box which I kept tucked in my underwear drawer. Truth be told, I hadn't opened the ring box in several months, the jewelry box in even longer.

I sorted through the pieces until I came across what I was looking for, the dainty gold chain with its filigreed gold crucifix. Aunt Bessie had made sure to tell me it was made of real 18ct gold. Momma had rarely let me wear it, telling me it wouldn't be appropriate to wear something so gaudy every day. As a girl, it had killed me to let it sit in the box, and sometimes I'd sneak it out of the house and put it on after I got on the school bus.

Laying the chain across my palm, I studied the cross. Aunt Bessie had even had my initials engraved on the back. *RAG.* Lord knew I'd been teased mercilessly about that fact when the other kids in school found out. Which incidentally was when one of the mean girls in my class noticed my necklace and asked to try it on. I'd relented—anything to fit in with my classmates—but she'd taken one look at the initials and tossed it back to me with a nasty insult.

I hadn't worn it since.

I was done with letting people make me feel worthless. Sure it had happened in the sixth grade and Theresa Hopper didn't even live in Henryetta anymore, but the necklace would be a reminder to stand my ground.

I lifted the chain and fastened it around my neck.

Rose Gardner was done backing down.

Chapter Seven

When I got to the nursery the next morning, Violet was waiting with her hand on her hip. "You didn't think to call me about getting attacked? *Again.*"

I started to ask her how she knew, then stopped. Of course, it was big news, and Henryetta was a small town. It would have been more surprising if Violet *hadn't* heard.

I waved my hand as I tossed my purse behind the counter. "It was nothing. Mason thinks someone heard that poor Miss Dorothy died and tried to break in to steal her jewelry."

Violet's father-in-law showed up just as she was about to give me a tongue-lashing. Giving me the evil eye—which just about screamed *We're not done talking about this*—she turned to him with a smile.

"Thanks for letting us borrow your truck, Gary. If you want to take my car, I'll switch with you later today."

"Don't be silly, Violet. You're like a daughter to Shelia and me. We're so proud of what you and Rose have done," Gary told her with tears in his eyes. "I don't know what's going on in that fool boy's head, but I hope he doesn't think we're gonna turn our backs on you."

Violet teared up as she threw her arms around his neck, and her voice broke as she held onto him for several seconds. "Thank you."

I wasn't sure what Mike's parents knew, but as far as I could tell, there was plenty of blame to go round. I wasn't happy that Mike had left Violet, but I'd also seen the misery she'd put him through with years of belittling and badgering. Still, to be fair to

Violet, he'd just about squashed any thoughts she'd ever had of being anything more than a wife and a mother.

As we began to slide the flats of flowers on the pickup bed, we quickly realized it was going to take more than one trip. Gary drove the first load to the church, and I followed him in my car. After we set the first batch on the sidewalk, Gary returned to the nursery while I unpacked my gardening tools from the trunk of my car.

Violet and I had inherited our love for flowers and gardening from our father. We'd spent most of the warm weather months of our childhood outside planting, weeding, and pruning. Later, I realized it was my father's escape from my mother's razor-edged tongue. But as a child, spending time outside with my father was where I found most of my happiness. Since I still lived in my parents' house, my shed was full of shovels, rakes, pruning shears, and any other tools we might need.

While I waited for Gary to return, I called Neely Kate. I had several minutes to kill, and other than a few minutes we'd seen each other at the grand opening, I hadn't talked to her in over a week. I knew she'd be at the courthouse, but she hated her job so much she always answered, welcoming the distraction.

She answered on the second ring. "I was just about to call you. I heard about your incident last night."

"Is there anyone in Henryetta who hasn't?"

"Doubtful. You can tell me all about it at lunch this afternoon."

I groaned. "Oh no. I forgot. I can't. We got a big order to plant flowers and prune the landscape at the New Living Hope Revival Church." I eyed the church entrance. Jonah's car wasn't in the parking lot, but I was still keeping an eye out for him. He made me nervous, and I didn't want to be caught alone with him.

"I thought you just sold the flowers. I didn't know y'all did the plantin' too."

"We didn't plan on it, but that was the only way to get this job, and it's a big one. This is more money than we'd expected to make in a month."

"Well that makes sense, I guess, but are you planting 'em all yourself?"

"No, I hired David Moore and Bruce Wayne Decker to help. They should be here any minute."

She paused. "*The stoners?*"

I sighed, starting to doubt the wisdom of my plan. "I was desperate."

"Yeah, I guess so."

My gaze focused on the front doors of the church. I could feel Rhonda's eyes staring me down through the office window. I suspected she was gathering the rocks for my stoning later.

"So tell me about last night."

I told her everything, including the bit about the St. Jude's necklace they'd found in Miss Dorothy's backyard.

"Huh."

"What? You know something?"

"Well, maybe. Maybe not. My grandma was close friends with Miss Laura. Several days after the funeral her daughters got together to start cleaning out the house. But they noticed all her jewelry was missing as well as a few silver pieces. They called Grandma to see if she knew what Miss Laura had done with her things. She didn't have a clue. She suggested they call the police, but they told her they had a cousin who'd been hanging around Miss Laura, taking advantage of her kindness. They suspected she'd just given the jewelry to her, especially since there wasn't any sign of a break-in."

"We have to tell Mason."

"Nuh uh," Neely Kate groaned. "I ain't gettin' involved."

"Neely Kate!"

"It's a coincidence, Rose. I suspect Miss Laura's niece stole the jewelry or convinced her aunt to give it to her. Everyone knows she's addicted to meth. Which brings us back to your new employees."

"They're not addicted to meth. They simply have a fondness for pot."

Neely Kate laughed. "Call it what you like, but an addiction is an addiction." I heard someone in the background, then Neely Kate groaned. "I gotta get back to work, Rose. Call me if you find out anything else."

"You too." I hung up as Gary returned with the second load of flowers. We were halfway through unloading them when David pulled up in a beat-up yellow Pinto, with Bruce Wayne in the passenger seat. After they parked, they sauntered over to us, a wary look on their faces. In light of Neely Kate's comment and the way they looked this morning—like they were coming off some sort of bender—I was having second thoughts about hiring them. They might be able-bodied men, but I wasn't sure how *willing* they were.

"Thanks for showing up," I said, handing a flat of burnt orange chrysanthemums to David.

He took the tray, acting like something was going to jump out and bite him.

I motioned over to a partially-filled bed on the east side of the church. "You can set it on the ground over there."

David wandered off while I handed the next flat to Bruce Wayne.

He hesitated, looking down at the ground before peering up at me through his scraggly bangs. "I never got a chance to thank you." He cleared his throat. "For what you done for me."

My breath caught in surprise. "You're welcome, Bruce Wayne."

He didn't move, and I waited. I'd learned he was a nervous guy and pushing him wouldn't help.

"When David said you offered us a job . . ." He swallowed. "Thank you. I got one too many strikes against me in this town. I'll try my best not to let you down."

I'd never considered the fact Bruce Wayne might have difficulty finding a job with his history. One could argue he'd brought it upon himself, but he still had rent and bills to pay. "Well, that's all I can ask. And you both are helping me out more than you know."

"If you need anything, anything at all, Miss Rose, you just let me know. I'm your man."

His words shocked me. First, he called me *Miss* Rose, a term usually reserved as a sign of respect for older women. Bruce Wayne was older than me, so I knew he used it with the utmost respect. Second, the conviction in his voice told me he meant it.

If I needed help, he'd be there for me. But the problem with drug addicts is that unreliable is their middle name.

Nevertheless, a lump burned in my throat. I hadn't expected anything in return when I sought to clear his name of murder charges. I had done it because it was the right thing to do. "Thank you, Bruce Wayne."

He nodded and trudged after his friend.

Gary stood at the back of the truck, his hands on his hips, as he watched the guys setting the flowers next to the bed. "Be careful with those two."

I wiped sweat from my brow, keeping my gaze on them. "They're harmless."

"They're criminals." His tone was harsh and unforgiving.

I suspected half the town's attitude about me was harsh and unforgiving. *She's strange. She's a gossip.* They'd sure been willing to accept that I'd murdered Momma with little proof. Maybe that's why I felt a new kinship with Bruce Wayne. We'd both been discounted by the townsfolk of Henryetta.

Gary left to get the last load of flowers as I told the guys what I needed them to do. David balked at the instructions, but Bruce Wayne bobbed his head. "Yes, ma'am. We'll get it done."

"Hard at work, I see," Jonah drawled behind me.

Startled, I jumped. I hadn't seen him pull up.

He rested his hand on my arm. "I didn't mean to scare you, Rose."

I backed up, searching his face. "Sorry. I was just concentrating so hard, I didn't hear you walk up."

"I love that kind of dedication." He eyed the guys next to me.

"Jonah, this is David and Bruce Wayne. They're going to be doin' most of the manual labor."

To my surprise, Jonah reached out to shake their dirty hands. "Nice to meet you boys. Welcome to the New Living Hope Revival Church. I hope you feel at home here."

Bruce Wayne, who was used to scorn, latched onto Jonah's warmth. "Thank you."

"Do either of you boys have church homes?"

David snickered, but Bruce Wayne shook his head, looking Jonah in the eye. "No, sir."

"I'd be honored if you'd consider attending my church. We welcome everyone here." He paused to let his full meaning sink in.

Bruce Wayne bobbed his head, looking down. "Thank you."

Jonah clasped his hands together. "Well, I've got to get to work before Rhonda takes me to task. It's gonna be another hot one today. You boys don't be shy. Be sure to come inside and cool off or get some cold water. We can't have you coming down with a heat stroke. You make yourselves at home."

As Jonah walked off, I glared at David. "Don't you be goin' in there and taking a nap."

He scrunched his nose. "Who said I was gonna?" But he didn't look like a man who'd been wrongfully accused.

"Don't worry, Miss Rose," Bruce Wayne said. "I'll keep him in line."

I had serious doubts about that. What little I'd learned about their friendship dynamic during Bruce Wayne's trial was that David was the leader. Nevertheless, I didn't have time to stay here all day supervising. "Bruce Wayne, I'm gonna leave you in charge. I've got to run back to the nursery, but I'll stop by after lunch to check on your progress."

"You bringin' us lunch?" David asked.

I sighed. "I'll bring you something, but you have to get the beds on this side of the building cleaned out and pruned before you can eat it. I'll be back in about three hours." I had serious doubts they could do it, but maybe the incentive would work.

When I got back to the nursery, Violet was talking to a customer about azaleas. She looked up and smiled. She seemed unusually happy today, but then again, she had reason to be: Business was going well, and she had a date.

She pulled me aside. "I haven't had time to get started on the pots for Reverend Jonah. Can you? Besides, I don't want to get too dirty. Brody is picking me up from here to go on our date."

"Oh." I still had a hard time imagining her with someone besides Mike. "You know I love making planters." And we both knew that she'd be better at dealing with the customers. It was an unspoken agreement between us. "Where are you two going?"

A smile softened her face, and I was surprised how shy she looked. "He said he was taking me out to dinner."

"I'm happy for you, Violet."

Tears filled her eyes. "Really?" Her chin trembled. "I know how hard this is for you and everyone else. It's gonna be an adjustment."

I pulled her into a hug. "This is your life, Violet. You deserve to be happy."

"Thank you, Rose. I've been so envious watching you and Joe together."

My lips parted. "Envious of *me*?"

"You two are just so happy and in love. You have no idea how much I wanted that. I'm so happy to have found it too."

I narrowed my eyes. "But you and Brody just met."

Fear and guilt slid over her face, and then it was replaced by a mask of fake happiness. How had I never noticed that either? How long had my sister been hiding behind the masquerade of her life? I missed the Violet who'd been my confidant and best friend. When had I lost her? I suppressed a sigh. In some ways, I had lost her when Momma died. When I decided to start taking control of my own life.

Violet wiped imaginary dirt off the counter and scrunched up her nose. "How's it looking out at the church?"

She was hiding something, but I decided to let it go for now. "They were just getting started when I left, but Bruce Wayne seems determined to repay me for helping exonerate him by doin' a good job."

"And the other guy?"

I shrugged, unwilling to admit to my doubts. "Jonah seemed pleased to meet them, and he welcomed them to come inside to cool off when they get too hot."

She scowled. "They'll end up spending most of the day inside that church."

I could see why she might think so, but I decided to trust Bruce Wayne.

The next several hours flew by as I did what I loved. Working with flowers. I'd been so busy with the chaos of life lately—Momma's murder, dating Joe, being picked for Bruce Wayne's jury, opening the nursery—I hadn't had much time for my hobby, now my business. But putting my hands in the cool soil and transferring the plants to new containers—to new lives—I experienced a peace I'd never found with people, not that I'd had many people in my life before Momma's murder.

Joe had changed all of that.

I missed him more than I cared to admit. How could I live twenty-four years without a man, and then find myself so attached to him after four months that I found it difficult to breathe when I wasn't sure he was safe? Worry for his safety was a constant, anxious current beneath the surface of my skin. But Mason's revelation that he knew about Joe's secret, along with what Joe himself had said, raised it to a higher level. Everyone was ashamed of something in their past. Lord knew I had plenty of regrets. But I'd shared all my painful secrets with Joe. There was hardly any part of me he didn't know, yet I couldn't say the same about him.

Mason's suggestion that Joe should have told me was nipping at my faith.

But wasn't faith believing in something even when you didn't have irrefutable proof? What was I doubting? Joe's love for me? No, I was as sure of Joe's love as I was that the sun would rise in the morning. The scary realization was that I wasn't sure who Joe really was. It was no secret that his job was pretending to be someone else. What if Mason was right? What if the Joe I knew wasn't really the Joe I thought I knew?

Nausea bubbled in my stomach. I needed to stop this and focus on what I *did* know. Joe loved me for all he was worth. What did it matter if something had happened in his past? The truth was, I was a totally different person before Momma's murder, and he wasn't holding *that* against me. I needed to give him the same trust.

After I prepared six pots, I decided to take them to the church when I went back with the guys' lunch. But fitting them in my old Chevy Nova proved to be a challenge. There was no doubt a few of them could fit on the back seat, the question was how to fit them in the door without ripping off the blooms. I put a hand on my hip, staring at the car. I was sure this wouldn't be the only time we had this issue, and we couldn't count on Violet's father-in-law to help us out every time. Especially if she was gonna start dating again.

Joe had been after me to sell the Nova for months, but it had been Daddy's car, and I'd gotten it by default when he died my freshman year in college. Violet was already married and had a car of her own, and Momma had quit driving by then. I loved the car, despite its size and gas-guzzling ways, mostly because it had been Daddy's and was full of happy memories. But the few times I'd driven to Little Rock to see Joe, he'd been a nervous wreck, worried the car wouldn't make it there and home. Maybe it was time to consider getting something else. Not a sedan like Joe had been not-so-subtly implying that I should buy (he e-mailed me links to local used car lots daily), but a pickup truck. We needed one for our business anyway.

When I went inside and mentioned the idea to Violet, she rolled her eyes. "What do you know about driving a pickup?"

"What's there to know? It drives like a car."

She dismissed me with a wave. "It's bigger than a car. You could run something over."

Something rose up in my chest and overflowed into my head, filling me with an overwhelming urge to stand up for myself. "You know this isn't the last time we're gonna need a truck. I'll buy one and put the business name on the side. It will be like free advertising." The more I thought about the idea, the more I liked it, despite the fact that it would mean spending even more money on the nursery. I'd already invested so many hundreds of thousands of dollars that I couldn't think about it without hyperventilating.

"You don't know the first thing about buying a truck."

"You're buying a truck?" Mason asked, coming through the doorway at just that moment.

I turned around and smiled. After not seeing him for weeks, I'd seen plenty of him in the last couple of days. "I'm considering it."

Violet rolled her eyes. "Mr. Deveraux, tell her what a ridiculous idea it is."

Mason kept his eyes on me, a teasing glint in them. "I don't know. I can see you driving a truck. A shotgun in the window for when you get into trouble." He winked.

Violet's eyes widened.

"Driving a truck isn't hard. It's just bigger and higher up," Mason added.

"She doesn't know the first thing about buying a car," Violet laughed, taking a new angle. "Or a truck, as the case might be. She thinks she's just going to waltz in there and negotiate a deal."

Why was she trying to make me look like a fool? And why was I just now seeing what she was doing? This was far from the first time she'd pulled a stunt like this, and it had always infuriated Joe to no end. He claimed Violet was jealous of me. I'd always told him the idea was preposterous, but now I wasn't so sure. Well, starting the nursery might have boosted Violet's confidence, but it had boosted mine too.

Mason turned an expressionless gaze on Violet. "I'm sure Rose is capable of doing anything she sets her mind to."

Violet wasn't sure what to say to that, and I took the opportunity to change the subject. "Is there anything we can help you with, Mason?"

He turned his full attention to me, practically ignoring Violet. "Actually, my mother is coming to visit this weekend, and I wanted to get her a gift, so I thought about your shop. I remembered you sold indoor plants. She's always trying to grow something, despite her black thumb. I thought you might be able to recommend a plant that will take her longer to kill."

I laughed. "Flowering or non-flowering?"

His eyes widened. "Uh . . ." A strange look crossed his face. "We'd better stick to non-flowering."

"Okay. Does her house have a lot of light?"

"Not particularly. She lives in an older house in Hillcrest. Lots of older trees and shade."

I walked to the back corner of the store where we kept a variety of indoor plants. "Hillcrest. That's one of the historic neighborhoods in Little Rock, right?" Joe had driven us through it on one of my visits to see him.

"Yeah."

"So you grew up there, then?"

He smiled. "I did."

"Does your mother have any pets? Any grandkids?"

Wariness washed over his face.

What was the deal with the men in my life and their secretiveness? "I'm not pryin'. I need to know for the plant. Some are poisonous to pets and children. If that's an issue, we obviously want to stay away from those."

"Oh. None of either."

"Then there are several plants you can choose from that like low light and are fairly hearty. One is a dieffenbachia." My fingertips brushed the thick dark green and yellowish leaves. "They can get to be quite tall. Or if you want something smaller and even hardier, you could go with a zeezee plant." I pointed to a plant that looked like a small bush. "They're also called eternity plants since they're considered nearly impossible to kill."

Mason pointed to the latter. "Definitely that one."

"That was easy."

"I'm not that difficult to please. Contrary to what you might have thought after our first encounters."

I smiled up at him. "I'm glad you loosened up. I thought we were going to be friends."

His smile fell. "I told you that I regret the agreement I made with Joe. Have you talked to him? Does he know I'm no longer avoiding you?"

I squirmed. "We talked about it briefly before he left yesterday. He's on an undercover assignment, and I can't talk to him right now."

Mason's mouth pursed.

I had a feeling he wasn't telling me something, but pressing for more information was pointless. "Thanks for backing me up with Violet," I said in an undertone. "Sometimes she . . ."

"Acts like an older sister?" He teased, his earlier playfulness returning.

"Yeah."

"For what it's worth, I think getting a truck is a great idea. Do you have much car shopping experience?"

"No, but I've considered trading the Nova in for a newer used car."

"If you're worried about getting a good deal, feel free to take me along. There's nothing as intimidating to a car salesman as negotiating with the assistant district attorney."

I had been making a real effort to do more things on my own, and I was succeeding, but negotiating for a car made me nervous.

He sensed my hesitation. "If it makes you feel any better, I helped my cousin Neal negotiate for his last car. I'm not sure anyone can get a better deal than I can."

I crossed my arms and smirked. "I bet you were the captain of the debate team, huh?"

His mouth twisted into a smug grin. "Well, of course. Pulaski Academy wouldn't have gone to the nationals in forensics without me."

"Such a humble man."

He lifted his eyebrows in an exaggerated manner. "I know. I keep telling everyone that, but no one listens."

I shook my head with a laugh. "Imagine that." Against my better judgment, I was thinking about letting him help. "Isn't your mother coming for the weekend?"

"Not until Saturday morning. I'm taking off early tomorrow afternoon. We could go then."

"Are you sure? If you got an afternoon off, surely you want to spend it doing something other than haggling over a truck."

He pointed to himself. "Hello. Have we met? I'm Mason Deveraux III, and I love to argue for the fun of it."

I grinned. "Okay. You've got a deal."

"I get off at noon. Do you want to meet at Merilee's for lunch first?"

I had worked through lunch for the past two days, and Violet would be taking off early tonight. I figured I could go to lunch without feeling guilty. "Sure. Sounds good."

Mason's smile widened. "Great."

I started to pick up his plant to take it to the counter, but he took it from me and carried it instead. While I rung up his purchase, I told him the latest courthouse gossip Neely Kate had shared with me, and he confirmed that about ninety percent of it was true.

He shook his head in amazement. "The Henryetta Police Department should hire her as some kind of informant."

I considered telling him about Miss Laura's missing jewelry, but it didn't feel right, especially if it got her niece into trouble. It was most likely a coincidence. "Neely Kate has a way of knowin' things."

At that moment, a vision pushed its way to the surface. Panic sent an urge to resist it, but that never did any good. I'd deal with the fallout when it was done. I saw an attractive, well-dressed elderly woman. Her mouth opened in happy surprise as I handed her the plant Mason was buying. "I love it!"

The vision faded away, and I looked up at Mason. "Your mother is going to love the plant," I said automatically.

He smiled. "Thanks to your help, I think she will."

Thank the Lord above I hadn't seen anything embarrassing. Mason still didn't know about my visions, and I hoped to keep it that way.

Picking the plant up off the counter, he headed for the door. "I'll see you tomorrow at noon."

Violet had been assisting someone outside, but she came back in when Mason left, watching him over her shoulder. "You do know what just happened there, don't you?"

My back bristled. "I know you don't approve of me getting a truck, but Mason—"

"Not that, Rose." A smug smile lifted her mouth. "Your lunch date."

I squinted in confusion. "What about it?"

"It's a lunch *date.*"

"What?" I paused as the full meaning of what she'd said slipped in. "*Oh.*" No, she was wrong. "Mason and I are just friends."

She laughed. "That's how it starts. Then the next thing you know . . ." She walked outside, leaving her sentence unfinished.

Just minutes ago, she had hurt me for sport. Was this comment any different? When had she become this person? Where was the loving, supportive person who would have done anything to protect me?

Watching her through the window as she returned to her customer, all sweetness and sugar, I wondered again if I knew her at all.

Chapter Eight

When I got back to the church, I was surprised by how much progress Bruce Wayne and David had made. They were about finished with digging up the weeds and turning over the soil. I'd brought them deli sandwiches, chips, and lemonade, and they sat under the shade of a mimosa tree to eat their lunch and enjoy the breeze that had kicked up.

I took advantage of some time alone. I grabbed a shovel and finished turning over the ground before we added fertilizer and planted the flowers.

"I see you're hard at work. I thought that was what those boys were here for."

I jumped at the sound of Jonah Pruitt's voice and spun around to face him. "Reverend Jonah. You caught me by surprise."

"I didn't mean to sneak up on you. You were very intent on your job."

"Oh, I love working with the dirt and plants."

"Nothin' wrong with being one with God's creation."

That was one way to put it. "Yeah."

"I noticed your necklace this morning." He pointed to the base of my throat where the cross laid. "You weren't wearing it yesterday. I hope this means you're considering coming to church on Sunday."

I reached up and grabbed the crucifix self-consciously. What was I going to tell him? Thankfully, he plunged on without waiting for an answer.

"The boys made tremendous progress," Jonah said. "I had to force them to take a water break a little while ago."

"Bruce Wayne is determined to do a good job."

"I can tell," Jonah cast a glance at the guys under the tree before turning back to me. "I found his desire to impress you rather curious. It didn't seem to be something as innocent as a crush."

I wasn't sure why his announcement ticked me off so much. Perhaps because Bruce Wayne's motivations weren't any of Reverend Jonah Pruitt's business.

"I can see I've upset you, Rose. That wasn't my intention."

I exhaled, trying to keep my cool.

"It's my business to know what makes people tick." He paused. "I know it seems nosy, but that's how I figure out what people need."

"I'm not sure why you care what his reasons—"

Jonah's voice lowered. "Rose, a pastor takes care of his flock. To do that, I have to know how they're hurting. Otherwise how can I heal them?"

"With all due respect, Jonah, isn't it the Lord's job to heal them? And technically neither of us are part of your flock."

To my surprise, he laughed. "You are like a breath of fresh air, Rose Gardner, just sayin' what you think."

I wasn't so sure about that.

He sobered. "I know about your connection to Bruce Wayne Decker."

My chest tightened. "What does that mean?"

"I know you were responsible for getting the murder charges against him dropped."

I felt like my privacy had been invaded, but I wasn't sure why. It was public knowledge. Jonah had moved his church to Henryetta at about the time of Bruce Wayne's trial. For all I knew, he remembered the trial. But it was far more likely he'd been snooping.

Jonah sensed my train of thought. "Rhonda made the connection. I swear I wasn't prying. But I confess that I did do a bit of investigation after I found out."

I spun to fiddle with the shovel some more.

"Can you tell me why you did it?" He asked, his voice softer and more anxious than I'd expected. "You were put in jail for trying to prove his charges should be dropped. What convinced you he was innocent?"

I put my foot on the shovel and pushed it deep into the dirt, then twisted to glance up at him. "I just knew. And because I knew, it was the only right thing to do."

"I hear you *know* things." He was behind me now, so close I'd elbow him if I put some effort into turning over the dirt.

Icy dread slid through my veins.

"How do you know things, Rose?" he said, pushing me with his words.

Suddenly Bruce Wayne was next to me, picking up a shovel. "I'm ready to get back to work now." He turned to Jonah. "It's coming along, ain't it?"

Jonah smiled, but for the first time, it wasn't genuine. "That it is," he said, then turned around and went back into the church.

What had Jonah Pruitt heard about me, and why was he so interested? Was he just another in a long line of preachers determined to rid me of my demon?

"Are you okay, Miss Rose?" Bruce Wayne asked in a hushed tone.

I released a nervous laugh. "Of course. Why are you asking?"

"It looked like he was upsetting you."

Suddenly, I felt foolish. Everyone in town knew I'd helped free Bruce Wayne. Of course the reverend had been curious. "I'm fine. Men of the cloth just seem to find me lacking."

"Me too," he said quietly before he pushed his shovel into the dirt.

Bruce Wayne and I had more in common than being accused of murders we didn't commit.

I had planned to stay for the rest of the afternoon, until Violet needed to leave the store, but I was worried Jonah would come back and try to continue our conversation. What did he think he knew about me? I told Bruce Wayne to finish the east side, then show up early tomorrow to receive the flower shipment and start on the west. We'd tackle the short south and north sides on Saturday and Sunday afternoon if needed.

Violet was surprised to see me when I walked through the door. "I thought you wanted to help with the planting."

"I did. But I changed my mind. They're making good progress without me."

Violet took me at my word and turned her attention to some paperwork on the counter. I went outside to check on the flowers. To keep the plants in the flats looking lush and healthy, we had to water them multiple times a day. Watering them now seemed like a good time filler since I didn't feel like telling Violet about my interaction with Jonah. If I hung around inside, she'd be able to tell something was eating at me, and she'd pry it out of me. I really needed advice on how to handle the situation, but Violet was the last person I wanted to talk to about it after our earlier interactions, and Joe was unavailable for who knew how long. Besides, I knew perfectly well what he'd say. Quit. But the money was too good to pass up, and Jonah hadn't done anything bad. He just made me feel uncomfortable. I was probably being too sensitive.

When I went inside, I leaned against the counter. "Vi, maybe you should go out to the church tomorrow to check on the progress." If she went, I wouldn't have to see Jonah.

Her head lifted, surprise in her eyes. "Why?"

"Well . . . it's your name and reputation on the line too. Maybe you should give it your stamp of approval."

She laughed, pulling off her apron and washing her hands in the nearby sink. "I saw the plan you drew up. It was great. Why wouldn't I like it?"

How could she do that? How could she tear me down in one breath, and then build me up in the next?

"You don't want to see it at all?"

She looked up and smiled. "I trust you. You're really good at landscaping, so I'll just see it when it's done. You can surprise me."

I wanted to protest and tell her I refused to go back out, but then she'd want to know why.

Violet grabbed her purse as a black sedan pulled into the parking lot. She put her hand on her chest and took several deep breaths. "Brody's here." Her skin was flushed, and she looked more excited than a person had a right to be about a first date. "Thanks for closing up, Rose. I'll see you tomorrow."

"Have fun," I said, but a heaviness had settled on me. I knew part of it had to do with Violet's entanglement with Brody and my lingering worry over Joe's secrets, but I couldn't help thinking it was more than that. Something below the surface. I just couldn't figure out what.

After I closed up the shop, I went home, feeling guilty because I hadn't let Muffy out since I'd left for the day. I'd been so distracted by Jonah that I'd forgotten to swing by in the afternoon. Muffy was ecstatic to see me, jumping up and licking my hands and face when I bent down to pet her. We stayed outside for a long time as I mulled over my thoughts, wallowing in hurt and confusion. I didn't usually allow myself to wallow, but this seemed like a good night for it.

While I was sitting on the porch, a car turned into Miss Dorothy's driveway. Had the intruder come back to finish what he started? Surely he wasn't stupid enough to return in broad daylight and park a car in the driveway. Nevertheless, I was curious, so I slid off the steps and walked into the yard, which gave me a perfect view of the house. A woman got out and stomped up to the front, heading inside without even knocking. She obviously knew Miss Dorothy wasn't home.

Miss Mildred came out of her house carrying her watering can, and for once it wasn't because of me. Her glare was firmly fixed on the car in Miss Dorothy's driveway.

"Do you know whose car that is?" I asked her against my better judgment.

She kept her gaze on the house for so long I thought she was going to pretend she didn't hear me. "I suspect it belongs to Christy, her niece. A ne'er-do-well who moved to Shreveport a few years back."

"Why isn't she staying with her mother?"

"Because I suspect she's here to claim what she thinks is hers."

"She's inheriting the house?"

"Well, she thinks she is. But what she thinks and what's true are two different things in this case."

"Aren't she and her mother Miss Dorothy's only living relatives?"

"Yep."

I squinted in confusion. "Then who—"

Miss Mildred set her watering can down on the porch and started down the steps. "Come with me, and you can find out right along with Christy."

I put Muffy inside, and then fell into step behind Miss Mildred, surprised she'd not only had a semi-conversation with me, but actually invited me along. Which made me highly suspicious. Still, my curiosity overruled the warnings ringing in my head.

Miss Mildred hobbled up the steps and rapped on the door.

Christy answered it, an amused look on her face. "Hey there, Mildred. Where's the casserole? Ain't you God-fearing Baptists known for your condolence casseroles?"

Miss Mildred gasped. "How dare you stand in your aunt's doorway making blasphemous comments about casseroles!"

"Well, you aren't known for offering your compassion, so if you aren't here with a casserole, you're here to snoop."

I would have loved to bask in the revelation that I wasn't the only recipient of Miss Mildred's contempt, but the situation felt like it was escalating quickly. I needed to diffuse it if I had any hope of getting answers.

Offering a smile, I said, "Hi, I'm Rose, and I don't think we've met. I live down the street. I just came over to tell you how sorry I was to hear about your aunt."

"You're Rose? Aunt Dorothy mentioned you." Christy pushed open the screened door and looked me up and down. "You look normal to me."

My face burned with embarrassment.

She shrugged. "I'm not surprised. Aunt Dorothy was as thick as thieves with this one here." She pointed to Miss Mildred. "And she ain't got one damn good thing to say about anybody."

Christy's words hurt. While Dorothy had always preferred Violet, she'd been nice to me. I hadn't realized she'd thought I was strange, although everyone else did, so I wasn't sure why it was surprising. "Have the police contacted you since last night?" I asked. "I wanted to make sure you heard about the attempted break-in."

Her eyes widened. "What break-in?"

"Someone tried to get in the back—"

Miss Mildred seemed to have regained her gumption. "It don't matter to you who tried to do what in this house," she said, her head jutting forward like a bobble head. "Since you don't own it and will never own it."

Christy put her hands on her hips. "What fool nonsense are you talkin' about, old woman? I'm her only kin, after my momma. And if she got it, she's givin' it to me."

Miss Mildred smirked. She loved lording information over people's heads. "So you've read the will?"

"I ain't got to read the will to know it's mine."

Miss Mildred's mouth lifted into a grin that made her look like she had a raging case of constipation. "Well, it might be that there's a surprise waiting for you when you attend the reading of the will. Until then, you're trespassing on private property."

"What the hell are you talkin' about? I'm only here in Henryetta a few days. I gotta make hay while the sun shines. I'm gonna start packing up boxes."

"If you stay in this house another minute, I'll call the police and have 'em forcibly remove you."

Christy laughed. "You wouldn't do that."

What did Miss Mildred know that Christy didn't? She liked to stir up trouble, but I didn't think even she would kick Christy out if she didn't think she had the right. "I guarantee you that she will," I said. "She calls the police on me at least twice a week."

Christy looked me up and down again, really studying me this time. "*You?* What on earth for?"

"Kissing my boyfriend in my front yard."

Christy laughed. "It's only because she's jealous she ain't gettin' any."

It was my turn to gasp.

She turned to Miss Mildred. "Get off my porch, old woman. I ain't warning you twice."

Miss Mildred poked her finger into Christy's chest. "We'll just see who has the last laugh."

Christy looked like she was about to punch Miss Mildred, so I grabbed the old lady's arm and gave it a gentle tug.

"Miss Mildred, this isn't accomplishing anything. You've had your say, let's get going."

Mildred jerked her arm free from my grasp. "Don't you be telling me what to do, demon woman."

Now I regretted not letting Christy punch her.

"I'll go when I want to go," she went on. "Dorothy was my friend, and I won't see her house violated by filth like that woman." But even as she muttered the words, she was descending the steps.

"That's right," Christy called after her. "Crawl back under your slimy rock!" Then the screen door slammed shut.

Miss Mildred hobbled down the drive to the sidewalk, and I wasn't sure whether to stay with her or get out of her line of fire. I decided to ask her the question that was burning in my brain. "Were you serious when you told Christy she didn't inherit the house?"

Miss Mildred turned to me with a sneer. "You callin' me a liar?"

"Well, no . . ."

"Dorothy changed her will last week. I know for a fact she didn't leave the house to that low-life druggie. Dorothy wanted to do everything in her power to make sure she didn't get it, and she even told me the house had already been turned over, whatever that means. She went to her attorney last week to sign the papers. I drove her there myself."

"Who'd she leave it to?"

Miss Mildred's face puckered in contempt. "Someone not much better."

"Who?"

"I don't see how it's any of your business. Don't you have something to do other than pestering me?"

I stopped in my tracks at the edge of the driveway, watching her make her way down the sidewalk. If I lived to be a hundred years old, I'd never figure that woman out. Why'd she share the information with me if she wasn't going to tell me to the whole story?

I couldn't help thinking it was a strange coincidence that Miss Dorothy had died a week after changing her will. I considered calling Mason, but what was he going to do with that?

"It's too bad that old bat wasn't killed too."

I jumped at the male voice behind me and spun around to see Thomas standing next to the open door of his car. "Thomas! That's a terrible thing to say!"

He shrugged. "I'm just sayin' what everyone's thinkin', and you know it. This neighborhood is full of old bitches, but she's the biggest of 'em all."

How could I argue with that? "Still, it's not right to wish anyone dead."

"Don't worry," he said, bending down to get into his car. "She'll get what's comin' to her."

His engine revved as everything went black, and a vision overtook me. I stood in a dark room across from a beefy Hispanic man who was sitting on the edge of a table. "You got the stuff?"

"I had problems."

The bulky man stood, towering over me. "I ain't got time for problems. Get your ass back out there and get it."

"But I think the police are starting to figure things out."

He held his hands from his sides. "You're just full of problems, amigo. Figure it out."

Thomas's car came back into focus as it backed out of the driveway. "You've got big problems," I said out loud.

I nearly stumbled over from shock, thankful that Thomas was speeding away and wouldn't get suspicious about my remark. What kind of trouble was he in? What did he mean that Mildred was going to 'get hers'? I suddenly remembered something he'd said— *It's too bad that old bat wasn't killed too.* The police and the media were claiming the women had died of natural causes, but Thomas had used the word *killed*, not *died*. Now I was even more curious.

I hurried home and locked my doors, suddenly feeling more unsafe than usual. I tried to imagine scrawny Thomas murdering someone. It didn't seem to fit. And even if he had killed Miss Laura and Miss Dorothy, how had he made it look like natural causes? God help me, but that boy just didn't seem that bright.

I couldn't think of anything useful I could draw from our talk or my vision. It was too abstract to take to the police or even Mason. I needed to keep it to myself for now.

But I could do something with the information that Dorothy had left her house to someone other than her niece. And I knew someone who could help me find out more.

I grabbed my cell phone and pressed Neely Kate's speed dial button.

"Say, Neely Kate, can you look up something official for me?"

"Sure."

I loved that about her. She didn't even think to ask what it was before agreeing. "Can you look up the beneficiary of a will? Since you run the personal property department, I figured you might keep track of that sort of thing."

"We only keep records on the actual owners, not the beneficiaries, and the courthouse wouldn't have a record of that until the family files probate."

"Oh." So much for that idea.

"Why're you asking?"

"You know my neighbor who died yesterday and someone tried to break into her house? Well, it turns out there's more to the story. Her niece showed up today, and Miss Mildred went over to confront her. She told Christy that she needed to wait for the reading of the will before she could start packing up the house."

"That doesn't mean anything. You know how cranky she is. She's probably stirrin' up trouble like usual."

"I wondered that too, but then she told me that Miss Dorothy changed the beneficiary of her will. Miss Mildred drove her to the attorney's office last week so she could sign the papers. In fact, she said the house had already been turned over."

"Who'd she leave it to?"

"Mildred told me it was none of my business, but she said that whoever Miss Dorothy ended up picking wasn't much better."

"Why do you care who she left her house to?"

"Because it's just too weird. Two old women have died from supposed natural causes, but their air conditioners were turned off and their windows were shut. And then Miss Laura's jewelry went missing and someone tried to break into Miss Dorothy's house last night, probably to steal her jewelry. What if a serial killer is on the loose?"

"A serial killer in Henryetta, Arkansas?" Neely Kate sounded incredulous.

"Stranger things have happened."

"And you're wondering if the new beneficiary has something to do with it."

"It *is* quite a coincidence."

"Why don't you just tell Mason?"

"I don't want him to think I'm any more of a fruitcake then he already does. I wanted proof."

"First of all, Mason Deveraux does not think you are a fruit-cake, and second, the fact that Mildred said the house was already taken care of made me think of something. Dorothy might have added the new beneficiary to the deed of her house to avoid probate issues. That way the new beneficiary would already own the house. But she would have needed to file a quit claim deed. My grandma added my mother and my aunt to hers last month. I can check to see if one was filed for Dorothy."

"There'd be a record of that in your department?"

"No, but I have connections."

"I don't want to get you into trouble."

"Please." Neely Kate scoffed. "Have we met? You know I can find out *anything*. Besides, I'd love it if they fired me."

Chapter Nine

The next morning, I checked on Bruce Wayne and David on my way to the nursery. I hadn't expected to find them there at 8:45 in the morning, I just wanted to see how far they'd gotten the night before. I was also hoping to avoid Jonah, which was silly. I was gonna have to see him at some point, if only to get our final check. But I wanted to put that off as long as I possibly could.

To my amazement, both men were digging up dirt and pulling weeds. They'd finished the east side of the building, and it looked amazing.

"You guys are doing great!" I said, walking around the side of the church to greet them.

Bruce Wayne leaned his arm on the top of his shovel. "Thanks, Miss Rose."

"I might not be around much today. I'm hoping to buy a truck."

"Oh yeah?" David's head popped up. "My uncle Ernie has a used car lot outside of town on Highway 82. You should check it out and tell him I sent you."

I knew which lot he was talking about, and I wasn't sure if mentioning that David had sent me would get me a better deal or a worse one. "Thanks, David." I smiled. "If you have any questions or need anything, call me on my cell phone."

When I arrived at the nursery, Violet was already there, humming as she watered the flowers on the sidewalk.

I cast a sly glance at her. "Your date must have gone well."

Her grin was mischievous. "Mhmm."

"What did you guys do?"

"Brody took me to Jaspers for dinner, and then we drove over to Magnolia to see a movie."

"Sounds fun."

She smiled. "We're going out again tonight."

"What about Ashley and Mikey?"

Cocking her head, she lifted her eyebrows. "Well . . . now that you mention it . . ."

"Oh." She wanted me to watch them.

"With Joe being gone, I figured you wouldn't have anything else to do."

She was right, and I loved my niece and nephew. They'd help fill the empty evening ahead of me. "Sure, why not? But I don't know when I'll be back from truck shopping."

Violet rolled her eyes. "That again? How are you gonna fit their car seats into your truck?"

"Seeing as how I'm not their mother, I don't suppose I need to worry about fittin' their car seats in my truck."

Her mouth dropped in surprise at my snippy tone.

I couldn't believe I'd said that to her.

She stared at me, clearly waiting for me to apologize, but I just stiffened my back, staring at her.

I suddenly wondered if I was being fair. Violet was my sister and her husband had left her. She needed help from time to time, and why should I begrudge her that? A good sister would offer without resentment. "Look, Vi. A truck seats three people, so of course the car seats will fit. Besides, I did a little research on the Internet last night and lots of trucks have a back seat. We can fit the car seats there if not in the front."

My answer somewhat appeased her, but she gave me the cold shoulder most of the morning. When I took off my apron to meet Mason for lunch, she eyed me up and down. "I didn't mention how pretty you look today. I like your hair like that."

Since I hadn't planned on working at the church, I'd worn a sundress, and I'd pulled my hair back into a loose French braid that Neely Kate had taught me how to do. But I wasn't sure how to address her obvious insinuation. For someone who wanted me to watch her kids, she was acting pretty spiteful. "Thank you."

"You're gonna be back in time to watch the kids, right? You can pick them up from Mike's parents' house."

I paused, picking up my purse. "You're not bringing them over?"

She scrunched up her face. "Why do you think I mentioned the car seats? Mike's parents have them."

I stared at her for a full five seconds, wondering where in tarnation my sister had gone, because the woman on the other side of the counter wasn't her.

"Any other instructions?" I'd meant it as a snide comment, but it went right over Violet's head.

"Just bring them here tomorrow morning. We'll let them play for a while, and then we'll send them off with Mike."

Since the beginning of our joint venture, I'd wondered how she was going to make the nursery work with her kids. At the moment, it seemed as though her plan was to ship them off to everyone else. But that wasn't fair. Violet was a single mother, trying to build a business that would support her and her children. It was obvious she would have to spend a lot of time away from them. I had just expected that it would bother her more.

I was so frustrated with her that I didn't even tell her goodbye when I left. I tried to settle down by the time I found a parking spot on the town square, only one block from the restaurant. I arrived early and was seated by the time Mason showed up at the door. He spotted me right away and made his way through the narrow aisle, a wide grin on his face.

"Ready to get a truck?" he asked, sitting across from me.

"Yeah." Trying to find enough excitement to match his.

His eyebrows lifted. "Are you having second thoughts? We don't have to do this today if you want to take more time to think it over."

"No." I looked into his face and smiled. "That's not it. The more I think about it, the more I know getting a truck is the right thing to do."

"So what's the problem?"

The waitress came over and took our order before I could answer Mason. A vision popped into my head. When it was done less than a second later, I was staring up at her. "Your mother-in-law is going to call you tonight."

"Excuse me?" she asked.

Mason's eyebrows rose.

The waitress put her hand on her hip. "Why would you say that?"

I cringed in embarrassment and lowered my gaze to the table, my hands shaking in my lap. "Just call it a hunch."

"What a strange thing to say," she muttered, walking away.

Mason studied me for several seconds as I willed my racing heart to slow down. It had been inevitable that I'd have a vision in front of him sooner or later. How he reacted to it would determine if he'd remain my friend.

He ignored the bizarre interaction, picking up the thread of our previous conversation instead. "Rose, I can't help noticing that you're not very enthusiastic about this. If you'd rather go alone, I understand."

"No, I want you to come. I just wish my sister understood."

"Ah." He picked up a sugar packet and twisted it around with his fingers. "What's the real reason she doesn't want you to get a truck?"

"Honestly, I don't know."

Mason set the sugar on the table and lowered his head so his eyes were level with mine. "The relationship between siblings is fascinating, don't you think?"

"I'd never really given it much thought."

"I bet you and your sister fight? Right?"

"You don't know that half of it."

"And you drive each other crazy."

"Yeah."

"But you'd do anything to protect her if you could, right?" he said with a hitch in his voice.

Something in his eyes grabbed my heart. "Yes," I whispered.

I wanted to ask him about his sister. Mason had told me something really bad had happened to her, but I didn't know what. I couldn't help thinking that Joe was somehow involved. I wasn't sure why, maybe because this was Mason's deep, dark secret, and Joe had a secret too. How many deep, dark secrets could there be? But somehow I knew what had happened to

Mason's sister was twined with Joe. It was a deep, gut instinct. And that knowledge scared the bejiggers out of me.

"Well, look at you two!" Neely Kate squealed next to me. She must have seen us and ducked into the restaurant, and I'd been too busy in my staring contest to notice. "Got room for one more?"

Mason looked up at her with a friendly smile. "Of course. You must be the infamous Neely Kate."

She put a hand on her hip, grinning. "One and the same, Mr. Deveraux."

"Call me Mason, please." He stood and grabbed a chair from another table, holding it behind Neely Kate and waiting for her to sit. "I know we've seen each other before—the time you applauded after Rose told me off outside my office comes to mind—but I don't think we've been introduced."

If I were in Neely Kate's position, I'd probably die of embarrassment, but she was an entirely different girl. "It seems to me you deserved every bit of that tongue-lashing. In fact, there are still people all over the courthouse who lament that it wasn't caught on video."

Mason burst out laughing. "Maybe next time Rose will alert someone to whip out their cell phone."

As Mason slid in Neely Kate's chair, she shot me an amused and surprised look. The waitress gave our table a wide berth, casting a wary glance my direction, but Mason grabbed her so Neely Kate could make her order.

After the waitress left, Mason turned his attention to my best friend. "We were just talking about you yesterday."

Her eyebrows shot up. "Were you, now?"

I laughed, thankful Mason was being so nice to her, especially after her declaration. But there was no denying that several months ago he'd been a bear in the courthouse. He was better now, but he was still the assistant DA. His position was probably considered higher than hers. It could have been awkward, but he was going out of his way to make sure it wasn't.

"Rose was telling me about all the intel you've gathered about the goings on in the courthouse, and I confirmed that most of it was true. You have a remarkable accuracy rate."

She pursed her lips into a smug smile. "I have a way of knowin' things. But not like Rose. Hers is a true gift."

Mason's smile faltered. "What do you mean?"

Neely Kate was lifting a glass of tea, and her hand froze. "He doesn't know?"

The blood drained from my head, and I struggled with what to say. How could I talk my way out of this one?

Mason continued to watch me, his face becoming expressionless. Every second that passed made it even more impossible to escape this conversational black hole.

Neely Kate set down her glass and turned to me. "I'm so sorry, Rose. I thought he knew."

"So I'm not the only one with secrets," Mason finally said, indecision in his eyes as he scooted his chair back, his gaze on me.

I wanted to cry. I had to tell him now. We'd finally started talking again, and now he was going to either call me crazy or think I was lying. Any way I sliced it, this was sure to end badly.

Neely Kate turned to Mason, steeling her back. "If you want her to tell you, you better wipe that hurt look off your face. She's only told a few people. I only thought she would have said something since you two are friends . . ."

"He's been avoiding me since the trial." I pushed out.

She rolled her eyes. "Well there you go. You haven't been around for her to tell, have you?" Her eyes narrowed. "She only tells people she trusts. Can she trust you with her secret, Mason Deveraux?"

He turned to me, leaning his forearms on the table. "You can trust me with anything, Rose."

The way he said it made me think he meant something more than just this secret. But it still wasn't easy.

A lump burned my throat. "You know I don't have a lot of friends here in Henryetta. But you don't know the reason why."

"I thought it was because you tried your best to annoy them all," he joked, but it fell flat. The fact he was trying to help ease me into this gave me hope he'd understand.

"Ever since I was a little girl, I've *known* things I shouldn't know."

He watched me, waiting for me to continue.

"I don't ask for it." I looked down at the table and took a deep breath. "They're visions, like a movie playing in my head. But it's never for me. It's always for whoever's next to me." I paused, still shocked that I was telling him this. "And after the vision is over, whatever I saw just falls out of my mouth." I bit my lip and looked up to him hesitantly. "When I told you yesterday that your mother was going to like the plant, I'd just had a vision. I saw her—she's very pretty by the way—and she was thrilled when you handed it to her."

Mason swallowed, offering me a weak smile. "Well, that's good to know."

At least he hadn't run away yet.

"And the waitress when she took our order?" he prodded.

I nodded, wanting to cry. "That was a vision."

"She can't usually control the visions," Neely Kate added. "They just pop into her head. That's how she got into the whole Daniel Crocker mess. She was working at the DMV, and he was her customer. She had a vision of herself dead."

His eyes narrowed in confusion. "But you didn't die, obviously."

"My visions aren't set in stone. They can change if I alter my behavior based on what I see. I saw visions of myself dead three times during that whole mess, and I—or Joe—did something different than what we would have normally done to change things. The second time, Joe disobeyed orders from his supervisor and saved me when I went to meet Daniel at The Wagon Wheel. Crocker had threatened to kill Violet if I didn't show up. He thought I had a flash drive with information. Joe gave me a flash drive with false information, but he still suspected Crocker was going to murder me, and I think he was right. I had seen a vision of myself lying in the woods at night with a bullet hole in my forehead. Joe snuck me out the back and hid me when Crocker's men came looking for me."

Mason paled. "That had to be terrifying. Seeing yourself dead."

"You think I'm crazy."

He shook his head and swallowed. "No. I don't. This is just a lot to process. Give me a chance to catch up."

"Okay."

After several seconds, he sighed. "You told me that you knew Bruce Wayne Decker was innocent because you'd overheard a conversation about the case in the men's bathroom. You really had a vision."

"Yeah, but I didn't know what it meant until the lapel pin I saw in the vision came up as evidence in court."

He nodded, deep in thought.

"You believe her?" Neely Kate asked.

"Of course, I believe her," Mason said softly. "Rose isn't a liar, and she's not prone to exaggeration. If she says this is true, then it is. But you have to understand that my world is based on black and white. What you're telling me falls squarely into gray territory. I just need to wrap my head around it, is all."

"Thank you." I choked out.

His head shot up. "What did you think would happen when you told me?"

"I thought you'd call me crazy and never talk to me again."

"No, Rose. Now that we're friends again, it's going to take a lot more than that to drive me away."

The waitress came to the table with our food, and we all watched as she put our plates in front of us. I'd lost my appetite.

Neely Kate squirmed in her seat. I'm sure she was worried I was angry with her. I sort of was, but she was right. If Mason really was going to be my friend, he had to know. Especially if I was going to spend any considerable length of time around him.

I picked at my salad with my fork. "People don't like me knowing stuff. They think I'm a snoop or a gossip, but it's like Neely Kate said—I can't control the visions. They just happen. Other people think I'm demon-possessed. It just became easier to hide away and avoid people when I could. So now I'm the weird Gardner sister. I'd figured I'd probably grow old alone and live in my mother's house with a pack of feral cats."

A smile lifted his mouth. "I can assure you that you won't die alone."

"Violet has always encouraged me to hide the visions. She's spent most of her life protecting me. But Joe thinks I need to trust people more. He'll be happy to know I told you."

Mason snorted. "I highly doubt that." He looked into my eyes. "But Joe's right. Your visions are part of who you are and how God made you. Don't hide that Rose. You need to find people you trust and tell them. You might be surprised to find they accept you, visions and all."

"Thank you."

He grinned, looking down at his sandwich. "I'm starving."

The tension still hung over the table as we ate. Mason was still adjusting and Neely Kate was palpably nervous. Finally Mason shot me an exasperated look. "Will you go ahead and tell Neely Kate you forgive her for spilling your secret? Otherwise, I'm sure to get indigestion from all the nerves at this table."

I laughed self-consciously. "Neely Kate, there's nothing to forgive. You didn't mean to let it slip, and I'm glad Mason knows. Really."

She pulled me into a hug. "Thank you."

I looked at the two people sitting at the table with me, wondering how I could have felt so lonely the night before. The good Lord was blessing me with more people in my life than I'd ever thought possible before Momma's death. I needed to count my blessings.

Chapter Ten

Before Neely Kate went back to work, she told me in cryptic terms that she'd probably have the information I was waiting on later that afternoon. "I'll call you. And don't forget I'll be working at the nursery with you tomorrow."

Violet and I hoped the weekends would be busier, so we'd decided to hire some extra hands. Neely Kate had agreed to help out, taking plants for her new house as payment. "Oh, wait." I called after her.

She stopped on the street corner, waiting to cross the street.

"I might not be at the shop tomorrow. I'll probably be working at the church."

"How's that going?" she asked suspiciously.

I hesitated, unsure of what to say, especially with Mason standing next to me. "It's going good."

"What about the stoners?"

I cringed at her choice of words, but Mason was well aware that Bruce Wayne and David were inclined to smoke pot recreationally. "Bruce Wayne seems determined to pay me back. He's makin' sure they do a great job."

"Well, there you go. You just never know a person, do you?" Waving, she crossed the street toward the courthouse.

"You hired Bruce Wayne Decker to work for you?" Mason asked.

I glanced up at him, surprised at the lack of recrimination in his voice. "You going to tell me you disapprove? Go ahead. Everyone else has."

He shook his head. "No, I think it's a great idea. I firmly believe everyone deserves a second chance, and I'm thankful for it . . . otherwise, I wouldn't be standing here next to you." He grinned. "Where's your car?"

I pointed down the street, and we headed for it.

"Who's been giving you a hard time?"

"Violet, Neely Kate." I supposed that list wasn't long enough to encompass *everyone*, but the reality was it included most of the people in my world.

"Not Joe?"

Pursing my lips, I shook my head. "No. I hired them after he left. He doesn't know yet." I suspected he wouldn't approve either.

"What are their objections?"

"Neely Kate worried they wouldn't get anything done. Violet said the same thing, and she also thinks they'll steal the church blind."

"Do *you* think they'll steal?"

"No. Call me crazy, but I don't. I trust Bruce Wayne to keep his word." We reached my car, and I looked at him over the hood. "Do you think I'm foolish?"

"No, definitely not. I've recently learned to go with my instincts. If your instincts tell you to trust him, listen to them."

"And did your instincts tell you Bruce Wayne was guilty? You were the one prosecuting him."

His eyes clouded. "My instincts were clouded by extraneous circumstances."

My eyebrows rose. "What does that mean?"

"It means I needed someone to remind me that everything isn't always as it appears. I knew it, I just needed reminding."

We got into the car, and I rolled down my window. The day was cooler and the air conditioner wasn't working as well as it had in the beginning of the summer. I asked Mason if he thought it would hurt the trade-in value of my car.

He shook his head with a smirk. "No offense, Rose, but this car is so old, I bet we could take it in on cinder blocks and still get you the same deal."

"Oh." My heart fell a bit with that news. While I knew the car was old, it still had sentimental value.

He cleared his throat, looking uncomfortable. "It's probably a good thing I'm going with you to negotiate. I'm not sure you could get a good deal in town on your own."

Indignation rose. "Why? Because I'm a girl?"

"No, because the town thinks you have money."

I pulled to stop sign at the town square. "*What?*"

"Word got out that you put a lot of money down on the business."

My breath came in short pants. "That's personal information. How does anyone know?"

"It's a small town, Rose. People talk."

Didn't *I* know that firsthand? My hands gripped the steering wheel. "What are they saying?" I shot him a glare. "And don't sugar coat it."

He paused. "They say your mother left you a bunch of money, and that you stole it from your sister. You've opened the nursery, but you're forcing you sister to work there, taking advantage of her vulnerable state."

I took in several deep breaths. This must be what Violet had alluded to the day before we opened the nursery. "Do you believe that?"

"Are you really going to insult me by asking that question?"

"Part of it's true, but it's not what they think. Momma left the house and everything else to Violet. But she left me the contents of a wood box." I sighed. "The contents of that wood box got me into trouble with Daniel Crocker, and now it looks like it's getting me into trouble again."

"What was in the box?"

I looked at him. "The truth."

He didn't answer, waiting for me continue.

"My momma wasn't my birth mother. I was adopted."

"Oh."

"But it's more complicated than that. My father was my birth father, but he left my momma for someone else, Dora Middleton. She got pregnant with me, but she died in a mysterious accident when I was a baby, and my momma raised me. Everyone in town thinks I'm hers."

"*Oh.*"

"I didn't know until I opened the box. I was so hurt when I found out she left everything to Violet. Violet was always her favorite. Momma hated my visions. She was sure I was demon-possessed, but it turns out she hated me even before I started seeing things."

"What was in the box besides the truth?"

I shot him a half-hearted grin. "You're perceptive."

He shrugged. "It's my job."

"My birth mother's will was in the box. She left me her family farm and some oil stock. But my uncle had taken over the stocks and had made me over a million dollars by the time I found out. Turns out I had more money than Violet."

"So you funded the nursery."

I nodded. "But my uncle set my finances up so that I can only take out chunks at a time. After I buy this truck, I'll have used up my allotment for the next several years."

"How are you dealing with all of that information? Finding out your mother wasn't your birth mother?"

"Honestly, I try not to think about it."

"Rose." Mason's voice was low and serious. "You can't push this out of your head. What you discovered was earth-shattering. Life-changing. You have to face that and deal with it before you can move on with your life."

I gaped at him. He was the first person to ever suggest such a thing. Everyone else seemed okay with me sweeping it under the rug. And by everyone, I meant Violet and Joe. But when we found out, Violet had been terrified that I'd no longer think of myself as her sister, even though we'd been raised together and we shared a father. And Joe, maybe Joe never thought I needed to deal with it because he seemed to be running from his own past.

But the problem was that I could see the truth in Mason's words. I knew I had to face the truth and wrestle with what it really meant. I just wasn't ready to do it yet.

"I know," I finally said. "I just don't have the first clue how to go about it."

"I can only share my own personal experience, but at first, I tried to pretend the bad thing in my life had never happened. Eventually I realized that I could ignore it all I wanted, but it didn't make it any less true. All it did was leave a festering wound that would never heal. I started letting myself absorb it in bits and pieces. And after a while, once I got used to it, it was easier to deal with. I can never accept it, but I'm learning to live with it."

I couldn't believe he was sharing so much of himself with me. Sure, he still hadn't told me what exactly had happened, but this was just as important. "Thank you."

His eyes widened in surprise. "For what?"

"For sharing something so personal with me."

He was silent for a moment, and then he offered me a soft smile. "I hadn't intended to, but then you never intended to share something so personal with me either. It felt right." He paused. "Would you ever have told me about your visions on your own?"

"Don't take it personally, Mason. You have to understand that I've told very few people, and most people haven't responded very well. I didn't want to lose you as a friend."

"Joe knows?"

"Of course. I told him during the whole Crocker mess. And Neely Kate guessed after I told her that her flower girl was gonna come down with chicken pox."

"You've been friends with Neely Kate for years, and you just told her recently?"

"No. Neely Kate and I only met on the jury."

"You two are so close . . . I just assumed you'd known each other forever."

I shrugged. "I know, but sometimes you meet someone and you just know they're perfect for you, you know?"

"Yeah, I do." A wistful look crossed his face before he turned to look out the passenger window. He was silent for a moment. "So the visions really just come to you?"

I squirmed in my seat. "Yeah."

Mason sat up straighter. "If you don't want to talk about—"

I shook my head. "No, it's fine. I'm just not *used* to talking about it."

"How often do you get them?"

"Several times a day."

"And you can't control it?"

"I wish to God I could. Especially since I automatically blurt out what I've seen."

"Do you ever try to have a vision?"

I resisted the urge to sigh. "I've only tried twice. The first time Joe asked me to, and I saw him dead. But that was good because I knew what to do to stop it from happening."

"And the second?"

"Neely Kate's wedding. It was a good vision. I don't have many of those. But it was the best vision I ever had."

"Why was it so special?"

"I don't know." I paused. "Maybe because I just let it happen without being anxious about it, so it was longer than usual. And it was filled with happiness. Neely Kate walked down the aisle, and she was bursting with joy." I turned to him. "That was the first time I ever felt overwhelming emotion in a vision. I'm glad it was a good one."

"Do you have bad ones very often?"

The worry in his voice caught me by surprise. "No, not really. When I was younger, I saw upsetting things, but nothing really bad, like someone cheating on his wife or my momma losing the blue ribbon at the county fair for her pie. The first time I ever saw something *really* bad was when Daniel Crocker came into the DMV last May. And that was the first time I saw a vision about myself. I was sitting on my momma's sofa with my head bashed in and blood everywhere. When I saw it, I passed out at my desk from shock."

"I can't even imagine how frightening that must have been."

My throat burned at the memory of that day, but I swallowed to clear it. "I didn't know what to do or who to tell. I just waited for it to happen. And then it happened to Momma instead."

"You just waited for Daniel Crocker to murder you? Why didn't you tell the police?"

"What was I going to tell them? They would have never believed me."

We were silent for several moments before Mason spoke. "Do you ever talk about what happened? With Joe or your sister?"

I tensed, feeling defensive. Violet didn't want to hear it, and I didn't want to worry Joe. "No."

Mason sighed. "Rose, you can't let these scary things happen to you without talking about it."

"There's no one to talk to about it, Mason. I'll just upset or worry everyone, and a psychologist would think I was crazy."

"You can tell *me*."

I pinched my mouth, unsure of whether it was a good idea.

"Why don't you tell Joe?"

I turned to him for a moment. "I don't want you to get the wrong idea. It's not that Joe doesn't want to hear it."

"But does he ever ask?"

I hesitated. "No."

"I'm not judging him or you. That's exactly how a lot of people handle traumatic situations, but we're friends, and as your friend, I think you should talk about it. And I'm volunteering to listen whenever you're ready."

"I'll think about it."

"Thank you." His voice hardened. "But if you ever have a vision in which you see yourself physically harmed, I want you to call me immediately."

"Mason . . ."

"Rose, I'm the assistant DA. I have the power to protect you."

"Not without proof."

"Just promise you'll tell me, and I'll sort out the rest."

"Okay."

I pulled into David Moore's uncle's used car lot. There were a lot of clunkers and a few newer cars and trucks. A sign reading *Henryetta Moore for Less Used Car Lot* leaned to one side, threatening to topple over onto the road. Mason and I stayed in my car, staring out through the windshield.

"I should have asked you if you had any idea what kind of truck you want or how much you want to spend."

"I have no idea what kind of truck. And price? I know I want something reliable. I don't want something that's going to break down all the time."

"Then this might not be the place to get a truck." He pushed open his car door. "But let's check it out. If we don't see anything, we'll drive to Magnolia."

"Okay."

A short man with a large belly waddled out of the small building. Back in the day, this lot was a gas station. It had been converted to a used car lot about ten years ago.

"Can I help you young folks?" the salesman asked, wiping his hands on his jeans and smearing orange powder down his legs. There were still chip crumbs on his chin. "You two look like you're in the market for a nice sedan." His eyes lit up as he cocked his head to the side. "Or maybe a minivan? Getting ready to start a family?"

I looked down at my stomach. Was he insinuating that I looked pregnant?

"No, actually," Mason said. "We're looking for a pickup truck."

"Ho boy!" the guy said. "So we're shopping for the man of the household today. Just brought the wife along to keep you company, aye?"

I expected Mason to correct the guy, and he did, but not about our relationship. "The truck is for the lady."

"Oh."

It wasn't unusual for women to drive pickups in Fenton County, but they usually owned farms.

He extended his hand and Mason shook it. "I'm Earl."

"Mason."

I shook Earl's hand next. "I'm Rose."

"Can I just say that you two make a really cute couple?" Earl grinned.

A blush rose to my cheeks. "Actually, we're—"

"Looking for truck that has working air conditioning. Also it has to have less than sixty thousand miles." Mason turned to me. "Do you care if it has stick shift?"

"Uh . . ."

"Do you know how to drive one?"

"No."

He turned back to Earl. "We won't discount a truck with stick shift at the moment, but we'd prefer an automatic."

Earl led us to the section where the trucks were parked, and I glanced up at Mason with confusion.

Trust me, he mouthed.

Turned out I was trusting Mason Deveraux with lots of things.

Chapter Eleven

It also turned out that Mason knew what he was doing. Between what he knew about trucks and what he learned on the Internet browser on his phone, he decided a Ford F150 with a backseat and a longer truck bed was my best option on the lot.

When I gave my driver's license to Earl so that we could take it for a test drive, Mason handed his over too. As Earl was writing his name in a binder, Mason said, "That's Mason Deveraux III, the assistant district attorney."

Earl looked up, wide-eyed, before glancing at the papers again, his hand shaking as he finished writing.

Mason winked at me.

Earl let us take the truck on a test drive alone, saying he was supposed to go with us, but if he couldn't trust the assistant DA, who could he trust?

Mason chuckled as we walked over to the vehicle. "I bet he's in there hiding all evidence of his illegal activities while we're on this test drive."

"Why would you let him get away with that?"

"No harm in putting the fear of God into him. Besides, you never know. This incident might scare him straight."

"Do you really think so?" I asked.

We reached the back of the truck, and Mason tossed the keys to me. "Nah, but hope springs eternal. Contrary to popular belief, it is not my goal to put half of Fenton County behind bars."

I got behind the wheel, nervous to be driving something so big. Maybe Violet was right. Maybe it would be ridiculous for me to buy a truck.

"Oh, no you don't." Mason said, buckling his seat belt.

I turned to him in surprise.

"I know what you're thinking, and your sister is wrong. There is no reason on earth you can't drive this truck. In fact, I won't let you out until you drive it around Henryetta."

I laughed. "You think you can keep me in here until I drive it?"

"I don't know if you've noticed, but I'm probably the most stubborn man in southern Arkansas. You're driving this truck. You may decide you don't want to buy it, and I'm fine with that, as long as it's not for the wrong reason."

"And what's the wrong reason?"

"Fear. It's okay to be frightened trying something new, but don't let fear stop you from living your life."

Fear had been my enemy for my entire life, and although I'd vowed not to let it stop me anymore, I realized that was exactly what was happening right now. "You're right."

Mason's face lit up with a smug smile. "About damn time someone admitted it, now drive."

I pulled out of the parking lot, terrified that I was going to run over a mailbox or small car, but once I got on the road and got the feel of driving the pickup, I not only got used to it but liked it.

"Well?" Mason asked after we'd driven around Henryetta and were on our way back to the car lot. "What do you think?"

"I think I like driving a truck."

"You look good driving it too."

"You're just saying that."

He laughed. "You'd probably look good driving just about anything."

I cast a sideways glance at Mason, looking at him in a new light. Did Mason like me as more than a friend? If he did, I knew I shouldn't lead him on, but I really valued his friendship. Selfish or not, I wasn't willing to give that up. Besides, I was probably imagining things. Violet was right. I was terrible at this kind of thing.

After I parked in the lot, Mason stopped me as I was about to get out. "Do you want me to see what kind of deal I can get you for this truck or do you want to think about it?"

I shook my head. "I'm not sure what there is to think about. I need a truck. I like this one. Let's do it."

"Okay."

As I grabbed the door handle, everything faded to black, and I was in the courtroom facing Judge McClary, the judge who'd presided over Bruce Wayne's trial. He was looking over the bench at me, his face red with anger. "I can't believe you tried to submit this as evidence given what you know about the questionable chain of custody."

The parking lot came back into view. "The judge is going to throw out your evidence."

Mason's mouth dropped open, and my face flushed.

He immediately laid a hand on my shoulder. "Rose, don't do that. Don't be embarrassed by something you can't control."

"I'm sorry. I . . . I just . . ."

"You didn't do anything wrong. Can you tell me what you saw?"

I studied my hands in my lap. "I was in the courtroom where Bruce Wayne's trial was held, and Judge McClary was looking over the bench at me, which means he was looking at you. Then he said he was throwin' out the evidence due to a questionable chain of custody. He looked really angry."

Mason sat back in his seat. "Well, I'll be damned."

I looked up in confusion. "Are you mad?"

"Mad? Why would I be mad? You just helped me."

"What? How?"

"There was some question about a time stamp in the chain of custody on a blood sample for a DUI case I'm prosecuting next week. I won't submit it as evidence now."

"Oh. But my vision might not be true."

"But there's a good chance it is. I was worried about building my case on it. Now I'll take a different tactic." Mason's eyes locked on mine. "Don't let people belittle you, Rose. Don't be ashamed of who you are."

Joe and Neely Kate had told me the same thing. So why had Violet always believed the opposite? Mason had given me something to think about. "Let's go buy a truck."

Mason was right about getting a better price because he was the assistant DA. I paid less for the truck than I'd anticipated, partly because Mason got a better trade in for the Nova than I'd thought possible. When Mason was satisfied, I signed the paperwork and wrote a check.

After we were finished, we got into the truck, and I sat behind the steering wheel, shaking my head. "I can't believe I just did that."

"You did it. Now you need your business name on the side. Do you know who's going to do that for you?"

"No, I hadn't thought that far ahead."

"Stan runs the body shop on Third Street, and he'd do a good job. Tell him I sent you, and he'll give you a deal."

My eyebrows rose as I looked at him.

Mason shrugged. "I helped him collect on some hot checks. He'll help you."

"Thanks."

"No problem."

My cell phone rang before I put the truck into reverse, so I pulled it out of my purse, hoping it might be Joe. It was Neely Kate.

"You were right, Rose." Her voice was hushed but determined. "A quit claim deed was filed last week on Dorothy's house."

"Who'd she put on it?"

"You're not gonna believe this part. Jonah Pruitt."

I cast a glance at Mason, trying to contain my shock. "So he owns her house now."

"It looks like it."

Mason had noticed my change in demeanor and was outright staring at me.

I tried to ignore him. "Can you find about the other . . . person?" I didn't want to say Miss Laura's name or he'd know for sure what I was talking about.

"One step ahead of you. When I found out about Dorothy, I asked Marta to look into it. I'll let you know when she gets back to me."

"Thanks, Neely Kate. I'll talk to you later."

"Anytime."

"Is everything okay?" Mason asked when I hung up the phone.

"Yeah. Fine." I wasn't sure what to do with this information. I needed to let it sink in before I decided how to tell Mason, so I focused on something else. "Why didn't you correct the salesman when he thought we were a couple?"

"Rule number four of negotiating a deal: Never correct the other person's assumptions. You never know when you might be able to use it to your advantage, one way or the other."

"Hmm . . . okay."

"What are you insinuating? I'm well aware that you're with Joe. I would never stand in the way of your happiness."

"I didn't mean—"

"Rose, it's no big deal. We're friends, all right? I like us being friends."

"Me too."

I parked at the square, close to Mason's car. The truck was wider than the Nova, but not by much. It was easier getting into a parking spot than I would have thought.

"What are you going to do now?" he asked.

"I'll get the big pots Violet and I made and deliver them." I really didn't want to go back to the church now. What if Jonah was involved in Dorothy's murder? What if he killed Miss Dorothy and Miss Laura to get all their money? Heavens knew he was throwing money around like it was holy water.

"What's bothering you?"

I lifted an eyebrow. "How do you know something's bothering me? Are you a mind reader?"

"No, I can read your face. It's my job to read people."

His words sent a shiver down my back. "Funny," I said, "that's what Jonah Pruitt said to me."

Mason stiffened. "When did you talk to Jonah Pruitt?" His eyes widened with realization. "Oh. You're working at his church."

I nodded.

"Rose, I'm not sure it's a good idea to do business with him."

Given Neely Kate's news, I wasn't so sure either. "What do you know about Jonah Pruitt that makes you concerned about me doing business with him?"

"Rose, you know I can't give you the details of an active investigation."

My mouth dropped. "So you're investigating him too?"

It was his turn to be surprised. "*Too*? Who else is investigating Jonah Pruitt?"

I closed my eyes and shook my head. I wondered if I should tell him, but I was already in this deep. I might as well tell him what I knew. "The state police must be looking into him. Joe warned me to be careful, but he insinuated that I'd be okay as long as I got the money to cover my costs up front. When I asked for details, he gave me the same crappy answer you just did."

"I think Joe's right, but I also don't think you should spend much time alone with Jonah." Mason stared at me for several seconds. "But there's something else you're not telling me. What did Neely Kate just call you about?"

I twisted my hands around the steering wheel, avoiding his gaze. "I think Miss Dorothy added Jonah Pruitt to her will last week. Miss Mildred said she drove her to her attorney's office to change the document."

"Holy shit." He sat back in the truck seat, staring out the window.

"That's not all."

He sat up. "There's more?"

I turned to him. "She added him to the deed on her house. She filed a quit claim deed last week. That part's been verified."

Mason shook his head. "From the way he's been courting the elderly women in his town, I suspected he was up to something like that." His eyes narrowed. "Why are you only telling me this now?"

"I just found out. You heard me take the phone call."

"You know that's not what I'm talking about. Why did you have Neely Kate check on it instead of telling me?"

I expected to hear anger—Joe would have been angry—but there was no anger, just curiosity. "Did Detective Taylor find out anything about the shouting?"

"He said he asked around when he questioned the neighbors about the attempted break-in, but no one heard anything."

"Hmm."

"Rose, I told you that I'm not putting a four-year-old boy on the stand."

"I don't want that little boy on a witness stand either, but I don't believe Miss Dorothy died of a heart attack. I think someone killed her. I think someone killed Miss Laura too."

Mason looked deep in thought for several seconds, and then pulled out his cell phone.

"Who are you calling?"

"I suspect you're right. I'm going to arrange to have your neighbor's body shipped to Little Rock for an autopsy."

"But the funeral is tomorrow."

Mason grimaced. "Not anymore." Then he cursed under his breath. He called the coroner and the police department while still sitting in my truck. They talked about digging up Miss Laura's body and doing an autopsy on her too, which inspired more cursing from Mason, but in the end they decided to wait on Miss Dorothy's results first. In light of Miss Dorothy naming Jonah Pruitt as her beneficiary, Mason told them to investigate any connection Miss Laura might have had with the minister. When he hung up, he asked. "You're planning on going to the church this afternoon, aren't you?"

"It's the main reason I needed the truck right now."

He re-buckled his seat belt. "I'm coming with you."

"Mason, you and I both know that you going to the church is a bad idea. Besides, I'm a big girl. I can take care of myself."

"But if Jonah Pruitt murdered Dorothy Thorntonbury and Laura Whitfield, he's a dangerous man."

"If Jonah murdered them, he did it to get their money."

"And I suspect Jonah thinks *you* have money."

"*Oh.*" I hadn't considered that. Of course, I hadn't suspected that half the town thought I had money either. Was that the reason for Jonah's interest in me? "Maybe so, but I haven't signed a quit claim deed or made him the benefactor of my will. Murdering me wouldn't do him any good."

"Just be careful, Rose. And if you run into any sign of trouble, let me know. Call my cell phone number. You still have it, right?"

"Of course I do." How come I always found myself in the middle of these situations? "Thanks again for helping me buy the truck."

"You're welcome. If you need help with anything else, don't hesitate to ask."

"Thanks, Mason. I will."

Mason climbed out and I backed up and headed toward the nursery. When I pulled into the parking lot, Violet came outside and crossed her arms. "Well, you went ahead and did it."

"It's great, isn't it?"

"You're gonna run over something."

"I'm not gonna run over something. I've already got the hang of driving it."

An evil grin lit up her eyes. "Joe's gonna have a fit."

Ice water chugged through my veins. I suspected she might be right about that one, but I wasn't about to admit it to her. "Joe's going to see how practical this is, and he'll think I'm a savvy businesswoman."

Dread set me on edge. I hoped he saw it my way. Maybe I should have waited to buy the truck, but in my defense, it was a business decision and I had no idea when I'd talk to Joe next. Given the secrets he was keeping from me, we had far more bigger problems than me buying a new truck. Or letting Mason help me. That was the part that worried me the most, but there was no sense thinking about it now. I could stew over it while I tried to go to sleep tonight.

After a bit of a struggle, I got the pots in the truck. Maybe I should have recruited Mason to help me load everything.

"Be sure to pick up the kids," Violet called out after me as I was about to leave.

"I know, Vi," I grumbled before pulling out of the lot. "I'd hate for you to miss your precious date."

On the way to the church, I picked up some lemonade from the Piggly Wiggly for the guys. I waved them over to some shade next to the parking lot when I parked and handed them the cups when they wandered over. Both men were sweaty, with dirt smeared on their legs, shorts, and faces. They drained their cups in less than a minute, and I poured them more, happy that I'd thought to buy a gallon.

"Thank you," David said, wiping his mouth with the back of his hand.

"You guys are making great progress." I was shocked to see that the west side was almost done—and done well.

"It's a bit rougher on this side," Bruce Wayne said after drinking a big gulp. "We've got the afternoon sun, so it's hotter."

"But Reverend Jonah has been bringing us water all day," David said, watching as a car pulled into the parking lot.

"That's mighty nice of him," I mumbled, trying not to sound sarcastic. *Good heavens, Rose.* When did I become so cynical? I was so suspicious of Jonah Pruitt that I couldn't take a kind gesture at face value. Besides, I didn't have proof that Jonah was guilty of anything other than sporting a 1980s hair style.

A woman got out of the car, and then helped an older woman out of the backseat. David took another big gulp of lemonade then lowered the cup. "Hey, ain't that Christy Hansen?"

Leaning forward, Bruce Wayne squinted. "Yep, I think it is."

While the name Christy Hansen didn't sound familiar, something about the woman *looked* familiar.

"What's she doin' here?" David asked. "I thought she moved to Shreveport."

"Her aunt died."

My attention kicked into high gear. "Is her aunt Dorothy Thorntonbury?"

"Yep." Bruce Wayne mumbled, taking a drink.

"How do you two know her?" She was old enough to be their mother.

"She was our math teacher in middle school," David said.

"You don't say."

"I saw her at the pool hall last night," Bruce Wayne added. "She told me about her aunt."

I put my hand on my hip. "What were *you* doing at the pool hall?"

Bruce Wayne's eyes widened in confusion. "I was playing pool."

"You weren't up to questionable activities?"

He realized what I was asking and shook his head. "No, ma'am. I gave that stuff up for good. But I still like playin' pool."

I wasn't about to call Bruce Wayne a liar, especially since he'd done everything in his power to prove how hard he was trying. But if he really had given up drinking and smoking pot, I couldn't help thinking that the pool hall wasn't a good place for him to be hanging out.

"Christy bought a round of drinks for everyone, saying she was about to be rolling in dough since her aunt had died."

A shard of guilt shot through my chest. Who was going to tell her that Dorothy had left the house to Jonah Pruitt? Maybe that was why she was here now. Could be she'd just found out.

"How'd she afford that?" I asked. Her beat-up Ford Fiesta attested to her financial status. "She doesn't have any money yet."

"Shoot, no." David chuckled. "She was trying to place a bet with Skeeter, but he wouldn't have any part of it. He said she didn't have the cash to back it up."

"So what was she doing buying everyone drinks?"

"That's Christy Hansen. Spendin' what she don't have," he said, amused.

I cocked my head to the side. "How do you two know so much personal stuff about your middle-school math teacher?"

"We didn't find this out as her students," David smirked. "We found out from partyin' with 'er."

My mouth gaped, unsure what to say. How far had she fallen? Mildred had called her a drug addict, and here she was trying to place bets with the local bookie.

"I can't believe Skeeter didn't throw her out." Bruce Wayne muttered shaking his head.

I turned to him. "Why would he throw her out?"

"When she left for Shreveport a couple of years ago, she owed Skeeter money. We all figured that's why she left."

If Christy owed money to Skeeter Malcolm, there was only one reason I could think of as to why. Christy Hansen was a gambling fool. And gambling fools were always needing money.

Chapter Twelve

At the moment, my biggest puzzle was what Christy Hansen and someone I assumed was her mother were doing at the New Living Hope Revival Church.

There was one thing I was certain of: Miss Dorothy hadn't died of natural causes. Someone had killed her—and likely Miss Laura too—and I suspected that they'd done it for personal gain. The most likely suspect was Jonah Pruitt. After all, he'd inherited Miss Dorothy's house and probably any money she had.

But then again, maybe he hadn't killed her. Christy was looking pretty suspicious too. She needed money, and she thought she was inheriting everything from her aunt. But was she capable of murder?

And what about Thomas? It was common knowledge on our street that Thomas and Miss Dorothy hadn't exactly gotten along. Up until about a half an hour ago, when Mason had ordered the autopsy, the police were still calling the elderly women's deaths natural causes. Thomas had insinuated they were murdered. How could he have known that, and did it have anything to do with my vision?

The guys helped cart the pots out of the truck and position them around the church entrance. Since I was wearing a dress, and I needed to pick up the kids from Violet's in-laws, I couldn't do much work. Instead, Bruce Wayne took me on a tour of the church grounds, showing me what they'd done, and what was still left to do. When we made our way to the front of the church,

I saw an old black Trans Am pull into the church parking lot and park close to the entrance.

I shaded my eyes to get a closer look. Sure enough, it was Thomas's car. "What's he doing here?" I mumbled under my breath.

"Thomas?" Bruce Wayne asked.

My mouth dropped open before I recovered. "You know him?"

A sheepish look spread across Bruce Wayne's face. "I've seen him around."

That could only mean one thing. They'd met under nefarious circumstances. I wasn't all that shocked Thomas was involved in illegal activities.

"But I wonder what he's doing here. At church."

"He was here yesterday afternoon too. Reverend Jonah hired him to do odd jobs. He brought David and me some cold water."

"And what did you guys talk about?"

Bruce Wayne stuffed his hands in his pockets. "Who said we talked?"

"I'm no fool, Bruce Wayne Decker. If you knew him before and he brought you water, y'all had to make some kind of chit chat."

He pressed his lips together. Apparently, I wasn't the only person to whom he felt loyalty.

"Did he tell you how long he's been working for Jonah Pruitt?"

Looking at the side of the church, he shrugged. "A couple of months."

"It seems odd that a boy like Thomas would be working for a reverend."

He shrugged again. He knew something but wasn't telling me. "Why do you wanna know?"

"He lives on my street. Next door to the woman who was killed a couple of days ago."

His eyes flew open. "Someone was killed on your street?"

"Yeah, Christy's aunt."

He shook his head in confusion. "But she said her aunt died of a heart attack."

"That may be what the Henryetta police are sayin', but Mason just ordered an autopsy. There won't be a funeral tomorrow."

Bruce Wayne released a low whistle. "Christy won't be too happy to hear that. She has big plans back in Shreveport."

I started walking toward the church entrance. "Nobody ever plans for a murder."

Unless they committed it.

When I intercepted Thomas on the sidewalk outside the church, he looked up in surprise, then annoyance. "What are you doin' here?" he asked.

"I could ask the same thing about you."

A cocky grin spread across his face. "The way I see it, it ain't any of your business."

"I know you're mixed up in trouble."

The smile fell off his face.

I had no idea what possessed me to say that. I suspected that Mason was right about not showing your hand, and if there was ever a time to keep what I knew to myself, it was now. But I couldn't help thinking that Thomas had gotten himself involved in something out of his control. Maybe he needed help getting out of it. "If you tell me what you're mixed up in, maybe I can help."

He snorted in disgust. "Ain't you datin' a state policeman? The one who busted Daniel Crocker? You know you pissed a lot of people off when you got involved with him and his business. There's a lot of people who'd like to see you pay."

It was my turn to be shocked.

"It looks to me like *you're* the one in a heap of trouble," he said.

The doors to the church opened behind me. "What's going on here, Thomas?" Jonah asked in a stern voice.

"Nothin', Reverend." Thomas said, trying to show remorse and failing miserably. "Rose and I was just catchin' up."

"You two know each other?"

"We're neighbors," I said, swinging my gaze to Jonah. Christy and her mother stood behind him.

"Well, it *is* a small world." Jonah said, but his voice was strained. "Imagine that."

"It gets even stranger when you take into account that Christy's aunt lived next door to Thomas."

"You don't say," Jonah muttered, but he didn't look all that surprised. "Thomas, I think Rhonda has some jobs lined up for you. Why don't you run on inside?"

"Sure thing, Reverend." He walked toward the door, but when he was behind Jonah, he turned and held his hand up like a gun, aimed it at me, then lifted his finger like he'd fired. He gave me an evil smile before heading inside.

What in tarnation was that all about? I'd never considered that Daniel Crocker's henchmen might hold a grudge against me. I resisted a shudder. Daniel had been locked up months ago, so surely I would have been threatened by now if there was any true danger.

Christy wrapped her arm around the reverend's. "Jonah, thank you for being such a support in my time of need." She glanced at her mother and added, "And, of course, for helping Momma too."

Jonah patted her hand. "Just doin' my job to console my flock. But rest assured your aunt was a God-fearin' woman. She's with her maker right now, lookin' down on us all." I could swear his accent was thicker than usual.

While Jonah walked Christy and her mother to her car, I watched to see if anything was amiss. The way Christy had hugged him told me she was still clueless about the ownership of Miss Dorothy's house. But with all my gawking, I'd missed my opportunity to escape. Jonah spanned the short distance between us, stopping only a few feet in front of me with his wide television smile.

I cleared my throat. "The guys are almost done. I think they might finish up tomorrow, in plenty of time for your revival on Monday."

"I hope you'll consider coming."

"Uh . . . I'm pretty busy with the nursery and all. I'll see if I can make it." I'd just lied to a minister, which I was sure put me on the slippery slope to my own damnation. I decided to change the subject. "That's just terrible what happened to Miss Dorothy."

Jonah pressed his lips together and shook his head. "All the more reason to make sure you're right with your maker. When God calls you home, there's no screening caller ID."

"I'm confused about why Christy and Miss Edna were here." I hedged. "I thought Miss Dorothy went to the Methodist church."

He folded his hands in front of him. "She transferred her church membership here. She had been a member for a couple of months at the time of her death."

"So will the funeral be here?"

"No, they don't expect a large crowd, so it's going to be held at the funeral home." He paused. "However, the police called during our visit and told Christy and her mother that they had decided to conduct an autopsy." Jonah didn't look all that unnerved by the prospect. Maybe he didn't think they'd find anything.

"An autopsy? Why would they do that? I thought the police said she died of a heart attack."

"That's a good question, and Christy was *very* upset over the matter."

"She didn't look that upset when I saw her leave."

"That's because I assured her that it was all part of God's plan. She had planned to head back to Shreveport on Sunday, but now she'll stay until the middle of the week and attend the revival."

There was no doubt Christy had set her claws in Jonah. Given her lifestyle, why she'd be interested in a man of the cloth was beyond me. Perhaps it was the allure of his cameras.

"Detective Taylor said he wants to interview all the people who saw her in the few days before her death."

Something in his voice piqued my interest. "Are they going to interview you?"

"Yes, although it's only a formality." He was looking me up and down as though he were studying me.

I suppressed a shudder. "When was the last time you saw her?"

"I do believe it was last Sunday, right after the morning service." He continued examining me. "Did you know Dorothy well?"

"She lived down the street, but no, I didn't."

"You feel alone in the world, don't you Rose?"

I crossed my arms, suddenly feeling exposed. "I'm not sure why you think that."

His lowered his voice and moved closer. "I can see it in your eyes. The eyes are the window to the soul. I can help you, Rose. You can share your burden with me."

I remembered what Mason had suggested, that Jonah Pruitt might be after the money he thought I had. The breeze kicked up and goose bumps broke out on my arms. "I don't really have any burdens, Reverend. My life is great. I have a boyfriend and a new business. I'm happy."

He shook his head. "You can pretend all you want, but I can tell you're troubled. I'm here to help you, not just as a pastor, but as a friend." He put his hand on my bare shoulder.

I tried to stuff my panic, feeling uncomfortable with the direction this was heading. I turned and saw Rhonda standing at the door. Her arms were crossed beneath her bosom, and if she scowled anymore, her face would get stuck in a permanent pucker.

I took a tiny step back and forced a smile. "Thank you, Reverend. I'll keep that in mind."

He watched me for a few uncomfortable moments. "I hope you do. I'd like to get to know you better." Then he turned and walked back into the church, but Rhonda kept her vigil, making no attempt to hide the hate in her eyes.

As he walked away, a vision blackened everything around me.

Rhonda stood in front of me, her face red with anger. "That girl is trouble, Jonah."

"Who I talk to is none of your business."

"We came here with a plan, and you're getting distracted."

My hands clenched at my sides, and my words came out clipped. "Let's not forget who's in charge here."

She gritted her teeth and looked down, mumbling, "Yes, I know."

"You need to have more faith, Rhonda. Our ultimate goal will be obtained."

The brick exterior of the church came back into view, and Rhonda stood in the open doorway now. "You're fighting with Rhonda over me."

Rhonda's mouth dropped open, and then she quickly got ahold of herself and took a step toward me, still holding onto the door. "I told you I know your kind, and I won't stand back and watch you ruin that Godly man."

This judgmental woman was ticking me off. "I don't have any interest in Jonah Pruitt other than as a businesswoman."

"Don't you go trying to pull the wool over my eyes. I can see what you're doing as clear as day." She pointed her finger at me. "I won't stand for it. When you finish this job, don't you ever set foot on this church's grounds again."

I stuffed down a laugh. "I thought Reverend Jonah was all about acceptance and turning no one away."

"Sometimes the reverend forgets himself and needs someone to watch out for him."

"Funny, he seems perfectly capable of taking care of himself." I spun around and stomped off to where the guys were working.

My encounter with Jonah had shaken me, particularly the vision. I considered calling Mason, but what was I going to tell him? That Jonah's secretary hated me? That didn't exactly seem like DA material.

Instead, I told Bruce Wayne and David goodbye for the day and drove across town to pick up Ashley and Mikey.

They were playing in the front yard of Mike's parents' house when I showed up. Mike's mother sat on the step, watching the kids. Ashley was blowing bubbles, and Mikey was chasing after them. They let out squeals of excitement when they saw me pull up in the truck, and they ran over to check it out. Mike's mother's brow wrinkled in confusion. "Violet said you were thinking about buying a truck, but she led me to believe it was an old clunker."

That didn't surprise me a bit. "No, Mason Deveraux, the assistant district attorney, helped me get a good deal."

Her eyebrows rose at my statement, but she didn't comment.

When the kids settled down, we set up the car seats in the truck's backseat and strapped them in. Once they were settled, Mike's mother turned to me, her face pale. "Do you think that Mike and Violet will ever get back together?"

I cleared my throat, stalling. But there was no sense in hiding what I thought. "It doesn't look promising, does it?"

"We love Violet like a daughter, but I'm not sure we can watch her start dating." Her voice broke. "It's just too painful."

I nodded. I understood better than she knew. "I feel exactly the same way. I love Mike and miss him terribly. But I also love Violet, and I need to let her make her own decisions. Mike seems to be moving on and she wants to do the same, as difficult as it is for me to accept."

She bit her lip. "I don't want to lose my grandchildren."

I pulled her into a hug. "You won't! Violet loves you and Gary, and she would never let the kids lose you. Besides, not only are you amazing grandparents, but you're the only ones they have."

She sniffed and patted my arm. "You're a good girl, Rose. I wasn't sure about you when Mike and Violet first got married—you were always so quiet and self-contained, like you didn't have time for anyone else—but you've really come out of your shell and grown into yourself."

Her comment caught me off guard, and I wasn't sure what to say. "Um . . . thank you."

After she put the kid's bags into the truck, she went inside the house, leaving me a little dazed. Had people stayed away from me because they thought I wasn't friendly? Had I been the one to create the barrier between myself and the world?

"Aunt Rose! I'm hungry!" Ashley shouted from the backseat.

She shook me out of my musings, and I climbed inside. "Then let's get you something to eat. Do you like my new truck?"

"Ru," Mikey said, clapping his hands together.

"I'll take that as a yes. How about you, Ashley?" I cast a glance at her as I backed out of the driveway.

Her brow wrinkled. "I guess it's okay. Barbie drives a pink car."

"Well, Barbie doesn't own a nursery."

"But she's a vet. And a teacher."

I laughed. The logic of a five-year-old. "I suppose a pink car works for that, but I got a blue truck, and I like it."

"But boys drive trucks, like my daddy."

"Girls can drive trucks if they want to. They can do pretty much anything a boy can do."

"They can't pee standing up. I tried it, and Mommy got really mad because I made a huge mess."

I tried not to laugh. She was using her serious voice, and I didn't want to hurt her feelings. "True, they probably shouldn't pee standing up, but girls can do just about anything else."

"Are you going to marry Joe?"

I wasn't sure how we'd changed topics so quickly, and this one caught me by surprise. "Well, he hasn't asked me officially, but yeah, I think we'll get married someday." The thought filled me with happiness. I pictured me and Joe in my tiny house with a baby, and tears sprang to my eyes. How could I go from being so miserable five months ago to this happy now? I kept expecting to wake up from a dream.

Ashley talked about her day with her grandparents, and Mikey made sounds like he wanted to join the conversation, but was having a hard time getting a word in edgewise with his talkative sister. I kept my eyes on the road, my nervousness about driving something so big dissipating with each mile.

When we got home, Muffy was excited to see the kids. It was hard to tell who was happier—her or them.

I made a quick dinner of hot dogs and carrots and let the kids have a picnic on the front porch while Muffy chased a bug in the yard. I was sure Joe would teasingly disapprove of our meal. He always gave me a hard time about rarely cooking for myself, even though I used to do all the cooking when Momma was alive.

A pang of regret struck like a sharp stab. After what Violet's mother-in-law had said to me, I was starting to question everything about my life before, and a brand-new thought struck me: Was my poor relationship with my mother partially my fault?

My cell phone rang.

Ashley picked it up and looked at the caller ID, staring at it for two rings. I resisted the urge to snatch it from her as she tried to read it. "Joe," she finally said, and I took the phone, quickly pressing answer.

"Joe?" I answered, hoping I hadn't missed him.

"Hey, darlin'. I miss you."

I leaned my shoulder into the support post on the porch, my heart aching at the sound of his voice. "I miss you too."

"I wanna talk to Joe!" Ashley said.

"Joe. Joe." Mikey mimicked.

My eyes widened in surprise. I'd never heard him say Joe's name before.

"Does my fan club miss me too?" Joe teased.

"Not as much as I do."

"Let me say a quick hello, so I can have you all to myself."

"Good idea." I handed the phone to Ashley.

She grinned from ear to ear. "Guess what, Joe? We get to spend the night at Aunt Rose's house and play with Muffy while Mommy goes out with her new friend. And we took a ride in Aunt Rose's new truck."

Oh, crappy doodles.

Ashley was silent for several moments. "When are you gonna come back and play with me?" She paused. "Okay, bye Joe."

She handed the phone back to me, and my stomach balled into a knot of nerves. "That was short."

"You got a truck?" He didn't sound happy about it, but he didn't sound upset either. It was like he was testing the water, dipping his toe in to gauge the temperature. Or perhaps it was the other way around.

I took a deep breath. "Yeah, we got that job with Jonah, and we needed to haul things to the church. Violet's father-in-law brought his truck to help, but I realized that we needed our own." I waited for him to answer.

He hesitated for a couple of seconds. "That's probably a good idea."

My shoulders relaxed.

"If you'd waited, I would have helped you."

"I know, but I didn't know when you'd be back. You said it could take a couple weeks or more. Does it still look like it's gonna take that long?"

Joe sighed. "It's hard to say. I hope it gets wrapped up soon. I miss you."

"I miss you too."

"Did you have trouble negotiating a deal on the truck? Where'd you get it?"

"The Moore For Less Used Car lot."

Joe groaned. "Earl Moore? He's a crook, Rose. He probably ripped you off."

I suppressed a groan. I was gonna have to tell him. "No, I had some help."

"Who? Violet? I know she thinks she knows everything, but—"

"No, it wasn't Violet. It was Mason."

Joe was silent for so long I thought he'd hung up. "Let me get this straight." His voice was tight and controlled. "I told you that I was worried about you talking to Mason Deveraux, and as soon as I leave town, you ask him to help you buy a truck? After I've been after you to buy a new car for months?"

I squeezed my eyes shut. "I know this looks bad, Joe, but I promise you it just happened."

"It just happened." He sounded so detached.

"I saw Mason after they found Miss Dorothy dead—"

"The Miss Dorothy on your street?" At least he sounded concerned about that. "How'd she die?"

"They ruled it as natural causes, but after I got tackled by someone who was trying to break into her house, I called—"

"Whoa! How did you get tackled? What were you doing around her house?"

"Muffy ran into her backyard. She must have heard the guy breaking in. Even though she was on her leash, she bolted and I chased her around back."

"Are you okay? Did you get hurt?"

"I'm fine, other than my pride being wounded after getting knocked on my behind. Mason came to check out the crime scene, and he told me Muffy scared the intruder off before he got in."

"Let me get this straight." His voice was strained. "Mason showed up for a simple breaking and entering? That seems a little beneath his position."

Oh, dear. This was getting worse. I knew I should tell Joe that I'd been the one to call Mason, but his tone made it clear that it would be a bad idea. The truck was probably safer territory. "Anyway . . . I was telling Violet I thought we needed a truck when Mason showed up at the nursery looking for a gift for his mother. He heard and offered to help me negotiate."

"I bet he did." Joe's tone was dry. "And you accepted."

My anger riled up. I didn't like what he was insinuating. "I told you that I would have waited for you, but I didn't know when you'd be back."

"I've been begging you for months, Rose—*months*—to get a safer vehicle. And then as soon as Mason offers to help buy you a truck, you run out and buy one."

"It wasn't like that. We went the next day."

"Well there you have it," he said mockingly. "You went the next day."

"Joe, please try to understand."

"I think I do understand." His voice was strangely quiet.

Panic rose up, but it was liberally flavored with irritation. "What are you insinuating, Joe McAllister? Do you think I'd send you off on a dangerous undercover operation, and then cheat on you with Mason Deveraux? Do you think so little of me?"

"After what happened between Deveraux and me in Little Rock, it's not you I'm worried about."

"And maybe this conversation would mean more to me if you'd bother to tell me what happened."

His breath was heavy in my ear. "You're right." He paused. "I'll tell you about it the next time I see you, I promise. I don't want to have this conversation over the phone. Trust me, okay?"

Joe had never given me reason *not* to trust him. If anything, he'd given me every reason to give him my absolute blind faith. But this deep, dark secret scared me. "I love you, Joe. You know that."

"I know." His voice broke. "I just don't want to lose you."

Something about the way he said the words made me wonder if the threat was entirely on my end. "What's goin' on there? Are you safe?"

"Darlin', you know every time I put on my badge—"

"Joe. Stop. Is this more dangerous than usual?"

"You know I can't talk about my job." I heard the tired smile in his voice.

My heartbeat sped up. "Quit."

"I already told you that I'm planning on it."

"No. Right now. Tell your boss you're done and come home to me, Joe."

"Oh, Rose," he said. "You know I can't do that."

I knew, but I was still upset that he was choosing his job over me. But that wasn't fair, and it wasn't true, either. Joe couldn't just quit in the middle of an assignment—that wasn't the type of person he was. And that was one of many reasons I loved him. "I know. I'm sorry."

"I'm sorry too. Just please be patient with me."

"I'm just scared."

"I know, darlin'. I am too. But not because of my job."

"I'm not goin' anywhere. I'm here waiting for you."

"I'm counting on that." He sighed and his voice was tight. "I trust you, Rose. I'm sorry if I insinuated anything different. That wasn't my intention. It's just that . . ." His voice trailed off.

Tears clogged my throat. "I love you, Joe. Only you."

"I know, darlin'. I never doubt that. That's what's getting me through this."

"You're job?" My breath hitched with my rising terror. What was he doing in El Dorado?

"No, darlin'. Not my job. It's okay. I didn't mean to scare you. I'll explain it all when this is done." The timber of his voice deepened. "I have to go. Whatever is going on there with Miss Dorothy's death, stay out of it. Sometimes I think you scare up more danger than I do."

Sometimes I wondered if he was right. But this time, the danger I was facing wasn't the bad guys lurking outside my door.

Chapter Thirteen

The kids played all night with Heidi Joy's boys and Muffy. I tried to have fun with them, but I was too upset. Once again, it felt like there was sand shifting under my feet. I barely had time to get used to the new way of things when everything shifted again. Violet and Mike's world had changed, but that didn't mean mine had to. Once Joe finished this assignment, he'd get the job at the sheriff's department and come live with me. We'd build our life together in Henryetta. But would Joe really be happy living here?

Thankfully, the kids went to sleep pretty easily after getting worn out by the rowdy boys next door. When I went to bed, I checked my phone, grateful that Joe had sent me a text.

I miss you. XO

I tossed and turned and spent half the night trying to get everything out of my head. When I woke up the next morning, both kids were laying across the bed, waiting for me to wake up. We snuggled for several minutes, and I let my mind wander to the thought of starting a family with Joe. Now that I knew we were on the same page about kids, I wondered what it would be like to lie in bed with Joe and our own children.

Mikey burrowed his head into the space between my arm and chest, and I leaned over to take a whiff of his hair. He'd outgrown that sweet baby smell, and had begun to smell more like a little boy, but this morning, a hint of the baby scent lingered. I wondered how Violet could give up this moment with them, how she could pick Brody over her own children, but I knew that wasn't fair. She'd had years with Ashley and plenty of mornings with Mikey. Besides, I'd been around enough to know it wasn't all peaches and cream at the Beauregard house most mornings. I only hoped that Violet would have a few dates, get it out of her system and try to get back with Mike. I suspected I was wishing for the moon.

After I made the kids pancakes for breakfast, I loaded every-one into the truck, Muffy included. I hated leaving her so much that I decided to try taking her with me to the shop. If nothing else, she'd entertain the kids until Mike showed up. And I could put her in the back room if need be. Besides, I missed my little dog. In the event that Violet didn't approve, I'd pull my fifty per-cent ownership card out. Of course, the fact that I'd put up most of the financial backing gave me a higher percentage of owner-ship, but I'd never throw that in her face. Still, if it came down to it, I'd stand my ground. Muffy was coming to work with me from here on out.

Violet was already at the nursery when we got there. She gave the truck a dirty look, but her face broke into a smile when she caught sight of the kids. They squealed with excitement when they saw her.

"Mommy! I missed you!"

"Momma," Mikey said, stretching for Violet.

I quickly unfastened his car seat straps while Ashley unbuck-led herself and leapt out of the truck and into her mother's arms. Mikey reached for Violet as soon as I lifted him from the seat. Muffy looked on from the front seat, her tail wagging.

"We brought Muffy to work!" Ashley said.

"I can see that." Violet's gaze had moved to Muffy, and thankfully she smiled.

My shoulders relaxed, and I was surprised by how worried I'd been about her reaction. "They had pancakes and chocolate milk for breakfast."

"You had food in the house?" Violet teased.

Grinning, I shrugged. "Joe was home on Tuesday night."

Her eyebrows rose, and I was grateful my old sister was back, even if only for a while. "Well, thank God for that man or you'd starve."

"Mommy, I got to talk to Joe on the phone," Ashley said. "He was really surprised Aunt Rose got a truck."

"I bet he was," Violet snorted.

I expected her to say more, but she took the kids inside, asking more about their night at my house.

After I uncovered the flowers on the sidewalk, I started watering the flats. I was still at it when Neely Kate's car pulled up. I offered her a bright smile as she walked over to me.

She stopped a few feet away. "I wasn't sure you would want me here after I told Mason your secret yesterday."

Violet emerged from the shop and sidled next to Neely Kate, grinning slyly. "What secret?"

"I told Mason about my visions," I said.

Violet's smile fell. "Do you think that's a good idea?"

Neely Kate put a hand on her hip. "He's her friend, Violet. She should have told him months ago. Why keep it a secret?"

Violet glared. "To save her from ridicule, of course. Do you have any idea the torment our poor girl went through in school? Kids didn't even know her secret, and they still teased her mercilessly."

Neely Kate tilted her head, a determined look on her face. "And maybe they wouldn't have been so mean if they'd known the truth."

"Rose isn't like you, Neely Kate." Violet smiled and batted her eyelashes, her voice syrupy sweet. "She doesn't like bein' the center of attention. I know you find this hard to believe, but not everyone wants to have some supernatural talent. They want to be *normal*. What is it for you this week? Tarot cards? Voodoo dolls?"

I gasped at Violet's rude behavior.

Neely Kate clenched her fists and stood her ground. "Maybe she'd know if she wanted to be the center of attention if you didn't always try to steal it from her."

Once again I wondered why I was constantly on the sidelines watching other people battle for me.

"Enough." I stepped between them. "Neely Kate is right. There's no reason to keep such an important part of me from people

I trust. Secrets cause more harm than good. You of all people know that, Violet."

Fear filled Violet's eyes. "What is that supposed to mean?"

So she *was* keeping something from me. I quickly recovered. "You know," I said. "Like Momma keeping the information about my birth mother from us. And Daddy leaving her for Dora. We didn't know any of that until after she died and look how upset we both were when Aunt Bessie told us the truth."

Violet took a deep breath, relief flooding her face. "Of course that's what you meant."

I wanted to ask Violet what her *other* secret was, but I stopped myself. She'd never tell me in front of Neely Kate, and it wasn't fair to ask.

Violet lifted her chin, her smug demeanor returning. "You do what you think is best, Rose. Over the last few months you haven't listened to a word I've said anyway. I might as well be talking to a brick wall." She turned around to go inside.

"Violet," I called after her, but she ignored me, watering the plants inside.

"Let her go sulk," Neely Kate said with a scowl. "I don't know what her problem is lately."

"She means well." Funny how defending Violet had become a habit, even when I doubted my own words.

Neely Kate helped me water the flats. "I thought you said you were going to be at the church this morning."

"I planned to . . ." My voice trailed off as I tried to figure out what to tell her.

"What happened?"

"What didn't happen?" I looked through the window to see if Violet was within hearing distance, but she was occupied with the kids.

Neely Kate saw what I was doing. "She's busy. Spill it."

I lowered my head closer to hers. "I told Mason about the quit claim deed, and he ordered an autopsy on Miss Dorothy, but there's so much more."

Excitement lit up Neely Kate's eyes. "Like what?"

"I didn't tell you about Thomas, the teen who likes to rev up his car and drive like a maniac down our street."

"He's involved?"

"After Miss Mildred confronted Christy on the front porch, Thomas told me it was too bad that Miss Mildred hadn't been killed too. Killed as in murdered."

"Why would he say that?" Neely Kate whispered.

"I don't know, but then I had a vision, and he was with some mean-looking guy. Thomas told the guy he had a problem, and the mean guy told him he was going to *give* him a problem."

"That doesn't sound good."

"But wait, there's more." A car pulled into the parking lot, and a young couple climbed out, three kids in tow. We didn't officially open for ten more minutes, but I wasn't about to turn a customer away. They started browsing, and I kept my eye on them as I talked. "I was walking around the church grounds with Bruce Wayne yesterday afternoon, and Thomas showed up. I guess he works for Jonah Pruitt."

"You're kidding."

"Nope. And not only that, but he told me that Daniel Crocker has some supporters who are upset with me for getting him incarcerated, and they're out to get me."

Neely Kate's face puckered. "Do you think that's true?"

"I don't know. I'd have heard about it sooner, don't you think?"

"You should tell Mason."

"I'd rather tell Joe, but who knows when I'll see him again, and he's upset with me for getting a truck with Mason."

"Oh." She grabbed a hose to water the flowers. "I can see how that could happen."

"Everything's such a mess, Neely Kate. Joe told me he was going to tell me his deep dark secret the next time we see each other."

"Well, that's good, right? Just like you told Violet, secrets only lead to trouble."

I leaned my hip against the table. "But I'm scared to hear it. Joe's worried I'll leave him over it."

"We both know Joe. What on earth could he have done that's so bad?"

I chewed on my lower lip. "I don't know; that's what scares me. Both he and Mason insinuate it's really bad. And to make it worse, I think it has to do with Mason's deep dark secret too."

"Even more reason to get it all out it the open." She started spraying the flowers. "But none of that explains why you're here and not at the church. Unless you're scared Thomas will be there?"

I took a deep breath. "Did you know there are rumors going around town that I have lots of money?"

Neely Kate squirmed. "Well . . ."

"Why didn't you tell me?"

"What good would it have done?"

"I had a right to know."

She looked me square in the eye. "You're right. I'm sorry."

"Whenever I go over to the church, Jonah Pruitt pops out of the woodwork and starts hanging around me, asking questions and getting personal."

She snickered. "You've gone from no men in your life to half a dozen."

"Neely Kate, I'm pretty certain Jonah Pruitt heard the rumors."

Her brow wrinkled in confusion before her eyes widened. "Oh. You need to tell Mason."

"He's the one who put that part together. After I told him about Miss Dorothy's will and he ordered the autopsy."

"That's a good thing! But if Jonah Pruitt had something to do with the deaths of those women, you'd better be careful."

"Jonah Pruitt might be opportunistic, but a murderer?" I shook my head. "People jumped to conclusions about me and Bruce Wayne without knowing all the facts. I'm not going to do that with Jonah."

"You never know, he could just be interested in you."

"I don't think so. I know I'm inexperienced—as Violet loves to point out—but I always feel like a mouse in a trap when he starts hanging around. He's after something. Although his secretary sure hates me. She thinks I'm Jezebel reincarnated."

Neely Kate laughed. "As if."

Then customers started to roll in, and we got too busy to keep talking. I was helping a customer carry a potted flower arrangement to her car when Neely Kate caught my attention while she helped someone load a cart with flats of flowers.

"Look who just walked up."

From her tone of voice, I was half afraid to look. The last person I expected be walking straight toward me was Miss Mildred.

Crap.

I forced a cheerful greeting, "Good morning, Miss Mildred."

"There ain't nothin' good about a morning when murderers and thieves are running around our neighborhood."

She had a point.

"Is there something I can help you with Miss Mildred? Do you want me to get Violet?"

"No. I came to see you."

I took an actual step backward in shock. "Me?"

"I just said so, didn't I?"

"Well, yeah . . ."

"I want to know what progress you're making in solving Dorothy's murder."

I blinked. "Excuse me?"

"I know you're looking into her murder. I want to know what you know."

I wasn't sure what the police department was saying about her death now, but I sure didn't want to get into this with Miss Mildred. Denying it seemed the best way to get rid of her. "We don't know it was a murder."

She shook her head. "Poppycock. Of course it was a murder and I want to know what you've dug up."

I shook my head. "I'm not investigating her death."

"Why the Sam Hill not?"

"*What?*"

"You've solved two murders this summer, and you can't be bothered with the murder of your neighbor?"

I held up my hands. "Wait! No. It's not like that. I just fell into those other two cases. The police will take care of this one."

Mildred's face scrunched in disgust. "You really think the Henryetta Police Department can find evidence laying right in front of their noses?"

"Well . . . no . . ."

"I know you've been snoopin' around. I've seen ya, and I hear things. I heard you got the new DA to get an autopsy, and as much as I hate the thought of them cutting up that poor woman, maybe they'll finally find out for sure what killed her. I also know you started working for that high falutin' TV minister just about the time Miss Dorothy died, so don't you tell me you ain't investigating."

"Well . . ."

"What are you gonna do about it?"

I leaned closer and lowered my voice. "Miss Mildred, with all due respect, I'm flattered that you think I can find out who killed Miss Dorothy and Miss Laura, but my boyfriend will kill me if I try."

Her face scrunched in disgust. "The guy you spend all your time fornicating with in the front yard? Maybe you two can take a break so you can find the killer." She turned and walked away, and my mouth dropped open as I watched her get into her car and leave. She hadn't even gone through with the pretense of buying something.

"What just happened there?" Neely Kate asked.

"I have no idea," I muttered. "Miss Mildred thinks I should try to solve Miss Dorothy and Miss Laura's murders."

"Well, are you going to?"

I swung my gaze to her. "No. Of course not."

"Yes you are."

Irritated, I put my hands on my hips. "Why does everyone keep insisting that I am? Shoot, Joe almost broke up with me over my involvement with exonerating Bruce Wayne. I know when to leave well enough alone."

"Deny it all you like, but you and I both know you're already involved."

I pursed my lips. "Whatever you think I've done has been accidental. I'm leaving this for the police."

"You're really not going to try?" she asked, incredulous. "You *do* realize that you have something the police don't have that can help you find her killer, right?"

"Wits?"

"No," she laughed. "Your gift."

"My curse. And no, there are so many problems with that idea. For one thing, I have to be right next to a person to have a vision. And two, I have to concentrate if I *want* to have one.

That won't look suspicious at all. And three, you know what I see comes out of my mouth instantly. They'll know I know. How dangerous is that? And who's to say I'll even see anything incriminating? Not to mention that the police can't press charges based on what I see."

"But Mason knows about your visions. He might be able to use them."

"How? He can't mention something like that in court. And you still didn't address the fact that what I see is like Russian roulette. I can't choose my visions."

"That's because you need to practice more. You purposely had a vision with Joe and with me. How many other times have you done it on purpose?"

I turned away and began to straighten up flats on the shelves. "None."

"Why not?"

My eyes widened with frustration. "Because it's a horrible thing, Neely Kate. I fight it every day of my life. Purposely using it is crazy."

Neely Kate grabbed my arms and pulled me to the end of the aisle. "No, Rose, it's not a horrible thing. God gave you this talent, and you should use it. When you used it with Joe, you saved his life. What if you hadn't used it? He'd be dead right now."

My eyes filled with tears at the thought. This went against everything I'd believed to be true my entire life. Momma had literally beat it into me that my visions were evil. While part of me was beginning to think differently, it was a hard lesson to unlearn.

"Your vision for me and my wedding was a beautiful thing. You said so yourself. You said it made you so happy. How can that be bad?"

I shook my head, no retort springing to mind.

"God gave you this for a reason. Rose."

"And what if Momma was right? What if it's a demonic talent?"

"You seriously don't believe that, do you? You're the sweetest person I know."

I glanced away. "I don't know."

"Just think about it, okay? I hate to see you do this to your-self. Violet is wrong. Hiding yourself from people close to you can't be a good thing and you know it. You need to give people a chance. You're just presuming the worst of 'em."

I nodded. Deep down, I knew she was right. But knowing it and believing it were two different things.

Chapter Fourteen

A little after lunchtime, there was a lull in customers, so I snuck away to check on Bruce Wayne and David. I'd intended to visit before the nursery opened, but I hadn't wanted to bring the kids. Muffy had done great around the shop, and she'd entertained several children while their parents shopped, but I decided to take her with me to the church.

When I pulled up the guys were sitting in the shade, eating their lunch. Bruce Wayne started to stand, but I waved him back down. "Don't get up. I'm just here to see how you're getting on."

"We're almost done." David said through a mouthful of sandwich.

Muffy jumped out of the car and made a beeline through the grass.

"What is that?" David asked, watching her.

"It's my *dog*."

"It's an ugly thing, ain't it?"

If one more person besmirched Muffy's looks, I wasn't going to be held responsible for my actions. "Beauty is in the eye of the beholder." I frowned my disapproval. I was a firm believer in if you can't say something nice, don't say anything at all. "She's a good dog." I added defensively.

Muffy wandered past David, and he began frantically waving a hand in front of his face. "I thought you said it was a dog. She smells like a skunk."

I shrugged. "Muffy has some fiber issues."

Bruce Wayne chuckled as Muffy stopped next to him, and he scratched behind her ears. "I think she's cute."

Somewhat appeased, I spun around to appraise the front of the church. "It looks beautiful." And it did. I had a good view of the front of the church along with the east side. It had been an overgrown mess, and they'd cleaned out the weeds, trimmed the bushes, and planted the flowers.

"All that's left is the mulching," Bruce Wayne said, getting to his feet.

I hadn't brought it to the job site yet since I hadn't thought they'd be this far along. "Bruce Wayne, don't let me disturb you on your break."

"I'm nearly done." But the half-eaten sandwich in his hand told me otherwise. Muffy followed him as he walked toward me.

"Are you gonna need help loading the mulch in the truck, Miss Rose?" Bruce Wayne asked.

"Um . . ." I hadn't thought that far ahead, distracted by everything else.

"How about I ride back with you to the nursery and help load?"

"What do you have left to do here?" From the looks of things, they were almost done.

"We've got a small batch of flowers to plant. David can take care of that while I go with you."

To my surprise, David agreed. "I can handle it." Maybe he was worried I'd make him help load the truck. He might have gotten out of the loading, but he was going to get plenty of opportunity to unload. I kept that part to myself.

Bruce Wayne gathered the rest of his lunch and got into the truck with me. Muffy sat between us, studying Bruce Wayne, who was quieter than usual.

"Everything okay?" I asked.

He swallowed, glancing at me before looking straight ahead. "Yeah." He reached for Muffy's head and began to rub.

"Thanks for all your hard work this week. You've really helped me out of a bind."

"No, thank you. It feels good to be working. I like this job because I can see that I'm doing something that makes a difference. I'm making something better, even if it's just plants."

I smiled. "I understand. I started gardening when I was a girl. One of the reasons I loved it was because I could plant something and take care of it and watch it grow. It was magical. It still is."

"Yeah, I get that," he said softly. "I like that too, but I also like how I *feel* when I'm working."

"And how's that?"

He took a deep breath. "It's hard to explain. I ain't necessarily good with words."

"That's okay, try."

He twisted his hands in his lap. "It's like I'm someone else when I'm working with the dirt. I feel like I'm important." He swallowed again. "Like I've found somewhere I belong."

I'd spent my entire life searching for that feeling. I'd only ever known it with Joe and the nursery. "I get that," I finally said.

"I like this work. I know it ain't David's thing—he hates manual labor and sweating—but I like it. I'd like to keep working for you if you'll have me."

My shoulders cramped. I didn't have any other work for him at the moment, but I wondered if I had anything else he could do. Bruce Wayne had finally found a place he fit, and I didn't want to be the one to take it from him. "You've done a great job. If we have more work when this project is done, you'll be the first person I hire. But I don't have anything at the moment."

He nodded, his mouth drooping with disappointment.

"I'll be happy to give you a reference too, so that you can get another job until I have more work for you." I turned to him. "I'm sorry. I wish I had something now."

"Don't be sorry," he insisted. "You're the only one who thinks I can make something of myself. You and Reverend Jonah."

"Do you like Reverend Jonah?"

"I ain't sure yet. He's been nice to David and me, but I don't like how he's sniffing around you."

I could tell it pained him to tell me that. I'd seen how Jonah treated him, but Bruce Wayne was also protective of me. "I'm glad he's been kind to you two."

He was quiet the rest of the way to the nursery, and he insisted on loading the truck by himself when I went in to check on how things were going. Violet was craning her neck to get a glimpse of Bruce Wayne.

"Is that *him*?"

"Don't talk about him like that. He's not an ax murderer, Violet."

Her eyebrows shot up. "That you know of."

"Stop it. I like him. He just needs someone to believe in him and give him a chance."

"And that person is you?"

"It's not just me who thinks that. Reverend Jonah has been nice to him too." I figured that would have some effect on Violet, and I wasn't wrong.

"Well . . . Still, be careful."

I rolled my eyes, then glanced around the shop. "Where are the kids?"

"Mike picked them up while you were gone."

"Oh." I was sad I hadn't seen him. Violet might be the one most likely going through the divorce, but I'd lost him too.

Neely Kate came inside, wild eyed. "Is that him? Bruce Wayne Decker?"

I nodded.

"How come you didn't jump down her throat when she asked?" Violet protested.

"Maybe because she looks at him as a celebrity instead of a criminal."

Violet's mouth puckered before a customer walked up to the counter to check out, and then her face burst into happiness. It was scary how fast she could transform herself.

"So he's working out, huh?" Neely Kate asked, watching Bruce Wayne load the truck.

"He's a hard worker, and he's really trying to do a good job. He asked me if he could keep working for me, because he really likes it. I wish I had something for him to do."

"Have you read that book about gettin' what you want?" She craned her neck as Bruce Wayne walked to the side of the building to grab another bag. "You're supposed to just put it out there in the universe." She stretched out her open hand. "And the universe gives it to you."

I squinted in disbelief. "Let me get this straight. I just tell the universe what I want, and it's supposed to give it to me? What if everyone asks for a million dollars? How would that work?"

She shook her head in irritation. "Why do you have to always be so literal? I'm sure it has something to do with karma. Have a little faith."

"Faith? I'm supposed to throw my secret desires out there into the universe and some genie will answer my requests?"

Laughing, Neely Kate smacked my arm. "I didn't say it has to be a secret. In fact, I think you're supposed to tell people." She gave me a wicked grin. "Now tell the universe what you want."

I didn't see the point, but I also didn't see how it could hurt. "I want to have enough work to give Bruce Wayne a job." I turned toward her. "So what do I do?"

She shrugged. "You just did it."

"You're kiddin' me. That's it?"

"Yep."

I already knew it would never work. The job with the New Living Hope Revival Church had been a fluke. We weren't a full-service nursery. For one thing, we didn't have the stock for it. We hoped to expand our inventory next spring, but at the moment, we were just feeling our way around owning a nursery. There was no way Bruce Wayne could wait that long for a job.

When he finished loading the truck with as many bags as the truck bed would hold, we went back to the church, Muffy coming along again. David didn't seem very happy about unloading the mulch, but he didn't complain about it either. He'd finished planting the last of the flowers, so he had nothing else to do, not to mention that once they finished this job, they'd be officially done.

It didn't take them long to spread out the mulch, and Muffy had fun running around and sniffing the musty-smelling wood chips. When they finished, I wrote each of them a check. David stuffed his into his jean shorts pocket, but Bruce Wayne held his in his hands, staring at it. "I've never loved working for a paycheck as much as I did for this one."

David shook his head, tossing gardening tools into the back of my truck. "You are *crazy*."

Bruce Wayne winked at me then tucked his check into his wallet. "Crazy like a fox."

"What the hell is that supposed to mean?" David asked.

"Hell if I know, but it sure sounded good."

I shook my head laughing. "I'll be in touch, Bruce Wayne."

He nodded, turning solemn. "You do that."

Muffy and I headed back to the nursery, me feeling like I'd let Bruce Wayne down. Not long after, I was assembling some potted plants in the back of the shop when I heard Violet call out, "Well good afternoon, Reverend Jonah."

My breath stuck in my chest. That man made me nervous, even on my own turf.

"Call me, Jonah. I insist."

"Of course. Silly me." Violet giggled. "What can I do for you, Jonah?"

"I was hoping to see Rose."

I cringed. *I'd* been hoping to avoid him.

"She's in the back. Let me get her." Violet poked her head into the open doorway leading to the back room. "Someone's here to see you," she sing-songed.

Groaning, I set the plant I was holding on the work table, not stopping to wash my hands.

"Well there she is, the miracle worker!" Jonah beamed.

I shook my head. "Bruce Wayne and David did all the hard work."

"But they were only implementing your vision. You have definitely found your calling, Rose."

"I helped," Violet said, her voice rising.

Jonah turned to her and smiled his TV smile. "Of course you did." Then he turned back to me, leaving a stunned Violet in his wake. She wasn't used to people dismissing her so easily, and she sure as Pete didn't like it. "I'd really like for you to come to church as my special guest tomorrow for the late service. I want to introduce you to the congregation."

"Isn't that your televised service?" Violet asked.

"It sure is."

I took an involuntary step back. "Oh . . . I don't know . . ."

"We'll be there." Violet said, walking around the end of the counter and wrapping an arm around my shoulders. "Should we be there at a special time?"

Jonah's smile faded a tiny bit. "The service starts at 10:30. Perhaps you could come at 10:15, so we can make sure you're seated in the front."

As soon as I got Jonah Pruitt's check, I didn't want to be anywhere near him. But Miss Mildred's lecture had been nagging at me all day, along with what Neely Kate had said to me. What if I could find out something about Miss Dorothy and Miss Laura's murders? If I had that ability to figure out what happened, wasn't it my obligation to do just that? And if Jonah Pruitt was the murderer, then going to his church was a good opportunity to try digging up some information on him.

"Okay," I agreed, but try as I might, I couldn't make it sound enthusiastic. "Thank you for inviting us."

Jonah clapped his hands together. "Well, now that that's settled, I have one other thing to discuss." He leaned closer.

Oh, dear Lord. I hoped he wasn't going to ask me out on a date.

Neely Kate slipped inside, her eyes wide with anticipation.

"You did such a wonderful job on the church that I'd love to have you work on the parsonage too."

I blinked, stunned. "You mean your house?"

He grinned. "While I *do* live there, it belongs to the church."

"And you want the Gardner Sisters Nursery to do some work there?"

"Well, I was hoping *you* would do it." He took my hand in his, and I stopped myself from jerking it back.

Violet looked confused, as though she wasn't sure whether she should be happy we got the business or upset that he specifically requested me. But then again, Violet was more a weeding type of girl, while I'd always been of the get-my-hands-dirty variety. Maybe she was relieved.

Neely Kate was practically jumping up and down in the doorway, reminding me that there was more at stake here than just me. This was a chance to give Bruce Wayne more work.

"Why thank you, Reverend." I said, uncomfortable that he was still holding my hand. "I'd love to see what we can do with the landscape of the parsonage."

"Now, now, what do I keep telling you about calling me Jonah?" He laughed and looked back over his shoulder at Neely Kate. "Isn't she something else?"

Neely Kate smirked. "She sure is."

Jonah turned back to face me. "Wonderful. Why don't you plan on coming by the parsonage on Monday morning at nine?"

I forced a smile. "I can't wait."

"But first you're going to be my special guest tomorrow!" Thankfully, he dropped my hand.

The way he kept saying special guest reminded me of Hansel and Gretel for some reason. Was Jonah planning something devious? No, I told myself. My imagination was running wild. He was just being friendly.

So he could get me to sign over all my worldly possessions.

Violet's smile spread so wide it was a wonder her face didn't crack open. "We wouldn't dream of missing it, now would we?" She jabbed her elbow into my side.

"Can't wait."

"Well, I'll see you lovely ladies tomorrow." Jonah turned around and left. Neely Kate could barely contain her squeal.

"I told you!" she whisper shouted. "I told you it would work!"

"What would work?" Violet asked, narrowing her eyes.

It occurred to me that Violet probably wouldn't approve of me wanting to provide more work for Bruce Wayne, but I didn't care. This was my business too, and the way things were turning out, it looked like I would be in charge of offsite business while Violet was in charge of the store. That meant I could hire whomever I wanted.

"Rose was saying how bad she felt that Bruce Wayne loved working for her so much that he asked to keep working for her, only she didn't have anything for him to do. So I told her to just put it out there in the universe." She thrust her hand forward. "If you put it out there, the universe will provide."

Violet squinted, looking at Neely Kate as though she were a crazy person. "That's awfully New Age, isn't it?"

Neely Kate ignored her. "Didn't I tell you to do that, Rose?"

"You did. And it worked." Only I was sure the cosmos was playing some big practical joke by sending the business via Reverend Jonah Pruitt.

Chapter Fifteen

Violet and I had agreed to meet in the parking lot of the New Living Hope Revival Church. We usually rode together to things like this, especially since Mike had left, but I realized why as soon as I pulled up.

Violet was with Brody MacIntosh.

Irritation prickled my insides, and I fought the crankiness ebbing its way in. Brody was a nice guy. And Violet had every right to date again. But she'd just started dating him. Did they have to do *everything* together?

I sat back in my seat, grabbing onto the steering wheel as reality hit me. Isn't that what I had done when I started dating Joe? I'd spent every spare moment with him. I turned to catch a glimpse of them out the side window. Brody had his hand around her waist and was leaning in to whisper something in her ear. Violet laughed, looking up into his face with eyes shining with happiness.

I gasped.

Violet was in love with Brody MacIntosh.

How could she fall in love with him so quickly? They'd just started dating a few days ago. Did people fall in love with each other that fast?

I spied on them a few seconds longer, feeling like a peeping Tom, but desperate to prove my theory wrong.

The thing was, they clasped hands like two people familiar with each other, people who had been together for weeks or even months.

Oh dear God. Violet hadn't just started dating Brody. This had been going on for some time. *This* was Violet's secret.

Violet caught sight of me and motioned for me to get out, her face beaming. An internal skirmish began brewing inside me. I got out of the truck and walked toward them, trying to hide my disapproval.

"Rose, you look beautiful this morning," Violet said as I approached.

I involuntarily smoothed the skirt of my peach dress. "Thank you, Vi. You do too."

She smiled at my compliment, and then turned to include Brody. "Look who I found in the parking lot." Violet gushed. "The mayor himself."

"Good morning, Brody." I forced myself to smile at him.

Brody dropped his hold on Violet, his hand flopping to his side as though it didn't know what to do with itself. "Good morning, Rose. I hear the Gardner Sisters Nursery had a very successful first week."

"That it did." I tilted my head toward the front entrance. "Shall we go in?"

"Sure."

It was funny how different the church felt today. It might have been because the lot was full of cars and people were going inside, but I didn't think so. A sense of foreboding washed over me that hadn't been there all week, even when Jonah had made me uncomfortable. Then I realized what it was . . . I used to get this feeling every Sunday, back before the preachers stopped trying to expel my demon.

Maybe I was worried Jonah Pruitt would do something similar.

I told myself to relax. Special guest or not, I would leave if he made me uncomfortable. Rose Gardner was done with letting people make her feel badly about who she was.

As I reached for the front door, I heard a voice call out from behind me.

"Rose! Wait up!"

I looked over my shoulder to see Neely Kate hurrying to catch up with me, dragging her husband behind her. She wore a gauzy floral dress and Ronnie had on a suit and tie. I was

secretly pleased that he was dressed better—and looked better—
than Brody.

I was surely going to hell. I hoped I didn't burst into flames
when I walked into the sanctuary.

Violet grimaced. "Who invited her?"

"It's a church, Violet. It means that technically anyone
is welcome."

"That's not what I meant, and you know it. Do you think
she's trying to get on TV?"

I shrugged. "I don't know. Maybe."

"Well, she's not stealing my limelight." Violet tugged on
Brody's arm. "It's hotter than blazes out here. Let's go inside."
She went through the double wood doors, leaving me at the top
of the stairs.

Neely Kate was breathless when she reached me, and I
hugged her tight, grateful for her presence. "What are you
doin' here?"

"Like I would miss my chance to be on TV?" She wrinkled
her nose, waving her hand as though she were batting away that
nonsense. "I don't think so."

So Violet was right, not that I cared. I didn't understand
their desire to be seen. I'd spent my entire life trying to hide.

Neely Kate leaned closer with a knowing look. "Besides, I
didn't want you to be alone in case you start investigating. You
might need me for back up."

"What exactly do you think I'm gonna do?"

She shrugged. "I don't know, but I've got your back."

I shook my head. Neely Kate's imagination had run wild
again. Ignoring it seemed the best option. "Hi, Ronnie." He
stood behind his wife, surveying the parking lot. "You look quite
handsome today."

He tugged at this neckline. "Thanks." Ronnie was a
mechanic, and I knew he hated dressing up. Neely Kate must
have done some serious bribing to get him in a suit.

I suddenly wondered what Joe looked like in a suit. I'd seen
him dressed up in nice shirts and even a tie, but never a suit. Like
Ronnie, Joe seemed more comfortable in casual clothes.

A wave of melancholy washed over me. I hated that we'd had a disagreement the other night, especially when he was in a dangerous situation. The thing was, I understood why Joe was upset when I stepped back to look at the situation. I didn't blame him. At the same time, I didn't think I'd done anything wrong. How could we both be right? Or wrong.

Neely Kate and Ronnie followed me into the church foyer. Violet and Brody were still in the foyer, waiting with Rhonda, who had a clipboard tucked in the crook of her arm and a frown tugging at her mouth. "You're late."

I clutched my purse to my side, feeling defensive. "Jonah said to be here at 10:15."

"And it's now 10:16." If possible, she scowled even more. "And it's Reverend Pruitt to *you*."

I kept the fact that he insisted I call him Jonah every time I saw him to myself. She already hated me enough.

A harried-looking guy wearing a headset came over. "Rhonda, we're having problems with camera two."

She put a hand on her hip. "Why are you telling *me*? That's the production manager's job."

His shoulders scrunched up around his ears as his face reddened. "I only know what I was told."

Rhonda turned her evil glare on me before she started to walk way. "Wait here and don't be wandering off," she called over her shoulder.

Neely Kate leaned into my ear. "Is it my imagination or does that woman not like you?"

I sighed. "That's Jonah's secretary. I told you that she thinks I'm a jezebel."

Neely Kate giggled just as Bruce Wayne walked through the door into the foyer. His eyes widened as he looked around. He'd been in the building multiple times over the last few days, but he looked as lost as I felt. He caught sight of me and headed for us.

"I'm sorry I'm late." He wore a long sleeve dress shirt that was too big for him and a poorly knotted tie.

I offered him a welcoming smile. "Bruce Wayne, what are you doing here?"

"Reverend Jonah invited David and me, but David couldn't make it."

I was fairly certain David couldn't make it because he was either still sleeping or he was hungover. Or both.

"Well, I'm glad you came. You two did the hard work." I looped my hand around his arm and pulled him aside. "And I have some good news. I have another job for you. Probably starting Monday."

His eyes widened. *"You do?"*

"Jonah asked us to work on his parsonage."

"Oh." He seemed hesitant. "Okay."

"Does that bother you?"

He paused. "No. A job's a job."

Rhonda came back, looking more irritated than ever as she cleared her throat. "We need to get you seated." She opened one of the big wooden doors to the sanctuary and waved us in.

The parking lot was full, so I wasn't sure why I was surprised that the church was already packed to the brim. Rhonda waved to a half-empty pew toward the front. "We hadn't planned on all y'all. I'm not sure you'll fit."

We walked down the aisle, and I glanced up at what was supposed to be the altar. Instead of a pulpit or a choir section, there was a stage with lights hanging from the ceiling. I stopped in shock when I saw a man wearing a T-shirt and jeans playing an upbeat rock-sounding song on an electric keyboard on the right of the stage.

Jeans and a T-shirt in church. Momma had to be rolling over in her grave.

Violet gave me a little push, and I continued toward the pew, taking in the cameramen stationed around the church. They wore headphones with mikes extending around their cheeks.

No matter what I thought of Jonah Pruitt, this was proof that he was a big deal.

When we reached our row, Violet brushed past me, dragging Brody by the arm. She scooted in, making sure she didn't get set somewhere else. Bruce Wayne and I followed with Neely Kate trailing in behind us. We all fit, but it was cozy, and Violet didn't look pleased.

The rest of the band joined the keyboard, and my mouth dropped open in surprise. I'd heard them practicing the night I'd stopped by for the deposit, but this went against everything I'd been raised with. I was used to "Amazing Grace" sung by a choir, not a rearranged rock version played by a band, complete with swaying backup singers.

Over half the church was filled with younger couples and families, and I could see why. No wonder Jonah was doing so well. If I didn't suspect him of one or possibly two murders, I might have considered joining his flock as well. What surprised me was the group of older people sitting in a section in the middle, all focused on what was happening on stage. Smack dab in the middle was Miss Opal. And Mildred sat with her.

After fifteen minutes of music, Jonah came onto the stage, his megawatt smile lighting up his face as well as the crowd. The people broke into loud applause as he moved front and center, waving and smiling. "Good morning! Welcome!"

Jonah started his sermon, and it was easy to see that while the music and the lure of the cameras drew the crowd to fill the pews, it was his charisma that kept them there. He was the perfect speaker, raising his voice when needed, showing emotion throughout, and talking about love and acceptance instead of shouting about fire and brimstone. When he finished, I realized that most of the people in the congregation had latched onto every word of his twenty-minute sermon. He took a story about one of the Marys washing Jesus's feet with her hair and made it fresh and relevant to the people of Henryetta.

My heart felt like it had been filled with ten pounds of lead. I wanted Jonah Pruitt and this church to be real. Just like all the other people who filled this sanctuary, this is what I'd been looking for.

He seemed to be wrapping up his message when he held out his hand. "I've told y'all to become the Marys of our modern world. How about I give you a real example? Did you all know we have our very own Mary in church today?"

The people began to look around, trying to figure out who Jonah was talking about.

"This week, a local business opened its doors." He took a step backward and to the side. "Here, let me show you."

My heart slammed into my ribcage as the lights dimmed and a video appeared on the giant screen at the back of the stage. Jonah's voice echoed throughout the room.

"Marys are hidden everywhere." A montage of people assisting others played on the screen. "But sometimes they're in our midst without our knowledge." A video of Jonah at our grand opening appeared next, and then Jonah's voiceover returned. "The New Living Hope Revival Church's decision to support a local organization turned out to be so much more."

The screen filled with an elderly woman talking about Bruce Wayne and his past.

Bruce Wayne let out a gasp, and I reached over and grabbed his hand, squeezing for dear life. If Jonah Pruitt was digging up the dirt on Bruce Wayne, I wondered what was coming up for me.

Neely Kate turned to me, raising her eyebrows in question, and then leaned in toward my ear. "Did you know about this?"

I shook my head, a metallic taste coating my tongue.

The screen filled with headlines about Bruce Wayne's arrest and trial.

Bruce Wayne's head lowered as he studied his lap.

A white hot anger ignited my insides. Jonah Pruitt was exploiting us for ratings. I wasn't sure why that surprised me. I knew he was swindling the older women in town out of their fortunes, and possibly much worse. This wasn't much different.

My face appeared next, a photo of me at the grand opening. "Enter Rose Gardner, a shy, soft-spoken woman who stands in the shadow of her sister." The screen cut to me standing behind Violet as she cut the ribbon with Brody.

Violet was going to be furious.

"Rose was picked as a juror for Bruce Wayne's trial, but somehow she knew Bruce Wayne was innocent, and she set out to prove it."

A headline from the Henryetta Gazette filled the screen. *Juror Jailed on Obstruction of Justice, Mistrial Averted.*

"But Rose didn't stop there. She worked tirelessly to free a man she didn't even know." Next were headlines about Jimmy DeWade's arrest and Bruce Wayne's release from prison. If I was on edge already, the next screen caught me totally off guard. It was a shaky video of me. Jonah's voice on the video asked, "Can you tell me why you did it? You were put in jail for trying to prove his charges should be dropped. What convinced you he was innocent?"

I answered him, a soft look on my face as I looked up at the camera. "I just knew. And because I knew, it was the only right thing to do."

Where could the camera have been hidden? We'd had that conversation on the side of the church! What was Jonah Pruitt up to?

The video faded and the lights turned up. "It was the right thing to do," Jonah said, his eyes burning with conviction. "Why did Mary wash Jesus's feet?" Jonah crossed the stage as if he was searching the crowd for the answer. "Because it was the right thing to do." He stopped pacing. "Be the Marys of the world. Help your neighbor with his overgrown yard. Help the single mother who is overwhelmed with responsibility. Help those who can't help themselves. Live the example Rose Gardner has set for you. Do the right thing."

Then Jonah called for the collection plates to be passed around and for the people to do the right thing for the church.

Violet's mouth pressed into a tight line, and I realized Bruce Wayne and I were still clutching hands. I let go, suddenly self-conscious. People who realized we were in attendance had begun to stare. Every part of me screamed to get up and leave, but I knew it would make the situation worse. Bruce Wayne had spent most of his life flaunting public perception, though, so he felt no need to stay. He started to get out of his seat, but I pulled him back down.

"I didn't know, Bruce Wayne. I swear I didn't know he was doin' that."

He nodded, his eyes glassy. "I know Miss Rose, but I need to get out of here. I'll see you at Reverend Pruitt's house tomorrow. Is nine okay?"

I nodded, no longer sure whether working on Jonah's parsonage was a good idea. Still, he had us between a rock and a hard place. Bruce Wayne needed the work, and I wouldn't back out for the same reason my butt was still firmly planted in my seat. I wasn't ready to lose face yet.

As soon as the service ended, I stood and hurried for the aisle, pushing past people in my haste to get away.

"Rose," Mason called out in the foyer. I stopped, surprised he was here, and even more surprised to see his mother was with him. She was more beautiful in person than she'd been in my vision.

I lifted my chin, resisting the urge to cry. "Mason, what are you doing here?"

"I couldn't resist the chance to hear one of Jonah Pruitt's sermons. I didn't realize you'd be part of it."

I shifted my weight, looking down. "That makes two of us."

"Are you okay?"

I nodded. The last thing I wanted to do was talk about the video that had just been played.

"We haven't officially been introduced," Mason's mother extended her hand, a warm smile on her face. "I'm Maeve Deveraux."

I took her hand, surprised at how gentle her touch was. "I'm Rose, but then I guess you already know that from that demonstration inside."

"I knew about you long before Reverend Pruitt put on his show. Mason speaks very highly of you."

Mason's cheeks reddened, and I couldn't help but grin. "Did he tell you about our first encounter, and how I asked him if his mother knew about his rude behavior?"

To my surprise, Mrs. Deveraux burst out laughing. "No, he most certainly did *not*. I'm sure he was worried about the repercussions."

"Well, don't hold that against him. His behavior has greatly improved. You've raised a fine Southern gentleman."

"Can we change the subject now?" Mason asked, glancing around. "You two are ruining my reputation as the intimidating assistant district attorney."

I laughed, thankful that the horror of what had happened in the sanctuary was fading.

Violet emerged from the double doors, Brody following close behind. She was heading straight for me when she spotted me with Mason.

"Do you have plans?" Mrs. Deveraux asked. "Mason and I are going out for lunch before I head back to Little Rock."

I hesitated. Part of me was drawn to Mrs. Deveraux's friendliness, but I was already in a mess with Joe over Mason. I couldn't imagine how going out to lunch with them was going to help matters. "You have no idea how much I'd love to join you." I hoped my sincerity came through. "But I'm going to have to take a rain check today."

"But of course," she said. "I plan on visiting Mason more often, so this won't be our last opportunity."

"Good. I look forward to it. Now if you'll excuse me, I have to appease my sister." I turned around, but Mason touched my arm.

"Rose."

I spun at the waist to face him.

"I want to talk to you later." He looked worried.

"Sure. Call me after your mother takes off for Little Rock."

I headed Violet off before she reached Mason.

Her smile was tight. "Why didn't you prepare me for that little *show*?"

I lowered my voice. "Because I had no idea he was gonna do that. If I'd known, I wouldn't have come."

"I don't think he even mentioned the name of the nursery."

"Our sign was in the video, with the footage of you and Brody cuttin' the ribbon. You both looked very nice, by the way."

Brody grinned, but Violet wasn't so easily swayed from the topic. "That man is far too fascinated with you."

Finally, she was seeing what I'd been trying to tell her all week. Her jealousy could actually be useful. Maybe she'd insist that the nursery shouldn't work on Jonah's parsonage. Relief washed through me, guilt quickly on its heels. I might be more comfortable that way, but Bruce Wayne would be out of a job. "Well, I didn't ask for it."

She frowned. "I'd tell you not to take that parsonage job, but you know we need the business." Her eyes studied mine. "Unless you feel threatened by him. Then we'll make do. I don't trust him."

"I'm okay with it for now. Bruce Wayne needs the work."

Brody's eyes squinted in confusion. "Why wouldn't you trust Reverend Pruitt? He's the second best new business to hit Henryetta." He kissed Violet's cheek. "The Gardner Sisters Nursery being the first, of course."

While Brody might be the most eligible bachelor in Henryetta, he wasn't the sharpest tool in the shed. At least Mason had looks *and* brains.

Violet smiled at him. "Thank you, Brody. Just call it women's intuition."

Mildred hobbled over, Opal following with her walker. "You can't just come to church and mind your own business?" she said to me.

"If I'd known Jonah was going to do that, I never would have come."

"Then why did you come?" She glared.

I locked eyes with her. "I think you know." I had a sinking suspicion that's why she was there too. I turned to Miss Opal, who was leaning forward on her walker. "I was surprised to see you here Miss Opal. I thought you were a long-time member of the Presbyterian Church."

"I was until Reverend Jonah invited me to coffee one day and convinced me to try his church. I've been coming here ever since."

"Has Jonah ever talked to you about bequeathing your worldly possessions to him?"

Opal looked offended. "No. Of course not. Why would you insinuate such a thing?"

"Because Miss Dorothy did." Now I was confused. I was fairly certain Miss Opal had more money than Miss Dorothy. Not that you could tell by the way they lived. Then again, maybe that was my answer right there.

I caught Jonah out of the corner of my eye, heading my way. "It was really nice talking to y'all. I have to get goin'." I took off for the doors.

"Hey," Violet called after me. "Aren't you going to get lunch with us?"

"I'll take a rain check," I shouted over my tensed shoulders. I didn't look back until I pulled my truck out of the parking lot.

Chapter Sixteen

I spent the rest of the drive stewing over the mess that had become my life. Jonah Pruitt, Violet, and all my unresolved issues with Joe. I didn't know how to resolve any of them, which made me feel even worse.

When I turned down my street, I gasped. Joe's car was parked in my driveway.

He was home.

I tried to settle the raging butterflies in my stomach. Could he be done with his assignment?

But when I pulled into the driveway and saw his face, my stomach balled into a lump that weighed ten pounds. He was sitting on my front porch waiting for me. And he didn't look happy.

I opened my door and climbed out as he came down the porch steps. "Joe, I know you were upset—"

Before I could finish my sentence, his arms were around my waist, pulling me to his chest as his mouth found mine. I reached for his face, holding him close in case he changed his mind.

But he covered my hands with his and lifted his head, searching my eyes. "I don't care about the stupid truck, Rose. I only care about you. I'm sorry."

"I'm sorry too. I could have waited, but—"

He kissed me again, long and deep, letting me know exactly how much he'd missed me. "No more talk about this mess. I only have a few hours, and I don't want to ruin it."

My heart seized. "You're not done with your job?"

He shook his head. "Not yet, darlin', but we're close. I had a break for the afternoon, and I drove straight here when I found out. I tried calling you, but you weren't answering your cell phone." He took in my dress. "Where've you been?"

"Church. How long have you been here?" I hated that I'd missed a single minute with him, especially after what I'd been through.

"Not that long. Maybe fifteen minutes. Since when did you start goin' to church?"

"This morning was a one-time thing I hope to never repeat. I'll tell you about it later." I pressed my lips to his. "I can think of something better to do with our time."

Joe grinned. "Then why are we still outside?" He lifted me up so that I straddled his waist, pulling the back of my dress down to cover my behind.

I giggled, swatting his shoulder "Joe, what are you doing? I'm about to flash the neighbors."

"I've let Mildred down by not giving her a show. I plan on making up for it."

"Well, it's all for nothin'. She's not home yet. She was at church too."

His eyebrows lifted, a suspicious look covering his face. "You and Mildred were at church together?"

"It was sort of a coincidence. Let's leave it at that."

Joe didn't look convinced, but he must have decided he'd rather focus on his conjugal visit because he climbed the steps, still holding me like I weighed nothing until he reached the front door. Then he slid me down his front while he pushed through the door. Muffy followed behind him, jumping up on my legs and wanting to be petted.

"Not now, Muffy," Joe mumbled against my lips as he slammed the door and unzipped the back of my dress.

I grabbed his cheeks, kissing him as he pushed me backward down the hall. He paused in my room, tugged my dress off my shoulders and let it drop to the floor so I was only in my underwear.

"I don't want to lose you, Rose." His eyes were filled with fear.

"I'm not going anywhere." I caressed his cheek with my fingertips.

He kissed me again, and we spent the next half hour proving how much we loved each other. Afterward, I lay in his arms, staring up into his face. His mouth was drawn down, and his eyes were full of worry.

"Joe, I'm sorry I bought the truck without you. I know how much you wanted to help me."

He shook his head slowly. "I'm glad you got a truck. Really, I am. You're right. It'll come in handy with the business. I'm not sure why *I* didn't think of it sooner. You have every right to be friends with Mason Deveraux. I was worried he'd tell you my secret before I was ready, but then I realized he's hiding from his past too. I have no right to ask him to stay away from you as long as he's not making any moves to try to steal you away from me."

I chuckled. "Steal me away from you? What makes you think he'd do that? We're *friends*, Joe."

His fingers swept stray hands of hair from my cheek. "You're a beautiful woman, Rose Gardner. I'm surprised you don't have a line of men trying to win your heart."

I laughed, shaking my head. "Now you've lost your mind. You know most of the people in this town think I'm odd. You were the first man who ever paid any attention to me."

"But you're different now. You were pretty before, but you dress differently now and your hair's styled. But more importantly, you have a confidence you didn't have before. You've grown into yourself, and people are noticing . . . men are noticing." He swallowed. "I admit that it makes me nervous. What if you decide you've outgrown me? What if you decide that Violet was right, that you should date other men? We're starting to look at a future together. I worry that you'll think you need to experience life more first. Life without me."

"No! I can't imagine my life without you."

He kissed me gently, and then lifted his head. "I was so worried that Mason Deveraux was trying to take you away from me, I never once stopped to ask you what *you* wanted. No one can steal you from me unless you're willing to go."

"I don't want to be with anyone else. I want to be with you."

Fear filled his eyes. "You might not say that when I tell you what happened in Little Rock."

I brushed my thumb along his lower lip. "I love you, Joe. Nothing's going to change that. You and I both know I'm not proud of who I was before I met you, but you don't hold that against me."

A tiny smile appeared as his eyes turned glassy. "That's entirely different, Rose. You were beaten down into believing you were nobody. You've become the person you were meant to be."

"And you say Joe Simmons is different than Joe McAllister. Maybe Joe McAllister is who *you're* meant to be."

"It's not that neat and tidy. I promised I'd tell you, and I want to do it now."

Whatever Joe was going to tell me was about to change everything. I knew it deep in my marrow. I wasn't ready for that yet. I needed to prepare myself.

I sat up. "I'm hungry."

Joe rolled over and pushed up on one elbow. "What?"

"I didn't get breakfast, and I'm starving. I'll make us lunch."

Joe's eyes narrowed. "Since when do you back away from a problem?"

I got up and pulled a T-shirt and jeans out of a drawer. "The old me used to do it all the time."

"Rose . . ."

I put on my bra and turned to face him. "Look, I know this is big, whatever it is, and I really am starving. I think I can handle it better if I've got some food in me. I promise, I'm not running. I'm preparing myself."

He nodded, getting off the bed. "I'll cook."

I wrapped my arms around him and pulled him into a hug. "Not this time. I'll cook, and I'll tell you about what's been going on around here. And when we're done eating, you can tell me. Okay?"

His arms tightened around me. "Okay."

"When do you have to go? Do you have time?"

"I have to leave in two hours. I have time."

"Good. How about some spaghetti?"

"What?" His eyebrows rose in mock surprise. "No sandwiches?"

"You know darn good and well I can make things other than sandwiches." I tried my best to sound playful, but his news hung over my head like a storm cloud. "I just don't cook when it's only for me."

He turned serious. "I know."

Maybe waiting was a bad idea.

I went into the kitchen and started a pot of water boiling, then searched for the ingredients to make sauce from scratch. I wasn't sure I would have everything, but I did, mostly because Joe always went grocery shopping when he came to see me.

He walked into the kitchen and stood behind me, wrapping his arms around the front of my waist.

I looked up over my shoulder at him. "I don't thank you often enough for all the grocery shopping you do. And cooking. Not to mention your help with the nursery. I appreciate everything you do for me, Joe."

He spun me around to face him. "Hey, enough of that. I love doing things for you, just like you love doing things for me. Like when you take care of my laundry. And the sweet texts you send me. You have no idea how much I love getting those."

I tried to squash my fear down. Joe had to be exaggerating when he said there was something terrible in his past. Maybe it was like my visions. They were a huge deal to me, but once everyone else got over the shock, the people who truly care about me accepted them. Maybe his secret would be like that.

But I knew it wouldn't.

"Let me help." He grabbed an onion and a knife. "I take it this is for the sauce?"

"Yeah." I started to chop a green pepper, my hands shaking.

Joe leaned down and gave me a soft kiss. "I love you."

"I love you too."

"Tell me about Miss Dorothy."

I filled him in on Mildred finding her body, Keith telling me he'd heard shouting from her house, and me telling Mason.

Joe sighed. "Mason's right. There's not a damn thing he can do with that."

"There's another death that might be related." I told him about Miss Laura. "I overhead Mason asking the police to see if she had a connection to Jonah."

He nodded. "That's a good idea."

I'd been throwing Mason's name around a lot, but thankfully Joe didn't seem upset.

"Tell me more about the break-in."

I filled in the skimpy details I'd given him on Friday night.

"You need to be more careful. You can't be running into dark alleys and backyards."

"Joe, it's my neighborhood. I've lived here all my life. It's safe." Or at least it used to be before Momma's murder.

"Apparently, it's not safe at all." Fear filled his eyes . . . and guilt.

"It was nothing."

"The hell it was. I should have been here with you."

I put down the knife. "Joe, I'm fine."

"Do you have any idea what could have happened to you? And I was over a hundred miles away with no way of knowing . . ."

I wrapped my arm around his neck and pulled his mouth to mine, kissing him gently. "Shh. You're doing your job, and it's a lot more dangerous than me getting tangled up in sheets hanging from a clothesline."

"I'm trained to handle dangerous situations, Rose. You're not. Why did you go back there?"

"Joe. That's like asking me why I walked into my kitchen last May when I found Momma dead. Muffy ran back there, and I went to get her. Why would I think anything bad would happen?"

"I should have been here," he repeated, his shoulders tense. "I hope to God that deputy sheriff position comes through."

"Me too." I kissed him again with longing. I was about to get everything I wanted.

His arm tightened around my waist as his other hand found my cheek. "Do you have any idea how much I miss you when I'm not with you?"

I grinned against his lips. "I think I do. Now do you want to hear the rest?"

"Yes, but I'm beginning to think sandwiches would have been a better idea. I like having you in my arms."

I wiggled free, feeling kind of sorry I'd suggested cooking. "Let me just get the sauce started, and then we can sit down. I still haven't told you about Thomas." I went on to tell him about Thomas's involvement in the whole mess, including what he'd said about Daniel Crocker. "Do you think Daniel Crocker is a threat to me from behind bars?"

Joe took a deep breath. "I haven't heard anything, but now I'm more worried about you than ever. Daniel Crocker is batshit crazy, and he holds a grudge like a pack rat hoards."

"Oh." I'd expected Joe to tell me there was nothing to worry about.

"Last I heard, he was in the county jail, awaiting trial."

"The same jail I was in?"

"Sort of. You were in a holding cell. He's somewhere more permanent." Joe was silent for a moment. "I'll do some digging. The sheriff's office might know something."

"Okay."

"I sure wish the Henryetta Police weren't a bunch of thick-headed Neanderthals who refuse to believe they aren't infallible. I'd feel better if someone smart and prepared was watching out for you."

I offered him a weak smile. "I've got my rolling pin."

He scowled, not appreciating the reminder. "Why were you at church this morning?"

"I kind of got roped into it."

"By Violet?"

I grimaced. "Her too."

From the look on his face, Joe was starting to put things together. "You went to Jonah Pruitt's church."

I nodded as I scraped the chopped onions, peppers, and garlic into a skillet, suddenly grateful that I could keep my back to him as I sautéed the vegetables.

He didn't say anything for a long moment, so I thought he'd decided to give it up. Then he finally said, "How'd it go working on his church this week?"

"Good. The guys got it all done before our deadline, with plenty of time to spare."

Joe grabbed a beer out of the refrigerator and leaned his hip against the counter. "What guys did you hire to help you?"

"David Moore and Bruce Wayne Decker." I glanced over my shoulder to see his reaction.

"You hired the guy you kept out of prison and his drug-addicted best friend?"

"They did a really good job, Joe."

"Uh huh." He took a sip of his beer. "So you're done with your job at the church?"

"Yeah, but we have a job at the parsonage that we're starting on Monday."

He shook his head. "I think doing any more work for Jonah Pruitt is a bad idea. Especially in light of this new information."

"We deposited the money from the church grounds job into our bank account right away. We didn't lose any money. And we'll deposit the second check tomorrow. Jonah brought it by the store yesterday."

"I'm more worried about losing *you* than I am about your money. This is starting to look really fishy."

"Like I told Mason, if Jonah Pruitt had anything to do with Miss Dorothy's death, he did it to get her money. I don't have a will, and I don't own this house. He's got no reason to kill me."

His eyes widened. "Is that supposed to make me feel better?"

I'd be the first to admit I wasn't crazy about working for Jonah again, but admitting it to Joe wouldn't help me plead my case. "Bruce Wayne is counting on me."

He sighed, turning so that his butt rested against the edge of the counter. "Your responsibility to Bruce Wayne Decker ended the moment he stepped out of jail."

"But no one will hire him, Joe. And he *really* likes landscaping."

He shook his head in confusion. "Why do you care so much about what happens to him?"

I turned to face him. "Because he's so much like me."

"When were you ever a drug addict?" Joe asked sarcastically.

"Not that, and you know it. He's an outcast, and no one wants to have anything to do with him, let alone give him a chance. He needs something to make him feel good about himself. Working with the earth and plants makes him happy. He feels like he's accomplishing something. I don't want to take that away from him."

"Rose, he needs to take charge of his own life, just like you've taken charge of yours."

"I may have taken charge of it, but I've had your love and support, and Violet's been there for me too, in her own way. Bruce Wayne has no one." He started to say something, but I stopped him. "I don't want to argue about this. I don't want to argue with you at all."

His face softened. "I'm sorry. I know how important this is to you, and it's just one of the many reasons I love you. But I'm scared for you, Rose. I think you're taking an unnecessary risk. Just tell me you'll consider turning down the job."

Joe didn't have to worry. I was still weighing all my options. "I'll think about it."

He kissed my forehead, his lips lingering longer than necessary. "Thank you."

I nodded.

When the spaghetti was done, we sat at the kitchen table and I picked at my food. I'd been starving earlier, but I was getting closer and closer to finding out Joe's secret.

Eating lunch first had been a bad idea.

Chapter Seventeen

I dropped my fork on my plate. "I can't do this."

Joe's hand stopped mid-air, and he carefully set his fork on his plate. "You can't do what?"

"I can't pretend everything's okay. It's not okay. I'm ready for you to tell me now."

He wiped his hands off on his napkin and stood. "Let's sit in the living room."

This really was serious.

I nodded, swallowing the lump in my throat. He followed me as I moved into the other room, as though I were being led to my execution. I sat on the sofa, expecting him to sit next to me, but he sat in the chair to my left, resting his hands on his knees.

"You've already figured out that Mason and I have history."

I forced my lungs to inflate so I wouldn't hyperventilate.

He opened his eyes, looking sad. "You also know that Hilary and I grew up together and she followed me to Little Rock. We were seeing each other off and on. We've done that a lot since we were in high school."

"You say that like you plan on seeing her again."

"Not a chance. We are *definitely* done." His face paled. I'd never seen him look so nervous, not even during the whole Daniel Crocker mess. "But we were on a break, and I started seeing this other woman."

I had a hard time picturing Joe with other women, so the jealousy that reared its ugly head caught me by surprise.

"I met her at a bar." His hands began to rub the denim over his legs. "I drank a lot then." He looked into my eyes. "I wasn't happy, Rose. In fact, I was miserable, and I was looking for something to fill the hole in my heart. Anyway, I met Savannah, and there was something between us that felt deeper than with most of the women who paraded through my life when I was on a break from Hilary."

I didn't like how this was going.

"Savannah and I started seeing each other. She was in Little Rock going to law school at the University of Arkansas, and I'd graduated from law school a few years earlier, so we had that in common." He swallowed.

I wasn't sure I wanted to hear the rest. I didn't particularly care to know details about his former dating life.

"Hilary and I weren't really done yet at the time. I couldn't bring myself to cut my ties to her." He ran his hand over his head. "Hilary came over late one night and begged me to come back. She had some hold on me then that I can't describe. Savannah was better for me, but I was too stupid to see it, so I ended things with her and went back to Hilary." Joe stared out the window, refusing to look at me.

"That's not so bad," I finally said.

"That's not the bad part." His voice cracked.

"Okay." My stomach fell to my feet.

"Savannah didn't take it well, and I have to admit that I didn't handle the whole thing the way I should have. I was a coward. She started calling me, making excuses for me to come over to her place. I went the first few times. She told me I'd left some clothes and tools there. Then I'd show up, and she'd try to convince me that Hilary was stringing me along, that I needed to move on. With her." He shook his head, his jaw clenching. "She was right, but I was too stupid to see it. I told her that she and I were over, and I asked her to quit calling me. I wasn't very nice about it. In fact, I was downright mean. But she kept calling, and Hilary started to get pissed. And a pissed Hilary was something I tried to avoid at all costs."

My breath was coming in short bursts. What if Joe decided to go back to Hilary now? Would I beg him to come back to me? Would he treat me like that?

He leaned back in the chair, still avoiding my gaze. "Savannah ran out of excuses, and she stopped calling for a while, but then one day she called to tell me that someone was following her, that she'd seen this person lurking outside her apartment. She said she was getting a lot of hang up calls too. She wanted to know what to do about it. I figured it was her way of trying to get me back. So I told her to call the police, which she did. But I hung out at the same bar as the guys in the Little Rock PD. I'd told them all about Savannah and how she'd been looking for excuses to get me over to her place. They checked it out and said they found nothing. Turns out she called them several times."

I felt like I was going to throw up.

"One night Hilary and I had a fight over God knows what. She was still pissed and I was drinking, trying to make myself feel better, not that it ever did any good. It was late when Savannah called." He swallowed again, his face pale and clammy. "She told me there were noises outside her apartment, and she wanted me to come over and check it out. I refused and told her to call the police. She said, 'They never take me seriously. I need your help, Joe.'" He laughed, but it was an ugly sound. "I told her to leave me the hell alone and call 911. I found out later that she did. They came over and did a cursory check, then left."

My hands were shaking. I knew that something bad was about to happen, and I was positive I didn't want to know anymore, but there was no way to stop him.

He leaned forward again, wringing his hands. "She called me again, around three in the morning. I was in bed, and it took several rings for me to wake up and answer. Hilary was livid. I was about to hang up, but her breath was coming in short pants. 'I think there's someone in my apartment,' she said. Something in her voice made me listen this time. So I told her I'd come over."

"Hilary told me not to bother coming back if I walked out the door. And I almost didn't go, but somehow I knew that Savannah was in real trouble." He grabbed the sides of his head. "I should have called 911 myself, but I was still kind of drunk and not thinking straight. I definitely shouldn't have been driving." He paused. "I ran into a ditch when I was a couple of blocks away and banged up my car pretty good. But I was still determined to check on Savannah. So I walked the rest of the way and when I got to her apartment, the front door was wide open." Tears streamed down his face.

"Joe, you don't have to tell me anymore."

I put my hand on his knee, but he pushed it off and stood, turning his back to me. "Yes, I do. I need to tell you. I don't want to hide it anymore."

"Okay."

He took several gulps of air. "When I went inside, I saw signs of a struggle, but I didn't see Savannah. When I called her name, she didn't answer." His eyes sank closed "I found her in her bedroom. She was lying on her bed. She'd been repeatedly stabbed." Joe's voice broke. "She was still alive though, and she reached for me, whispering 'I knew you'd come.'" Joe's shoulders shook as he cried harder, his back still to me. "She'd expected me to come save her all along, and I'd ignored her. I had convinced the officers on patrol in her area that she was only trying to get attention. But she wasn't, Rose. A guy from a coffee shop she went to had started stalking her."

I knew I should do or say something, but I was too overcome with horror to react.

"I finally got my act together enough to call 911, but it was too late. She died before the ambulance showed up. She died holding my hand." Joe's head hung forward as he cried.

I watched him for several seconds, waiting to see if he was going to add more. "I don't see how this involves Mason." But as soon as I said the words, I knew. I sank back into the sofa cushions, squeezing my eyes shut as though to block out the horror playing out in my living room.

"Savannah was Mason's sister."

I started to cry.

"Mason was furious, and he blamed me for his sister's death. I alternated between blaming and recusing myself. Hilary took me back, of course, but I decided I was done with her for good and moved out."

"When did this all happen?"

"Last March."

My mouth dropped in shock. "*That recently?*" It had been less than a year ago.

He nodded, still refusing to look at me.

Neely Kate had told me that Mason had come to Henryetta because something bad had happened to him, something that had been buried so deep even she couldn't figure out what it was. It had to be part of this mess, but why would he hide his sister's death? There had to be something else. "What happened to Mason?"

Joe's head lifted. He turned toward me but still refused to look at me. "What do you mean?"

"Neely Kate said he was exiled here because of something he did in Little Rock. What did he do?"

"He beat the shit out of the guy who killed his sister."

"Can anyone blame him for that?"

"He put the guy in a coma."

This just got worse and worse.

"The DA was about to file assault charges against him, which was an embarrassment to the Little Rock prosecuting attorney's office as well as his prominent family. My father used his political connections to get him out of it."

"Why would he do that?"

For the first time, Joe looked at me, bitterness in his eyes. "Because I was such an embarrassment to *my* family. My father swept everything under the rug that he could reach with his political broom. Mason got out of the charges and moved to Henryetta. Only he was pretty bitter about it. He had a very promising career in Little Rock. Moving to Henryetta was the death of that."

No wonder Mason had been so cranky when he first moved here.

"Do you have any questions?"

Did I? I wanted to know how long he'd dated Savannah, how serious they'd been. If he'd been cruel to her. But I also *didn't* want to know any of those things. Part of me wished I didn't know any of it. "No."

He watched me, a variety of emotions playing across his face. "Say something."

I bit my lip as tears burned my eyes. "I don't know what to say."

"Do you hate me?"

I stood, then shook my head and threw my arms around his stiff shoulders. "I could never hate you, Joe."

Some of the tension in his back faded.

"I'm sorry."

His head lifted, incredulous. "Why are *you* sorry?"

"I'm sorry you had to go through this."

He shook his head, crying again. "I never wanted you to know, but I realized how wrong that was. If I didn't tell you, our life together would be based on a lie. I'm a different man with you, Rose. When I'm Joe Simmons, I'm hard and jaded. But Joe McAllister is kinder and gentler. I want to be that man."

"You *are*." I kissed him softly, moving my hands up into his hair and holding his face close to mine. "I love you."

He closed his eyes, resting his forehead on mine. "I don't deserve you."

"Stop that nonsense, right now. You're a good man."

"You make me feel like I can be one." His lips found mine and he clung to me, kissing me desperately, as though I might disappear, and he had to make every moment count. "That's one of the reasons I want to quit the state police. My job makes me cynical. But I'm worried that moving to the sheriff's department won't be enough of a change."

"You're not cynical with me. You know I want you with me all the time. But I don't expect you to quit your job either."

He looked into my eyes, incredulous. "You still want me, even after everything I've told you?"

"You know I love you, Joe. My feelings aren't that shallow."

"If knowing what happened changed how you felt about me, it wouldn't make you shallow, Rose. It would probably make you smart."

Was that his plan? That he could make me send him away? "My love for you isn't like a light switch I can turn off and on."

He pushed me against the wall, his hands sliding under my shirt as his mouth claimed mine. He found the button on my jeans, unfastened it, then unzipped them and pushed them to the floor. I stepped out of them, and his hands cupped my butt, pulling me against him.

I twined my fingers into his short hair, surprised at his intensity. We had an active and healthy sex life, but Joe had never been this possessive before, and we always ended up in a bed. Clearly that was about to change. Joe tugged his own jeans down and kicked them off, then pushed me back against the wall, lifting me so my legs straddled his waist. I wrapped my arms around his shoulders as he claimed me then and there.

I felt wicked and wanton. Good girls didn't have sex against a wall, but right or wrong, the way Joe wanted me so intensely made me want him even more.

Our libidos kicked into overdrive, and it didn't take long until we leaned into each other, breathing heavily and feeling sated.

His face lifted and guilt was etched across his features.

I grabbed his cheeks and kissed him passionately. As he kissed me back, matching my eagerness, I knew our relationship had just crossed a threshold.

The threshold to what remained a mystery.

Chapter Eighteen

We took a shower together, touching each other as though we were never going to see each another again. We were usually playful after sex, but this time we were reverent. Joe hardly spoke, watching me with a seriousness that both scared me and turned me on.

After we dressed, we sat on my sofa, my legs draped across Joe's lap. We didn't speak, just held each other. I was worried about Joe going back to his assignment, but his news still swirled around in my head, all the pieces trying to sort themselves out. What he was thinking seemed obvious—he was scared I'd change my mind.

He reached up and caressed my cheek, leaning in to kiss me. "Since you haven't kicked me out yet, there's one more thing I've been worried to bring up."

My heart pounded against my chest. I wasn't sure how much more I could take. "Okay."

"My mother has demanded that I bring you to meet my family."

"Oh."

"I told you they keep pestering me about it, but they've become insistent. I think the best thing to do is to get it over with. If you're willing."

Meeting Joe's family was the last thing I wanted to do, particularly given what little I knew about them, but Mason's mother had been nice. Perhaps Joe's family would surprise me. Besides, Joe put up with Violet on a regular basis. Meeting his family only seemed fair. "Okay."

"Really?"

"Yeah, how bad can it be?"

His mouth pursed, and he didn't answer.

Crappy doodles.

"When?"

He sighed. "As soon as possible. This case is moving along faster than expected, so I should finish this job in a day or two, and then I'll have a few days off. Maybe we could go to El Dorado then. We'll just go for dinner. Will that work with the nursery?"

That soon? I swallowed the fear lodged in my throat. "Yeah."

"Thank you."

I waited for him to say not to worry or *they'll love you*, but nothing came. Only silence.

He closed his eyes and tightened his embrace. "I need to be leaving. I don't want to go with us like this."

"I know." Our relationship felt like we were in a snow globe we'd just shaken and were waiting for the dust to settle to see where we ended up. We hadn't landed yet.

"I'll be back as soon as I can."

"I know."

He kissed me gently. "Thank you for still being here."

"It's my house, silly," I tried to joke.

He didn't smile. "You know what I mean."

My smile fell. "I'll be here when you come back. Take care of yourself. I couldn't stand it if something happened to you."

He stood and pulled me to my feet. "You're the one I'm worried about. Leave the investigating to the police. I mean it, Rose."

"You know I don't purposely look for this stuff."

"That's not true, and you know it."

"Okay, in this case it is. But the autopsy hasn't even come back yet."

"We both know those women were murdered. Stay away from their houses. Stay inside and lock your doors and windows."

I snorted. "Like that does any good."

He looked scared. "You're right. I think you should go stay with Violet."

I shook my head. "Why would anyone be after me? Whoever did this went after two old women. I'm fine. Anyway, I've got Muffy, my guard dog."

Joe bent down and rubbed Muffy's head. "Take good care of her for me—will you, girl?" His voice broke and he stood, pulling me to his chest. His arms tightened around me.

I committed this moment to memory as I clung to the only man I'd ever loved. We'd get through this and be stronger than ever. I had to believe that. "You better get goin'. You don't want to be late."

He nodded.

My truck was parked behind his car. I half-expected him to check it out, but he didn't seem interested as he watched me back out onto the street. I gave him another hug and kiss next to his car door.

He handed me a business card. "I'm not readily available to you right now, and I don't trust the Henryetta Police Department at all. If you need help with anything, call this number. It's my friend, Brian. He's another state police detective, and he'll help you."

I had serious doubts a detective in Little Rock could help me if I needed it, but it seemed important to Joe. "Okay. Thanks."

"I'll be back as soon as I can."

"I know. Go already."

He reluctantly climbed in his car and drove away, waving as he left.

When I went back inside, the expected wave of profound loneliness washed over me. How was I going to make it through another few days without him, wondering if he was safe? Wondering if Hilary was trying to get back with him. I shook my head. Thinking like that wouldn't do any good.

My phone rang. I dug it out of my purse, thinking it might be Joe, but the caller ID told me it was Mason.

I sat down on the sofa and took a deep breath before answering. "Hey, Mason," I said. "Did your mother head back to Little Rock?"

"Just a few minutes ago."

After hearing about his secret, my heart ached for him. Within a few short months, he'd lost everything—his sister, his job, the future of his career. "Joe came to see me." The heaviness in my words surely told him everything he needed to know.

"Is he still there?"

"He left a few minutes ago too."

He was silent for a moment. "Can I come over? I know it seems presumptuous but—"

"Yes." My voice broke. "Please."

"I'll be right there."

I hung up and went into the kitchen, our lunch dishes still on the table. Tears blurred my eyes as I washed the plates and silverware and put them in the dish drainer. Now that Joe had left, everything he'd told me played in my head like a movie. Joe hadn't meant for anything to happen to Savannah, and I knew with all my heart that he'd change everything in an instant if he could. But the fact remained that she was dead.

But even more disturbing to me was the way Hilary had manipulated Joe, and how he'd let her do it. She'd made no secret that she wanted him back now. Even though Joe insisted he wanted to be with me, could I be sure he'd stay? He and Hilary had known each other since childhood, and his family expected him to marry her. Was it safe to bet on our future?

The knock at the front door shook me out of my pity party and shame burned my face. Feeling sorry for myself was not only selfish but a wasted effort. I had no right to feel sorry for myself. I was the least affected person in this whole mess.

When I opened the door, Mason stood on the other side, his face expressionless. He came inside, and I closed the door behind him, suddenly unsure of what to do. I wasn't used to entertaining guests. "Do you want anything to drink? I have some lemonade."

Mason spun around to face me. "He told you?"

I nodded, my chin quivering.

"Can we sit down?"

I nodded again and sat on the sofa, while Mason sat in the very chair where Joe had been sitting when he made his confession.

We stayed like that for several seconds, me staring at my hands in my lap, both of us quiet.

"Do you want to talk about it?" he finally asked.

His life was the one in ruins, yet he was asking *me* if I wanted to talk about it. I looked up, searching his face. "I'm so, so sorry, Mason."

His eyes widened, and he swallowed.

"I'm shocked by what Joe told me, and if I'm honest, I'm hurt and scared for lots of reasons. But when I start to feel sorry for myself, all I can think about is how selfish I am."

He leaned forward and grabbed my hand. "How can you say that? What on earth have you done that makes you feel selfish?"

"Joe's ashamed of what he did, and I can see it's eating him alive. I noticed that months before I knew. And Savannah . . ." My voice broke, and I swallowed the lump in my throat. I looked up into his face. "But you. You lost *everything*."

He closed his eyes and sank back into the chair, letting go of my hand.

"I think about how awful I was to you after we first met—"

He sat up, his eyes flying open. "Stop right there. Don't."

"But . . . I didn't know, Mason. I had no idea."

"I know. I didn't want you to." He let out a huff and leaned forward, resting his elbows on his knees. "I wish you didn't know now."

Guilt weighed down my stomach. "I'm sorry. I shouldn't have told you."

"No! You don't understand, and I'm doing a terrible job of explaining it." He took a deep breath. "I'm glad you know because now I have someone I can talk to about it. I've kept it bottled up inside for months, and it's killing me. If you'll let me, anyway."

"Oh, Mason. Of course."

His eyes found mine, full of sadness. "But when you look at me that way, with pity and helplessness . . ."

I looked down at my lap. "I'm sorry."

"Don't be sorry." His voice broke. "Just be my friend."

"We already are friends, Mason." I paused, wondering if I was pushing him too far. "Can you tell me about her? Savannah?"

Amazement covered his face. "You want to hear about Joe's ex-girlfriend?"

Funny, when I'd asked him that, I hadn't thought of her as Joe's ex-girlfriend. "No, I want to hear about *your sister*."

Mason broke down into sobs.

I sat on the sofa, watching him, unsure of what to do. If it were Joe, I'd sit next to him and wrap my arms around him, but

Mason wasn't Joe. And if we were going to make this friendship work, especially since I suspected he might have feelings for me, I needed to be sure to keep strong boundaries. But while I'd established that holding Mason wasn't acceptable, I hadn't come up with an alternative.

He looked up. "I'm sorry. You probably think I'm weak."

"Weak? How can you say that? Look what you did for her. You found the man who murdered her and got justice."

He shook his head. "No, I didn't get justice. I wanted cold-blooded revenge, and that's exactly what I got." His face paled. "He may not have died, but he's as good as dead. They don't expect him to ever wake up from his coma." He looked up. "If I wanted justice, I would have let the police arrest him and my boss convict him. They had a strong case. He would have gone to prison for the rest of his life. Maybe even got the death penalty. But I decided to seek my own punishment. And in the process, I lost who I was and what I stood for. Until you burst into my life."

"Me?"

"When you got thrown into jail for contempt of court, after Judge McClary found out you'd been snooping around the murder victim's house—"

I cringed. "I wouldn't call it *snooping* . . ."

"When I asked you why you did it, do you remember what you told me?"

"Because I loved bologna sandwiches?" I joked.

He gave me a soft smile. "No, you told me you were fighting for justice. You were the only person who believed Bruce Wayne was innocent, and you were going to prove it. You reminded me why I chose this career. I wanted justice, and I still do. Sure, you were fighting to prove Bruce Wayne was innocent, and I was fighting to put him away, but we both wanted the same thing. I'd lost that over the few months before the trial."

"Oh." I wasn't sure how to respond.

"Do you really want to hear about Savannah?"

"Yeah," I said softly. "I do."

Mason spent the next fifteen minutes telling me about his sister. They'd been close growing up, even though she was four years younger than him. They loved to argue and drove their mother crazy, so it was no surprise they both wanted to be attorneys. Savannah was outgoing and vivacious. And beautiful. "Our father died when we were in our teens. He and Savannah were close, and she took it really hard," Mason said. "After his death, Savannah began to look for attention from guys. Often they were destructive relationships, like the one she had with Joe." Mason's eyes widened. "Oh. I didn't mean you and Joe . . ."

I offered him a soft smile. "It's okay. I didn't take it that way at all."

He grimaced. "Yeah, until I apologized for it."

I shrugged. "Joe told me a little bit about their relationship. From what I heard, I'm not sure destructive is a bad description." I purposely avoided defending my own relationship.

"I'm sorry that you're caught in the middle of this mess."

Sighing, my shoulders slumped. "It is what it is."

"Are you still upset I didn't tell you?"

"No. You were right—it wasn't your story to tell. Joe's part anyway. It would have been easy to tell me as a way to get back at Joe."

"That would have hurt you in the process. There was no way I was going to do that. And as crazy as it sounds, I don't want to get even with Joe." He paused, looking out the window. "Not anymore, anyway." His gaze turned to me. "Do I think he's partially responsible for Savannah's death? Yeah, right or wrong, I do. But I don't want to punish him for it. I'm done with seeking my own retribution."

I twisted my hands in my lap. "Honestly, Mason, I think he's punishing himself enough for both of you."

Mason nodded, looking down at his own hands.

"So you ended up in Henryetta. Was it a coincidence Joe got sent here too? It seems pretty odd."

Taking a deep breath, he shook his head as he released it. "I don't know. I lost my job in Little Rock and part of me didn't even care, especially since my own boss was about to file assault charges against me. But then everything was buried. They weren't going to file charges anymore, and I was offered another job here in Henryetta. So I packed up and came. It wasn't until I got here that everything hit me. I left a promising high-power job to come to . . . this place. And I blamed it all on Joe. I was pretty bitter, which I took out on everyone. Especially you."

"Mason, you were still in shock."

He shrugged. "After I saw you in the jail cell, I was determined to get you out." Releasing a bitter laugh, he glanced up at me. "Imagine my surprise when I got a call from Joe Simmons, who happened to be your boyfriend. How in the world could that happen?" He sank back into the chair. "But I'd vowed to get you out, and the fact that your boyfriend is in the state police helped your case. Still, we weren't getting anywhere. Until Joe called his father and you were suddenly released within thirty minutes. And that's when I knew. Joe's father had gotten my charges dropped and had me exiled here to Henryetta. Did he send us both here to punish us?" He shook his head. "I have no idea."

"You could leave," I whispered. "If you hate it here so bad, you can get enough experience to put on a resume and leave this stupid town."

His smile wobbled. "I know, but I'm not ready to leave yet."

We sat in silence for several seconds.

"How's your mother handling all of this?"

"Better than I am, strangely enough."

"I like her. She seems very sweet."

"She is."

I twisted my hands. "Joe's parents are insisting they meet me. Joe says he can't put them off anymore. We're going to have dinner with them after his assignment is finished. I hope they're as nice as your mother."

Mason laughed. "No one is as nice as my mother."

"That's probably true."

"But don't get your hopes up. I don't know them personally, but after I figured out how I ended up here, I did a bit of investigating. Joe's from a powerful family, and they expect big things from him."

I sighed. "Joe says his father is upset because he wants him to join his family's business, the law firm."

Mason's eyebrows rose. "Is that what he told you? Sure, they're attorneys, but they're really grooming him to run for political office. They have big plans for him. They expect Joe to be the JFK of southern Arkansas."

My head felt fuzzy. "They want him to run for president?"

"Not at first, but that's their end goal. They'll settle for the state senate position that's about to become available."

Joe's father's big favor. "And they expect him to run. Even if he doesn't want to."

"They own him, Rose. Especially after what happened to Savannah. There was an internal investigation with both the Little Rock P. D. and the state police. Not to mention Joe was drunk when the police showed up at the scene." He took a deep breath. "They found his car a couple of blocks away and were going to file DUI charges. Those were dropped and buried too."

I felt like I was going to be sick. "They'll never approve of me," I whispered.

Mason remained silent for several seconds. "I'm sure they have certain . . . expectations."

I stood, suddenly feeling claustrophobic. "Violet was right."

"Right about what?"

"She told me his family would never accept me. That I wouldn't be good enough for them. Joe was so furious, I almost thought he was going to hit her." I started to pace.

Mason stood and grabbed my shoulders, staring me in the eye. "There is no doubt in my mind that he loves you. It's obvious to everyone. But you have to admit, he's caught between a rock and a hard place. He's going to have to ultimately choose—you or his family. And his family is hard to say no to."

My knees buckled, and I felt like I was going to pass out. Mason must have realized it because he helped me sit down. I gulped big breaths, irritated at myself. I thought I had grown past the almost-fainting stage of my life.

"What am I going to do, Mason?" I whispered.

Determination steeled his jaw. "You're going to go meet his parents."

My eyes widened in exasperation. "They're going to hate me."

"Maybe. Probably. But don't you dare let them intimidate you. They're bullies—rich and powerful ones—but definitely bullies. If I recall correctly, you don't back down to bullies." He smiled softly as he quoted my words when I told him off outside his office during Bruce Wayne's trial.

I shook my head. "I'm not sure I can stand up to them. They're too powerful."

"You can and you will. Say what you want, but you are not a coward, Rose Gardner."

I stared at him in amazement. "Why are you helping Joe?"

A frown pulled down the corners of his lips. "I'm not helping Joe. I'm helping *you*."

I covered my mouth with my hand. What had I gotten myself into?

"People only have the ability to make you feel badly about yourself if you let them. Remember that." He stood up. "I should probably go. I think I've said too much."

I tilted my head to look at him. "No. I need to know what I'm facing. Thank you for preparing me."

"If you need me for anything, don't hesitate to call. Okay?"

I nodded, then followed him to the front door. "Thanks."

He pulled me into a timid hug, kissing my forehead. "Are you sure you're all right?"

I offered a weak smile. "I'm fine. Quit worrying about me."

"Maybe we can meet for lunch again one day this week."

"I'd really like that," I said, surprised by how much I meant it. At least someone was telling me the unvarnished truth.

Chapter Nineteen

I woke up to strange sounds in the middle of the night, but Muffy was sleeping soundly next to me. I laid in the dark, my ears straining to make out the noise, but I only heard silence, broken by Muffy passing gas. I buried my face in my pillow. "Muffy!" I really needed to change her dog food. Again.

When the air cleared, I listened to the still night. When I didn't hear anything else, I fell back asleep.

I let Muffy out the side door the next morning and looked around, not finding anything amiss. I decided that it was probably just the wind blowing the tree branches against the house. I really needed to get the limbs on the back trees cut.

Only I was sure whatever I'd heard came from the front.

So I slipped my robe on and walked around the house, fully expecting to find nothing. And I did, except for a big rock in the middle of my front porch, sitting on top of a piece of paper.

I tiptoed over to it, although I wasn't sure why. It was a rock, not a snake, so it wasn't going to jump up and bite me. I was more worried about that piece of paper flapping underneath it.

Muffy ran around my feet, wanting me to pet her. Keeping my eye on the rock, I squatted and absently rubbed her head, wondering what I should do.

"I'm scared of a rock, Muffy. Have you ever heard of such foolishness?"

She wagged her tail.

My curiosity won out. It was a piece of paper, for heaven's sake.

The rock was almost too big to pick up with one hand. I pulled the paper out from underneath and dropped it on the porch.

The paper was white and had been pasted with letters cut out of a magazine that spelled *Stay Away.*

Stay away? Stay away from what?

Since I had no idea who or what I was supposed to stay away from, I had no idea who could have left the note on my porch. It could have been worse. At least they weren't destructive about it. They could very well have tossed the rock through my window.

The person who left the note had done it in the middle of the night, so I was sure there weren't any witnesses.

Or were there?

Muffy followed me as I crossed the street, and I rapped on Miss Mildred's front door.

The door cracked open and disapproval covered her face as she pushed her screen door open. "Has Henryetta turned to Sodom and Gomorrah overnight?" Her eyes narrowed as she stared at the hem on my robe.

I self-consciously tugged at it. How could I have forgotten I was still in a robe that barely covered my butt? "Speaking of overnight, did you happen to notice any strange goings-on in my front yard last night?"

"You mean other than the parade of cars coming and going from your house?"

I suppressed a groan. "Someone left a note on my front porch in the middle of the night."

"Probably some man tryin' to schedule time in your brothel."

"*Miss Mildred*, someone left me a note saying *Stay Away.*" I shoved the paper at her.

She grabbed it and held it in front of her as she read it. "Stay away from what?"

"I have no earthly idea. That's why I was hoping you saw something."

She held the paper out to me, some of her feistiness fading. "I didn't see or hear anything."

I snatched back the note and started down the stairs. "Thank you."

"You're on to something," she called after me.

I turned back to face her. "On to what?"

"Dorothy's murder. You've made someone nervous."

I shook my head. "I don't know *anything*. How could I make someone nervous?"

She pointed at my hand. "You must know something, otherwise why would someone come to your house in the middle of the night and leave you a note?"

I exhaled, my shoulders sagging. "I wish I knew what that something was." I started across the street. "I have to get ready for work."

Leaving the note on my kitchen table, I made a cup of coffee then took a shower. The thought of going to Jonah Pruitt's house made me nervous. I told myself that Bruce Wayne would be there too. I'd just make sure not to end up alone with the reverend.

At least I knew one person who *hadn't* left the note. Jonah Pruitt. Why would he rope me into working on his yard, then send me a note telling me to stay away?

So who could it have been? Thomas? Christy? Maybe I was looking in the wrong direction. What if the note didn't have anything to do with Miss Dorothy and Miss Laura's deaths?

What if it had to do with Joe's secret?

As I drove across town, Neely Kate called. "Rose, I only have a second, but I wanted to let you know that Miss Laura's inheritance and house went to her family. Not to Jonah Pruitt."

"Are you *sure*?"

"Yeah, my grandmother saw one of Miss Laura's daughters at Sunday evening service. They've already filed probate. She said the police had questioned her earlier that day."

"So that means that Jonah's not a suspect?"

"Well . . . Miss Laura had been going to his church. But that doesn't mean anything. Half the town's going there now. And besides, he didn't inherit a dime, so why would he kill her?" Her voice lowered. "I've got to go."

"Thanks, Neely Kate."

This whole situation just kept getting stranger and stranger.

When I turned down the street toward the parsonage, I suddenly wondered if Bruce Wayne would even be at Jonah's when I got there. Jonah had humiliated both of us with his video. Bruce Wayne might decide the job wasn't worth the embarrassment.

I was a few minutes late, but when I saw Bruce Wayne sitting on the front porch, I heaved a sigh of relief. He stood when he saw my truck pull up and walked toward me.

"Good morning, Miss Rose."

"Thanks for coming, Bruce Wayne. I was worried you might not show after yesterday."

"I told you I'd be here. I wouldn't let you down."

I wanted to hug him, but I was worried it would spook him. He didn't seem like a touchy-feely kind of guy. But I was certain of one thing: The next person who besmirched Bruce Wayne's character was going to get an earful from me. "Have you seen Jonah yet?"

He shook his head. "No."

I took a deep breath and let it out. "Let's get this over with."

Bruce Wayne stayed at the bottom of the front steps while I knocked on the door. Jonah answered before I could knock the second time. He must have been watching us.

"Lovely to see you, Rose," Jonah drawled then nodded to Bruce Wayne. "And you too, Bruce Wayne. It was wonderful to have you both in church yesterday."

I was so busy cringing, standing within three feet of him, that it took me several seconds to realize he wasn't wearing his usual business attire. He had on a T-shirt and a pair of shorts.

He noticed me staring. "Monday's typically my day off. Most people get the Lord's day off, but that's when I'm my busiest."

Crappy doodles. Jonah was going to be there all day.

"But the revival starts tonight, so I'll be going to the church later this afternoon."

I smiled at him. Thankfully, he didn't seem to realize it was in relief. "Why don't you tell us what you have in mind, and we can get started?"

Jonah took a step backward into his house. "You want to come in and have a cup of coffee first? It's always hard to jump back into work on a Monday morning."

"No, thank you. It's gonna be another scorcher today, so the sooner Bruce Wayne gets started, the better."

Jonah paused, his smile falling a bit. "Oh. I guess that's true."

We walked into the middle of the yard and turned to face the house, Jonah and I standing next to each other and Bruce Wayne behind us. The parsonage was a modest ranch house built back in the 1960s. The red brick exterior was in good shape, but the landscape looked like it hadn't been touched in years. Overgrown evergreen bushes blocked the lower half of the big picture windows. The trees in the yard were in desperate need of trimming, and the yard was full of weeds.

"What do you have in mind?" I asked.

"Well," he raised his hands palms up as if to present the house to me. "It's obviously a mess."

I tilted my head to the side as I studied it, trying to get some ideas. "It could use a little work."

Jonah laughed. "It could use a lot of work. That's where you and Bruce Wayne come in." He looked around. "Say, where's David?"

"He couldn't make it," Bruce Wayne said.

"I'm sure you'll be fine on your own." Jonah turned back to me. "So what do you suggest?"

"Well . . ." I took several steps closer to the house. "These bushes need to be pruned." I poked around the branches, then looked over my shoulder at him. "But they're so overgrown that there's no growth on what will be left of the inside branches. See?"

Jonah leaned next to me, his shoulder touching mine as he examined the branch I'd exposed. "Yes, you're right."

I dropped the plant and stood, taking a step backward. "I think all the bushes need to be replaced."

"Sure," Jonah nodded, studying the bushes as though they held the secret of life. "That's good. What should I replace them with?"

I quickly spouted off some ideas to put some lower height shrubs with several shade-loving perennials since the trees' foliage was so dense. I came up with a quick sketch, and he watched over my shoulder, standing too close for my comfort, but not close enough for me to push him away without being rude.

Jonah headed toward the porch steps. "That looks great, Rose. Why don't you have Bruce Wayne get started digging up the bushes, and you can come inside and give me an estimate?"

"Uh . . ." Wide eyed, I glanced back at Bruce Wayne, panic squeezing my chest. I didn't want to go inside and be alone with him.

"Oh, no. . . ." Bruce Wayne's voice trailed off as two Henryetta police cars pulled up to the curb. Detective Taylor got out of one car and Officer Ernie got out of the other.

My head went fuzzy as I scoured my brain for what I could have done to make the police show up at a minister's house looking for me. Then I had a moment of panic that they were there for Bruce Wayne. He must have considered the possibility as well. His face paled, and he took several steps backward.

Neither of us considered a third scenario, even though I had reason to. Detective Taylor's mouth pinched tightly when he saw Bruce Wayne and me, but his gaze quickly lasered in on Jonah. "Reverend Pruitt?"

Jonah froze on the steps, sweat beading on his forehead. "Yes?"

"We'd like to talk to you about the death of Mrs. Gina Morton."

Who was Gina Morton?

Jonah's face paled, and he stumbled before regaining composure. "Gina's dead?"

"Yes, sir. Her daughter found her body early this morning. We understand you spent the afternoon with Mrs. Morton yesterday."

"Well . . . yeah . . ." he stammered. "Gina invited me over for lunch after church."

Taylor's face puckered with disapproval. "We'd like to ask you a few questions."

Jonah's hand shook. "Yes, of course. Would you like to come inside?"

Taylor nodded and followed Jonah into the house.

Officer Ernie stood to the side, eyeing Bruce Wayne and me. "Are you two colluding with a murderer?"

I put my hand on my hip. "Are you allowed to ask questions like that?"

Bruce Wayne moved closer to me, looking like he was about to lose his breakfast.

I'd just about had enough of the Henryetta law enforcement thinking the worst of me. "Isn't that slander? Accusing someone of something when you don't have any proof?"

Ernie's jaw jutted forward as though he wanted to say something, but he stopped himself.

I looked over my shoulder at Bruce Wayne. "You haven't done anything wrong so don't let him make you feel like you have. And whatever you do, don't answer any questions."

Bruce Wayne swallowed and nodded.

I shot Ernie my meanest glare. "Some of us have actual work to do." I looped my arm through Bruce Wayne's and tugged. "Let's get started on the back."

When we got to the side of the house, Bruce Wayne lowered his mouth next to my ear. "Jonah didn't say nothing about working on the back."

"I know," I whispered. "But I don't like Ernie looking at us like we're criminals." I opened the gate and pulled Bruce Wayne with me. "And I hope to find out what Jonah and Detective Taylor are talking about."

Bruce Wayne's eyes widened. "You want to snoop?"

I tried my best to sound offended. "I can't believe you asked that of me, Bruce Wayne."

He snickered, the first sign I'd seen that there was a bit of spunk in him. "So, do you?"

"Well, yeah . . ."

We walked around the backyard, staying close to the house. There was a little landscaping here and there, and a set of windows in the middle of the house looked out onto the large backyard. When I got closer I could see Jonah sitting at a table with the detective.

"I want to get under that window to see if I can hear something."

Bruce Wayne looked worried. "I'll keep a lookout in case Ernie decides to come back here and check on us."

"Thanks."

Curtains hung on either side of the windows and would block any sight of me from the men inside, but the windows were higher off the ground in the back of the house. I spun around looking for something to stand on, but Bruce Wayne was a step ahead of me. He handed me a bucket.

"How did you know I needed this?"

He gave me an apologetic grin. "I've got some experience."

I didn't have time to stop and dwell on Bruce Wayne's former life of crime, nor the fact that I was possibly dragging him back down that road. But then again, I wasn't sure this was illegal. Rude? Yes. But illegal? Besides, most of the people in town already thought I was guilty of this very crime—eavesdropping. I might as well at least try it *once*.

I turned the bucket upside down and climbed on top, pressing my ear to the glass. I could barely make out their words. I had to close my eyes and concentrate.

". . . roast beef and potatoes." Jonah said.

"Then what happened?"

"Should I call my attorney?"

Taylor's voice lowered. "Have you done something that warrants calling a lawyer?"

Jonah didn't answer him.

"Did you discuss Mrs. Morton's money or her will?"

"I don't see why it matters what we discussed." Jonan tried to sound indignant, but his voice was shaking.

Detective Taylor's voice turned menacing. "We can do this down at the station if you'd prefer."

Jonah sounded like he coughed. "We did discuss how she planned to handle her affairs after she passed through the pearly gates. She was about to redo her will. She asked for my advice." Jonah sounded defensive and seemed to be regaining some of his confidence.

"Did you convince Dorothy Thortonbury to give you her inheritance?"

"No, definitely not."

"Her niece brought me her will, and it shows that you get everything. And wouldn't you know it, she signed it about a week before her death."

"I don't know anything about that." Jonah sounded panicked.

"What about Laura Whitfield? What's your connection to her?"

"She . . . she was a member of my church."

"How's your church doin' financially, Reverend."

"We're doing very well."

"I see you hired the new nursery to work on your church grounds. They did a lot of work. That had to cost a pretty penny."

"The church's financial records are available for church members to review. We have nothing to hide."

"Don't you think it's a bit coincidental that you hired a multiple offender to work on your property right around the time the elderly women in this town started dropping like flies?"

Jonah cleared his throat. "Jesus made himself available to the tax collectors and the prostitutes. A doctor doesn't treat healthy people. I'm here to help the downtrodden and the misguided. If some of my parishioners happen to have less than spotless records, well, I wouldn't be surprised."

"I'm talking about one in particular. Bruce Wayne Decker. In fact, I hear you're so taken with him that you featured him in a video in your service yesterday."

"Well, yes . . ." Jonah said. "I'm fascinated by his relationship with Rose."

"Rose Gardner?"

My heartbeat pounded in my head. I didn't like where this was going.

"Yes," Jonah drawled. "They have a loyalty to each other I'm still trying to understand."

"Yeah," Taylor said, sounding puzzled. "I'm trying to figure those two out too. Do you want to hear my theory?"

"Sure." But Jonah didn't sound so sure.

"Rose Gardner and Bruce Wayne Decker are part of your dirty little scheme."

"What scheme?" Jonah asked.

I gasped as my anger rose. *How dare he!*

"Is that an admission that they are?"

"There's no admission of any kind, Detective. I hired the Gardner Sisters Nursery to work for the church. Bruce Wayne is their employee."

"So what are she and Decker doing here now?"

"They're working on the church parsonage." Jonah sounded ruffled.

"How convenient that they're here the morning after a murder."

I couldn't believe him. How could he think of pinning this on me? And how dare he assume Bruce Wayne was involved without any evidence.

"Am I under arrest, Detective?"

Taylor paused for several seconds. "No, but don't leave town, Mr. Pruitt."

"That's Reverend Pruitt."

"We'll see about that."

The edges of my vision blackened, and I tensed. Now was a terrible time to get a vision.

I was in the police station, and Bruce Wayne stood in front of me pale as a ghost.

"I didn't do it. I swear."

I laughed, but it was an ugly sound. "Once a criminal, always a criminal, Decker. It was only a matter of time before I put you away again. Ever heard of three strikes and you're out?"

Bruce Wayne started shaking, backing up into a police officer standing behind him. "I've been good. I promise. I'm gettin' my life together."

"Yeah, tell it to the judge."

Jonah's backyard came into focus along with Bruce Wayne's panicked face.

"You're gonna get arrested." I said.

His mouth dropped open then he grabbed my arm and pulled me down from the bucket. "Ernie's comin' back here."

I bent over, pointing to a plant as Officer Ernie rounded the back corner. "This needs some serious attention, Bruce Wayne."

"Yes, ma'am." Bruce Wayne nodded. "I've added that to the list."

Ernie spread his feet apart, hooking his thumbs in his waistband. "Whatcha you two doin' back here?"

I straightened. "What's it look like we're doin'?" I hoped I sounded belligerent, because at the moment I was freaking out.

My question stumped him for several seconds. "It looks like you're poking around in some bushes."

"Since I own a gardening center, does it seem suspicious that I'd be poking around in some bushes?"

His forehead wrinkled. "Well, no . . ."

"Can we help you with something, Officer? Or were you just planning to watch us work?"

Ernie's face reddened, and he spread two fingers into a V, pointing them at his eyes then in our direction. "I'm on to you two."

Bruce Wayne trembled.

I went from intimidated to ticked off. How dare they do this to him? I put my hand on my hip, lifting my chin in defiance. "You're onto the fact that we're the best landscaping team in southern Arkansas?"

"No, that you're abetting a murderer."

"That's the most ridiculous thing I ever heard. Especially when you take into consideration that I've turned in every murderer I've ever come across."

Ernie's jaw worked again.

I turned to Bruce Wayne. "I think we're done here for now. Let's head back to the nursery and collect what we need."

He nodded, looking incapable of speech.

I marched past Ernie, offering him a syrupy smile as I passed. Bruce Wayne followed, slouching as though he hoped to sink into the ground and disappear. When we got to the front yard, I lowered my voice. "Get into my truck."

"Okay."

Detective Taylor appeared in the front door, Jonah standing behind him. Taylor watched as I drove off.

"They think Jonah murdered Miss Laura, Miss Dorothy, and the woman this morning." I shot a glance to Bruce Wayne. "And they think you and I are part of it." Had the autopsy results come back? What could have made them change their minds so suddenly about Miss Laura and Miss Dorothy's deaths? I might as well tell Bruce Wayne the rest, since I'd already blurted part of it into his face. "And at some point they are going to arrest you."

As soon as we turned the corner Bruce Wayne began to hyperventilate. "Why do they think that?"

"Do they really need a reason?" I sighed. "Their only piece of evidence connecting us to the deaths at this point is that we started working for Jonah at around the same time the women started dying."

"But we started working for him after they died! Well, except for this latest one."

"I know. We'll get this straightened out. I got you into this mess, and I'm going to get you out."

I drove to the town square and pulled into a parking spot close to the courthouse.

"What are you doing *here?*" Bruce Wayne asked, his voice rising.

"I'm going to find Mason."

"The assistant district attorney?"

I grabbed his hands and tugged. "Bruce Wayne, calm down. Panicking won't fix this."

"I can't help it." He started wheezing.

I believed it. Panicking had gotten him into his previous murder charges. If you overlooked the fact that he'd intended to rob the hardware store, it had been a simple case of being in the wrong place at the wrong time. I was noticing a pattern. "Mason is my friend. There's no way he believes I had anything to do with this."

"What about me?"

"Mason trusts my judgment. He told me so. If I trust you, then he will too."

He nodded, swallowing. "But I still don't want to go to the courthouse. It makes me itchy." He began scratching at his neck.

I understood. As far as I knew the last time he'd been in a courthouse was for his trial. "How about you wait at Merilee's? We'll order you some coffee and a breakfast, and I'll go talk to Mason and come back and get you."

He nodded with tiny, nervous bobs. "Yeah. Okay."

We went inside the restaurant and sat down at a table. "You go ahead and order whatever you want. I'll pay for it."

"You don't have to do that, Miss Rose."

I handed him the menu. "I know, but eating something might make you feel less lightheaded."

He squinted at me. "How did you know I felt like that?"

Telling him I felt the same way wouldn't exactly be confidence inspiring. "I just do. Stay right here, and I'll be back as soon as I can."

Bruce Wayne nodded, but he didn't look happy about it. "There's something I have to tell you."

"You can tell me when I come back."

"No. I saw something."

I rested my arms on the table and leaned closer, lowering my voice. "Saw something where? When?"

"At the church last week. I didn't think anything of it until this morning."

"What did you see?"

The waitress filled his empty coffee cup and took his order.

His hands shook as he tore the corner off a sugar packet and poured it into his cup.

"Bruce Wayne. What did you see?"

He scrubbed his face with his hands. "Nope. I don't think I should tell you." His hands lowered, and his eyes turned glassy. "They already think both of us are a part of this thing. If I tell you, they might use it against you."

"No. We're in this together. You can trust me."

His looked down at the table, his eyes peeking out through scraggly hair. "You're the one person I know I can trust, which is why I have to protect you."

I sat back in my seat, running my hand through my hair in frustration before turning back to him. "Just tell me this: Were you at the church when you saw whatever you saw?"

He nodded.

At least that was something. "Would you tell Mason?"

"I don't know."

"We can go to the courthouse together—"

His eyes widened. "No! I ain't goin' in the courthouse!"

I held up my hands. "Okay. How about if he comes here? You have to give me something more to go on, though."

"It's about that kid that was at the church."

"Thomas?"

"Yeah." He patted his chest, then his jeans pockets. "I wish I had a cigarette."

"When I come back, I'll get you some."

He didn't look so sure about waiting, and I had serious qualms about leaving him alone. I pulled my cell phone out of my purse, planning to call Mason to see if he'd meet us. But when I tried to pull up his number, I discovered my phone was dead. It was my first cell phone, purchased just a few months ago, and I wasn't sure I'd ever get the hang of remembering to charge it.

Bruce Wayne's leg bounced up and down. "I can't go back to jail, Rose. I just can't."

I covered Bruce Wayne's hand with my own. "Nobody's going to jail. I'll go get Mason. He'll take care of this. I promise. Wait for me here."

As I left him in the diner, I hoped I'd find him there when I came back.

Chapter Twenty

Mason's attractive young secretary didn't look happy to see me. She glanced at me from the corner of her eyes, and then looked back at her computer screen. "He's out."

"Do you know when he'll be back?"

Her eyebrows rose, but she kept her attention on her computer. "No."

"Is he in court?"

Her mouth puckered in disapproval. "I'm not at liberty to discuss Mr. Deveraux's schedule. Perhaps you should call and make an appointment like everyone else."

Why had I let my phone die? It was the only place I had his cell phone number stored, but I couldn't wait for it to charge. "Can you just call him and tell him that Rose needs to talk to him. It's important."

Folding her hands on her desk, she gave me a patronizing stare. "I'll be happy to take your name and number and *make an appointment for you.*"

"Can you just give me some idea how long it will be?"

She ignored my question, returning to her work.

I wasn't sure how long Bruce Wayne would wait for me. Resting my hands on her desk, I leaned forward. "I promise he'll want to know I'm here. Can't you just call him and leave a message on his cell?"

"Rose?" Mason stood in the doorway, surprise in his voice.

I looked up, and his smile faded.

"Is everything all right?"

"No."

He took my arm and pulled me into his office, shutting the door behind us. "What happened?"

"I don't even know where to start."

"Start at the beginning."

I paced the room as he sat on the edge of his desk. He looked more official and intimidating that way, with his blue dress shirt and dark grey tie and his stern expression. I expected the impression to make me nervous, but it gave me more confidence that he could help.

"I met Bruce Wayne at Jonah's this morning, and we were in the front yard discussing the landscaping job when Detective Taylor and Officer Ernie showed up. They said another woman had died, and they needed to question Jonah."

"Another woman died? They didn't call me." Mason looked livid.

"There's more." I took a deep breath. "Taylor and Jonah went inside and Ernie said something about Bruce Wayne and I helping a murderer."

"What?"

"Bruce Wayne and I went around to the backyard. I could see Jonah and Detective Taylor in the window, so I put my ear to the glass to hear what they were saying."

He grimaced. "I'm not sure I want to know that part."

"Mason, Detective Taylor thinks Jonah killed those women. And he thinks Bruce Wayne and I are part of it."

He stood. "That's the most ridiculous thing I've ever heard. On what grounds?"

"He says we started working for Jonah right about when the women started dying. And Bruce Wayne has a criminal record. I had a vision while I was listening."

Mason's gaze jerked up. "Did they hear you?"

"No," I shook my head. "But I saw Detective Taylor booking Bruce Wayne at the police station. Unfortunately, Bruce Wayne heard that part, and he's freaking out."

Mason walked around his desk and picked up his phone. "I'm getting this resolved right here and now." He angrily punched in some numbers and waited while I walked over to his window. His office had a good view of Main Street, and I could see Merilee's down below.

"You've got some explaining to do, Taylor. I hear there was another death and no one notified me to come to the scene." He paused. *"Excuse me?"*

I turned to look at him, and his face was red.

"On what grounds?" After several seconds, he shook his head. "Do you ever give *any* consideration to how you investigate a case? Is there even a logical thought in your head?"

Oh, dear. This wasn't going well. I looked out the window, watching the entrance of Merilee's in case Bruce Wayne left.

Mason's voice was tightly controlled. "My personal life is *my* business, Detective Taylor, and it has no bearing on this investigation." He paused again. "You will regret this decision." He slammed the phone down.

"What happened?"

"He decided not to summon me to the crime scene because I have a relationship with a suspect, and my personal feelings could cloud my judgment." He banged his palm on the desk. "Goddammit."

I jumped at his outburst. "Can he do that?"

"Sure, he can *forget* to notify me to come to a scene, but the DA and I are the ones who press charges. Taylor can bring whatever bullshit he wants to me. I'm not going to do a damn thing with it."

"Don't burn any bridges on account of me, Mason."

His eyes hardened. "This bridge has been burning for quite some time."

"I left Bruce Wayne in Merilee's. He refused to come into the courthouse. He says he can't go back to jail."

Mason rubbed his temple. "What a mess."

"He says he saw something at the church last week that he didn't realize was important until this morning, but he won't tell me what it was. He's worried that if the police find out I know, they'll have more proof of my involvement."

"Shit."

"I asked him to give me something to bring to you, and he said it involves Thomas, the boy who lives on the corner."

Mason stood and started for the door. "Is he still at the restaurant?"

"That's where I left him. I ordered him breakfast and told him I'd be back after I talked to you."

He held the door open for me, and as he passed his secretary's desk, he stopped and gave her the Mason van de Camp Deveraux, III death glare. "Cecelia, this is Rose Gardner. If I *ever* hear about you ignoring her request to talk to me again, you will no longer be employed by this office. Is that clear?"

She looked down. "Yes, Mr. Deveraux."

"Good. I'm leaving the courthouse for a bit." Mason looked up at me, resignation on his face. "Let's go find Bruce Wayne."

When we got onto the world's slowest elevator, I said, "You didn't have to do that. She was only doing her job."

His eyes burned with anger. "If she was doing her job, she would have called me immediately and told me you were there. She knows you receive top priority."

I'd never been in Mason's office before, although I'd been outside of it, and the few times I'd called him had always been on his cell phone. "Why?"

"Because you have a knack for finding trouble, and I know you well enough to know you'd only call if it was important."

"Well . . . thank you."

"Do you think Decker's information is credible?"

It took me a second to realize what he was asking. "You mean he might have been stoned and made a mistake? I suppose it's always a possibility with a drug addict, but if you're asking me if *I* think he was stoned, then no. Bruce Wayne's trying to stay clean, and I was with him enough last week to have noticed if he was high."

He nodded. "Good enough for me."

My stomach was a ball of nerves when we got to Merilee's, and my heart sank when I saw Bruce Wayne's table was empty. "He's not here."

Mason looked around the small café. "Could he be in the restroom?"

Cringing, I shook my head. "No. He was at this table and now it's cleared off. He must have took off right after I left."

"Do you know where he would go if he's scared?"

I wanted to cry. "No. I don't even know where he lives. I contacted him through David at the Piggly Wiggly. They just showed up at the job."

"Then let's go to the Piggly Wiggly and see if David's there. Maybe he knows where his friend is."

"He won't be there. I'm pretty sure he only works nights." I sank into the chair at Bruce Wayne's table. "This is all my fault. He was scared to death. I never should have left him."

"No more talk like that. This is not your fault. We'll find him."

I looked up at Mason. "They wouldn't think he was a suspect if I hadn't hired him and made him work there."

"You told me he was doing a good job. And he showed up this morning, right? Even after the stunt Pruitt pulled on you two yesterday."

"Yeah . . ."

Mason sat in the chair in front of me. "Men get pride from working and doing a good job. Seems to me that Bruce Wayne's had a run of bad luck. Sure he's brought a lot of it on himself, but he couldn't catch a break after getting arrested for a murder he didn't commit . . . until *you* gave him one."

I rested my elbows on the table and leaned my forehead into my hands. "Maybe I gave him one, but look what good it did him. He's about to get arrested for something he didn't do. Again."

"We'll find out where he's hiding and get this mess cleaned up, okay?"

I lowered my hands. "Why are you helping me? You don't even know him."

The corners of Mason's mouth lifted slightly. "Because it's the right thing to do."

The waitress came over, perkier than when she'd waited on Bruce Wayne. "Hey, Mr. Deveraux. Do you want your usual?" She flashed him a toothy smile.

He shook his head with a sigh and stood. "No. I'm about to leave. Thanks anyway, Brittany."

I got up, watching the two of them, surprised by how familiar they seemed. But then again, Mason was a single man who spent a lot of time at the courthouse. It stood to reason he ate here a lot.

She tilted her head as she studied me. "Weren't you with the guy who was sitting here just a little while ago?"

"Yeah," I pulled my wallet out of my purse. "I'm sorry he took off. Do I owe you any money for his bill?"

"Nah, the guys he left with took care of it."

My head jerked up. "What guys?"

"Two guys came in and sat with him. He looked nervous about seeing them, but he was jittery when you were with him, so I didn't think much of it."

Mason turned to her. "Do you remember what they did?"

She blushed and brushed the hair off her face self-consciously. "They didn't really do anything, Mr. Deveraux. They just talked. When I brought out the nervous guy's breakfast, all three of them were gone. The money was laying on the table."

Mason fixed his gaze on her. "Did you see where they went?"

"Yeah, I think I saw them going out the back."

"Do you remember what the two guys looked like?"

"Yeah, one was tall and bald with snake tattoos on his neck."

"Can you guess how old he was?"

She scrunched her nose as she pondered it. "I'm guessing in his thirties. The other guy looked like a kid."

"A little kid?"

"No, a teenager. Acne and all. He had long black, shaggy hair. He was kind of lanky. And some peach fuzz on his chin."

I put my hand on Mason's arm. "That sounds like Thomas."

Brittany scowled as her gaze pinned on my hand.

Mason didn't notice; his focus was on me. "You're sure?"

"Yeah."

Mason returned his attention to the waitress. "Did you see what kind of car they drove? What kind of clothes? Anything to help me identify them?"

"I didn't see what they drove. I just noticed them when they sat down at the guy's table. The kid wore jeans and a rock band T-shirt. But the bald guy had on a uniform. Like a work uniform."

"Do you remember anything about it? Like what color it was or if it had any writing on it?"

"It was a medium gray shirt. And it said something about a garage."

I felt lightheaded. "Weston's Garage," I half-whispered, worried I was right.

The waitress's face lit up. "Yeah! That's it!"

Mason turned around to face me. "How'd you know that?"

I tried to blink away the fuzziness in my head. "Daniel Crocker."

Mason's face hardened. "Daniel Crocker is in jail waiting for his trial."

"Thomas told me . . ." It all made sense now.

"Thomas told you what?"

"That Daniel Crocker is out to get me."

Chapter Twenty-One

Mason guided me back into my chair and sat across from me as Brittany went to wait on another customer. "Why do you think Daniel Crocker is out to get you?"

"Well, first I had a vision about Thomas. It was after I found out Miss Dorothy didn't leave her house to her niece. Thomas was in the front yard saying it was too bad Mildred hadn't been killed too. I thought that was strange, since the police were still calling it natural causes at that point."

"Yeah, that's odd."

"I told him it was a terrible thing to say, and he told me that no one liked her. I couldn't really argue with that. He was getting into his car when I had the vision. He was with some scary-looking guy, who wasn't happy. Thomas said he was having some problems doing a job, and the guy didn't like it."

"Sounds like he might have gotten himself in a bit of trouble."

"Yeah."

"But I'm still not sure what that has to do with Crocker."

"I saw Thomas at the church on Friday."

Mason's eyebrows rose. "Jonah Pruitt's church?"

I nodded. "I think he's working for Jonah. He told me a lot of people were upset about the part I played in shutting Daniel Crocker down, and they'd like to see me pay." I leaned my forearms on the table. "Thomas is always working on his car. It stands to reason that he might have some connection to Weston's Garage. Daniel Crocker's shop."

Mason looked angry. "Why didn't you tell me he threatened you?"

I shrugged. "He's a kid. I thought he was all talk. I mentioned it to Joe yesterday . . . before . . ." I closed my eyes, pushing the pain back down. Funny how worrying about going to jail had momentarily pushed my other troubles aside.

"I'm glad you told Joe, but he's not here, is he?" Mason's voice was cold.

My eyes widened. "What's that supposed to mean?"

"Joe is off doing who-knows-what who-knows-where while he's undercover. He can't do anything with this, Rose. I'm the one here in Henryetta. You should have told me too."

"I didn't think it was important."

"If someone says Daniel Crocker is threatening you, it's important."

"Joe said he was going to call the sheriff's department to see if they knew anything. And he gave me the contact information for a friend of his with the state police."

Mason look unimpressed.

"Do you think they took Bruce Wayne to Weston's Garage?"

"I don't know." Mason looked lost in thought, and then he pulled out his cell phone. "I'd love nothing more than to have the Henryetta police check this out, but we both know how well that would go over. I'd call the sheriff, but while Weston's Garage is on the outskirts of town, it's still within city limits. Henryetta police get jurisdiction. However, I plan to call them myself about the Crocker threat."

"Well, I can't just sit here and do *nothing*. What if they did take him? What if they hurt him?" My voice broke.

"All the more reason for you to stay as far away from them as possible." He stood. "Come on."

"Where are we going?"

"I don't know yet, but we're not accomplishing anything by sitting here." The waitress walked by, and Mason pulled a business card out of his coat pocket and handed it to her. "Brittany, if you remember anything else, would you give me a call?"

Giggling, she took his card and stuffed it in her apron pocket. "Sure thing, Mr. Deveraux. Is your home number on there?"

"Just my office."

Disappointment sagged her shoulders.

"But my secretary will put you right through to me if I'm available."

That seemed to make her happier.

We stepped out onto the sidewalk, the steamy air hitting me in the face. When was the weather going to figure out it was almost October? "You've got quite the fan club," I grumbled.

Mason stopped in front of me. "What's that supposed to mean?"

"Everywhere you go, women fawn all over you."

He shook his head in bewilderment. "*You're* the one who told me I was one of the most eligible bachelors in Henryetta. I never asked for any of this. Why do you even care?"

Fuming, I refused to answer him. Mostly because I didn't have an answer. I couldn't figure out why it ticked me off. The crummy weather and losing Bruce Wayne must have made me cranky. The best way to handle the situation was to change the subject. "So have you figured out where are we going?"

"The sheriff's office."

"I thought you were going to call."

Mason led me to his sedan and opened the passenger door for me. "I was, but a visit seems more in order."

"You're bringing me with you?" I asked in surprise.

"If I let you out of my sight, Taylor might catch wind that Bruce Wayne is missing and decide you're a flight risk and lock you up. That's the best case scenario. Worst case, the guys who took Bruce Wayne could come for you. What do you want to do?"

"Stay with you."

"Yeah, I figured."

The sheriff's office was in a little town about ten minutes outside of Henryetta. Everyone in Fenton County knew there was a rivalry of sorts between the two law enforcement departments. I was hoping that would work in Bruce Wayne's favor.

As we walked inside, Mason straightened his tie. "I'll show you where you can wait for me while I talk to the sheriff."

"Okay."

He sat me in a waiting area outside of a glass-enclosed box, like some gas station attendants sit behind when they work in a bad neighborhood. "Is that bulletproof glass?"

Mason cast a glance toward it. "I guess," he answered absently.

"Do they have many shootings out here? Why does the receptionist need to be behind bulletproof glass?"

"Rose, you're perfectly safe out here. Just wait for me."

Easy for him to say. He was the one going behind the glass, but it wasn't like I had any options. "I'm not going anywhere."

The sheriff's deputy led him into the back, and I took in my surroundings. A young guy sat two chairs down from me. He had headphones in his ears, and he tapped his fingers on his legs like he was playing the drums.

I picked up an old issue of *Better Homes and Gardens*, trying to find an article to read, but I really didn't care about making a Valentine's Day centerpiece. I tossed it back on the table next to me.

The outside door flew open, and a woman rushed the glass window. The woman behind the glass actually jumped in surprise.

The blond-haired woman beat on the glass with her fists. "I demand justice! I'm not leaving until I get what's mine!"

The receptionist, who had recovered from her initial excitement, now looked bored. She yawned and pushed a clipboard through the opening at the bottom. "If you have a complaint, I'll need you to fill out this paperwork."

"Paperwork?" The woman shrieked. "I'm past paperwork!" She pulled a handgun out of her purse and held it up in the air.

I was going to beat Mason Deveraux senseless the next time I saw him. Perfectly safe out here, my eye.

The receptionist had already bent over her paperwork, not even noticing the gun. And here I'd been pinning my hopes on the sheriff.

The crazy woman spun around to see who was in the room, and her gaze stopped on me.

I blinked. "*Christy?*" Miss Dorothy's niece was standing in the sheriff's office holding a gun. She must have lost her ever-loving mind.

"Rose?" Christy lowered the gun to her side, out of sight of the receptionist, who got up from her desk and walked to the back, leaving the front window abandoned.

I pointed to the gun. "What are you doing here?"

She shrugged, starting to cry. "I just need someone to listen to me." She looked like crap. Her hair was stringy, and her face was dripping with sweat.

"Waving a gun around the sheriff's office doesn't seem like the best way to go about it."

"I wanted to get the sheriff's attention."

I decided it wasn't a good idea to point out that I was the only person who had noticed. The little drummer boy was still beating on his leg, his eyes closed as he played through what looked to be a wicked drum solo.

"I heard about Jonah Pruitt getting your aunt's house."

She moved toward me, the gun still lowered. "It ain't right. It just ain't right."

"No, it's not."

Her face hardened. "Hey. You work for the rat bastard."

My heart nearly leapt from my chest. "No." I shook my head. "I don't really work for him. I'm more contract labor."

Her face lit up. "Oh, I think it's more than that. In fact, when I visited the church last week, you two looked downright friendly." She lifted the gun again and pointed it at me. "I bet you know all about it. You're coming with me. We're going to go talk to Reverend Pruitt together."

"I'm not sure that me talking to Jonah is going to help."

Her eyebrows shot up. "Jonah, huh? That's a little personal, isn't it?"

Crap.

"I think this might be a great idea." She moved next to me, pointing the gun into my side. "Let's go." Her eyes were wild, and her pupils were dilated. Christy was high on something.

Shit.

I looked desperately at the window, but the receptionist hadn't returned yet. The man with the beats was working up to a crescendo. I considered shouting or screaming, but Christy seemed agitated and strung out enough to actually shoot me.

Sighing, I headed to the door with her. How did I get myself into these situations? "I came here with the assistant DA," I said. "He's not going to be happy when he notices I'm gone."

While I thought that might help her change her mind, it seemed to have the opposite effect. The gun jammed into my ribs, and I cried out in pain and fright.

"The DA brought you here, himself, huh? Is he about to file charges against you *for stealing what's mine*?"

"No, he's protecting me."

She laughed. "He's doin' a shitty job of it, ain't he?"

I grimaced. "It's obviously not turning out as I had hoped."

Her car was close to the entrance, parked at an angle in the middle of the parking lot. She hadn't even bothered to find a parking space, blocking in Mason's car and several police cruisers.

Christy made me get behind the wheel while she sat beside me in the passenger's seat. "I'm sure you know how to get to *Jonah's* house."

I hated to admit that I did, but that seemed to be the least of my worries at the moment. "This is a stick shift."

"So?"

"So, I can't drive a stick shift."

"You're a lying whore. Drive."

Pointing a gun at me was one thing, but she had just besmirched my character. "A lying whore? Why are you callin' me *that*?"

Her eyebrows arched, and she stared at me like I was an imbecile. "Sleeping with a minister and stealing other people's money makes you a lying *whore*."

"I'm not sleeping with him. How do you get that from us talking to each other?"

"I know these things!" she screamed, jabbing the gun wildly in my direction. "Now *drive*."

My shaky hand turned the key over, and my mind raced as I tried to remember the one and only time I'd driven a stick-shift car. I'd visited Aunt Bessie and Uncle Earl on their farm, and Uncle Earl had tried to teach me on his old truck. Key word: *tried*.

Foot on the clutch. Move the stick. I followed my own instructions, and the car didn't move. Instead, it started rolling.

"What are you doing?" Christy shrieked. "Get going!"

"I told you that I can't drive a stick shift. I'm trying."

The car rolled, stopping when I banged into the sheriff's patrol car.

"You just hit a police car!"

"I didn't mean to! Stop shouting at me! You're making me nervous!" I let my foot off the clutch and the car jerked, hitting the patrol car again. "Crap!"

Christy grabbed the stick with her free hand. "Put your foot on the clutch and the brake."

I did what she instructed, although I wasn't sure why. Perhaps the gun she had pointed at me was all the persuasion I needed.

She gave me instructions, and we jerked and screeched our way onto Highway 82. The car made such a racket, I couldn't believe no one had come to investigate. But I was grateful they hadn't. I didn't doubt Christy would use the weapon if backed into a corner.

We made it to Jonah's house, and I parked at his curb while my mind scrambled to cobble together some kind of plan. Would she shoot Jonah? "Christy, I know you need money, but there's another way. I promise you."

She waved her gun around in the air. "Another way than gettin' what's rightfully mine? Good, then I'll have even more money. Let's go."

We walked up to Jonah's front door, and my palms started to sweat. If I went inside that house with her, I was sure this wouldn't end well. She knocked on the door, and we waited long enough for her to knock again. When he didn't answer, she jammed the gun into my side again. "Where is he?"

"How should I know?"

"You two are sleepin' together, ain't you? Surely, you know his schedule."

I cringed in disgust. "Eww! No! I am *not* sleeping with him." An image of Jonah Pruitt naked flashed into my head. I suddenly felt the urge to take a shower.

"Like you'd admit to it. Open the door."

I jiggled the door knob, grateful it was locked.

Christy kicked the door, and then yelped in pain. "*Where is he?*"

I tried to back up but she grabbed my arm, her fingers pinching my skin. "I don't know. The church?"

She pushed me toward the car, telling me to drive again. This was ridiculous. "You should drive," I told her. "I'm terrible at driving a stick. People in town are bound to notice. What if the police pull me over for drunk driving?"

"I can't drive and hold a gun on you at the same time."

"I won't do anything. I promise. Just don't make me drive."

She chewed on her fingers as she considered it. "Okay, but you can't run away."

I nodded, not actually saying the words.

We got back into the car, and she set the gun on her lap. Guilt ate at my conscience. The lying part of the *lying whore* was turning out to be true. But I had no choice.

I needed to distract her as much as possible, so I started peppering her with questions. "Aren't you supposed to be back in Shreveport by now? I thought you had to get back."

Her upper lip curled in disgust. "Did your *boyfriend* tell you that?"

I shuddered. "Jonah Pruitt is *not* my boyfriend. And no, Bruce Wayne and David told me that you needed to take care of your aunt's house so you could get back."

"You mean *my* house!" she shouted, veins popping out on her forehead. "That bastard stole it!"

"Is that why you killed Miss Dorothy? So you could get the money?"

She started laughing hysterically. "Do you really think I'd admit that to you? *Do I look like an idiot?*" She'd turned to look at me, so she didn't notice that the Suburban in front of us had stopped. Her car rammed into the back of it, throwing her gun to the floor.

The seatbelt dug into my shoulder and abdomen after the impact. My fingers fumbled with my seatbelt latch as Christy tried to orient herself. I reached for the door handle just as she figured out what I was doing. She grabbed a handful of my hair.

"*Where do you think you're going?*" She reached down beneath her, feeling for the gun.

The SUV driver had gotten out of the car and was shouting, but he stopped when he took in what was happening. I shoved an elbow hard into Christy's stomach, and she groaned and dropped her hold on my hair.

I pushed the door open and took off running. "Call 911!" I shouted to the SUV driver as gunshots rang out.

She was really trying to shoot me!

I ran for several blocks, zigging and zagging between houses and changing streets. I stopped behind a giant oak tree to catch my breath, looking around to make sure I'd lost her.

I was at the edge of downtown, which meant I was close to the nursery. But should I take a chance and go there? The police station was out. I considered going to Mason's office, but I didn't want to risk passing any police officers who might decide I was guilty before proven innocent.

I snorted. A crazy lunatic like Christy was walking around Henryetta shooting at people, but they were interested in arresting me and Bruce Wayne.

I doubted Christy even knew about the nursery, let alone that I was an owner. When I walked through the door to the shop, Violet was livid. "Where in the hell have you been?"

I wiped the sweat off my forehead. "I don't even know where to start."

"I've been manning the shop all alone. You didn't even call to tell me where you were, and your phone went straight to voicemail."

I stumbled to the back room and grabbed a bottle of water from the fridge, taking several gulps. "My phone's dead," I finally said, realizing I'd lost my purse somewhere in the last couple of hours. My phone along with it.

"When are you going to become a responsible adult and learn to charge your phone?"

I ignored her question and took another drink.

"Why are you so out of breath?"

"I was running from a crazy woman."

"Ha. Ha," she sneered, going back behind the counter. "Very funny."

I leaned against the counter. "I had to go to Jonah's this morning. Remember? We got that parsonage job."

Her eyes bugged in exasperation. "Well, why didn't you just say so? I forgot all about it. How's it going?"

I thought about everything that had transpired over the last few hours. "It's going fine." I went behind the counter. "Where's the phone book?"

"Why?"

"I need to call Mason."

"If you'd just charge your phone, you could call him on that."

I saw no point in arguing with her. I looked up Mason's office number and Cecelia answered on the second ring.

"Cecelia, this is Rose Gardner. Has Mason come back to his office yet?" I took the cordless handset to the backroom, out of Violet's earshot.

"No. Not yet." I could tell it was killing her to be nice to me.

"Will you give him a message? Tell him I lost my cell phone, but I'll call him back later to explain what happened. In the meantime, could you call the police and tell them Christy Hansen is running around town with a gun? I suspect she plans to put one of her bullets in Jonah Pruitt."

"*What*?"

"I know." I sighed. "Just tell 'em."

I may have gotten away from Christy, but as far as I knew, Bruce Wayne was still missing. I had to find him. I put the phone back in the charger. "Vi, I have to go back to the job. David's not working with Bruce Wayne, and he needs the help." Lying to Violet made me feel guilty, but it was a lot easier than explaining every-thing, not that she'd approve of me helping Bruce Wayne anyway.

"But you haven't even taken any plants yet."

I cursed under my breath. "Uh . . . there's a lot of digging out bushes and tree trimming. We probably won't get to planting until tomorrow. Or the next day."

She looked out the window. "Where's your truck?"

This day just kept getting worse and worse. My truck keys were in my purse, wherever that was.

I waved in the direction of the street. "Oh, you know. Out there."

She shook her head, looking at me like I was one of her mis-behaving children. "What does Joe think about you spendin' so much time with Mason?"

"He's just *fine* with it. He told me yesterday that he *trusts* me."

Putting her hands on her hips, she jutted out her hip. "What's that supposed to mean?"

I groaned. I didn't have the time or energy to deal with her right now. "Exactly what it sounds like, Violet. Joe trusts me." I headed for the door. "I don't know when I'll be back."

"Charge your phone!" she shouted after me.

Unsure what to do for transportation, I decided to check Merilee's for my purse since that was the last place I remembered having it. And if I couldn't find it there, I'd call a locksmith to get new keys for the truck. After that, I was looking for Bruce Wayne.

Even if it meant driving out to Weston's Garage alone.

Chapter
Twenty-Two

Thankfully the waitress at Merilee's had found my purse and put it behind the counter even though she didn't look too happy to see me. My cell phone was in it, but I hadn't put a charger in my new truck yet.

I drove to the Piggly Wiggly first. I hadn't expected to find David there, so I was pleasantly surprised to see him stacking cans on a shelf. He, on the other hand, looked surprised, but not so pleasantly.

"Bruce Wayne's in trouble."

David hung his head, rolling it from side to side. "What's that boy gone and done now?"

"Actually," I squatted next to him. "He hasn't done anything. It's one of those wrong time and place situations."

He pressed his lips together. "He seems to get into a lot of those pickles."

"Have you seen him?"

"Nope, not since he left for that preacher's house this morning."

"Do you know if Bruce Wayne had any dealings with Weston's Garage?"

David's shoulders slumped. "Don't tell me he's mixed up with those guys again."

My heart sunk. *Again*. So he had a history with them. "He left Merilee's with a couple of them this morning."

He shook his head. "I told him to stay away from those guys."

"What did he do for them?"

"Little jobs, mostly errands. He was in training to rise in the ranks."

"What does that mean?"

Sighing, he held out his palm. "Look, you can't just join one of those places. You have to work your way up, prove you're worthy. I'm surprised your boyfriend didn't tell you about it. He knows the drill. Why don't you ask him?"

"Because he's not here, and I need information now. When was the last time Bruce Wayne associated with them?"

"About the time he was arrested for murder. When he got out, Crocker had been arrested."

"Do you think he's working for them again?"

"I don't know. Maybe, maybe not. He was really trying to go down the straight and narrow, but it hasn't been working out too well."

I stood, brushing my hair from my face as I tried to figure out what to do next. "If you see him, will you ask him to call me? Tell him that I'm worried sick about him, and I want to help."

David's eyes narrowed. "Yeah, I noticed that. Why do you want to help him so bad? What's in it for you?"

"Maybe I want to help him because I like him."

A knowing grin spread across David's face.

"As a friend!" I added. "I've got more man troubles than I can handle. I sure as hades don't need any more." I looked around the store. "Do y'all sell cell phone charger cords? I lost mine."

"So you can take Bruce Wayne's call? We sure do . . ."

What in tarnation was up with people linking me to men in whom I had no interest? I rolled my eyes. "Where are they?"

He tilted his head to the left. "Aisle four."

"Thank you." I hurried over two aisles, trying to process what David had told me. The fact that Bruce Wayne had dealt with Weston's Garage in the past was a good sign. He might have actually gone with them willingly.

The menagerie of cords hanging in front of me was driving me crazy. I pulled my cell phone out of my purse, trying to match it to the cord ends on the chargers. Why did there have to be so many?

"We're in deep trouble." I heard Jonah Pruitt say. My eyes widened as I looked around to find him. When he spoke again, I realized he was one aisle over.

I grabbed the cord that seemed to fit my phone and followed his voice as it moved down the aisle.

"The police were at my door this morning accusing me of murder. I thought this was under control." He was silent for several seconds, and I couldn't be sure if he'd stopped or was still moving. Finally he spoke again, several feet ahead of me. "Well, that doesn't help . . . I had her right there within my reach before I got interrupted. When I finished with the detective nonsense, she was gone."

Was he talking about me? I was desperate to hear more, but he was at the end of the row and headed my way. I spun around to run the other way, but Jonah rounded the corner and spotted me before I could make good on my escape. He cast his gaze down and mumbled, "I've got to go." Then he stuffed his phone into his pants pocket. He'd changed out of his shorts and T-shirt into a polo and khakis. "Rose? What on earth are you doin' here? Aren't you supposed to be working on my yard?"

"Well . . ." I stalled. "We never came up with an approved estimate, so I put Bruce Wayne on another job today." The lies were rolling off my tongue today like butter off hot corn on the cob.

"I was disappointed that you were already gone when I finished my interview with Detective Taylor."

"Sorry, I had another job to bid." I shifted my weight. "What did Detective Taylor want?"

He waved his hand as though my question was nonsense and he was batting it away. "Nothin'. They just wanted to know if I noticed any suspicious behavior when I was at poor Gina's house. I guess I have another funeral to officiate."

"Did he mention how she died?"

His mouth twisted as though he was thinking about it. "Now that you mention it, he didn't."

Despite being in the middle of all this mess, I still didn't know how any of these women had *actually* died. "I ran into Christy Hansen this morning."

His smile fell. "Is that so? And how is she?"

"Angrier than a cat tossed into a bath. She's lookin' for you, and it's not to discuss Sunday's sermon."

He gulped. "Thanks for the warning."

"Yeah." I wasn't sure why I had told him. He probably deserved her wrath, but if she shot him, I didn't want to live with the guilt of knowing I could have helped prevent it.

"Well, I've gotta get going." I pointed my thumb toward the registers.

"Wouldn't you know it? I'm done too." He was carrying a basket with a loaf of bread and a block of cheddar cheese. "We can check out together."

Oh yippee.

We walked to the registers together, Jonah staying closer to me than necessary.

David looked up from stacking his cans, watching us with curiosity.

Placing my cord on the conveyor belt, I pulled out my wallet, purposely avoiding Jonah's gaze. "If Monday's your day off, how come you planned for the big revival to start tonight?"

Jonah released an exaggerated sigh. "The Lord may have had a day of rest, but my work never seems to be done. I wanted to get in five solid nights."

"Did you have revivals at your old church? I'm not sure where you were before you moved to Henryetta."

He stiffened. "Why the sudden curiosity?"

I wasn't sure, but if Jonah had anything to do with these deaths, maybe he'd swindled old ladies before. Maybe it was why Joe had warned me about him. The more I knew, the better my chances of getting out of this—and of helping Bruce Wayne. But Jonah wasn't going to just tell me for the sake of telling me. I'd been giving him the brush off, and I needed to be nice to him. I tried to give him a coy smile, but I wasn't sure if it worked or just made me look constipated.

The cashier leveled her gaze at me. "That will be $18.79."

I handed her a twenty, turning back to Jonah. "You know more about me than I know about you. That hardly seems fair."

He relaxed, resting his shoulder on a display rack. "I was in Texas before here. Homer, Texas. Ever heard of it?"

I shook my head and took my change from the cashier. "Can't say I have."

Laughing, he put his two items on the belt, but he looked nervous. "I'm not surprised. Most people haven't."

"So why move to Henryetta?"

"Oh, I don't know." He continued to look down at his merchandise. "It seemed like a nice town, ready for a spiritual revolution."

"You sure have added a lot of church members in a short time."

"I told you, it's our loving, accepting attitude."

The cashier handed me my bag.

Jonah looked up, and something in his eyes caught my attention. Desperation. "Rose, will you wait a second and let me walk you to your truck?"

"Uh . . ." I wasn't so sure it was a good idea, but Jonah seemed to have been forthright in his answer . . . well, as forthright as he seemed capable of being. I hated to lose an opportunity to gather more information. "Okay."

The cashier frowned in disapproval.

I stood at the end of the aisle. "I have to say I was impressed with your service yesterday. And I'm speechless you put me in your video." I was sure he'd take it as flattery.

"So you'll consider coming back?"

I tilted my head with a shy smile. "I'll think about it."

A grin spread across his face, and he looked almost genuine, like he wasn't a televangelist, just a happy man. He paid for his food and snatched up his bag, walking outside with me.

"Have you had lunch yet?" he asked.

"I . . ." I hadn't, but I needed to look for Bruce Wayne. But my stomach betrayed me, growling at the mention of food.

"I know you're a busy businesswoman, but you need to take time to eat. Besides I really need to talk to you about something. Lunch will be my treat."

Jonah was dropping his guard, and I had a chance to get more answers. Maybe he knew where Bruce Wayne was. "I can't stay for long."

He pointed to the park at the end of the street. "How about we grab something and go sit in the shade."

Being out in the open made me feel better, even if it was the park I'd escaped to the night of Momma's death. "Okay."

Jonah stopped at an authentic Mexican food restaurant that served takeout. I had recently noticed it next to the café I'd eaten at that fateful night months ago . . .

Everything always seemed to be swinging me back to Momma's death. Would it ever be behind me?

We ordered tacos and drinks, and then walked to the park, sitting on a bench overlooking the small pond. A small breeze kicked up, blowing off the water and bringing the temperature down several degrees under the tree branches.

"I love this park," Jonah said, handing me a taco. "I like to come here when I'm stumped on a sermon or I need to think."

"Do you get stumped very often?"

He laughed. "More often than you'd probably think."

I took a bite of my taco, surprised at how good it was. "I've never eaten at this restaurant. I didn't even know they were here until a week ago."

"Yeah, it's new. It opened a few weeks before your nursery, but they're Mexicans and they're pretty small, so they didn't get the same attention as you and Violet did with your business."

My hand stopped mid-air.

Jonah's eyes widened. "Oh, I hope you don't think I'm begrudging you the publicity. But I understand how it works; citizens with deep roots are the pillars in a community like this one. The transplants live on the fringe."

"You don't seem to be doing too badly."

He shrugged. "True. But I'll never fit in here. I think that's part of the reason I'm drawn to the outcasts and strays of society. I want to give them a place where they feel welcome and at home."

If Jonah Pruitt was giving me a propaganda speech, he was doing a mighty fine job. Sitting under the shade trees, he seemed different. The TV personality had faded away, leaving a man who looked a little beaten down.

"What was Thomas doing at the church on Friday?"

He took a bite, then swallowed. "I started an outreach program for teens on the edge. Kids who are getting into trouble, but not past saving." He turned to me. "Not that anyone is past saving; it's just easier to turn some back into productive members of society than it is with others."

"Oh." I was starting to rethink my assumptions about Reverend Jonah Pruitt.

He hung his head over for several seconds, looking very much like a defeated man, and then he sat up with a sigh. "It's been a rough week."

"You had two members of your church die in one week."

"Three in two weeks." He put down his food, suddenly looking nervous. "I know you helped Bruce Wayne, and that you were instrumental in putting Daniel Crocker in prison."

Leery, I rested my hands in my lap, wondering what he was getting at.

He focused on something on the other side of the pond. "This has happened before."

"What's happened before?" And then I realized what he was saying. "People dying? Is that why you left Homer?"

He nodded. "There were two deaths, but they were spaced months apart. No one noticed the connection to me, but it was why I left. I needed to make sure no one else got hurt."

I sank back into the seat, my voice hardening. "Did they leave their money to you too?"

His eyes grew wild. "I didn't know Dorothy Thorntonbury did that, Rose. You have to believe me. I was as shocked as Christy was when I found out."

"Did the others leave their money or houses to you?"

"I have no idea. No one has come to me about it yet."

"So other than coming to your church, what's the tie to you?"

He cleared his throat, looking uncomfortable. "I spent time with them."

"What does that mean?"

He squirmed. "Older women tend to get lonely . . ."

I scrunched my eyes closed. "Eww. I don't want to hear any more."

"No!" Jonah shouted. "Not like that! I just spent time with them is all. They like the company, and I like the cooking. Sometimes we play cards or watch TV."

"So why would you eating Sunday dinner with them get them killed?"

"I have no idea."

"Were the women in Homer both older?"

He shook his head, looking down. "No, the first one was an older woman whom I'd visited many times. I was quite fond of her." He paused. "But the second was younger. She was my age." He cleared his throat. "We'd begun spending time together."

"You two were dating?"

He nodded.

"And so you left? Just like that? You saw a pattern between two dead women that the police didn't, and you just *left*? Didn't you want justice for your girlfriend?"

"She wasn't my girlfriend. We had only gone out a few times." He hunched over, wringing his hands. "You don't understand."

"Then help me understand."

He kept his gaze lowered. "There's a reason I help troubled youth on the fringes of society. I was there once, and I have a criminal record to show for it. Jail time included. When I got out, I vowed to go the straight and narrow. If the police found out . . . let's just say I'd be their top suspect."

"Aren't you already their top suspect?"

He cringed. "If they find out, I suspect I'd get a trial like Bruce Wayne's. That's why I was checking into you and how you helped him."

What he was not saying hit me like a two-by-four. "You want me to help you." I shook my head. "I can't. I'm not a private investigator, Jonah."

"You helped Bruce Wayne."

I stood, facing the water. "That was different."

"Not really."

"It is. I knew he was innocent."

"I'm innocent. I swear it."

Something in his desperation made me believe him, but I still didn't quite trust him. "If I agree to help you, you have to tell me everything. The truth."

"Deal."

This was crazy. I helped put two murderers behind bars and now people expected me to solve crimes. What on earth were we paying the Henryetta police for?

I sat down on the bench and wiped my hands on my jeans. "Okay, but first I'm going to try something, and it's going to look and sound crazy."

He didn't even hesitate. "Okay."

I grabbed his hand and closed my eyes. This was insane. But what if Neely Kate was right? What if I could use my visions to see things that could help rather than hurt? Besides, if Jonah thought I was a loon, he'd send me away, and I could get out of this guilt-free.

"What are you doing?" he asked.

"You asked me if I knew things . . . Well, I do, and this is how. But you gotta keep quiet."

"Okay."

What did I want to know? If he was innocent, but also if he knew anything that would help me find Bruce Wayne and figure out who the killer was. I concentrated on Jonah and his time in Henryetta and how he'd come here from Homer. I waited for a good ten seconds, and just when I'd decided nothing was going to happen, a vision appeared in my head.

I was in a dark room. When my eyes adjusted, I saw it was a bedroom. The sound of heavy breathing filled the quiet, and it took me half a second to realize it was coming from me.

I moved to the door and called out, "Who's there?"

When no one answered, I grabbed a baseball bat from under the bed and opened the door, my hand shaking so badly it took several attempts.

"It's nothing. It's nothing. It's nothing," I mumbled over and over in a low chant as I tiptoed down the hall. Stopping at the entrance to the living room, I slowly spun around. I didn't see anything so I let out a loud exhale, my shoulders slumping in relief until I heard a low voice from the dark shadows of the dining room.

"I brought you a little present."

I nearly dropped the bat as I spun around to see who had called out. My heart beat against my ribcage when I saw a dark figure in the shadows, standing behind someone who was tied to a kitchen chair with rope.

The shadows hid the hostage's face, but I could tell that she was wearing what looked like a silky nightgown. Her feet were bare. Her hands were on her thighs, and the moonlight lit up the diamond ring on her finger. She had to be unconscious because her head was leaning forward, her long dark hair covering her face.

"Why are you doing this?" I asked in a whine.

The person with the hood held a gun to the woman's head. "You'll thank me later." Then a loud sound filled the room, and the woman's body jerked as blood splattered against the wall. I shouted my alarm, and the murderer handed the gun to me, to Jonah. "Take it. You have work to do, Jonas."

The vision faded, and my eyes flew open. "Someone's going to kill a woman in your kitchen."

His face paled. "How do you know that?"

The vision had sent an adrenaline rush through my body, but now it crashed and I started violently trembling as though it was thirty degrees outside and I was in a wet swimming suit. My stomach rebelled, and I leaned over the other side of the bench, vomiting onto the grass.

"Rose, how do you know that?" Jonah's voice rose to a high pitch.

I wiped my forehead with the back of my hand, tears streaming down my cheeks. I fought to catch my breath.

I'd just watched someone die.

I'd had visions of myself dead and Joe dying, but I'd never witnessed someone else's actual death. As violent as it was, I knew I could have witnessed far worse things. The poor woman could have been tortured. But this was the worst thing *I'd* ever seen.

"Rose, how do you know that?" Jonah was panicking.

I needed to get control. Freaking out wasn't going to do either of us any good. I took a deep breath. "I . . . I have visions. I can see things in the future. I saw a woman murdered in your kitchen."

Jonah made the sign of the cross. "Jesus, Mary, and Joseph."

I gaped. "I thought you were Protestant."

"My church is non-denominational, but I was raised Catholic. Some habits die hard."

Wrong choice of words. I threw up again.

Jonah was calmer. He'd gotten ahold of himself sooner than I had. But then again, he hadn't watched someone get shot in the head. "Why would you have *that* vision?"

When my stomach settled, I brushed back the hair hanging in my face. "I wanted to see if you were telling me the truth about being innocent. That was what I saw."

"So you believe me?"

I nodded, a queasy feeling still in the pit of my stomach.

"Who was the poor woman?"

I swallowed down a sob. "I don't know. The kitchen was dark, and she was tied to a chair. Her head was slumped forward, so I couldn't see her face."

"Are you sure she was murdered?"

The scene replayed in my head, blood and all, making me queasy. I nodded again, fighting to keep it together. "A person wearing a hood pointed a gun at the woman's head and shot her."

"Oh, God." Jonah started to hyperventilate. "Who killed her?"

"I don't know. I couldn't recognize the voice, and the person's features were completely concealed. He or she said that they'd brought you a present and that you'd thank them for it later. Then the person shot whoever the woman was and told you it was time to get to work."

"Work? Doing what?"

"I don't know."

Jonah rested his head between his hands. "We don't know anything."

"That's not true. I know you're not involved. You were confused and horrified."

"Can we keep this from happening?"

I squeezed my eyes shut. "Not everything I see happens, so there's a chance we can stop it. I just don't know how to at this point."

"Lord help us."

I needed to clear my head and think straight. I cast a glance at Jonah. "Why did the person in my vision call you Jonas?"

His face paled even more. "That's my real name. I changed it to Jonah when I became a minister because of my record. The biblical Jonah needed a big wakeup call to do God's work. It seemed fitting."

"Who around here knows your real name?"

"No one. I made sure of it." He paused. "Some people don't believe in rehabilitation."

"But you do. That's why you started the support group to give those kids a chance. Who shows up for it?"

"Teens and rehabilitated criminals who become mentors to the kids."

"How do you know they're rehabilitated?"

He shrugged. "They have to provide references. Like employers."

"Does anyone in the group work at Weston's Garage?"

His eyes flew wide at the mention of the business name, and then he tried to cover his reaction. "I'm not at liberty to tell you. All participants are guaranteed anonymity."

I grabbed his arm. "This is important, Jonah. Do any of them work at Weston's?"

He grimaced. "Several."

My fingers pinched his arm. "Define several."

He pulled loose from my grasp. "Rose, I've sworn to give them protection."

"Jonah, this could be the difference between life and death."

He rubbed his temples. "I can't believe I'm doing this." He swallowed. "Five, maybe six."

"Is there a bald guy that comes? With snake tattoos on his neck?"

Jonah tensed. "How did you know that?"

My chest felt like an elephant had sat on it. "I don't think you're running a support group."

"Of course, I am. You don't believe me?"

"I believe that you think that's what you're doing. But it sounds like your group is using it to recruit kids for Daniel Crocker's gang."

"What? No! I sit in on the meetings myself. They never discuss illegal activities. We have a Bible study."

"What happens after the meetings?"

He looked bewildered. "They leave."

"Do they hang around in the parking lot and talk?"

"Yeah, sometimes. Sometimes they just leave."

I didn't know what Bruce Wayne had seen at the church, but I was sure it involved the support group. "Did Bruce Wayne go to your support group last Friday after I left?"

Jonah stood and began to pace, looping his hands around the back of his neck. "Rose, I can't tell you that. This group is supposed to be anonymous."

"Jonah, do you understand the enormity of this? Telling me whether he went or not could mean saving his life!"

He closed his eyes and shook his head in frustration. "Yes. He came."

I jumped off the bench and headed to the park entrance. "I have to go."

"Wait!" he called after me. "Where are you going?"

"I don't know yet, but if you see Christy Hansen, run the other way. She has a gun, and I have no doubt she plans to shoot you with it."

"Wait!"

Exasperated, I turned, putting my hand on my hip. "*What*?"

"Does this mean you're going to help me?"

Was I? I didn't owe Jonah Pruitt anything, but if helping him meant preventing the death of the woman in my vision and finding out who killed the other women, how could I refuse? "I'll help you as best I can. I have to find Bruce Wayne first."

As I half-ran to my truck, I knew where I needed to go next. Weston's Garage.

Chapter Twenty-Three

When I got into the truck, I tore the charger cord out of the package and plugged in my phone. The thing was so dead I'd have to wait a while before I could make a call.

Mason was bound to wonder where I'd disappeared to, not to mention he was probably worried if his secretary hadn't given him my message. Had he figured out that I'd been kidnapped from the sheriff's office? I needed to tell him what I'd learned since leaving with Christy that morning.

Bottom line, I had to talk to him, and the sooner the better. But could I risk going to the courthouse? It was either that or call him. If I went to my house to use the home phone, Christy might be at her aunt's house, waiting for me. I could go back to the nursery, but I honestly didn't want to deal with Violet again. I also didn't want to wait for my cell phone to charge. What if Mason had news about Bruce Wayne?

The courthouse it was.

I parked my truck several blocks away. I worried about getting through security since both guards knew me, but Ol' Matt was on duty, and he greeted me with a big smile. "Second visit today, huh, Rose? Didn't you leave with Mr. Deveraux this morning? Here to see Neely Kate this time?"

"Nope, I'm here to see Mason Deveraux again. Do you know if he's come back?"

"I've been at this post since you all took off this morning, and I haven't seen hide nor hair of Mr. Deveraux since."

My shoulders slumped in defeat. This was the only entrance Mason would have used. "Thanks, Matt."

"You still wantin' to come inside?"

"Yeah, I might as well see Neely Kate since I'm here."

When I walked through the door to the personal property department, I found her sitting at her desk, thumbing through a pile of papers with a bored expression on her face. When she saw me, her face broke into a big grin. "Rose!"

I leaned my hands on the counter. "Can you take a break? I really need to talk."

Her smile faded. "Of course." She looked over her shoulder at the girl sitting at the other desk. "I'll be back soon."

The girl rolled her eyes.

"You can't find good help these days," Neely Kate muttered. I couldn't help thinking that Jimmy DeWade had probably said the same thing about her before he'd decided to start murdering people.

I would have laughed at the irony, but I was too on edge.

We took the stairs down to the basement and sat at a table next to the vending machines. The basement was chilly, and Neely Kate rubbed her arms. "Rose, you look like you saw a ghost."

"Close. I saw a murder."

"*What?*"

I squinted my eyes closed, trying to block out the memory. "I did what you suggested, Neely Kate. I made myself have a vision with Jonah Pruitt, and I saw a woman killed in his kitchen." I looked up at her, and my voice broke. "She was shot in the head."

Neely Kate's mouth formed an O as she stared at me in disbelief for several seconds. "So Jonah Pruitt really is a murderer."

"No, it was someone else. Jonah doesn't have anything to do with any of this."

"But what about Miss Dorothy's will? Her house?"

"He swears he didn't know anything about it. He says he found out after she died."

"And you believe him?"

I took a deep breath. "Yeah, I do."

She nodded. "That's good enough for me."

This was part of what I loved about Neely Kate. She took me at my word without a single doubt.

I told her about the rest of my morning, but I just couldn't bring myself to tell her about Joe coming home yesterday and confiding his big secret. She'd kill to know, and for all her gossiping ways, I trusted her to keep my secret. But talking about it made it more real. Right now I could pretend it was just a bad dream.

Neely Kate rubbed her arms. "So what are you going to do?"

"I have to help Bruce Wayne."

"Of course you do, but how are you gonna do it?"

"I'm going out to Weston's Garage."

Neely Kate narrowed her gaze. "Do you really think that's a good idea, Rose? What if Thomas was right? What if Crocker's guys are pissed at you?"

I wasn't stupid. The thought of going out there scared me to death, but I didn't have a choice. I had to see if Bruce Wayne was okay.

"Maybe you should wait for Mason. He seems pretty willing to help you two."

"Yeah, I know." What she said made sense, but it seemed wrong to sit around without doing anything.

"I know you." She leaned forward. "You're sitting here thinking about going out there anyway despite everything I just said."

A lump burned my throat. "I can't just sit here and leave him out there, Neely Kate. What if they kidnapped him? What if they're hurting him?"

She stared into my eyes. "Rose, you don't even know if he's there. For all you know, he's back home, kicked back in his Lazyboy and smokin' a reefer." She grabbed my hand, holding it tightly. "I know you feel responsible for him, but you can't just strut out there like nothin' can happen to you. Because *it can*. Just think it through a little bit before you do anything, and then think it through a little more. Okay?"

She was right, and I knew it, even if I felt like I was abandoning Bruce Wayne. Mason had gone to the sheriff's office to get them to go out to Weston's Garage. They had a much better chance of helping my friend than I did. But I had to make sure they'd followed through.

Neely Kate pulled me into a hug. "I don't know what I'd do without you."

"I'm not going anywhere." Then I shot her a glare. "But don't be asking me to try to force any more visions. I don't ever want to see anything like that again."

Neely Kate sucked in her lower lip, watching me and struggling with what she wanted to say. She shifted her weight. "Look Rose, remember when I told you I thought your visions were a blessing but you think they're a curse?"

"Yeah."

"Well, maybe we're looking at it all wrong. Maybe they're not a blessing or a curse, maybe your visions are a responsibility."

I pressed my lips together in irritation. "What does that mean?"

"You just saw a murder, which had to be shocking, and I'm so, so sorry for that. But you saw Joe's death, and you changed it." Her eyes burned with her earnestness. "You have the power to really help people, Rose. You have the power to save them."

I stood and turned my back to her. I didn't want that power. "That's not me, Neely Kate." Tears swam in my eyes. "I can't handle that kind of responsibility. I can barely take care of Muffy, and she's a dog." I shook my head. "You don't know what you're asking me to do."

She stood behind me and wrapped her arm around my back, resting her head on my shoulder. "I do know, and I'm sorry. You saw someone die. But what if you can stop it? What if you can save her life?"

I leaned my head against hers. "Joe will have a conniption."

"Like that's ever stopped you before."

I sighed. Neely Kate was on a roll. I took a deep breath and braced my shoulders. I'd cried enough. It was time to do something. "Okay."

"You need to tell Mason."

I shook my head. "You're like a ping pong ball. Mason won't approve of this."

She gave me a smug smile. "Don't be so sure of that."

We took the elevator, and I waved goodbye when she got off on the first floor, staying on so I could go to the second.

Cecelia was at her desk when I got to Mason's office. She took one look at me and frowned, but she quickly looked down to hide her reaction and kept typing.

I decided being extra nice was the best way to handle her. "Hi, Cecelia. Has Mason come back since I called you?"

She kept her eyes glued to her computer screen. "No."

"Has he called you since he left?"

Her gaze lifted, and her eyes hardened. "You are not allowed to know about Mr. Deveraux's official office business."

"I'm not asking about that. I'm asking if he's called you."

She glared at me for a moment. "Yes."

"And did you give him my message?"

"Yes."

"And . . . ? Did he say anything?"

She turned back to her work. "No."

I considered asking her to give me his cell phone number so I could call him from here, but I didn't want her to hear my conversation. And if I went into his office to make the call, I couldn't be sure she wouldn't eavesdrop. I might be getting bolder about my visions, but I wasn't ready to shout about them from the rooftop.

Matt waved to me when I passed through the security line. "You have a good day, Rose."

"Thanks, Matt." I stopped and spun back to face him. "If you see Mr. Deveraux, can you tell him I stopped by his office, and that I'm looking for him?"

"Shouldn't you tell his secretary?"

Apparently, that was a waste of time. "Everyone knows you're the most reliable employee in all of Fenton County."

He waved his hand. "Aren't you sweet? Of course I'll tell him. Even if you're exaggerating."

"It's not an exaggeration. It's the unvarnished truth."

My phone hadn't charged by the time I'd got back to my truck. Since I was used to charging it at home, I hadn't realized it wouldn't charge when the engine was turned off. I was practically back where I'd started.

I sat behind the steering wheel of my truck, staring at the courthouse. Neely Kate had a good point. If I wanted to save that poor woman, I needed to talk to Jonah again. Whoever was killing the women in Henryetta seemed to be targeting women to whom he was connected. He was getting ready for his revival, but I was sure he'd take a few minutes to talk to me.

The church grounds were bustling with activity when I pulled into the parking lot. A giant tent had been erected, and men were in the process of setting up chairs. We'd delivered extra pots of flowers, and they'd been set around the edges of the tent. I had to admit that the place looked great. Pride warmed my chest as I considered the part we'd played in the transformation.

When I couldn't find Jonah outside, I went into the church office. Rhonda was sitting at her desk still wearing her long sleeves despite the fact it was ninety degrees outside and the church wasn't very cold. She grimaced when I entered the room, looking down her nose and puckering her mouth in disapproval.

Why did secretaries hate me so much?

"Rhonda, I need to talk to Jonah."

Her face puckered even more. "That's *Reverend Pruitt* to you. And he's busy."

"This is important."

She picked up a stack of papers and tapped them on the desk. "Nothing is more important than the Lord's work. He's preparing for the service tonight."

"If you'll just tell him I'm here—"

"I'll be sure to tell him you stopped by, Miss Gardner. Good day."

Even though Jonah's door was closed, he might be inside. I considered ignoring Rhonda and just going in. She wouldn't reach me before I got the door open, although I wouldn't put it past her to tackle me when she *did* reach me. I decided to make a round through the church to look for him, and if he still didn't turn up, I'd come back and storm the door. The element of surprise would be on my side.

I left the office and headed for the sanctuary, thinking it might be a quiet place to sort through my thoughts and come up with a plan. Jonah must have been thinking the same thing because I found him sitting on the steps to the altar, his forehead resting in his hand. He didn't hear me until I was several feet away.

He looked up at me with a tear-stained face. "This is all my fault, Rose. All those women are dead because of me."

I sat on the step next to him. "It isn't your fault, but I think you're right. Someone is killing them because of you."

He released a moan and leaned over his knees.

"Can you think of anyone who has a grudge against you? Either here or back in Homer?"

He rubbed his mouth with his fingertips. "I don't know, Rose. My church isn't exactly conservative. I've ruffled a few feathers along the way."

"I'm gonna need specifics, Jonah. Anyone in particular come to mind?"

"I don't know."

"Think. This might help Bruce Wayne too." I gasped, an idea coming to me. "Could you have upset one of the guys in your troubled youth group? Could they be killing these women to try and make it look like you killed them?"

"Why would they do that? I give them a safe place to come and talk." Jonah's head rose, and he took in a deep breath. "Wait, there was an incident that turned ugly."

"What happened?"

"About three weeks ago, Sly, one of the older guys, a mentor, showed up to a meeting drunk. I told him that he was a negative influence on the teens, and he had to leave. He wasn't very happy with my request and started to throw chairs around." Jonah sighed. "I tried my best to calm him down, but I finally had to resort to calling the police. Sly went even crazier. He was shouting about how everything had turned to crap when Daniel Crocker got locked away." He lifted his eyebrows with a shy grin. "Only he didn't say crap."

"I bet."

"The police threw him in jail for destruction of property. I didn't press charges but he got into trouble with his parole officer. He blamed me for it, and I haven't seen him since."

"Was it the bald guy with the snake tattoos?"

He nodded.

This was good. A solid lead I could actually take to Mason. "If it happened a few weeks ago that was right before Miss Laura died. The only problem is how would Sly know about the deaths in Homer. Did you know him there?"

"No. And even if I did, no one—and I mean no one—pieced those murders together. Maybe it's just a coincidence."

"Do you really believe that?"

He didn't answer me.

"How did the women in Homer die?"

"They were poisoned."

Could the women in Henryetta have been poisoned? One more piece of information for Mason. "I think Bruce Wayne saw something here at your church last Friday, something that scared him. After we left your house this morning, Bruce Wayne stayed at Merilee's while I went to get Mason. But when we got back, Bruce Wayne was gone, and the waitress said that he'd left with two guys. One matches Sly's description and the other sounds like Thomas."

"Do you think they made him go with them?"

"I don't know. Maybe. Maybe not. The bald guy could have been his friend from when Bruce Wayne did some odd jobs for Daniel Crocker. Before he was arrested for murder last year."

Jonah shook his head. "No, Sly isn't anyone's friend. And if Thomas is with him, that's bad."

"I bet they took him to Weston's Garage."

He squeezed his eyes closed. "This is all my fault. What am I going to do?"

"You're going to pretend like you don't know anything, and you're going to have your revival tonight."

He shook his head, wild eyed. "I can't."

"Yes, you can. I'm going to go find Mason and tell him everything."

"Everything?"

"As much as I can without getting you in trouble."

"Okay." He sounded defeated.

I grabbed his hand. "Everything's going to work out. You'll see."

"Thanks, Rose."

I stood. "You coming out?"

"I think I want to just sit here and pray for a few minutes."

The church grounds were still bustling when I headed for my truck. Rhonda stood outside the tent with her clipboard pressed against her chest as she talked to several workmen. She shot a glare in my direction before she turned back to her task.

I needed to talk to Mason before I did anything else, so I decided to head back to the courthouse. I'd camp out in his office until he came back if need be.

Halfway to the courthouse my cell phone sprang to life. Before I could look Mason's number up, the phone began to ring, and I wasn't all that surprised to see who was calling.

Chapter
Twenty-Four

The moment I said "hello," Mason let loose.

"Where the hell have you been? Why did you leave the sheriff's office? You didn't even tell me you were going. I've been worried sick."

"I'm sorry." I didn't blame him for his anger. "I can explain."

Mason took a deep breath and replied much more calmly. "I'm listening."

"Did Cecelia give you my message about Christy Hansen?"

"What message?"

I groaned. "She told me that she did. I called her around lunchtime, as soon as I could get to a phone. Christy Hansen came into the sheriff's office with a gun, demanding justice. She was high as a kite. She saw me and remembered seeing me at the church. Somehow she came to the conclusion I was Jonah's girlfriend and took me hostage to go find Jonah."

"Oh, God." He sounded panicked. "Are you all right?"

"Yeah, I'm fine. I got away from her after we wrecked into the back of an SUV. I distracted her with the hope that she'd run off the road or something."

"That was good thinking, although you could have been hurt in the crash."

"We weren't going very fast. And I knew I had to get away. She's crazy. I have no doubt that she would have shot me." I pulled the truck into a parking lot since I didn't need to go to the courthouse.

"Why didn't you call me?"

"My cell phone was dead, and I didn't have your number. I ran to the nursery and used the business phone to call your office. I told Cecelia to call 911 about Christy running around town with a gun looking for Jonah. I also told her to tell you I was okay and would explain it all when I talked to you."

"Well, someone just spent her last day as a Fenton County employee, because she didn't breathe a word of any of that," he said. He paused, sounding worried again. "How in the world could you get kidnapped at the sheriff's station at gunpoint without anyone noticing?"

"The receptionist saw Christy come into the waiting room, then left to go to the back before she noticed the gun, and the guy sitting with me had his eyes closed and was wearing headphones." My voice hardened. "You told me I was perfectly safe sitting out there."

"I know. I'm sorry. I've never heard of anyone getting kidnapped in the Fenton County Sheriff's waiting room before. Leave it to you to be the first."

"Did you find Bruce Wayne?"

"No. I came up with a dead end."

"Did the sheriff deputies even go out there?" I asked, irritated.

"Yeah, they did. They questioned the guys in the shop, but they said they hadn't seen Bruce Wayne since he was arrested last year."

"Like they're going to admit they forced him to go with them."

"We don't know they forced him, Rose."

"True . . . I found out that Bruce Wayne used to do some jobs for Daniel Crocker before both of their arrests."

"How did you find that out?"

"I asked David. And I know a whole lot more than that."

"Where are you right now?"

"In the parking lot of the China Paradise Buffet."

"Do you have time to meet me somewhere and talk?"

The smell of Chinese food wafted out of the restaurant, making my stomach rumble.

"Sure, if you meet me here. I'm starving after I lost my lunch."

"I'm sure there's a story there. Go through the buffet without me. I'll be there in a few minutes."

Fifteen minutes later, I was fumbling with chopsticks and dropping lo mein on the table when Mason sat down across from me. I was the only customer in the restaurant so I knew he hadn't had trouble finding me. He'd lost his tie since I'd last seen him and his blue dress shirt was unbuttoned at the collar. His blond hair was rumpled like he'd run his hand through it and hadn't thought to fix it. Looking at him now, I could see why all the women in Henryetta were after him.

He grinned. "There's a trick to those."

"A trick I can't seem to master." I tossed down my chopsticks and picked up a fork. I was too hungry to eat one noodle at time.

He stared at me for a moment. "After you told me you were in an accident, I was worried about what you'd look like when I found you."

"My stomach and shoulder are a bit sore from the seatbelt, but no worse for wear."

He put his elbow on the table and rested his chin on his clasped hands. "I take it you've had a busy afternoon?"

"You have no idea." I put down my fork and searched Mason's eyes. "I'm about to tell you a secret about Jonah Pruitt, and you have to promise not to tell anyone."

His playfulness fell away. "Rose, you know that I can't do that."

I straightened my back in defensiveness. "I thought you were my friend, Mason Deveraux."

His face hardened. "You know damn good and well that I am."

"You also told me I could tell you if I saw something bad."

Leaning forward, he lowered his voice. "You had a vision?"

Tears filled my eyes, and I nodded.

"Was it about you?"

I took a deep breath. Crying wasn't going to help anything. I needed to save my tears for the funeral of the poor woman if I didn't figure out a way to save her. "No. I saw someone being murdered."

"You *saw* it happen?" Mason leaned forward. "Are you okay?"

I swallowed the lump in my throat. "I'm better now."

"What happened?"

"After I left the nursery, I went to the Piggly Wiggly to talk to David. I was buying a cord to charge my cell phone when I ran into Jonah. I warned him to watch out for Christy, and he asked me if we could go somewhere and talk. I thought maybe I could get some answers from him, so we picked up some lunch and took it into the park."

Mason looked concerned. "Do you really think that was a good idea? He's a murder suspect."

"He seemed desperate. And I told you, I thought I might be able to get some answers."

"So did you?"

I nodded. "He told me he needed me to help him like I'd helped Bruce Wayne."

"Did he know about your visions?"

"He didn't before, but he does now."

Mason was silent for several seconds, and then he said matter-of-factly, "You had your vision with him."

"Yes, but I did it on purpose."

"Rose." Mason frowned as he realized the seriousness of what I'd told him. "You said you never do that."

Closing my eyes, I rested my forehead in my hand. "I know. But he was desperate for help, and I didn't know if I could trust him. So I forced a vision. I touched him and thought about the murders and wanting to know if he was innocent."

"What did you see?"

Biting my lip, I took several breathes. "I was Jonah, of course. I was in his bedroom, and it was dark. He heard a noise in another part of his house and went to investigate. Someone was in his kitchen, but they were wearing a hood so I couldn't see their face." My voice broke. "There was a woman tied to a chair."

His hand found mine, and his voice softened. "You don't have to tell me now."

I looked up into his face. "Yes, I do."

He nodded. "Okay, but take your time."

I pushed my plate to the side. I'd lost my appetite, and I'd hardly had anything to eat. "I couldn't see her face. I think she was unconscious because her head was hanging forward."

"Do you remember anything about her clothes? Her shoes? What color hair she had?" he asked softly.

"Um." I rubbed my temple. "She had on a white nightgown, I think. It was kind of shiny. She didn't have shoes. She was barefoot."

"Any polish on her toes?"

I lifted my gaze in surprise. "I don't know." I closed my eyes trying to remember. "No, I don't think so. But it was dark. The only light was the moon streaming in from the window. It made the diamond ring on her hand sparkle."

"That's okay. This is good. What about her hair?"

"Dark and long."

"Do you remember if she was dark skinned or light?"

I shook my head, in frustration. "No, I don't remember."

His thumb stroked the back of my hand. "It's okay. You're doing great. You saw something really frightening so it might take a bit of time to remember it all. Take a deep breath and relax."

"I saw someone murdered, Mason. He shot her in the head. How can I relax?" I started crying and hid my face behind my hands in embarrassment.

Mason slid out of his seat and into the booth next to me, wrapping an arm around my back and pulling my head to his chest. "I'm sorry."

"It was so awful, Mason. He just shot her. And her head . . ." I sobbed harder, while he held me and let me cry. The terrible image just wouldn't go away. When I got ahold of myself, I took several breaths so I could talk. "The murderer told Jonah it was a present."

"So Jonah was involved?"

"No, Jonah was horrified and scared. And totally clueless. I was in his head, so I know that's how he really felt. He had no idea who the murderer was or what the murderer meant when they handed the gun to him and told him it was time to get to work."

"What did you do after you saw the vision?"

"I knew I had to save Bruce Wayne. And that I had to see you. I went back to the courthouse, but you weren't there." I decided to keep my conversation with Neely Kate to myself. "So I went back to Jonah to ask him if anyone had a grudge against him."

"Quite a few people have grudges against Jonah Pruitt," Mason muttered. "He's ticked off most of the ministers and

242

church boards in this town. And a lot of those church boards are filled with the more affluent Henryetta citizens. Trust me, I've heard quite a few complaints."

"You can't file charges for stealing their church members, can you?"

"No, that's not a crime. But coercing elderly women out of their inheritance could be. Dorothy Thorntonbury wasn't the first time this happened. The Henryetta police were starting to watch him, but I called the state police after you told me Joe warned you about Pruitt, and they said there were two instances in Homer, Texas, where Jonah Pruitt last established a church."

My heart stopped. Had Jonah lied to me? He claimed not to have known that Miss Dorothy had willed her money to his church. Maybe he didn't know about the instances in Homer either. For the moment, I had to go with my instinct that he was innocent. "Maybe so, but Jonah ticked off a guy named Sly who works at Weston's Garage. Sly used to be involved with Daniel Crocker." I looked up at Mason. "Sly is a big bald guy with snake tattoos on his neck."

Mason tensed. "Shit."

"But there's more. The part you can't tell anyone. And if you can't promise me, I can't tell you."

Mason dropped his arm and rested it on the table as he leaned down to look me in the face. "Rose, you can't expect this of me. You're putting my job on the line."

I cringed, my hopes sinking. "I hadn't considered that."

"You need to tell me anyway. People's lives are at risk. What you know might save them."

"He asked me to help him." My eyes pleaded with him. "He asked me not to tell."

"You don't owe him anything, Rose. Why are you doing this?"

I didn't answer.

Mason groaned, leaning his head back on the seat. "But you didn't owe Bruce Wayne anything either, did you?"

"I suppose not." I answered softly.

We were quiet for several moments before Mason sat up again, resting his arms on the table and not looking at me. "Can you just tell me the part you think is important?"

"Yeah. I think maybe I can." If what I told him wasn't enough, then I'd tell him the rest.

He nodded. "Okay, let's give it a try."

"Do you know how Miss Dorothy died?"

"We're not releasing that information to the public yet."

"Was she poisoned?"

Mason's eyes narrowed. "No."

"What if I told you something like this happened before, but the women were poisoned?"

"Hypothetically, it could be very important." He studied his hands as he absently rubbed his thumb across the back of the knuckle on his index finger. "Were they all older women?"

Taking Mason's cue, I leaned in closer to him. "Hypothetically, there were two women. One older and one younger—much younger. The younger one had dated a certain someone a few times."

He tensed, his fingers splaying on the table. "Only two? Did it stop without an arrest?"

"Yes. But someone moved."

"To Henryetta?"

I didn't answer.

Mason turned to face me, his eyes pleading with me. "You have to tell the police, Rose."

Indignant, I jerked away from him. "I'm not telling the police anything."

"Rose, listen to me. There could be a serial killer on the loose."

"I don't care." I pushed at him to let me out of the booth. "I'm not telling the police diddly squat."

Mason refused to budge. "You have a responsibility to tell them."

More responsibility talk. I was sick to death of it. "Mason, what am I going to tell them? That I saw someone murdered? *In a vision?*"

"You can tell them about what happened to Jonah Pruitt before he moved here. That's enough to help them with their investigation of this case."

"You and I both know the Henryetta Police are a band of imbeciles who look at a person's past and decide they're guilty before they know all the facts. I'm not putting someone else in that situation. No one should have to go through what . . ." My voice trailed off.

Mason's face softened. "What you did."

I pushed his arm. "Let me out."

"No." He lowered his gaze into my face. "No one should have to go through what you did, right?"

My hands balled into fists. "I'm not going to talk about this."

"The police assumed you'd murdered your mother because they thought you were odd. You knew things you shouldn't have known. They barely looked at the evidence, just presumed you guilty. They just had to wait to get enough evidence to arrest you."

Helplessness bubbled up in my chest, making me anxious. "Stop."

"Who believed you were innocent? Violet? Joe?"

"I don't want to talk about this." I didn't want to relive that awful time, when I felt so alone and desperate. I started crying again. "Mason, let me out. I just want to go home."

He grabbed my shoulders. "Jonah Pruitt isn't you, Rose. Bruce Wayne Decker wasn't you."

I pulled out of his grasp. "How can you say that? They're just like me! Everyone was ready to send Bruce Wayne to the electric chair."

"And what about you, Rose? What did people think about you?"

"*Why are you doin' this, Mason?*" I cried, my shoulders shaking.

He reached up and wiped away my tears. "Because I want you to look good and hard at why you're risking your life to help someone you hardly know." He lifted my chin, his jaw squared in determination. "Why are you really doing this?"

"I don't know."

"That's bullshit, and you know it. Tell me."

Why was I doing this? Because it really was the right thing to do. And because I wanted to save the woman in my vision. But Mason was right, it went deeper than that.

"Joe hates for you to take risks like this . . . hell, so do I. What makes you so determined to try to help someone you hardly know?"

"Because no one helped me." Resentment washed through me. "Every person in this town would have gladly sent me to prison." My jaw hardened. "No one fought for me."

His eyes softened. "I would have fought for you, Rose."

"Don't do this, Mason." I shook my head, my voice hardening. "You would have taken the pathetic evidence Detective Taylor collected, and you would have tried me before a jury of my peers." I lifted my gaze to his. "And you would have sent me to prison for the rest of my life."

His eyes widened in bewilderment. "How can you say that?"

My hands balled into fists, my anger raging. "Because you were doing exactly the same thing to Bruce Wayne when we met."

His face paled.

I pushed against him again. "I have to go."

"I don't want you to leave with things like this."

"Mason, please." My voice broke. "I can't do this right now."

Panic filled his eyes. "I pushed you too hard. I'm sorry. I'm scared for you, Rose. I can't stand back and watch you get hurt. I just want you to know what you're getting into."

I started crying again. "Mason. *Please.*"

He slid out of the booth, standing next to the table as I scrambled out. He started to follow me to the door, but the waitress shouted, "You can't leave before you pay!"

I kept running, but Mason cursed under his breath as he stopped to pull out his wallet. I was opening the truck door when he reached me. "Rose. Don't leave yet."

Shutting the door, I faced the window, refusing to look at him.

He stood behind me. "You're right."

I closed my eyes.

"I would have tried you." I could tell he was devastated to admit it. "I'd like to think I wouldn't have, but you and I both know I was a hard son of a bitch when I came here. And we also both know you're the one who helped me remember why I do this god-forsaken job." He leaned closer to my ear. "Maybe that's why I feel like I owe it to you to help you."

"Help me do what?" I spun around to face him. "Help me remember how awful it was?"

Pain filled his eyes. "Yes."

"Why would you do that, Mason? Why would you purposely hurt me? I thought we were friends."

"We *are* friends. That's why I'm doing it. You've been through more things in the last few months than anybody should have to go through, but you're not dealing with it. You're sweeping it under the rug, thinking it will go away if you just ignore it. But you can't do that, Rose. You have to face it. Every last ugly bit of it."

I shook my head, crying again.

"Until you face all the demons of your past, you'll never be able to move into the future." He pulled me into a hug, one hand on my back and the other digging into my hair. "I care about you Rose, more than you know."

I cried into his shirt for far too long before finally pulling back, embarrassed. "I've ruined your dress shirt."

"I don't care about my shirt."

I smoothed my hand across the wet spot on the blue oxford cloth. I knew he cared about me, and I was grateful for it. But I also realized he liked me more than a friend. As much as I knew I should send him away, I couldn't. I didn't want to lose him. What did that say about me? "Thank you."

"For making you cry?"

"No, for caring about me enough to risk our friendship to help me." I could see the truth in his words. I was stuck in my past. I needed to let it go so I would no longer hear the ghost of my mother telling me I wasn't good enough. So I'd start believing that I deserved the good things in my life.

"So we're okay?" he asked, but he still looked worried.

"We're good." But I felt terrible. My head hurt from crying. "But I just want to go home and take a nap."

"Okay." He hesitated. "But I want to call you later and check on you. Is that okay?"

"Sure."

He took a step back. "If you need me for anything, and I mean anything, call me. Promise."

"I promise."

I climbed into the truck and drove home, the memory of my vision still playing in my head. I was no closer to helping that poor woman than I was when I first saw it. Muffy was glad to see me when I got home, and as soon as she did her business, I told her we were going inside so I could take a nap.

She was so happy I was with her that she didn't put up a fuss, settling onto the bed next to me. I drifted off almost immediately, waking up to a muffled ring. Still groggy, I blinked as I tried to make out the alarm clock. It was five-fifteen. I'd slept for over two hours.

I realized the ringing was my cell phone, which was still in the kitchen. It had stopped ringing by the time I got up, but it started ringing again before I could reach it. I was surprised to see that it was Joe calling.

"Rose, why haven't you called me back?" he asked, sounding worried.

I rubbed my eyes, still feeling half-asleep. "I didn't know you'd called."

"I've been trying to reach you since this morning. You never answered." He paused. "I thought you decided you didn't want to talk to me."

"No." I sat in the kitchen chair, resting my forehead on my hand. "My phone died, and I couldn't get to a charger until this afternoon. I'm sorry."

"No, it's okay."

"What are you doing calling me and asking me to call you back? Are you done with your undercover job?"

"Yeah, we made an arrest early this morning."

I sat up, relief washing through me. "Does that mean you're coming home?" I needed Joe to hold me and tell me everything would be okay. The Henryetta police might not help me save the poor woman, but I felt certain that he would.

"Home." His voice choked up. "Are you still my home, Rose?"

"Of course, Joe. I told you how much I love you."

"I love you so much." He sounded like he was about to cry. "But I have a favor to ask."

Something in his voice set the hairs on my neck on end. "Of course."

He hesitated. "My mother . . ." He cleared his throat. "My parents have planned a dinner tonight, and they're insisting that I bring you to meet them."

My breath hitched. "In El Dorado?"

"You still have time to make it. It's at seven, and it will only take you about fifty minutes to get here."

I sat up, panicking. "Joe, I've had a horrible day, and I only have about forty-five minutes to get ready."

"I've seen you get ready in less than half that time."

I pushed down my fear. The last thing I wanted to do tonight was face Joe's family, especially with everything else I was handling. "Can't I come another time?"

"I wish you could, darlin'. And I wish I was with you so we come together, but she insists it's important. I'll meet you when you get here."

I wanted to ask him what would have happened if he were still undercover. How could he have gone then? Part of me wanted to tell them all no, to insist they needed to give me more notice, but I knew how much Joe dreaded this for me as well as himself. He wouldn't ask if it wasn't important. I sighed in resignation. "What should I wear?"

"They dress up for dinner, so wear something pretty."

"Okay . . ."

I heard voices in the background. "I have to go, darlin'. I'll text you the address, and I'll see you at seven."

"All right."

"I love you, Rose. When this is over, we'll start over."

I didn't trust the excitement filling my head. "What does that mean?"

"It means I got the deputy sheriff job. I told you this was my last undercover assignment, and I meant it. I'm coming home with you for good."

"Are you sure this is what you want, Joe?"

"I want to be with you all the time. This is the best way to make that happen."

"I don't know what to say."

"Say you're happy."

I smiled, happiness oozing through my words. "I'm happy."

His voice turned husky. "I can't wait to see you again."

A wave of desire washed through me. "I can't wait to see *you*."

"I'm going to make this up to you, Rose. All of it."

"I know."

I hung up and took a quick shower, mentally searching through my closet to try and decide what to wear. I settled on a gauzy, floral dress with a semi-attached under-slip. I curled my hair and put on my makeup, dread filling my stomach and feeling like a ten-pound anchor. Meeting Joe's parents was the last thing I wanted to do. But Joe wanted this so I'd do it to make him happy.

Even if it killed me.

Chapter Twenty-Five

I had plugged in the address of Joe's parents' house into my phone, but I was sure it had steered me wrong when I started down the street of older houses. Joe's parents were rich, and while the houses lining the street were much larger than my house, they weren't as pretentious as I'd expected they'd be.

I shouldn't have gotten my hopes up. At the end of the street sat a large brick and stone older house with landscaping that under other circumstances would have made me drool. A wrought iron fence surrounded the property, but the gates to the circular drive stood open. The brick-laid driveway was lined with luxury cars.

My blood turned to sludge. Joe and I weren't the only ones attending this dinner, apparently. Far from it.

I was five minutes early, and I considered driving around the block to kill time since Joe had told me he'd meet me at the door a couple of minutes before seven. Then I realized how silly that was and lifted my chin. Rose Gardner was done being scared.

I parked my truck behind a Mercedes and stood next to my truck, staring at the front door. I pulled out my phone and texted Joe that I was out front. When he didn't answer after a full minute, I took a deep breath, digging deep for my courage. I had nothing to be ashamed of. Joe's parents would either like me or they wouldn't. Standing outside another couple of minutes wasn't going to change a thing.

Nevertheless, I was flushed and out of breath when I pushed the doorbell. A long chime rang throughout the house, only adding to my anxiety. When an elderly man wearing a suit and an uptight attitude opened the door, looking me up and down like I was yesterday's trash, I knew I was in trouble.

He stared down his nose. "Can I help you?"

"I'm Rose." My voice sounded croaky, so I cleared my throat. "Rose Gardner. Joe's expecting me."

His eyebrows lifted slightly, and he backed up, opening the door wider. "Ms. Gardner." He drew my name out into a long drawl. "Everyone is in the living room."

My breath came in shallow pants, and I told myself I was being ridiculous. Joe's parents might have money, but that didn't mean they were any better than me. Why was I so scared?

But as I followed the butler, my heels clicked on the marble floor, echoing throughout the two-story entryway and around the double rounded staircase. Oil paintings hung on the walls, and the mahogany credenza under one of them was probably worth more than my truck. How had Joe grown up this way? The man I knew wasn't stuffy and pretentious. No wonder he never talked about his past.

The butler stopped at the entrance to a large room lined with ten foot windows that overlooked a garden comparable only to those I'd seen in magazines. But any admiration I felt was squashed by the fact that every person in the room was wearing a long evening gown or tuxedo, whereas I was standing in the doorway in my J.C. Penney's dress. And to make matters worse, Joe wasn't even here yet.

"Ms. Rose Gardner," the butler announced to the room.

My stomach fell to my feet as at least twenty faces stared at me with curiosity and disdain. Resisting the instinct to flee, I tried to smile. "Hello."

A middle-aged woman glided toward me, the picture of beauty and grace. Her dark hair was swept up, and her makeup was impeccable. Her black evening gown sparkled, matching the diamond pendant at the base of the throat. She looked like a model, even though I guessed her to be in her fifties. She extended her hand toward me as she looked me up and down, a cold expression in her eyes. "So you're the Rose we keep hearing about."

I swallowed, fighting the urge to wipe my palm on my dress before shaking her hand. "And you must be Joe's mother."

"Elizabeth Simmons, but everyone calls me Betsy." Her cold tone matched the chill in her eyes. "You may call me Mrs. Simmons."

Her ugliness stole my breath. It was going to be an uncomfortable evening.

An attractive man who resembled an older version of Joe moved beside her. Looking even less thrilled to see me, he shook my hand as well. "J.R. Simmons."

"Hello," I forced out.

The other people in the room were all openly gawking.

"Is Joe here?" I asked, angry with myself for sounding so timid. My gaze swept the room again.

Joe's mother gave me a cold, sly smile. "He'll be along in a moment."

As if on cue, a woman's laughter floated in the open door to the gardens. Hilary appeared in the opening, her dark red hair piled into a glamorous up-do. Her long, red, body-hugging dress was slit nearly to her hip and dipped low to show her cleavage, making her fair complexion look porcelain. She clung to a man who wore a dark gray suit and tie. When she saw me, Hilary broke out into a dazzling smile. The man looked up, and my face flamed with embarrassment and surprise.

She was with Joe.

Joe's mouth gaped in terror.

Everything in me screamed to turn around and run to my truck and drive all the way home. I might have done it if my feet hadn't been frozen to the floor.

Joe shoved Hilary's hand off his arm and pushed his way through the crowd. Moving next to me, he put his hand around my waist, leaning down to give me a chaste kiss. "Rose, I'm so happy you made it."

Feeling like a rat caught in a trap, I didn't answer.

Betsy turned to her guests. "Now that we're all here, let's move to the dining room."

Everyone filed toward the doorway as Joe took my hand and pulled me into the entryway, panic in his eyes.

"Joe," his mother called out to him. "You're needed in the dining room."

He ignored her, dragging me down the hall and pushing me into an office with paneling on the walls. Shutting the door behind him, he pulled me into his arms and lowered his face to kiss me.

I put my hands on his chest and took a step back. "No. Stop." I turned away from him and walked toward the desk at the back of the room. "I don't even know where to start."

"I didn't know my parents had invited all these people."

"I don't care about that." I shook my head. "No, I do. Why didn't you tell me it was formal? Do you know how stupid I look?"

He tried to wrap his arms around my waist, but I pushed them off. "Rose, do you even have any idea how beautiful you are?" He grabbed my arms and spun me around. "You don't need a four-thousand-dollar dress to make yourself more attractive." His hand slid up to my neck. "I don't care what you're wearing. You're the only woman I see."

My face burned with anger. "I could see that when you walked into the room." I was jealous, and I hated myself for feeling like that. Months ago Neely Kate and Joe had convinced me I had no reason to be jealous of Hilary, but after Joe's revelation the previous day, I was no longer sure of anything.

Regret filled his eyes. "Hilary?"

I didn't answer.

"I can explain."

"Why is she here, Joe?"

"I didn't invite her. I swear." His other hand clutched my cheek, keeping my gaze on him. "My mother insisted that I come to dinner tonight, and she said you had to come too. I didn't realize it would be a social function, or I wouldn't have asked you to make it. I figured she only insisted because she found out that I was in town, and I'm rarely here."

"Why didn't you call and warn me when you found out?"

A sheepish look filled his eyes. "I didn't find out until you were almost here. By then it was too late for you to change, and I didn't want to make you any more anxious than you already were."

"It wouldn't have mattered anyway. I don't even own anything that dressy." I glanced toward the door. "I bet they're all in there laughing right now." And I bet Hilary was having the biggest laugh of them all.

"Rose," he pleaded.

"Why were you alone with Hilary?"

"I wasn't with her, Rose. I swear. I showed up to a room full of people and had to get away from everyone so I went to the garden." His fingertips trailed along my cheek as his eyes searched mine. "I went out to my mother's rose garden. Every time I see the roses I think of you." His lips lowered to mine, and he gave me a soft kiss. "I love you, Rose. There's only you." He kissed me again, more insistent this time. "I was by the roses when Hilary showed up." His head lifted. "She told me that she was happy for me."

I pushed him away. "Then why was she hanging on you?"

"She wasn't. We were walking in together, and she must have seen you and grabbed my arm. She's trying to make you jealous. Don't let her win. Please. You have to trust me."

Two days ago, I would have believed it all. But Joe's confession had rocked the foundation of our relationship. I didn't know if that was fair to him, but I couldn't help the way I felt. "I walked into that room alone, Joe. I needed you. Why weren't you there?"

"I'm sorry, Rose. I didn't realize it was so close to seven. I just needed to get away from everyone for a moment."

I understood his need. I felt it now myself.

A knock on the door jolted me, and Joe turned around as the door opened. The butler stood in the doorway. "Mr. Simmons, your presence is immediately required."

Joe's eyes sank closed. "I'll be there in a moment."

I wanted nothing more than for this night to be over, but I'd promised Joe I'd come. Brushing past him, I walked to the doorway. "I don't want to stand out more than I already do, and everyone will be looking if we're late. Let's go."

We walked to the dining room in silence, but Joe slipped his hand in mine. I clung to him despite my anger. I needed him to get through this. But when we entered the room, everyone was already seated. The only two empty chairs left were situated at opposite ends of the table.

Joe's hand tightened.

His mother looked up with an icy smile. "Joe, you're seated next to the Wilders and Rose, we have you with our dear old friends the Whitehills."

Joe stood still for several seconds, his body tense, as he and his mother engaged in a staring contest. "Mother, seeing how Rose is my guest, I would prefer to sit with her."

She rolled her eyes. "Don't be ridiculous, Joe. Everyone is already seated. We're not going to shuffle our guests around like we're playing musical chairs." She shook her head condescendingly, narrowing her eyes at our clasped hands. Then she glanced up at my face. "Unless Rose feels so out of her element that she can't handle dinner without you holding her hand."

Joe's face reddened. All conversation in the room stopped, everyone's focus entirely on Joe and me.

I kept my gaze on Betsy. I knew what she was doing. Mason was right. People could only make me feel bad about myself if I let them. "Joe, it's fine."

"No, Rose. It's not."

I turned to him and forced a smile. "Don't be silly. I'm fine."

Finally, Joe gently pulled me toward the empty chair at the left side of the table. He leaned into my ear. "I'm so sorry."

Joe pulled out the empty chair while everyone watched. I looked up into his face, hoping for reassurance, but what I found there was barely contained rage.

"As soon as dinner is over, we're out of here, okay?" he forced through clenched teeth.

I nodded before I sat, my head pivoting to take in the people around me as I pushed down my panic. Betsy watched me with a saccharine smile.

Joe walked around to the other side of the table, his body tense as he sat in the chair next to . . . Hilary.

This just kept getting worse. I'd been so focused on where I was supposed to sit that I'd paid no attention to who was sitting at the opposite end of the table.

Hilary glanced up at Joe with a bright smile, which she then turned toward me.

I wished I had ten-foot-long legs so I could kick her.

Dinner was awkward as I tried to figure out which fork and spoon to use with which course. The older couple next to me made a limited attempt at conversation out of politeness, but gave up as soon as they realized that I was from Henryetta and had worked in a DMV until a few months ago.

When the roasted chicken breasts were served, Joe's mother looked down at me. "So, Rose, Joe tells me that you own a nursery."

I tried to smile. "Yes, my sister and I opened it last week."

"In Henryetta." I picked up on her condemning tone of voice.

I lifted my chin, tired of these people looking down their noses at me. "Yes, in Henryetta."

"They've done a great job with it," Joe added, his eyes on me, offering me support. "They took a rundown space and turned it into a thriving business in less than two months. They'd be a great model for your small business program, Dad."

Joe's father didn't look excited about the prospect. "Is your degree in horticulture or business?"

I took a drink of my water to stall, and then set the glass onto the white tablecloth. "Neither."

"Where *did* you go to college?" Hilary asked, smiling so wide her whitened teeth nearly blinded me.

Balling my hands in my lap, I leveled my gaze at her. "I went to Southern Arkansas University for a semester before my father died. Then I went home to take care of my mother."

Joe's mother's eyes hardened. "You don't have a college degree?"

"No, and I've managed just fine without it."

Joe looked tongue-tied.

A few people coughed.

"And what exactly do you mean by managed?" J.R. asked, his face hardening.

Joe's face reddened. "I don't see what difference it makes what her definition of managed is."

The woman sitting on the other side of Joe put her hand on his forearm. She looked like an older version of Hilary. "It's a fair question, Joe."

Joe started to get out of his seat.

"Now, now," Joe's mother lifted her hands. "He's right. We're interrogating the poor girl." Only she didn't look very sorry when she gave me a condescending look of sympathy.

Joe sat in his chair, watching me for some cue about what I wanted to do.

"This is a happy night, we don't want to mar it with poor manners," Betsy continued. "J.R. and Joe have a special surprise announcement tonight."

Joe's eyes flew open in surprise. He leaned into his mother's ear, but she didn't respond to whatever he said, intent on cutting up a piece of chicken.

His gaze turned to me. I snuck a glance at the people around us. Would it be more humiliating to sit through the rest of this disaster or get up and leave? Sighing in defeat, I offered him a tiny smile of acceptance. I had promised to come for dinner, and I wasn't going to break my promise. But after that, I never wanted to step foot in this house again.

Joe's shoulders slumped, and he barely touched the rest of his food throughout the rest of the meal, refusing to look at me. I tried to eat, but everything tasted like chalk dust. I would have given up, but Hilary kept flashing me her smile. She knew I was uncomfortable. I didn't want to make her any happier about that than she already was.

What was this big surprise, anyway? I could tell that Joe was caught as off-guard as I was. That scared me more than anything.

Everyone else ignored me, not that I minded. I was done with pretending and wanted this dinner to end so Joe and I could leave.

When dessert was over, Joe's father stood, motioning to someone standing in the doorway. One of the catering staff handed out champagne flutes while another poured champagne into the glasses.

J.R. raised his up, looking down at Joe. "As everyone knows, Mike Morgan was running unopposed in the state senate race, but he was forced to drop out due to health concerns."

I felt lightheaded. Mason's prediction was coming true, and there wasn't a darn thing I could do about it.

J.R. lifted his glass up. "It is with the utmost pride that I announce that my son, Joe Simmons, is entering the race for the Arkansas state senate seat!"

Joe's lips pressed together and his eyes hardened as everyone clinked their glasses together shouting, "Cheers!"

Hilary clinked hers with Joe's, but he ignored her, glaring at his father.

No one bothered to touch mine.

"It's already the end of September," Joe's father continued. "We only have a little over a month to get this campaign rolling, which means we need to take off running. We'll get started first thing in the morning."

Betsy stood. "If everyone wants to adjourn into the living room, we can discuss business in there."

All the guests stood and left the room as Joe jumped up and headed toward me, livid. But J.R. grabbed Joe's arm. He tried to jerk out of his father's grasp, but then J.R. leaned into his ear. Joe's face turned white, and his anger faded as he accompanied his father out of the room.

What had J.R. said? I started to follow, but Betsy intercepted me, blocking my exit. "I hope tonight was a satisfactory demonstration of what your life as a senator's wife would be like. I'm not sure how long you'd survive when you find it a struggle to answer the most mundane questions about your education and your breeding."

I finally found my tongue. "Breeding? Is being a senator's wife akin to being a horse? Do I need to provide my pedigree papers?"

She laughed, but the sound was brittle. "I can see Joe's attraction to you. You're a pretty little distraction from all his troubles over the past year. But it's time for Joe to resume his family responsibility. He's been groomed for this his entire life."

I shook my head. "Do you know if he even wants this?"

Her gaze hardened. "Do you?"

I didn't.

Her eyes glittered with victory at my hesitation, and she offered a smile. "Rose, this life isn't for you. I've watched you tonight. You struggled with what silverware to use. You're poor white trash, and you live in that cesspool Fenton County. It's no wonder you feel out of place and discouraged around Joe's family and friends." Her voice lowered. "The sad truth is that you'll never fit in here. You have your place, and Joe has his. The sooner everything gets back to the way it should be, the better off everyone will be." She patted my cheek. "I'm sure a street-smart girl like you can figure that out." Then she turned and left me standing alone in the dining room.

Angry, I stormed to the living room, expecting Joe to be in the living room setting everyone straight, but he stood in the middle of a group of men, all of them patting him on the back with congratulations. He didn't respond to any of them, looking shell-shocked.

Hilary stood to the side, her champagne flute in one hand. When she saw me, she lifted it and smiled, then took a sip.

I could either stand here and fight or turn around and leave. I wanted to fight. Fight for Joe and me. Fight and prove to every person who'd ever hurt me that I was done taking other people's crap. But Joe stood in the center of the group doing nothing.

Why wasn't he fighting for me?

I spun around and left the room.

Joe found me as I was climbing into my truck. "Rose! *Wait!*"

I hesitated, unsure of what to do. Part of me just wanted to go home.

But he caught up with me, grabbing my shoulders. "I didn't know he was going to do that. I swear."

I looked up at him, clenching my jaw. "You've been doing a lot of swearing tonight, Joe."

"You have to believe me. I didn't know about any of this."

I closed my eyes. "I believe you."

Part of me was so hurt by this evening, and the rest of me was angry. The angry part won out. "How could you let Hilary make me look like a fool?"

For the first time tonight, he didn't look apologetic. "We both know she asked you where you went to college to humiliate you, but asking someone about another person's education isn't usually considered a rude question. I was worried if I said something it would only make it worse."

His answer infuriated me more than her behavior. "Why are you standing up for her?"

He looked defensive. "I'm not."

"*Why was she here?*"

"I told you. Her family and mine have been lifelong friends."

I walked toward the front of the truck, looking at the massive house in front of me. The truth sinking in. "She's always going to be here, isn't she?"

"Well . . . I . . ."

"She is, isn't she?" I glared up at him. "You can't let her go, can you?"

"No. That's not true. I want *you*." He pulled me to his chest, his mouth crushing mine.

Despite whatever had transpired over the last two days, I loved this man. My anger faded as I sank against him, grabbing his suit and pulling him closer. I wanted desperately to make this work.

Joe's head lifted. "I love you, Rose. I want to marry you."

My eyes widened. "What?"

He dug into his coat pocket and took out a ring box. "I planned to do this tomorrow. I planned to come home to you and tell you about the sheriff's deputy job and propose then. Dinner and flowers and the whole works so I could make it romantic for you, but I don't want to wait." He pried the lid open, grabbing my left hand. "Rose Anne Gardner, I love you more than anything in this world, and I can't imagine a life without you. I want to wake up with you every day, and I want to go to bed with you in my arms every night. I want to fill our house with children, and our lives with love and laugher." He slid the ring onto my finger. "Rose, I've never been as happy as I am when I'm with you. I feel like I have everything I could ever want when we're together. Please say you'll marry me."

I stared down at the ring, a large square diamond in the center, surrounded by smaller ones. "What about the senate race?"

He didn't answer.

My heart sunk. "Joe, what do *you* want to do."

"I want to marry you."

I looked back at the house, but he tilted my chin to look up at him. "There's only you and me. To hell with my parents. I've let them rule my life for too long. I'm going to go inside and tell them I'm done."

"What did your father say to you when he dragged you from the room?"

Some of Joe's excitement faded. "He told me this was the payment for the scrapes he's gotten me out of. That I owed him." His breath came in short bursts.

Did he want to do this? "Joe . . . I'm not asking you to choose."

"I know. That's what makes you even more amazing. You're not the one who's insisting I choose. They are. And this time they've gone too far."

"Can you really tell him no?"

His body tensed. "He can't force me to run for the senate."

From what I'd seen of Joe's family, I wasn't so sure about that.

He caressed my face. "Why don't you go home, and I'll tell my parents off once and for all. I'll come home, and then tomorrow we'll start our life together."

It sounded so perfect, almost too perfect. But what he was offering was what I'd wanted my whole life. Was I really going to give it up without a fight? "Okay."

He kissed me again, pulling back reluctantly. "I love you, Rose. Go home, and I'll be there soon."

As I drove away, I looked back and saw him go through the front door, his hands clenched by his sides. Somehow, I knew that things would never be the same again.

Chapter Twenty-Six

It was close to nine-thirty by the time I got home. Muffy was overjoyed to see me, and once again, I was wracked with guilt for not spending enough time with her. But that would all change when Joe returned.

I wandered through the house, imagining what it would be like when he was here all the time, and my heart burst with a cloudy happiness. Now I wouldn't be lonely.

My home phone rang—a rarity these days—and I wasn't surprised that it was Violet. She was practically the only one who called me on it other than telemarketers.

"Rose, where have you been all evening?"

I sank into my sofa. "I went to meet Joe's parents."

"Tonight?"

"Yeah."

"Why didn't you tell me you were going?" She sounded wronged.

I sighed. "I didn't mean to hurt you, Violet."

She paused. "I know. You would never intentionally hurt me. Unlike me lately. I haven't been a very good sister these past few months, and I know it."

I really wasn't in the mood for a heart-to-heart right now. "Look, Vi. Joe told me this weekend that his mother was getting more insistent about meeting me, but then he called after five today and told me they wanted it to be tonight."

"You're kidding." Her voice was flat.

"No. And here's your chance to say I told you so, because it was beyond awful." My voice cracked, but I refused to shed any more tears over those horrid people.

"I don't want to say I told you so. I want you to be happy."

"Well, you've done a crappy job of showing it lately."

Violet gasped, probably as surprised as I was by my bluntness. "I know. I'm sorry," she finally said. "I think my guilt has been consuming me. That and jealousy."

"Guilt over what? Mike?"

She hesitated. "In a way, yes."

I sat up straighter. "What are you talking about?"

"Oh, Rose. I'm a terrible, terrible person. I'm afraid you'll never forgive me, but I feel like I have to tell you."

My heart started to race. I knew she had a secret. How many awful secrets could there be? "I love you, Violet. You're my sister. Nothing's ever going to change it."

I heard her take a deep breath. "Do you remember the day before we opened the shop, how you asked me what people were saying about you?"

"Yeah, you wouldn't answer."

"They were saying you inherited all of Momma's money, and I didn't get a dime. They were saying you were rich, and that you were making me work at the nursery for free."

I sank back into the cushions. "I already knew that, Vi. Mason and Neely Kate told me."

"They did?"

"Yeah . . . so, see? There's nothing to worry about."

"That's not all there is to the story."

"What else is there?" I asked tentatively.

"Some people confronted me with it, offering their condolences on how horrible you were being." She hesitated. "I didn't correct them."

I let her words sink in. "You let them think I was treating you horribly?"

"Yes," she whispered.

"*Why?*" I didn't know whether to be hurt or angry, so I latched onto both. "Why would you do that to me, Violet?"

"So people wouldn't notice what I was doing." Her voice was so quiet I could barely hear her.

My heart jolted again. "What were you doing?"

"I've been having an affair with Brody MacIntosh."

I'd guessed it, but to hear her confirm it still felt like a punch in the stomach.

"Say something," she whispered.

"How long has it been going on?" Maybe she thought going out with someone while you were separated counted as having an affair.

"Since April."

"Oh, God."

"I'm sorry." She started to cry.

"You and Brody were both still married then. Mike didn't leave until July."

"I know."

I took several deep breaths. "I don't understand. You just started dating Brody last week."

"No, we've been seeing each other at least twice a week since May. We just decided to start publicly dating last week."

Of all the people in the world I'd thought capable of an affair, Violet was the last in line.

"Say something."

A million questions ran through my head, but I had to pick one. "Do you love him?" That was stupid question. On Sunday, it had been obvious that she did.

"Yes, I love him." She paused. "But Mike found out that we're seeing each other and came over tonight to accuse me of having an affair." She hiccupped through her tears. "I denied it. I know I should have told him the truth, but he threatened to take the kids. He said he'd sue for full custody."

"Can he do that?"

"It happened to Sue Ellen Lewinski just last month."

"Oh, Violet." What a mess. "What are you going to do?"

"I told Brody I can't see him for a while. Not until things die down. I can't lose my kids, Rose." She broke down again.

"I know. Everything will be okay."

"I'm sorry I've been such a bitch lately."

"I know."

"Do you want to know the sad part?"

"What?" I asked.

"Brody asked me to marry him about an hour before Mike came over."

I wanted to cry. How ironic that both Gardner sisters had been proposed to on the same night. How ironic that both proposals were so bittersweet. "I'm sorry. Give it time. It will all work out."

"I was just so jealous that you and Joe were able to date out in the open. You're so happy and it just felt so unfair. I took it out on you. I'm sorry."

I had been happy . . . right up until a week ago. How quickly things changed. "I forgive you, Vi. Now go hug your kids and get a good night's sleep, and I'll see you tomorrow."

When I hung up, I stared at the ring on my finger for several minutes. Joe had proposed, and I was wearing the ring, but I hadn't really given him an answer yet. Was I going to say yes?

If he had asked me two days ago, I would have in a heartbeat. Now I was hesitating. The question was why.

I could give a million reasons for why I should marry him and part of me wanted to rush headlong into it, but I'd seen so many people run blindly into marriage, only to pay the price further down the road. I didn't want to be Violet and Mike, fighting over the custody of our kids.

Maybe instead of looking at the reasons I should get married, I should look at reasons *not* to.

I grabbed a piece of paper and put a magazine behind it as I laid back in the cushions and wrote *Why I Shouldn't Marry Joe*:

1. *He snores*
2. *He leaves his shaving cream gunk in the sink.*
3. *He forgets to close the bread bag.*
4. *He mixes up the laundry.*
5. *He buys the wrong salad dressing brand.*

I listed twenty-four items, and I examined my list. Was the fact Joe left his socks on the floor a real reason not to marry him?

This was a list of petty excuses. If I was going to write this list, I had to be honest with myself and look at the real issues.

25. *Joe's parents hate me.*

Their hatred was so palpable I didn't see how we could ever survive as a couple unless Joe disowned his family. And as poisonous as they seemed to be, I would never ask him to do that.

26. *I don't think I want to be a politician's wife.*

I couldn't say that I wouldn't, but I needed time to think about it. He couldn't just spring it on me and expect me to give up my entire life.

27. *He wants me to give up my entire life.*

That wasn't true, or at least I didn't have any proof of it. But I was smart enough to know that being married to a politician meant going to a ton of social functions, and I didn't think I was cut out for that.

28. *He hates when I help people who are in trouble.*

That wasn't entirely truthful either. He hated when I got mixed up in things that got *me* into trouble, but there was no doubt that if he had his way, I wouldn't have hired Bruce Wayne to work for me. He truly didn't understand my need to help people like me, even though, oddly enough, he loved me for it. Did I want to fight him on things like that all the time?

29. *He hates me talking to Mason.*

After tonight, I understood his reasoning. I hated for Joe to have anything to do with Hilary. But Joe and Hilary had known each other since they were kids, and for a lot of those years they'd been sleeping together. Mason and I had only been friends for a couple of months, and we had never been romantic. I sighed.

The truth was, if Joe and I got married, Mason and I could no longer be friends, especially since I knew Mason liked me. That wouldn't be fair to Mason or Joe. But if I loved Joe, why did the thought of giving up Mason hurt so much?

I wiped a tear off my cheek and wrote the next item.

30. *He's not over Hilary.*

He swore he was, but a sick feeling of dread burrowed deep in my heart at the very thought of her. It felt like I was just waiting for my world to be jerked out from underneath me. Would I feel that way our entire marriage or would it eventually go away? Did I really want to live like that?

Exhausted, I set the list on the table and went into my bedroom to undress, wondering if I should put on something sexy to greet Joe with when he came home or something more practical to sleep in since I was so exhausted. I kicked off my shoes, and then stripped the gauzy part of the dress over my head, tossing it on the bed as I tried to make up my mind.

Muffy whimpered.

I looked down at her, the hair on my arms feeling prickly. "What is it, girl?"

A scratchy sound came from outside my window. What was that?

My head jerked up as my cell phone rang in the kitchen.

I crept down the hall to get my phone out of my purse, my heart pounding in my chest. Had I locked the side door after bringing Muffy in?

I was being silly and paranoid.

The microwave clock read 10:15. Snatching up my phone, I locked the kitchen door as I answered, "Hello."

"Rose," Mason said. "I wanted to check on you."

I heard another noise outside my kitchen window. I was sure about it this time. "I think there's someone creeping around outside my house."

"Did you call the police?"

"I just heard it when you called."

"You need to call the police. But stay on this line and call them on your home phone."

Something felt really wrong. "Okay."

I put my cell phone on the counter. My hands shook so badly I had a hard time pressing the buttons for 911. When they answered, I told them I thought there was a prowler outside my house.

"We'll send someone over as soon as we can," the female dispatcher answered in a bored voice. "But Ernie's on a drunk and disorderly out by the Wagon Wheel."

I hung up, panic rising from the pit of my belly as I picked up my cell phone again. "I don't think they're coming, Mason. She said Ernie's on another call."

"I'll be there as soon as possible." He sounded anxious.

My breath came in short bursts. This is what happened to Mason's sister. The police didn't believe her, and Joe came over too late. "You won't get here in time."

"Stop that right now!" he shouted. "You're going to be fine."

I nodded, trying to convince myself that Mason was right. "Yeah, it's probably just my imagination." But I knew it wasn't. The paper I'd found that morning, now sitting on the kitchen table, caught my attention and my terror rose. "I forgot to tell you about the note. How could I have forgotten to tell you about the note?"

"What note?"

"I found it on my porch this morning under a rock. It said *Stay Away* in cut magazine letters."

Mason's voice sounded tight. "Rose, are all of your doors locked?"

"Maybe I should go over to Heidi Joy's."

"No! Stay inside." He was out of breath. "What's Muffy doing?"

"She's whimpering."

"Call 911 again."

Tears flooded my eyes. "They won't come, Mason."

"I'm on my way."

The whole house went dark, the lights flickering out into blackness. Muffy began to growl. "Mason, my lights just went out. I'm going to Heidi Joy's."

"*No.* Stay inside. You're safer inside."

I heard a noise in the back of the house. "Mason, if something happens—"

"Nothing's going to happen, Rose. I'm not going to let it."

I wrapped my free arm across my chest and gasped when I felt the silk against my skin. "Oh, God." I was wearing the white slip part of my dress, and my feet were bare. But the most telling of all was the ring on my hand.

"*What?*"

"The woman in the vision is me." My knees started to buckle, and I grabbed the counter.

"Why do you think that? What are you wearing?" He sounded panicked.

I grabbed the ring on my finger and tried to pull it off, but the band got stuck beneath my knuckle. "I can't get it off."

"Can't get what off? *What are you wearing?*"

"What I saw in my vision." I started crying.

"No, calm down." His voice softened. "It doesn't mean it's going to come true. You said so yourself."

I nodded, taking deep gulps of air as I opened my kitchen drawer and pulled out my rolling pin. I wasn't going down without a fight.

Muffy growled again, and I moved to the kitchen sink to look out the window. I didn't see anything lurking outside, but my vision shifted, and I saw a shadow image creeping up behind me in the reflection. I screamed, then turned around swinging, connecting with the intruder's shoulder and dropping the phone in the process.

"Rose!" I heard Mason's panicked voice coming from the phone on the floor.

But my strike wasn't strong enough to stop my attacker. I felt an electrical jolt rush through my body followed by intense pain as my muscles cramped.

And then there was only darkness.

Chapter Twenty-Seven

I woke up face down in the seat of a car, my hands tied in front of me. Every part of my body felt so heavy I could hardly move. A wave of panic raced through me before I took a deep breath and told myself to calm down. Panicking wasn't going to help me. However, the hood over my head wasn't helping either.

Just when I'd calmed down enough to start assessing my situation, the car stopped. Moments later the door next to me opened and rough hands grabbed my arms, pulling me out of the seat. My legs wouldn't support my weight, so I lost my balance. I fell to the ground, concrete scrapping my knee.

Two thoughts came to mind: One, I was in Jonah's driveway. And two, I didn't remember seeing a scrape on my knee in the vision. If the future was already diverging from what I'd seen, I still had a chance at surviving this.

Something pointed and metallic poked into my side. "Don't even think about shouting. I'll shoot you right where you stand."

I had no doubt he would—only *he* sounded like a *she*. He or she, I'd watched this person shoot me in the head. My knees buckled, and my head swam at the thought. Now was *not* the time to pass out.

A hand jerked me up, but from the angle, I could tell that the kidnapper was surprisingly short, further evidence that she was a woman.

"You're a sluttin' whore. I knew it the moment I saw you. What you're wearin' right now is proof of that. Now start walking."

Had Miss Mildred gone rogue and kidnapped me?

Then I realized who had taken me and icy fear crawled up my back. "I'm not interested in Jonah . . . I mean Reverend Pruitt. We're friends is all. I have a boyfriend. Did I tell you that? His name is Joe, and he's a state police officer."

The gun jammed into my side again. "Shut up and keep walking."

"There's been a misunderstanding here. If you just let me go, we'll forget all about it."

"You're just like all the others." Rhonda said. "They thought they were fooling me since they were so much older than my boy. But they all wanted to steal him away. Just like you do."

"I don't, really I don't."

"I'm not blind. I've seen you with him. Hanging around him at the church of all places." Her voice lowered into a hateful tone. "And don't think I didn't see you with him in the sanctuary." Something hard hit me square in the back, and I cried out in pain as I fell to my knees.

"Get up, whore." She jerked me upright again. "Jesus carried his cross on his back for miles after he'd been beaten. If I had time, I'd make you suffer his miseries as penance."

I fought the hysteria bubbling up in my chest. "Maybe we could pray for my soul. Would you pray with me, Miss Rhonda?"

She leaned around me, and a door opened as she leaned down into my ear. "I'll pray with you all right. I'll be praying over your dead body. Now keep quiet, or I'll shoot you right here. And that's not an empty promise."

Was it better to get shot now or let her tie me to a chair, knowing without a doubt what would happen? Running seemed like a better option. I started to bolt, but something hard came down on the middle of my back again, and I cried out.

"Keep your mouth shut."

She dragged me through the doorway and gave me a shove. I stumbled into a table, which made a screeching noise as it scraped across the floor. That was good. It hadn't been in my vision either.

The hood was jerked off my head, and I blinked as I took in my surroundings as quickly as possible. We were in a dark kitchen just like in my vision, and the moonlight was streaming in through the window. Rhonda held the gun out toward me, the hood of a sweatshirt over her head.

"Sit in the chair," she hissed, waving me toward the table.

The last thing I wanted was to sit in one of those chairs. "I think I'll just stand."

Before I realized what was happening, Rhonda pulled a stun gun from her jacket pocket with her left hand and aimed it at me.

I cried out as the pain flooded my body, but I fought the darkness at the edges of my vision. I needed to keep conscious.

Rhonda pulled the barbs out of my skin and dragged me over to one of the chairs, not an easy task given the fact that all of the muscles in my body refused to work. My head hung forward as she wrapped a rope around my chest, securing me to the chair. "If you'd just done this the easy way . . ."

"Mother?" Jonah asked from the doorway.

Mother? Rhonda was Jonah's mother? I tried to lift my head, but my body refused to cooperate.

"Mother, what are you doing? Who is that?"

None of this happened in my vision. I nearly cried with happiness.

"That slut who keeps sniffing around you at the church. I saw through her just like I saw through all those other women."

"*Rose*?" Jonah's voice broke. "What other women?"

"Those church women who tried to lure you away from your mission."

"Oh, Mother." Jonah sounded devastated.

"Jesus was celibate. He devoted his entire life to his ministry. I know you can't be a real priest now, Jonas, but you can still act like one."

"Momma, give me the gun."

The energy started to flow back into my muscles, and I could lift my head enough to see Jonah extending his hand to Rhonda.

"That's a good idea," she said. "*You* can kill her. You can prove your loyalty to your calling."

I could see Jonah's hand reaching for the gun.

Rhonda backed up. "No." She sounded disappointed. "You're not strong enough to do it. All these women have made you weak. It's up to me to save you."

"I swear to you that Rose hasn't done anything. I asked her to help me. If anyone should be shot, it's me." Jonah dropped to his knees, pleading with his mother. "God the Father sacrificed his only son for the salvation of the world. You can do the same." He reached for her but she stayed just out of reach. "You can sacrifice your son for the souls of the damned. The whores and the drug addicts and the thieves."

She hesitated, finally, shaking her head. "No. They don't deserve such a sacrifice."

"But did the prostitutes and tax collectors deserve Jesus's attention and love? If anyone should die, it should be me, Mother, so I can follow Jesus's example."

I shook my head, although it took more energy than I'd expected. "No. Jonah, don't do it," I said, but my words came out slurred.

Rhonda turned to me with a glare and whacked the side of my head with the butt of her gun. "Keep your heathen mouth shut!"

White light burst into my vision, but I clung to consciousness, even though my stomach rebelled.

Jonah cried out. "Mother! No!" He stood and crept toward her, his eyes wide. "There's another way."

She held the gun to my temple, and I fought a sob rising in my throat.

Jonah held up his hands. "Wait! Wait." He was close to hyperventilating. His gaze turned to the doorway, and Rhonda's followed, even though she was still holding the gun to my head.

Mason stood there, a shotgun in his hand, his face deadly calm. "Put the gun down. I can assure you that I won't hesitate to use this."

She sneered, "I know who you are. You're the assistant DA. You won't shoot me."

A murderous gleam filled his eyes. "Don't be so sure about that. I beat a man into an irreversible coma. Shooting you wouldn't begin to faze me."

Her hand shook, jabbing the tip of the gun into the place where she'd hit me. Bolts of pain shot through my head. I started crying harder.

Jonah reached out his hand. "Momma, just hand me the gun, and everything will be okay. *Please.*"

For the first time, she faltered in her conviction, tears filling her voice. "I just want what's best for you, Jonas."

Mason still stood in the doorway, his gaze turning to me for a moment. When he saw the blood dripping down the side of my face, his eyes hardened.

Jonah moved closer. "I know you do, Momma. You always have. That's why we're here. You realized I was about to get in trouble in Homer, so you suggested we move here."

Rhonda nodded. "Yes! It needed to be done, Jonas. I needed to keep you pure. But I didn't want people to blame you for killing those women. But women in this town are so much looser." Her voice hardened again. "Like this one here, throwin' herself at you."

Mason turned the shotgun toward Jonah. "How much do you love your son?"

Rhonda gasped.

I tried to shake my head, but pain sent spots into my vision. "Mason. Stop!"

"I assure you, if you kill her, I *will* kill your son."

Jonah lifted his hands in resignation. He would truly die to help save me.

The gun dug into my head. "You wouldn't," Rhonda challenged, but she didn't sound so certain.

"Are you willing to risk his life to find out?"

I couldn't sit here and let Jonah get killed or Mason ruin his career again, especially over me. I also knew Rhonda was too crazy for there to be any hope of reasoning with her.

The effects of the stun gun continued to fade. My body no longer felt like it weighed a thousand pounds. If I could create a distraction, I could keep the two of them from getting hurt. The problem was I needed to move quickly, and I wasn't sure how well my muscles would cooperate.

"You poisoned the women in Homer, but what about the women here?" Jonah asked, his voice cracking. "How did you kill them?"

She laughed. "It was so easy. I used my taser on them. The first one died of a heart attack, but the others had to be smothered as they laid there incapacitated."

"What about the windows?" Mason asked. "Why were their windows closed and their air conditioning turned off?"

She wrinkled her nose in disgust. "I wanted them to see how hot hell was going to be when they got there." She turned back to me. "I have special plans for you."

"I changed my mind," I said. "I don't want someone as evil as you to pray with me."

Anger filler her eyes, and her open hand connected with my cheek. But as she hit me, she lowered the gun. Then next thing I knew, Mason dropped his shotgun and both men lunged for her, all three of them falling to the ground and wrestling. A gunshot filled the room, and everyone stopped moving.

"Mason!" I cried.

I heard a moan, and Jonah rolled to the side, holding his arm. Blood seeped through his sleeve, and he looked like he was about to pass out.

Mason still lay on the floor with Rhonda. My breath caught in my chest as I waited for him to move. Finally, he pushed up off the floor with one hand and groaned, holding her gun with the other. "I'm getting too old for this nonsense."

Rhonda rolled from her stomach to her back, her face a mask of hate as she stared at me.

"Mason, thank God . . . I thought . . ." I started crying harder. Sirens sounded in the distance.

Mason knelt in front of me, fear in his eyes. "Are you okay?"

I nodded and winced.

"We have to stop meeting like this," he teased, but his hands began to shake as he untied me.

Ernie and another officer rushed through the doorway, then headed straight for Jonah.

"Not him," Mason barked, pointing to the floor. "Her!"

They pulled Rhonda to her feet as Mason turned back to me. "I'm taking you to the hospital. Do you want to go in the ambulance or my car?"

"Your car." I didn't want to go, but I knew there was no point arguing with him. Besides, it looked like Jonah needed the ambulance more than I did.

Mason took my hand, paused when he noticed the ring on my left finger, and then put an arm around my back so he could help me outside. "What did she do to you, Rose?"

I forced myself to walk without falling on my face. "I think she tased me in my house because I felt a jolt of electricity before I passed out and woke up in the back of car. The second time she tased me was in Jonah's kitchen."

"And the side of your head?"

I shrugged. It seemed obvious enough.

We rode the short distance to the hospital in silence, mostly because I kept trying to fall asleep, but Mason always woke me up, asking me some stupid questions. When we got to the hospital, he didn't even find a parking space. He pulled right up to the emergency room's sliding doors. He opened the passenger-side door for me, and I looked up at him in annoyance. "You're not supposed to park here."

"This is one of the few perks of my thankless job. Don't tell me you're going to begrudge me that."

When we got through the door, Mr. No Nonsense was back. "I need someone to look at her immediately. She keeps trying to go to sleep, and I'm not sure if it's the effects of the stun gun or her head wound."

Someone brought a wheelchair and made me sit in it while they took me behind the double doors. Mason stayed in the waiting room, and I protested all the way back. When they tried to lift me up on to the gurney, I refused to cooperate. "I want Mason back here with me."

The nurse's eyebrows lifted in confusion. "You mean Mr. Deveraux? I'm sure he'll be back to question you later."

"No, I want *Mason* Deveraux. My friend. Just tell him. If you don't, I'm gonna get up and leave right now."

The nurse shook her head and looked at the aide who was helping her. "Go see if Mr. Deveraux wants to come back."

Mason came through the door moments later with a look of disapproval that turned to relief when he saw me. "You're nothing but trouble, Rose Gardner."

I tried to laugh, but it hurt my head. "You know you like me this way."

His smile fell. "Usually, but you scared the shit out of me tonight."

"I had the shit scared out of me too."

The nurse watched our exchange in annoyance, and then her eyes widened as they landed on my hand. "I didn't know you were engaged, Mr. Deveraux."

Mason glanced at the ring on my hand again. "Rose isn't my fiancée. We're just friends."

She looked relieved as she picked up my chart. "Well, that's good to know for the rest of us single girls out there."

"You're still the second most eligible bachelor in Fenton County," I teased, but my heart wasn't in it. Mason's reaction to my ring bothered me.

"Second to Brody McIntosh, of course." But the teasing was gone from his voice too. Mason sat in the chair by my bed. "I suppose congratulations are in order."

I self-consciously grabbed the ring, and then I looked into his face. "I didn't really say yes."

"But you're wearing his ring," he said, grabbing my hand.

I leaned my head back on the bed, so exhausted I was sure I could sleep for twenty years like Rip Van Winkle. "It just all happened so fast. We were at his parents' house, and they—"

"You were at Joe's parents' house tonight?"

"They insisted I come to dinner. Once I got there, I immediately understood why." I opened my eyes and sighed. "They announced that Joe is running for the state senate seat. You were right."

"I'm sorry." His hand tightened around mine. "Joe didn't warn you?"

"He says he didn't know. He found out when I did. When his father made the announcement to all their dinner guests."

"You didn't mention going to see them when I talked to you this afternoon." He sat back in his chair, looking defeated. "Although it's pretty presumptuous to assume you would."

"Mason, I would have told you, especially after our talk on Sunday. But Joe called at around five and said his mother wanted me to come. When I showed up, they had about twenty of their oldest and closest friends there. Including his ex-girlfriend."

"Ouch." He paused. "After the day you had, why didn't you say no?"

"Because Joe really wanted me there. And I wanted to get it over with. When his father announced he was running, Joe really was completely caught off guard."

Mason remained silent, still staring at the ring on the finger of the hand he was holding.

"Joe's family hates me. You were right about that too."

He glanced back at me, sadness in his eyes. "I take no pleasure in being right about that, you know."

"I know." I sighed. "They tried to make me look like a fool at dinner, but when I thought about what you told me—that no one can make me feel bad unless I let them—I realized I have nothing to be ashamed of."

"Good. Because you don't."

"Where do they come off being so hateful and judgmental? Your mother has money, and she doesn't hate me."

"No, I can assure you she doesn't."

"I'll never be good enough for Joe's family."

Mason didn't answer.

"I don't think I want to be a senator's wife," I whispered.

"Did you tell Joe?"

"It's partially my fault his father forced him into this."

Mason shifted in his seat. "How do you figure that?"

"Part of this is the favor Joe's father expects him to repay. I was one of the scrapes he got Joe out of. If he hadn't used his father's political clout to get me out of jail, he wouldn't be stuck now."

"He's not stuck, Rose. And he had plenty more scrapes than you and Savannah. If Joe doesn't want to run for the senate, then he needs to grow a pair of balls and tell his father no."

"Mason!" I sat up, pain shooting through my head.

His expression softened, and he started to pull his hand away from mine. "Maybe I should go."

"No, don't leave me." I squeezed his hand. I hadn't noticed we were still holding hands. But I did now, and I was surprised at how comforting the gesture was. But then again, he'd just saved my life. That had to count for something.

"I'll stay with you as long as you let me."

I was pretty sure he meant something else. It wasn't fair to ask him to stay when I knew how he felt, but I couldn't bring myself to send him home either.

We were silent for a few moments, and I stared at our joined hands. I could always count on Mason to be there when I needed him. Especially if I was in trouble. "How'd you know where to find me?"

He leaned forward, resting his arm on the bed. "You told me your vision was coming true. You said it happened in Jonah's kitchen. So once I got to your house and you were gone, I knew where to find you."

"What made you bring a shotgun?"

"I'm a Fenton County boy now," he teased. "All us good ol' boys carry shotguns."

I shook my head, then winced from the pain. "No, really."

A fierceness filled his voice. "Because if someone hurt you, they were gonna have hell to pay."

I turned to my side and looked into his eyes, asking softly, "Would you really have shot Jonah?"

Mason's eyes hardened, and his jaw tightened. "I guess we'll never know."

An orderly came in and took me to x-ray for a CAT scan. I wondered if Mason would still be there when I got back, and he was. He was sitting in the same chair, his chin on his chest as he dozed.

He roused when the aide helped me onto the bed. "Everything go okay?"

"It was fine. They said they'd tell me the results soon." He settled back into the chair, obviously tired. "Mason, you don't have to stay with me. Go home and go to bed."

"Someone has to make sure you get home okay," he teased.

The door opened and Joe walked in, looking irritated. "Yeah, that someone is me."

My heart leapt with either fear or joy, I wasn't certain. Maybe both.

Mason gripped the arms of his seat, clearly holding back what he wanted to say.

Joe turned to me, concern on his face. "What happened?"

I waved my hand. "Oh, you know. The usual. Kidnapping, attempted murder." But inwardly I cringed, waiting for Joe to blow up.

"Are you okay?"

"I'm fine. Really. Just bruised and banged up."

He moved away from me, his face twisting with anger. "How did this happen. Again? Why can't you leave these things alone?"

I wasn't sure how to answer that.

Mason stood. "I don't like how you're talking to her."

Joe turned around. "What are you still doing here? When did it become the job of the prosecuting attorney to hold a vigil with a victim?"

"Joe," I warned.

"She doesn't think about the consequences of what she's doing, and you damn well know I'm right."

Mason stood his ground. "Are you suggesting that she brings this on herself?"

Joe ran his hand through his hair, looking even more frustrated. "I'm saying she's going to get herself killed if she doesn't stop and think about her own safety."

Mason's chest rose and fell as he fought to control his fury. "Perhaps if you were actually here to witness what goes on in her life, you'd see that she did nothing to bring any of this upon herself."

Joe's back stiffened. "You've made damn sure you're close at hand, haven't you, Deveraux?"

Mason moved next to the bed. "I'm not doing this to Rose tonight. She's been through too much trauma." He leaned over and kissed my forehead. "You know how to find me if you need me."

I smiled up at him, despite Joe's glare. "Thanks, Mason."

Joe's face tightened, turning his attention to the wall and not looking at either of us. "Thank you." He cleared his throat. "Thank you for saving her."

Mason stopped in the open doorway, his back rigid. "I'll always be there for Rose when she needs me."

When Mason left the room, Joe sat on the bed next to me, picking up my hand. All the fight rushed out of his body, leaving a profound sadness in its wake. "You're still wearing my ring."

"Yeah."

He looked like he was about to cry. "What happened tonight?"

I wanted to ask which part. So *much* had happened, and there was so much he didn't know about.

"Detective Taylor said Jonah's mother kidnapped you and threatened to kill you."

"That sounds about right."

"I told you that Jonah Pruitt was trouble."

"Jonah Pruitt is the furthest thing from trouble I've met in ages. He's just as much a victim as those poor women are."

"You collect them don't you?" He sounded disappointed, but somehow I knew it wasn't directed at me. "You can't help yourself."

"What are you talking about?"

"The outcasts. Bruce Wayne. Jonah Pruitt . . ."

I sat up. "If you add Neely Kate to that list, I'm liable to hurt you." Something about him had changed over the last week, but I couldn't figure out exactly what it was. "When did you get back to Henryetta?"

"Just a few minutes ago."

I looked up at the clock. "But it's almost two in the morning. Have you been with your parents this entire time?"

He avoided my gaze. "Yes."

And then I knew.

"You're running for the senate aren't you?"

He didn't answer.

"What about us?" I asked.

He picked up my hand and kissed my palm, then looked into my eyes with a ferocity that reminded me of Joe McAlister, not

Joe Simmons. "What about us? I still want to marry you, Rose. Nothing's changed there."

"I'd make a terrible politician's wife, Joe. What if I have a vision at an important event? What if people ask me about my education?"

"Not everyone is like my parents."

I started to cry.

He lifted his hand to my cheek and carefully wiped my tears. "Don't cry, Rose. Nothing's going to change the way I feel about you. I don't care what anyone says." But something was missing from his words. This wasn't my Joe.

I stared into his eyes, afraid of my sudden decision. "I want to have a vision." I might not see anything useful, but I was hoping I'd see us happy, so I'd know things were going to work out.

He looked surprised. "Of me?"

I nodded.

"But you hate doing that."

"I tried one on purpose today, and now I want to try it with you."

Joe took my hand. "Okay." He was more certain than I was.

I closed my eyes and concentrated on Joe and the senate race and our future. Sure enough, a vision filled my sight. I stood on a stage, waving to a huge crowed. Joe's dad stood next to me, beaming from ear to ear. "I want to present the next Arkansas Senator to the United States, Joe Simmons!"

I waved to the roaring crowd again, then turned to my left. A very pregnant Hilary walked toward me, placing a kiss on my cheek. "I told you we could win this."

"I never doubted you."

My eyes flew open as my tears choked the words that came out of my mouth.

Joe looked scared. "What did you see?"

"You won," I finally managed to say.

"The senate race?"

"I don't know about this one. The one I saw was for the US senate."

Joe still looked scared. "Are you really that upset about me running for office?"

"No, there's more."

He swallowed. "Okay."

"You were married. To someone else." I searched his eyes. "You were married to Hilary, and she was pregnant."

Joe stood up, anger pouring out of his body. "*No!*"

I didn't know what to say.

"I love *you*, Rose." His words were muffled with tears. "I don't love her."

I still didn't say anything.

"You know damn good and well that what you see doesn't always come true. What was the vision you saw earlier?"

"My murder tonight. Rhonda shot me in the head."

Joe pulled me against his chest. "Oh, God. Why didn't you tell me?"

"There wasn't time with the dinner and the announcement. Besides, I couldn't see my face, so I didn't know it was me until Mason called to check on me, and I told him there was some-one outside and the police weren't coming." I bit my trembling lip. "I think we both knew it was similar to what happened to his sister."

"So you talked about his side of things."

"We're friends, Joe. If it weren't for Mason, I really would be dead right now."

The door opened and the ER doctor came in, looking momentarily confused by how Mason had been replaced by Joe. "Ms. Gardner, we have good news. There's no sign of concussion, but we'll need to stitch up your head wound. It's close to your hairline, so the scar should be hidden." She came over and leaned me forward to examine my back. "These will hurt for several days but there's nothing I can really do about it other than have you ice it and give you some ibuprofen."

"Thank you."

"We'll be in to stitch you up in a minute, and then we'll send you home."

When she walked out of the room, I looked at Joe. "You're right. My vision didn't entirely come true. But a lot of it did."

"We can change it, Rose."

"Do you care about her?"

"We've known each other for a long time, so it's hard not to hope she's okay. But we're over. Your vision is wrong."

"Do you want to run for the senate, Joe? If your father and I weren't involved, what would you want to do?"

He sat in the chair, his hands clasped under his chin but not looking at me. "I think I can make a difference." But something in his voice told me he didn't totally believe it. Why was he doing this?

I wanted to cry, but I held it together as a nurse practitioner walked through the door. "Let's get you stitched up and send you home."

Joe held my hand as the nurse put four stitches in my head. After I signed some paperwork, he took me home, and I promptly fell asleep on my bed after I changed out of the bloody underslip and into one of Joe's T-shirts. Joe took care of Muffy, but I awoke when he climbed into bed beside me, pressing his stomach to my back and wrapping his arms around me.

"I love you, Rose." He kissed my neck with a tenderness that brought tears to my eyes.

"I love you too."

I only hoped it was enough.

Chapter
Twenty-Eight

By nine the next morning, word had spread about my escapade the night before. I got out of bed and discovered Joe in the kitchen fielding a call from Violet.

"I don't know all the details, Violet. I told you, I didn't get here until she was in the hospital." He was silent for a moment. "No. Mason knew where to find her. He got to her before the police." I could see it pained him to admit it.

I walked over to him, and he snaked an arm around my waist, gently pulling me to him and kissing the top of my head.

"Thank you," I mouthed.

He grinned and mouthed, "You can repay me later."

My heart leapt, thrilled that my playful Joe was back.

"She won't be in for the rest of the day. She still has to give a *lengthy* police statement." He shot me a stern look, but the corners of his mouth lifted into the hint of a smile. "Apparently, she's about to supply them with all the evidence Deveraux needs to try this case. But even when she's done, she needs to rest. She's pretty beat up."

When Joe hung up, he turned his phone to vibrate and tossed it on the kitchen counter. Lifting my chin, he tilted my head one way, and then the other. "You look more beat up on the right side, but it obviously could have been much worse. And you have two horrible bruises on your back. You need to take it easy today."

"If it means I get to spend the day with you, it sounds wonderful."

His smile fell. "I'm going to have to run back to El Dorado in about an hour."

My happiness burst. "So you're really doing this?"

Fear and sadness flickered in his eyes. "Yeah."

I wrapped my arms around his neck, burying my face into his chest. I was losing him. I knew it.

"What about the sheriff's deputy job?"

He hesitated. "That's on hold for now."

I turned away from him. "I need coffee."

"I'm going to make you breakfast too."

"If you're leaving in an hour, I'd rather just spend the time with you."

"Okay," His subdued tone matched my own.

A knock at the front door made me jump. Joe tenderly stroked my arm. "I'll get it."

He went to the front door, and I heard muffled voices while I poured a bowl of cereal.

"Rose, it's for you."

Worried it was Detective Taylor, I took my time getting to the front door, but I exhaled in relief when I discovered Bruce Wayne on my front porch.

When he saw me, he hung his head. "I'm sorry for stirring up so much trouble for you yesterday."

I leaned against the doorjamb. "What happened to you? I was worried sick."

"I got scared. I didn't want to go back to jail."

"But the waitress said you left with Sly and Thomas."

His mouth dropped. "You haven't been running around telling everybody that, have you?"

"Well . . . only a couple of people."

"I heard you were planning on going out to Weston's Garage." His voice lowered. "It's a good thing you didn't. There's a lot of people out there who don't like you."

I scowled. "Friends of yours?"

He shrugged. "They've helped me out from time to time." He shuffled his feet. "Look, I left with those guys, but they didn't force me. I wanted to go. They offered to hide me until this was over. I was okay."

"You have to tell me the next time something like this happens, Bruce Wayne. You can't leave me so worried."

"I will, Miss Rose." He paused. "So are we still doing the parsonage job or not?"

"I don't know." I rubbed my forehead and winced. "I'm sure Jonah's busy dealing with the fallout of his mother's arrest, not to mention he was shot in the arm. I'm not sure when—or if—he'll want us back."

He grinned. "Then we'll just wait for the next job."

"Yes, we will."

"Oh, I heard about Christy taking you from the sheriff's office at gunpoint. I'm not sure if you heard that Ernie arrested Christy yesterday afternoon. He found her high and shooting stop signs in Jonah's neighborhood. Oh, and Jonah said he was reverting all of her property back to her because his mother had coerced Miss Dorothy into willing her things to the church. She wasn't the only one, either. Miss Rhonda fooled a lot of people."

"So I heard." There was one piece of the puzzle I didn't have the answer to yet, but I suspected Bruce Wayne might. "Do you know anything about the break-in at Miss Dorothy's?"

His eyes widened, and he held his hands up. "I didn't do it. I swear."

"I know *you* didn't do it, but I suspect you know something about it."

He sucked in his lower lip and kept his gaze down. "Let's just say it didn't have anything to do with Miss Rhonda or Jonah, but it had a whole lot to do with the houses being empty."

"Houses? You mean this isn't the first time?"

His face lifted, and his eyes pleaded with mine. "Stay out of this, Miss Rose. You don't want to get messed up with Crocker's guys right now."

So Crocker's guys were breaking into the homes of the deceased, which explained the missing things at Miss Laura's house too. The news didn't surprise me at all. "Don't worry, Bruce Wayne. I'm done solving murders. I'm officially just a garden shop owner. So be ready to get back to work soon."

He grinned. "I will." Shifting his weight, he hooked his thumbs on his pants. "You take care, Miss Rose. You're one of the only people in this town who gave me a fair shake. Twice. I won't ever forget it."

"Thank you, Bruce Wayne."

After he left, I found Joe in the kitchen making an omelet, his back to me. I knew him well enough to know that something was bothering him.

"I told you that you didn't have to cook, Joe."

"I know darlin', but I wanted to make sure you ate something filling, something that's not cereal." Grabbing a plate, he slid the omelet out of the pan, setting it in front of me. He sat down next to me, looking uncomfortable.

I stabbed my eggs, taking a big bite, not realizing how hungry I was until the food was in my mouth. "Go ahead and spill it. I can always tell when you're worried."

"This senate race might be tight."

My food felt like a bowling ball in my stomach. Would I ever be able to just eat a meal in peace? "I thought the race was unopposed."

"Someone else is going to declare he's running later this morning. Frank Delany. Delany's a family man, so they'll be comparing me to him."

I glanced at the ring on my finger. "Is that why you asked me to marry you?"

"No. God, no." He took my hand, searching my face. "I told you that I planned to ask you today. Before I knew about the senate race."

"What does that have to do with what you're worried about?"

"My mother is concerned."

I set my fork down.

"You're from a lower socio-economic class than the opponent."

Resentment simmered in my gut. "And you." I looked up at him. "I'm *much* lower than you."

His eyes hardened with determination. And desperation. "But we can spin that as a positive. Look at the nursery that you and Violet started. Voters love that kind of stuff. I told my mother that you might actually be an advantage. We can pull in voters who relate to you and your humble roots."

I couldn't believe what I was hearing. I squared my shoulders. "I believe your mother called it 'poor white trash.'"

Joe cringed.

"Why are you doing this?"

He looked at me with a blank expression, but I could see the fear in his eyes.

"Where's my Joe?" My voice broke. "Because he would never talk about using me for votes."

Scrunching his eyes closed, he shook his head. "That all came out wrong. I'm doing this all wrong."

"Joe McAllister couldn't give two figs about a political office. Joe McAllister wanted to be with me and barbeque and take picnics and walk Muffy."

He turned his head to look out the window.

"Your mother called me a pretty diversion from all the bad things that had happened to you this year." I swallowed the lump of fear in my throat. "Is that true? Is that what I am to you?"

"God, no." Pain and tears filled his eyes. "How can you ask that?" His hand tightened around mine. "Do you even know how much I love you?"

"You know, you were right." I sat back in my chair, pushing my plate away. "You're very obviously two different men. Joe McAllister—my Joe—and Joe Simmons—the man you've fought so hard not to be. You're turning back into him."

His face hardened. "You're the one who told me there was only one me."

He was right. And so was I.

"So you plan on using the story of our entrepreneurial spirit in the campaign?"

He hesitated. "If you agree."

"What else do you want me to do?"

His jaw tightened and he refused to look at me. "You'll need to distance yourself from characters like Bruce Wayne and David for a while."

"And what about Neely Kate?" I asked without emotion. I couldn't believe I hadn't blown up yet.

From the way Joe was answering, neither could he. "I'm not sure yet."

I tilted my head. "So I need to cut the few friends I have out of my life. Mason too?" When he didn't answer, I swallowed my disgust, but kept my voice expressionless. "I guess I can work at the nursery since it will help your campaign."

"For a while anyway, until we get married. We can't live in Henryetta since it's not in the same jurisdiction." He wouldn't look at me but his hand held onto mine as though he'd drown if he let go. "I guess we'll live in El Dorado when we're not in Little Rock."

"Okay," I said, waiting to see how far he'd take this.

"Okay?" his gaze swung back to me, his eyes wide. He stood and grabbed the edge of the counter in front of the sink, his back to me. "Are you *even listening* to what I'm asking you to do?" He spun around to face me, horror in his eyes. "Are you seriously considering *doing* it?"

My mouth dropped open, my head muddled in confusion.

"I'm sitting here listening to the words coming out of my mouth and even *I* can't believe I'm asking this of you." He ran his hands over his head, his face contorting in agony. "I can't believe I even tried to make this work. I was so stupid. But I couldn't face losing you."

Fear coursed through my veins, and I stood in front of him. "Don't do this, Joe. I *know* you. You don't want to do this."

"I'm not strong enough to fight them, Rose." He shook his head, fighting his tears. "You're the strong one. Not me."

"What are you talking about?" I grabbed his hands. "That's not true, Joe. I've spent four months with you. I *know* you."

His eyes glassed over. "No. You knew the me I so desperately wanted to be. A man free to live his life without family obligations. Free to love you." His chin trembled.

"They're holding something over your head," I whispered. "That's why it took you so long last night. You were telling them *no thank you*, and they threw something bad at you to make sure you did what they said." What could be bad enough to make him do this? "It's about me."

His eyes sunk closed.

"No more secrets, Joe. We can't make this work if we have secrets."

"You don't want to know," he pleaded. "Just let it go. Let *me* go."

"Let you go? No! We can fight this together."

"Rose, my parents are terrible people." His face paled, and he rested his forehead in his palms. "It's not just about you and none of it's true. But the media doesn't care. They'll run with it, and no one pays any attention to retractions."

"What is it?"

"They've concocted some nonsense about Mike bribing county officials for his construction business."

My heartbeat sped up. "Oh, that's bad."

"They have photos of Violet with Brody McIntosh coming out of a motel. They plan to say they had an affair and left their spouses for each other."

"Oh, God." *They knew about Violet.* I couldn't let them expose her affair. My stomach tumbled. "What about me?"

"It's not true."

"I know. What is it?"

He looked green. "My father has set up an account in your name, and he had someone postdate the opening for last May."

"Why would they do that?"

"He also postdated a money transfer for last May."

"I don't understand." I was starting to panic, and I didn't even know why.

"Rose, they transferred the money into one of Daniel Crocker's bank accounts. They set it up to make it look like you hired Crocker to kill your mother."

My head felt fuzzy, but Joe pulled me onto his lap as he sat down in a chair, his voice breaking. "I was gone so long because I begged and pleaded for them to not do this, not to take you away from me." He looked down into my face, tears in his eyes. "You're the only good thing I've ever had in my life. *I want you.* You have no idea how much I *need* you." He stared into my eyes. "But I can't destroy you." He kissed me and moaned. "Oh, God. I can't believe I even considered it." He clung to me, crying into my shoulder. "If I love you, I'll let you go."

I shook my head, my panic rising. "No! I don't want you to let me go."

"If I don't, they'll destroy you. They've agreed for me to have a test engagement to see how the voters respond to you, but the things they expect you to do and not do will make you miserable. You'll end up resenting me for it. The life they expect me to live isn't you."

I grabbed his face between my hands. "But it's not you either. Can you tell me that you'll be happy?"

"Rose, it doesn't matter if I'm happy. My parents don't care."

"But *I* care. I can't let you do this, Joe. I can't let you throw us away."

"Don't you see?" he pleaded. "If I don't run for this senate seat, my parents will ruin you. There won't be any *us* because you'll be in prison. Not to mention what they plan on doing to Violet and Mike."

My fingers dug into his arm, holding onto him for dear life. "Then I'll do what I have to do to be with you. I'll follow their rules."

He gave me a bitter smile. "You think you can pretend you don't know Neely Kate and live with it? You can ignore someone who needs help? It will eat you up inside. Why do you think I was so messed up before I met you?"

"Joe, there has to be a way!"

He leaned his forehead against mine. "I wish there was." He kissed me lightly. "This is the only thing I can do to protect you, and for once I'm man enough to do it. The irony is that I'm losing you in the process."

I showed him the ring, frantic for him to listen to me. "You asked me to marry you. That means something, Joe."

"Of course it means something. Losing you is like losing a part of myself." His voice broke again and he kissed me in desperation and grief.

I clung to him, kissing him back and trying to show him how much I needed him.

How could I live without him?

He lifted his head, and took a deep breath. "No." He pried his hands from my neck then slid me off his lap and stood. "I'm just making this harder for both of us."

Still in shock, I followed him to my room. He grabbed the bag he kept in my closet, opening drawers and shoving the clothes he kept at my house into his duffel.

How could this be happening?

"Joe, *please.*" I grabbed his hand, but he shook it off.

Although his face hardened, he ignored me, stepping around me when I tried to block his path. "Joe, stop! *Please.* We can figure something out. We'll go somewhere together. We'll run away, go somewhere your parents will never find us."

He froze, the features on his face softening.

Encouraged, I looped my arms around his neck, pressing my body against his. "We can go anywhere. How about we live on a beach where we can live in our swimsuits? Me half-naked all the time. You'd like that." I tried to give him a saucy smile, a difficult task when he was breaking my heart.

His body relaxed into mine, and he closed his eyes.

I lifted my mouth to his, and he wrapped his arms around my waist, pulling me to him as he kissed me with urgency. One of his hands buried in the hair at the nape of my neck, tilting my head back to give him better access.

I reached under his shirt, my hands skimming up his back and his hold on me tightened. "I don't want to lose you, Joe."

I had said the wrong thing. He froze, horror on his face. His arms dropped, and he tried to break loose of my hold.

I held on tight. "You keep saying I'm the best thing that's ever happened to you. If that's true, then why aren't you fighting for me?"

"Don't you see that I am? I'm fighting so you don't lose *you.* If I let you become the person my mother wants you to be, not only will you resent me for it, but you will no longer be the woman I love." A sad smile covered his face. "I don't *want* you to change." He gently pried my hands from his back. "One day you'll thank me for this."

He picked his bag up off my bed. I couldn't imagine never waking up with him again. Or just cuddling on the sofa watching TV. Or making love with him. I couldn't imagine a life without him. "What do you want from me, Joe?"

Joe stopped in front of me. "I want you to move on with your life. I want you to be happy."

"*Happy*? How can you expect me to be happy without you?"

"Promise me you'll try."

I refused to answer. He was really going to do this. And I was going to let him.

I reached for my ring and started to tug it over my knuckle.

His hand covered mine. "No. I don't want it back. I bought it for you, Rose. It's yours." He tilted my face up to his. "I want to look at you one last time."

"I'm bruised and swollen. I don't even have on makeup. *This* is how you want to remember me?"

He tried to smile, but his chin quivered. "You're beautiful. Yes, this is how I want to remember you, just like this. Brave and strong and willing to stand up for what you believe in. Don't ever let anyone change you to be what they need. Me included, Rose." He leaned down and placed a gentle kiss on my lips, then headed for the door.

"So that's it?" I asked, my voice breaking as I followed him into the living room. "It's over, just like that?"

He opened the front door and held it open, turning around to look at me. "It was over from the beginning. I've just been waiting for my past to catch up to me." He pressed his lips together and swallowed, tears filling his eyes. "Goodbye, Rose."

I stood in disbelief as I watched my world walk out the door.

Acknowledgments

Thank you to my critique partner, Trisha Leigh, who helped me smooth out some minor tweaks that produced major impact. Also thanks to my slew of beta readers who so willing and eagerly offered their opinion. I was nervous about releasing this book and you made it easier. But I would be remiss if I don't mention Rhonda Cowsert. She's a faithful beta reader, whose insight is invaluable. I trust her judgment and opinion above all others.

Thank you to my children who endure Mommy getting lost in her plothead when she gets sucked into a story. Hopefully, one day they will understand.

Thank you to all my readers who love Rose and beg me for more. May we have many more Rose Gardner Mysteries together.